PENOBSCOT COUNTY, MAINE, 1861-62

BLUE HURRICANE

By F. van Wyck Mason

BLUE HURRICANE

GOLDEN ADMIRAL

PROUD NEW FLAGS

CUTLASS EMPIRE

EAGLE IN THE SKY

RIVERS OF GLORY

STARS ON THE SEA

THREE HARBOURS

CAPTAIN NEMESIS

THE COLONEL NORTH STORIES

THE CASTLE ISLAND CASE

BLUE HURRICANE

F. VAN WYCK MASON

J. B. LIPPINCOTT COMPANY
PHILADELPHIA AND NEW YORK

PRINTED IN THE UNITED STATES OF AMERICA

FIRST EDITION

Library of Congress Catalog Card Number 54-9417

To those sterling friends

WARREN *and* KATHERINE WEBSTER

and

To the bright memory of

LIEUTENANT WARREN WEBSTER III, USA,

killed in action in Korea, 1953

FOREWORD

For a long time it has seemed odd to this writer that the great "River War," as it was fought along the Tennessee, Cumberland and Mississippi in 1862, should have been so shamefully neglected not only by historical novelists but by formal historians as well. One has but to recall that the only land victories of real importance won by the Union during the first year and a half of our Civil War were rendered possible largely through the tactical and strategic assistance afford to the Northern Armies by the Western Flotilla of the Mississippi Squadron.

Just as a majority of the Corps of Officers in the old United States Army resigned in order to fight for the South so it became the North's good fortune to find that most officers of the Regular Naval Establishment were determined to cast their lot with the Union. Therefore the Union Navy, from the outset, was better led, served and officered than that of its antagonist.

It was the hard fighting of Flag Officer Foote's gunboats at Forts Henry and Donelson and at Memphis which decided the fate of Kentucky and western Tennessee. This little flotilla of hastily built ironclads formed the upper claw of a great strategic pincers which eventually met the lower claw of U.S. naval forces fighting northwards from the Gulf of Mexico under Rear-Admiral David G. Farragut. At Vicksburg this pincers eventually split the Confederacy vertically in half and made possible a further breaking up of the South into militarily ineffectual segments by Lieutenant-General William T. Sherman.

No part of the year-long research done for this book proved to be more fascinating than a study of the political and social conditions obtaining in St. Louis at the start of this war. Here partisanship became so violent that martial law soon had to be imposed, for to this thriving metropolis swarmed hordes of embittered and generally penniless refugees from southern and western Missouri as well as from Kansas. It was in St. Louis that were constructed four of those famous Eads ironclads with the service of which this book deals in so large a part. Yankee ingenuity, energy and a burning patriotism produced the armored hulls of these clumsy yet effective ironclads in a matter of forty-five days—a production miracle only to be equalled generations later, during World Wars I and II.

Any detailed study of steamboating along the Mississippi and its tributaries is both infinitely rewarding and fascinating. Verily the color of steamboat life upon these waters is unsurpassed anywhere in the American scene.

Victory over the multiple hazards of navigation, faulty engines and valiant enemy action should bestow long-overdue laurels upon the officers and men, North and South, who fought the most unusual naval campaigns recorded in history. Off the city of Memphis, Tennessee, the North's Western Flotilla and the South's River Defense Squadron fought the only true fleet engagement of the Civil War.

Due to an intensive research the dimensions, armor, armament and the names of even minor officers serving aboard the Western Flotilla are authentic. Of course the memoirs of various eyewitnesses and participants vary considerably as to fact and time. This necessitated a critical winnowing of fact from conjecture. This resulted in the incorporation of that data which appeared the best substained.

Families mentioned in this tale are imaginary although certain surnames were selected because they were known to exist in the general locality in which their bearers are described. All the principal characters appearing in this tale, with the exception of obviously historic personages, are fictional.

The various legal points raised in this story have been studied and approved by a number of competent lawyers, including two gentlemen at present practicing in the State of Maine.

It has been my intention to describe this decisive "Water War" through the eyes and reactions of persons typical of that era but with a faithful adherence to historical fact. I hope I have not failed the reader in this ambition.

Very sincere thanks go to Rear-Admiral John B. Heffernan, U.S.N., Ret., who furnished me with excellent details concerning the construction and operation of *Carondelet;* to Mr. Robert C. Black III, of West Hartford, Connecticut, for his information concerning the railroads of the day and their operation. I wish also to thank the St. Louis Historical Society for contemporary maps and for invaluable aid regarding a reconstruction of the city during that period.

Again it is my pleasure to acknowledge the great assistance afforded by my old friend Robert H. Haynes, Assistant Librarian of the Widener Library, Harvard College, and by my secretary, Jane West Tidwell, who has been, as usual, cheerful and efficient in the preparation of this volume.

F. VAN WYCK MASON

GUNNERS' HILL

RIDERWOOD, MARYLAND

CONTENTS

Book One

PENOBSCOT COUNTY, 1861

Book Two

THE WESTERN FLOTILLA

Book Three

THE WATER WAR

BOOK ONE

Penobscot County, 1861

I THE BLIZZARD

"HOWDY, MATT. NEVER guessed ye'd drive in through a storm like this one," drawled the grocer peering shortsightedly over square-lensed spectacles. "Must have run near out o' vittles."

"Hardly. It's growing brisk outside, and that's a fact," Matthew Hovey had to bend his head in a snow-flecked fur cap to enter. Momentarily his rugged outline filled the doorframe. After closing a door fashioned of pine slabs he lingered on the threshold to kick loose lumps of snow clinging to heavy, knee-high boots. "Drove in to fetch the mail and stock a few groceries."

"This is the most promisin' tempest I ever see hit Penobscot County so early in fifteen years. Yessir, 'pears like we're in for a long, cold winter. Each year the winters git worser." Moving with the stiff and angular movements of a confirmed rheumatic Ephraim Parker pushed aside the brown, pink and white slab of bacon he had been slicing to fix red-rimmed eyes upon a succession of silvery flurries whirling and billowing beyond this log structure's single window.

"Aye, Mr. Parker, expect this blizzard soon will be raging fit to blow the bushes flat so I'd better do my errands in jig time and get for home." Matt Hovey used a blue-mittened hand to rub high and prominent cheekbones honed bright red by the storm. Tiny snow crystals still clung to straight sandy eyebrows and somewhat darker eyelashes. "Mail in?" he demanded, while slapping snow from his brimless cap of red fox fur.

"Yep. Uptrain jest about did git through. Saul said it's beginning to drift something fierce opposite the Bradford place." The grocer's shaggy gray head swayed when he shuffled out from behind a counter heaped high with a miscellany of merchandise which included everything from padlocks to a pair of faded pink corsets. "Saul never should have felled that section of spruce. Told him so myself. Wind roars straight across the valley there."

"No. Mr. Bradford never should have," Matt Hovey agreed. "Specially as he got no good price for that timber, either." He could visualize that spot bordering the Maine Central's right-of-way very well because every time he called on Phoebe Whidden he went by it. Azel Whidden farmed down the road a short piece from his mother's neat white clapboard cottage. Nowadays quite a few such were being built—mostly to replace log cabins which had sheltered Dexter's original settlers.

Bending his sandy blond head slightly to avoid a cluster of steel spring traps dangling from a roof beam, Matt Hovey crossed to a big pot-bellied stove that glowed red-hot and, much like a dog, shook himself to rid his heavy brown wool jacket of melting snow. Small, angry hissing sounds and brief tiny puffs of steam resulted while anxiously Matt watched Mr. Parker enter a small, wire-protected enclosure sacred to the United States Mails, and dump the meager contents of a slim canvas sack onto a counter. He squinted shortsightedly at a packet of letters secured by a length of brown twine.

"Yer ma's letter's here," informed the grocer over his spectacles. "Beats all how they come like this, reg'lar as clockwork." Almost shyly the older man's red-rimmed eyes and the steady, dark brown ones of his customer engaged. "Yessir. Ever since I been here they've showed up right on the dot; first of November, March and July. That's a real mystery—indeed it is."

Over his shoulder he queried, "Say, is your ma still ailing? Azel Whidden said he heard she was right poorly yesterday."

Young Hovey's long, powerfully formed features contracted. "Mother's still dreadful feverish and I'd never have left her except she took to fretting so over this letter."

A puff of vapor escaped Mr. Parker's bearded lips, swirled up to dissipate among some hams dangling among the spring traps, trace chains and horse collars. "Had the saw-bones to see her?" Despite the glowing, pot-bellied stove this one-room store remained pretty chilly, what with the blizzard beating cold air through loose chinks between the logs.

On clumsy cowhide boots into the tops of which well-patched woolen trousers had been tucked, young Hovey approached the counter. "No, more's the pity. Mother wouldn't hear of it, but I stopped in at the Larrabees' on the drive over. Mrs. Larrabee's promised to send the doctor over the minute he gets back from Adam Fitch's."

"Wonder who's been took sick at the Fitchs'. Bet it's the boy. He's been looking mighty peaked ever since he took the typhoid last spring."

"No. Mis' Larrabee said 'twas one of their girls—the one called Charity. Seems like she somehow got lost last night in the start of this storm and fell into a brook. Got her feet frostbitten."

The grocer's hand, brown-splotched and gnarled by rheumatism, shoved a letter sealed in red wax over the mail counter. Without looking Matt knew exactly what to expect. The missive would arrive in a strong brown envelope, registered and addressed to Mrs. Abigail E. Hovey, Dexter, Penobscot County, Maine, in a bold, angular and arrogant script. Only concerning the postmark was he uncertain. On this occasion it was dated October 28, 1861, and a handsomely engraved yellow-and-black stamp depicting George Washington's likeness had been heavily cancelled in purple by a bull's-eye design undoubtedly hand carved out of a cork stopper. Exactly three hundred dollars in crisp, new twenty-dollar banknotes would be found within that long, pale brown cover. Just the money and nothing else at all. Ever since Matt could recall, similar envelopes had appeared three times a year but never once had his mother made even the least comment, although on each occasion her habitually serene and gentle expression faded into sad lines and she would wear for a long time a thoughtful air.

"Now this one here is postmarked Brunswick, Maine," observed Mr. Parker, peering up over his spectacles. "Ain't had one from 'way over there in the longest while. Brunswick's a mighty pretty little town, heard tell."

Matt in grinning exposed clean but slightly irregular teeth. "You figured this time 'twould come again from Portland, didn't you?" To predict the next point of mailing had developed into a sort of game between them. The most distant had been Boston, in March of 1859, but the great majority of these mysterious envelopes were mailed in some small town in the State of Maine.

"You needin' anything else?" Ephraim Parker queried while wiping a juicy, sharp red nose on a blue bandanna handkerchief.

Matthew nodded, pulled out a list. "We want a tin of coal oil, some yeast, molasses—I've our jug outside—a paper of pins, some beeswax for sewing and two pounds of raisins; make sure they're the Spanish kind Mother favors."

When Matt went out to fetch in the Hovey kerosene tin and molasses jug old man Parker shuffled over to peer out of his little window. Lord, how furious were these snow squalls! They completely obscured a row of dark, wind-tormented firs swaying beyond the village of Dexter.

"Good thing you're hitched up to a pung. Come another half hour you'd have a main hard time moving on wheels." With laborious care he then drew off a gallon of coal oil, impaled a small potato on the spout and, grunting, heaved Matt's tin onto the counter. Meanwhile his customer had set his jug under the molasses barrel spigot and stood watching the slow, golden brown stream descend.

The grocer-postmaster, always somewhat crippled with rheumatism, today moved with such deliberation that Matthew began fighting down a sharp impatience. After all, he was anxious to get started back towards that snug little white clapboard cottage set in the middle of two cleared acres indenting the primeval forest. There could be no denying he was feeling uncommonly anxious because never before had his mother appeared to be even half so ailing. Godfreys! How almighty frail she seemed lying there in her narrow spool-bed.

"You still carpentering at Bell's joining mill?"

"Yes."

"Thought you were set on attending that Divinity School in Bangor."

"I still am." Matt's nod set his collar-length, sandy-hued hair to gleaming in the half light. "I plan to start studying come the spring term. The Reverend Mr. Enoch Pond feels moderately confident I'll meet the Seminary's requirements."

In exasperating deliberation Mr. Parker commenced to count the various supplies into Matt's sturdy, hickory splint basket and check them against his list. "Well, there you be. Oh, you forgot to sign for that registered letter." He shoved forward a pen the steel point of which was lumpy with rust and dregs. "I hope your ma perks up real quick. She's a mighty fine Christian woman and the finest school teacher we'll ever see hereabouts. Wish she hadn't retired last year. My grandson Lemuel will start his schooling come next fall. You tell her we'll pray for her at meeting tonight."

"Thanks, I will," Matthew slipped an arm through his basket's handle —it had been fashioned by poor old Polly Porcupine, one of the few Penobscot Indians still lingering in the vicinity of Dexter. Polly claimed to be over a hundred years old but of course she couldn't prove it.

He pulled on his red fox fur cap and tied its ear flaps snugly beneath his jaws. Godfreys! Right now it certainly was blowing a first-class blizzard. And so early in the winter.

If Toby, the Widow Hovey's horse, hadn't been so sturdy and if his mother weren't so sick Matt guessed he'd likely have holed up in Dexter for the night. To lose one's way amid such a howling, blinding tempest was all too easy and he didn't relish travelling those four and a half miles home.

The tall young carpenter's hand actually was raising the slab-door latch when it swung sharply inwards and he had to step back fast in order to avoid a solid figure clad in a long, dark blue cloak and a black slouch hat that bore a brass hunting horn on its front. Cloudlets of snow fine as powdered sugar commenced skittering across the grocery's calk-pitted floor and sent a large tiger tomcat leaping resentfully up onto the counter to avoid the draft.

"Dear God! What a storm for early November!" Energetically the newcomer shook snow from a double-caped and scarlet-lined military cloak then brushed a heavy powdering of crystals from curly black side whiskers. Several bright brass buttons winked to his movements.

"Well, it if isn't Rob Ashton," grinned Matthew. "Blamed if I recognized you in that pretty blue uniform."

"Small wonder. Scarce recognize myself," grunted the other as he strode over to warm himself at the stove. "I close to squandered my last cent among those Boston tailors." Rob Ashton had gone to grade school with Matt but had received his later education in Boston. His father still lived and earned moderate bread as a doctor in the village of Garland, lying a scant six miles east of Dexter.

"Then you've finished study at the Massachusetts General Hospital?"

"Yep. I've graduated." Rob Ashton's wide and ruddy features formed a stiff grin. "Accidents will happen."

" 'Pears like you've joined the Army?"

"Last week. The Sanitary Corps needs doctors the worst way."

"Too bad," grunted the grocer. "Hereabouts we been figuring on your settin' up practice. Not that old Doc Larrabee ain't all right," he amended hastily, "but he's growing a mite feeble."

Dr. Ashton, looking young despite heavy sideburns, unhooked the caped overcoat and in so doing revealed a single line of gilt buttons descending a dark blue tunic belted above trousers of a lighter blue. "Well, Mr. Parker, that family of mice still nesting in your cracker barrel?"

"Guess so; ain't looked lately. Rob, should I call you Doctor—or should I say Lieutenant?"

"Neither. Just Rob—as usual," young Ashton said. "Funny you should have said that just now—I really *had* planned to open a practice around here."

"How come you changed your mind?"

"There was a parade along State Street in Boston and they had a mighty fine band. When it played 'Yankee Doodle' I got so worked up I went right over to the Sanitary Corps Office and signed up for a lieutenant's commission."

Matt stared at this young physician's chunky, blue-clad figure. "You got a commission just like that?"

"Just like that. A major there told me to go get measured for some uniforms and granted me time enough to travel home and bid Ma and Pa good-bye."

Matt rested his basket upon the counter. "Where are you ordered?"

"God knows. Expect I'll find out when I report back to Boston. Maybe I'll get sent down to Virginia or maybe away out west to Illinois or Missouri." Ashton stroked the big tomcat and smiled on the familiar hodgepodge of dusty horse collars, barrelled nails, pickles and corned beef. "Turns out the Rebels make damn'-sight better soldiers than Abe Lincoln's generals figured on."

Matthew winced at Ashton's use of the word "damn" but guessed that maybe about a metropolis like Boston the occasional use of profanity wasn't considered really wicked.

Rob Ashton, just as he had when a gangling youth, dipped into a blue-and-gray stone crock of gingersnaps and selected one, just one—which was all the largesse Mr. Parker ever permitted—and commenced to nibble thoughtfully. "What say, Mr. Parker? Is old Number Nine likely to pull out for Newport Junction this afternoon? I'm supposed to report at the Sanitary Commission in Portland by tomorrow night."

"Mebbe she will, but more likely she won't. Saul claimed he had a real rugged uptrip. 'Taint just a spring snow squall that's blowing outside."

All three men crossed to the grocery's white-rimed window and peered out at the depot, a small log structure at the terminus of the Maine Central's spur to Dexter. Through wildly spiralling flurries they glimpsed huge piles of lumber, logs and rough-dressed timbers awaiting shipment. A wind-torn streamer of bluish smoke rising beyond the depot revealed Number Nine which, having fetched up the mail, a long string of flat cars and a party of drunken lumbermen, was awaiting instructions before backing down to Newport Junction where the Maine Central, running northwest from Augusta and Portland, gave over to the Penobscot Railroad.

Carefully Rob Ashton brushed gingersnap crumbs from among the gilded buttons and shot his former schoolmate a quizzical glance. "Tell me, Matt, you still aiming to enter the ministry?"

Matt flushed a little. "I still figure I'm cut out to be a clergyman. Why?"

"Oh, I just wondered," the young doctor replied pleasantly. "As a lad you were always ready with your fists and your temper came to the boil pretty quick." He kicked melting snow from black, square-toed shoes. "Funny, what with all these ninety-day enlistments running out and the country being so hard-pressed for volunteers to replace them, I'd have sworn you'd be one of the first to go."

"I've learned to hold my temper and I'm not a fighting man by nature," Matt explained steadily. "Did you know Mother's been mighty sick abed?"

"Your mother's very sick?"

"Yes, for over a week. Heaviest cold she's ever taken."

"How is she faring?"

"Poorly." He heaved up the basket and lifted his kerosene can. "Nice to see you again, Rob, but I've got to be making tracks whilst I still can get out to our place."

Ashton placed a restraining hand on Matt's arm. "Wait here. I'll be back in a minute." The young doctor snatched his hat off the counter, hooked his cape, then clumped down three snow-covered steps outside and trotted over to the log depot.

"Now what ails Rob to go rushing off like that?" queried the grocer.

"Rob's gone to learn whether Number Nine will pull out tonight."

"Seemed considerable upset about your ma."

"Rob has set great store by my mother ever since he learned the three R's from her. Always sends her a Christmas present, even when he was away at that medical school."

Mr. Parker smoothed the tiger cat's glossy fur, then shuffled over to lift the tin reflector of a huge kerosene lamp dangling overhead. He lit it with a paper spill ignited at the stove–matches were still a sight too costly to be wasted on such a routine. The grocer glanced over his shoulder.

"As schoolteacher your ma was a shining wonder; even the worst little hellions we've ever raised hereabouts would eat out of her hand." He fumbled along a shelf, took down a long, orange-colored box. "Matt, here's some cough syrup feller sold me last summer. Swore it's considerable effective."

"May as well try it. How much?"

"Nothin'. It's for her. My compliments."

Young Hovey stared his amazement. Crabbed old Ephraim Parker was famous for being "nearer than near."

"Why, why–Mother will be mighty pleased. But you oughtn't–"

"Know it–" grunted the bent old fellow. "But me, I'm kinder partial to Mrs. Hovey too."

Dr. Ashton appeared in the doorway. "Saul allows he's not going to try it–not in the face of this full blizzard that's raging and night coming on. So I guess President Lincoln's Army will just have to forgive me if I'm tardy. Saul figures Number Nine won't start down till about eight tomorrow morning; by that time the plow should have showed up from Newport. Come along, Matt, let's take a look at your mother."

The two had literally to fight their way out to Mr. Parker's stable shed under which Matt's horse stood snorting apprehensively and shivering under a thick winter blanket. Now the screaming wind was driving sharp-edged crystals before it that stung like spent pellets from a shotgun. Successive blasts out of the northwest lashed near-by junipers, firs and spruces like surf beating on a lee shore and whirled up the already-fallen snow to create a blinding, cutting haze that limited visibility to a few yards.

Rob Ashton turned up his cape collar and, bent well forward against the blizzard, lugged his physician's bag out to the stable shed.

Matt heaved his supplies into the rear of a light pung, then lashed down its faded tarpaulin with care.

"Mighty good of you to come along, Rob," he shouted over the sibilant turmoil of the wind. "What with this storm Dr. Larrabee's hardly likely to get to Mother tonight."

"Anybody 'tending Mrs. Hovey?" yelled Ashton while stowing his bag under the pung's single lumpy seat.

"Only Polly Porcupine, the half-breed Penobscot who lives back of our hardwood tract."

Reluctantly Toby settled himself into the collar and commenced floundering through drifted snow. Matt noticed that lights glowed in the windows of the hundred log and frame dwellings which composed Dexter and, although it was only four of the afternoon, employees already had begun struggling out of Abed Thompson's steam sawmill and Levi Reed's furniture factory, for all that both concerns were swamped with war orders.

On the edge of the village the storm gained force and a succession of drifts that often rose high as the horse's belly barred the road for home. Matt hunched deeper into the upturned collar of his now quite inadequate homespun jacket and raised a mittened hand visor-like to shield his eyelids from the savagely stinging crystals. Godfreys! These icy blasts seemed ready to tear the breath right out of his lungs and the hairs on the inside of his nose commenced to grow stiff with frost.

Now and then a clump of fir trees towered right over the road and so afforded brief respite which was lacking when the wind came roaring across cleared and burnt-over land on which irregular rows of blackened tree stumps suggested sable tombstones. Twice Rob Ashton attempted to speak but gave up and waited until it became necessary for them to throw aside the pung's mangy black bearskin lap robe and help the horse through drifts now rising waist-high. It was growing dark with alarming rapidity.

"Worst storm I can remember," the young doctor bellowed while tying down his hat with a muffler.

"We'll have it easier from now on," Matthew encouraged him once they had gained the shelter of a spruce grove in which the snow lay level and easily two feet deep. Soon darkness had all but closed in and, sensing that his stable came nearer with every floundering stride, Toby lowered his snow-plastered head and churned onwards at a smarter clip until, at last, through the pitiless, lashing flakes a yellow glimmer shone beyond a stand of towering hemlocks. Presently the pung's iron-shod runners grated over a boulder which had yet to be removed from Mrs. Hovey's ungraded and winding driveway.

"Here's old man Parker's syrup. You'd better go right in, Rob,"

Matthew begged, "I'll come along soon's I've unhitched and dried Toby down."

II *IN DELIRIUM VERITAS*

A PAIR OF BRASS coal-oil lamps, boasting round ground-glass globes fringed with prisms, glowed brightly; but a faint oily reek attested the fact that their wicks could not have been properly trimmed since Mrs. Hovey had taken to her bed. Scrupulously clean yellow-and-white flowered wallpaper amplified the lamplight but caused old Polly Porcupine's deeply wrinkled flat and leather-hued features to appear shades darker than they actually were. Tonight the Penobscot woman appeared positively mummified save for the quick play of very small black eyes. Clad in the same shapeless gown of gray linsey-woolsey she had worn for years on end, the shrivelled old creature padded about the sickroom on moccasined feet, silent as an owl in flight.

Matthew, scarlet-faced and numbed with cold, had only to glance at Rob Ashton's expression to tell that his mother certainly couldn't be any better. The Army physician had tossed his scarlet-lined cape onto a rocker upholstered in black horsehair and his hat lay on its side upon the floor. The line of brass buttons descending his tunic's front and the gold edging of his buff velvet shoulder straps glinted when, without taking his eyes from the patient, he removed his jacket and, having rolled up his sleeves, paused, intently studying that tiny figure breathing so stertorously beneath a thick yellow puff tufted with goose down.

Next, Ashton went to flex his chilled hands before a Franklin stove in which a cheerful fire of white birch logs snapped and flared. Matt stripped off cap, mittens and coat and watched the physician bend over the bed's spool maple headboard and peer intently into Abigail Hovey's gentle and delicate but strangely sunken features. He noted the parched and cracked condition of her lavender-hued lips.

"How long has Mrs. Hovey been like this?" demanded the young doctor.

"She sleep so—long, long time," Polly Porcupine's guttural voice carried over the soft wailing of wind about the eaves.

"Mrs. Hovey isn't asleep," Rob Ashton said and suddenly looked years older. "She's in a stupor—which is bad." He turned to Matt towering so tall in the sickroom that his crisp, blond hair brushed the ceiling.

"Your mother was conscious when you left for Dexter?"

"Yes, Rob."

"When was that?"

"About half after one, I guess."

In helpless anguish Matthew lingered at the foot of the bed while the snow melting from his heavy cowhide boots created dark stains on an oval rag rug.

"Take off that comforter," Rob directed while searching in his brand-new, black leather bag.

Polly complied, turned a head still blue-black despite her obviously great age and inquired of Matt, "You fetch letter? Miss Abbie ask two, maybee t'ree time."

"I've got it. Well, Rob, how bad is it?"

All the answer he received was a premonitory shake of Rob's dark head as he bent above the patient and inserted a tiny thermometer into a corner of her mouth. Gently then he tested Abigail Hovey's forehead. "Her influenza's gone into lung fever, I'm afraid, and it's pretty far advanced," he announced. "She's fairly burning up, Matt. Um-m. Now about her pulse." Pulling out a watch he bent forward and lifted a limp, thin and blue-veined arm from beneath the covers. The patient's eyelids fluttered and she emitted a little gasping sigh when Ashton removed the thermometer and went striding over to a lamp to read it. His reaction was a worried frown.

The windows rattled louder than ever in their frames; heavy white rime had sketched elaborate frost patterns over nearly all of their neat little panes. "The temperature reads just over a hundred and four degrees."

"Is—is it bad?"

"Very. For a woman of her age that's mighty serious."

"Isn't there anything you can do?"

"Were she conscious I'd attempt to administer a decoction of chinchona bark which might reduce her fever. As it is, I guess I'll try cupping but—" he cast Matt a penetrating look "—there's really precious little to be done when lung fever reaches this stage."

From his bag the Army physician produced a gleaming glass vacuum cup and selected a lancet from his surgical kit.

"Rob—isn't there something I can do?"

"Polly had better fetch some bandage," came the reply, "and you'd better refill that wood box. Then you can pray—maybe that will help."

After he had lugged in a couple of armfuls of birch logs from the shelter of a long shed which served to join the cottage to its barn, Matt sought his bedroom at the top of a flight of very steep and narrow stairs. It was the only room on the second storey except for a little "poke hole."

On its rust-tinted plaster walls were hung a fine steel engraving depicting "The Passion at Gethsemane," by some English artist, and a certificate from Mr. Burton's Academy at Newport Junction which attested to the fact that Matthew Hovey had completed, to the faculty's satisfaction, courses in Latin, mathematics, English literature and Bible study.

It was downright cold in here. His breath went whirling away in a golden-gray cloud beyond the candle's flame. Obviously Polly Porcupine had forgotten to refuel his small chunk stove of cast iron, but a few embers still glowed within and, mechanically, he fed strips of birchbark and sticks into the firebox. When the fire blazed up Matthew Everett Hovey drew a deep breath and, dropping onto his knees at the bedside, clasped hands in intense supplication. God would heal Abigail Hovey if only he prayed earnestly enough. Of this he remained sublimely confident.

As always, he prayed aloud, pouring out his poignant anxiety, grief and fervent hope in classic and sonorous phrases acquired from the King James version of the Bible. His deep, clear voice, however, became distorted by the eerie moaning of the blizzard. Puffs of wood smoke, beaten back down the chimney, soon created a pale blue haze. He had almost completely unburdened himself when, during a lull in the wind's uproar, he thought to recognize outside a sound something like the clink of metal.

"Amen!" Hurriedly arising he rubbed a windowpane clear of frost and peered out. Good Lord in Heaven! A horse and sleigh were halted outside the kitchen door and someone was alighting in the yard. He pounded downstairs barely in time to unlatch the kitchen door for a stocky figure who stamped stiffly inside. The man's square-cut gray beard was whitened by snow and little icicles dangled from the ends of long, walrus-like mustaches.

"Dr. Larrabee! I never reckoned on your getting here tonight."

"Nor I either, and that's a fact," he shouted over the rattling of a loose shutter. Unbidden and without removing his black bearskin coat the doctor tramped over to the kitchen stove and poured himself a cup of steaming coffee. "Wild horses couldn't have dragged me out in a tempest like this for anybody saving Abbie Hovey. I'm plumb tuckered out."

All of a sudden Matt became uneasy. What would Dr. Larrabee say when he discovered another, and a greatly junior, physician in attendance on his patient of long standing? He started an explanation of Rob Ashton's presence, but the old man already had picked up his chafed and stained medicine bag and was stumping off towards the front of the house all humped over and resembling nothing so much as a mangy old bear. Over his shoulder he called, "Matt, just you trot out and 'tend to poor old Hephzibah—she went down twice among them murdering drifts."

Dr. Larrabee's ancient nag really needed attention; her eyes were almost frozen shut and she was wheezing pitifully so he took time to fetch out an iron teakettle that always simmered at the back of the stove and stirred up enough hot bran mash to give Toby a good measure as well. He was using a strip of old blanket to rub down Dr. Larrabee's mare when the stable door banged open and Polly appeared, hooded in a dark gray shawl. "Mist' Matt!" she croaked. "Medicine men say come *quick!*"

Matt ran so fast through the dark that he tripped over one of those big, pink-lipped seashells with which his mother had bordered her driveway and went sprawling deep into a smothering white drift and so burst into the house suggesting an animated ghost.

"Polly, you wait outside," Dr. Larrabee directed in a penetrating undertone. "Matt, come over here by the bed."

While hastening to obey, Matt became aware that his mother's fine dark eyes had opened but that she was staring fixedly at the ceiling. Next he noticed that those lavender-hued lips were in motion. Both Rob Ashton and Dr. Larrabee stood bent low over a Jacob's Ladder quilt which now covered the patient. Directing an agonized glance at his former schoolmate, Matt dropped onto his knees and took his mother's hand; vaguely he was aware of its being chill, no longer burning hot as it had been when he'd departed for Dexter.

"I'm here, Mother. I'm Matt," he cried, then choked off a sob when Abigail Hovey gave no sign of recognition.

"Don't talk—just listen carefully," Dr. Larrabee warned. His shadow, projected in gigantic proportions onto the ceiling, mimicked his movements. "I think she wants to say something."

Silence fell in which the brisk crackle of birch logs and the storm's wild symphony dominated the cheerful little bedroom. Mrs. Hovey's large dark brown eyes shifted, came to rest on Rob Ashton as he bent big and red-faced over her.

"That's a good boy, Matthew," she muttered, but her voice sounded faint as the fluttering of a moth against a windowpane. "South Paris. I've never seen quite so many jonquils before Eastertime— Church is prettily decorated I think. Papa, your sermon was inspired, everybody said so."

When the wasted figure fell silent Dr. Larrabee used a napkin to moisten his patient's fever-dried lips. She commenced speaking again in a shallow but much stronger voice. "Oh, no, Joe! *Oh, no!* There *must* be some mistake—it can't be so!" Again her voice deteriorated into breathless incoherencies; then, by bending very low, the three men heard her gasp, "Of course we were married, by the Reverend Mr. Adams. Yes, the Reverend Mr. D. Adams--all a mistake you say? Believe me— Papa! Papa! In Heaven's name have pity, Joe! Can you forget—I'm soon going to bear your child?"

The Widow's thin voice swelled astonishingly despite her labored breathing. "No! Joe, *no!* You can't do anything so wicked—so unfair. Judith, dear, where are you? Make him understand—poor little child."

Abigail Hovey's speech faded but then she struggled high on her pillows and lucidity entered her eyes. Smiling at her son she said very distinctly, "May God bless you, Matthew, and may He guide you ever in the path of righteousness. Forgive me for I—for I—I have sinned greatly, if unwittingly, against you. Dear Lord, please have mercy and receive my soul."

Abigail Hovey had just time to smile once more before lapsing into unconsciousness. She died just as a few rays of light feebly commenced to penetrate angry snow clouds still scudding low over the dark evergreen forests of Penobscot County.

III ASHES TO ASHES

After sunup the blizzard gradually petered out and rays of dazzling sunlight came slanting down to sketch bright blue shadows behind such familiar snow-shrouded objects as the Hoveys' privy and pump house. The former, for instance, at this moment suggested a crystalline bower in which a bunch-of-grapes design cut into its door loomed black as ironwork.

The two physicians roused themselves from armchairs in Mrs. Hovey's sitting room in which they had slept and, yawning, threw off shawls that had covered them. The little living room was neat and cheerful—its walls having been done in pink and light gray stripes and the usual "A Yard of Pansies" and a "God Bless Our Home" motto in cross-stitch hung above its two entrances.

Rob Ashton inquired deferentially, "Will you go see how Matthew is, sir, or shall I?"

"You'd better," yawned Dr. Larrabee. He rubbed a hand over cheeks silvered by a two days' beard and suppressed a faint smile. "Since you were first on the case I expect you had better make out the deceased's death certificate."

Rob Ashton's dark head swung sharply about. "Oh no, Doctor. I—I really couldn't. Mrs. Hovey was your patient. I only came here because Matt feared you might get stormbound—and I loved his mother dearly," he added and commenced to pack his instrument case. "Besides, I'll have to hurry if I'm to catch Number Nine and I must. I was ordered to report at Camp Ligonia last night."

"Ligonia? Now where in Tunket is Camp Ligonia?" The older man coughed, knuckling small, faded blue eyes swollen by windburn and reddened through lack of sleep.

"Right outside of Portland, Doctor. They've plenty of sick there, too. The scarlet fever seems everywhere."

"Aside from Quincy's *Dispensatory* and Innes on muscles, what did you study especial during your studies down to Boston?"

Ashton blushed like a schoolboy caught in mischief. "I expect you'll think me crazy, but I, well, I wanted to learn more, a lot more, about the relief of pain through the use of ether."

"H-humph! Been listening to that charlatan, Willy Morton, eh?"

"Although plenty of good men will agree with you, sir, there are others, Dr. Henry J. Bigelow of the Massachusetts General and Dr. Warren, who deem Dr. Morton no humbug."

A scrabbling noise at the hall door preceded the intrusion of Polly Porcupine's seamed brown face. "Breakfast," said she, then popped back as though expecting a billet of firewood to be hurled at her head.

"She's a loyal old savage, for all she smells like a fox's den," Larrabee muttered and groped under his beard to do up his collar of celluloid. "Suppose you go up to young Matt and tell him he's got to eat something. Poor feller. He and his ma were closer than close—too close, maybe. Near's I know, Matt's never been further away from Dexter than Newport Junction—barring timber cruising to the north. All right. I'll make out the certificate. Oh, you'd best notify the Reverend Mr. Holcomb on your way to town."

Rob Ashton completed the buttoning of his tunic of dark blue serge. "I'll do that after I talk to Matt. I expect I'd best borrow a pair of snowshoes and light out for Dexter. Can't afford to miss the train."

He had started for the door when Dr. Larrabee remarked, "By the way, you've a couple of brothers in the Army?"

"Had," came the sober reply, "but Charlie fell at Bull Run—serving with Colonel Erasmus Keyes' Second Maine. They reported that Edward, he was in the Third Volunteers, was captured. Ma's not heard a word from him, so she's almighty worried. If I get ordered to Washington I'll try to find trace of him."

"I'm mighty grieved, son, to hear this," said Dr. Larrabee closing his medicine case. "That makes five of our boys who've been captured or killed. Township can't stand many more such losses."

After gulping hot, if slightly stale, coffee and a mouthful of soggy brownbread, Dr. Larrabee tramped out to the Hoveys' stable and stroked Hephzibah's velvet-soft nose before he set about buckling on her weathered harness. Lord, how exhausted he felt—not a whole night's sleep in ten days. Jerusha! That dratted long, cold, wet spell before the blizzard certainly had raised hob.

Talking all the while to the horse Dr. Larrabee backed his mare from the guest stall then slipped the trace eyes over his cutter's manure-splashed whiffletree and finally shovelled four inches of snow off its floor.

Presently he tucked the cutter's buffalo lap robe about his aching legs, then his heavy blue-and-red mittens gripped the reins.

Dr. Larrabee cast a thoughtful glance at the dead woman's little white cottage. Matt would take his bereavement mighty hard. In all his years of practice he guessed he'd never observed deeper, if undemonstrative, devotion than that which had existed between Abigail Hovey and her son. When he thought of the widow's delirious talk he winced. Poor Matthew!

To avoid a five-foot drift gathered behind a neat white picket fence he guided Hephzibah over a flower bed in which nasturtiums, and pregnant-appearing love apples had glowed during the summer.

When Rob Ashton pushed it open the door creaked gently and he saw Matt Hovey prone on his bed. Although the stove was giving off hardly any heat the young carpenter had not pulled up the coverlet.

"You awake, Matt?" he called softly.

Abigail's son must have been dozing but instantly he sat up, blinking dazedly, his long, sandy hair all of a tangle.

"Matt, I've just got to pull out for Dexter right away. You know I'm ever so—" Ashton's voice faded but his blunt, capable fingers closed gently over Matthew's, then he said, "Hope you've got a spare pair of snowshoes tucked away somewhere."

Matt scrambled to his feet. "I'll drive you in to Dexter, Rob."

"With all those drifts piled up during the night we'd never get through," said the Army doctor. "On snowshoes I can make it easy and I'll stop at the minister's. Say, when I reach Newport shall I inform Mr. Stetson?" Mr. Stetson, he knew, was Mrs. Hovey's lawyer.

"Yes, I guess you'd better."

"And I'll tell Mr. Parker what's happened. He'll soon pass the news."

"*The news?*" Matthew's face flamed. "Oh, no, Rob. Promise you'll never repeat a word of what Mother said last night."

"You're addled if you think I meant anything but the news of your mother's—passing. Now you listen to me and heed what I say." He looked Matt squarely in the face. "Always remember this: Your mother was delirious, completely out of her mind, when she babbled certain things last night. It was not really she who was talking, understand? In fact, neither Dr. Larrabee nor I recall a thing she said. Dr. Gould taught me that good physicians never hear or remember a lot of things."

Over-energetically he commenced to hook up the scarlet-lined blue cape. "Hate like the devil to rush off like this but, well, I've no choice. Remember now to tell me when you join the Army—"

"I'll never go to war! I just couldn't bring myself to kill anyone," Matt burst out passionately. "She—" he nodded towards the front of the cottage, "she wouldn't want me to. 'Thou shalt not kill' remember?"

For a long moment the stocky, blue-clad figure remained silent. "Maybe so, but since the other side didn't set much store by that commandment at Fort Sumter and Bull Run, I reckon we need not respect it, either." The physician's bearded jaws tightened. "Guess you don't know what it means to lose a couple of brothers you were fond of." Almost harshly he inquired, "Where can I find those snowshoes?"

"They're hung to a peg above the oat bin. The harness should be all right. I oiled it only last week."

Rob Ashton offered his hand and spoke quietly. "If I were you, Matt, I'd call on Phoebe Whidden and her folks to help you in your trouble. Phoebe's one in a hundred and I know she sets great store by you."

Cloudlets of gray-white vapor commenced to eddy about the young doctor's black slouch hat when he stepped out into the diamantine world stretching away from the kitchen door. "Know something? Phoebe's been sweet on you ever since we all were to school together, so send Polly over to the Whiddens' right away; you won't be so damnably alone." He turned and stalked away so abruptly that his cape's lining flashed. Then he halted and called back, "Remember, Matt, *neither Dr. Larrabee nor I can recall one word your mother said in delirium.*"

For quite a while Matt remained motionless standing in the center of the kitchen floor. He was becoming aware that Rob Ashton had been quite right about his feeling alone—miserably, terrifyingly alone. Then he saw his friend stride past the window, managing his snowshoes with the ease of one reared in the North woods, and disappear in the direction of Dexter.

Behind a small, square-steepled church built of white-painted clapboards and standing almost across the road from that single-room schoolhouse in which Abigail Hovey had taught for nearly twenty years, the neighbors gathered. Among stumps and snow-trodden blueberry bushes sprouting in the tiny churchyard, loomed quite a few oblong mounds and headstones of varying sizes. There were only two stone monuments in the whole cemetery; Phineas Shaw's and old Mrs. Todd's.

The Reverend Mr. Holcomb was suffering from a heavy cold and sniffled continually during the service he conducted at the grave's edge. The hole was rimmed with raw earth and dirty snow which had been melted by charcoal in order to thaw the ground sufficiently to permit the use of spades. However toneless and uninspired the Reverend Mr. Holcomb's reading of the burial service might have been, his eulogy of the departed neighbor was as beautiful and eloquent as it was sincere and poignant.

Phoebe Whidden, looking very pale in a second-best black cloak of her mother's, gained Matt's side. The girl's finely modelled and classical features appeared more perfectly chiselled than ever beneath her bonnet of black velvet and a few curls of red-gold hair. During the eulogy she bent her head and sobbed softly for the first time during these past three dreadful days.

Early on the morning of his mother's death Matt had been heartened to see the whole Whidden family, Phoebe, her mother and father, shovelling through a drift on their way to Abigail Hovey's place. As soon as Polly Porcupine had travelled the half mile on snowshoes and had brought the sad news they had left their own farm in charge of a next-door neighbor who allowed he'd tend to the Whiddens' stock and keep the fires going.

Odd that Phoebe and Matt were about the two "only" children residing in Dexter township, though Azel Whidden had lost three offspring through typhoid. It was Phoebe who, with Mrs. Whidden, assisted in dressing her former teacher's small, frail figure in the Widow's lace-trimmed best gown of lavender watered-silk. That first night after Azel Whidden had driven back up the road to his farm, Phoebe remained in the dead woman's neat little sitting room and read aloud consoling passages out of the New Testament. Together Matt and Phoebe had knelt before the fireplace and prayed for over an hour.

Now, beside the grave, Phoebe stood looking gravely, gently, up at him with red-gold hair framing rather long and pointed features delicately pink beneath her black bonnet. The girl's large, dark blue eyes then swiftly lowered themselves.

"'I am the Resurrection and the Life.'" Only faintly did those familiar words penetrate Matthew Hovey's consciousness. Then finally, "'. . . ashes to ashes and dust to dust. . . .'" He was hardly aware of Phoebe's chilled fingers slipping inside the cuff of his rabbitskin mitten and exerting a comforting pressure on his.

Later he stood with eyes fixed in uncomprehending wonder upon that dark oblong of earth banked with fresh green fir boughs. Memories flooded back to torment his mind. Under that heap of boughs lay all that remained of his mother. Unlike the rest of the children around Dexter he had never called her "Ma." He saw her applying a cool witch-hazel compress to a bump on his head; teaching him appreciation of the works of Shakespeare; lighting candles on a tiny Christmas tree that time they had moved into the little house of white clapboards where, for years far happier than he had realized until now, they had lived peacefully, serenely, together.

Never had he journeyed from home farther than Newport Junction and that far only to attend Mr. Burton's Academy or in connection with so pressing a matter as having a tooth pulled.

As the Reverend Mr. Holcomb's voice died away, somebody coughed loudly and the women's sobs became painfully audible.

Mrs. Whidden said, "You'll come home with us tonight, won't you, Matt? It would be too painful for you to be in that house all alone."

Fearful that his eyes would overflow, Matt nodded dumbly. He still couldn't get it through his head that his mother wouldn't be bustling about their home and discussing news of national importance. For years the Widow had maintained a subscription to the *Bangor Daily Whig & Courier* and had manifested deep, if covert, interest in the booming lumber trade of which Bangor was becoming the capital.

"Dear Matt," Phoebe murmured, "I'm so pleased you will come home with us. With God's help we will attempt to make things easier for you during the next few days."

His anguished dark brown eyes finally raised themselves and swung to meet Phoebe's level blue ones. "Thank you," said he, "when you spoke just now, you sounded like Mother."

IV STETSON & STETSON, COUNSELLORS-AT-LAW (I)

NEWPORT JUNCTION HADN'T been much of a town until 1856 when its first steam sawmill and joining factory had commenced to operate. Since the outbreak of the great Rebellion initiated by a parcel of overly hot-tempered South Carolinians, all manner of new industries had come to town. Wheelwrights, wagon builders and boxmakers hurriedly erected factories of raw pine planks and set about hiring everybody in the vicinity who could employ hand and foot. How loudly these new manufacturers cursed whenever another able-bodied native climbed aboard the Maine Central's cars, grimly headed for recruiting stations in Portland or Bangor! After the inexplicable Union defeats of Bull Run, Ball's Bluff and at Wilson's Creek in far-off Missouri there had been mighty little cheering around the station platform.

On a day early in November a pale sun had broken through high, light gray clouds just enough to melt some of the snow on the rooftops and to sketch a pattern of weak, bluish shadows between the original log houses and newer frame dwellings.

In crossing the Penobscot Railroad's right-of-way, Matt Hovey barely anticipated passage of the morning train, southbound from Bangor. Its locomotive came chuffing into sight all the while erupting geysers of sparks from a huge, bell-shaped smokestack. Most of the cars it drew carried freight or lumber, but coupled to its end bumped a solitary passenger coach.

At a glance Matt saw that this car was crowded with men of all ages. Most sat staring moodily out over the trampled snow near a tall fir forest still hemming the Junction, but a gay, freckled-faced young fellow lifted down a placard and held it to a window. It read, "Abe Lincoln's Boys on their way to hang Jeff Davis." Another proclaimed, "Death to the Rebels!"

It came over Matt, all at once, that up in Dexter folks maybe didn't quite understand how seriously their State was taking part in this struggle to preserve the Union. Why, up to home about everybody reckoned that before the year was out all those Rebels would have run home. But it hadn't turned out like that. Not at all. Instead, had come sickening tidings of the Union disaster at Bull Run and the shameful news that the Maine First and Second Regiments had bolted in panic-stricken rout, along with almost all the other Militia. A lot of Maine men had either been killed, wounded or taken prisoner, which many people said was about as bad.

To steamy, strident whistlings the cars for Portland rolled to a halt on a siding, there to wait, with the engine panting gently, for the Bangor-bound train to pass. Matt tramped across the frozen and snow-filled ruts of Main Street towards a row of new two-storey shops and office buildings, all of which had been painted either white or light yellow.

He paused before Number Twenty Two and anxiously scanned a flight of stairs leading to certain offices located above A. H. Dean's Hardware, Coal & Feed Store. At the top of a gritty, calk-chewed staircase he read "Stetson & Stetson, Counsellors-at-Law" painted in bright gold upon a door which, to Matt's expert eye, had been fashioned out of prime white pine.

Diffidently he rapped, then tramped inside to become confronted by a low barrier. A bent and aged clerk wearing a green eyeshade glanced reluctantly upwards. "Morning. And what might your business be, Mr.–?"

"I'm Matthew Hovey from up Dexter way. I've come to talk to Mr. Edwin Stetson."

The old fellow's watery eyes narrowed and he nodded to himself.

"Hovey? Oh, to be sure. 'Twas you sent that note down yesterday. Pray take a seat, sir." He arose, shuffled past a tall bookcase filled with row upon row of well-used, calfbound legal books.

"Mr. Edwin will see you now," he announced almost immediately and readjusted black bombazine cuff-guards climbing to his elbows. "Don't let him forget he's due over to the Court House come eleven. He's to defend that Frenchy who got so drunk last week and nigh stabbed Abner Sailer to death."

Mr. Edwin Stetson's office proved to be about as bare and only slightly warmer than the henhouse back home. The only concessions towards decoration were a steel engraving of a bust of Plato, an oleograph depicting "The Surrender at Yorktown" and a framed degree granted by some law school over in New Hampshire.

Edwin Stetson himself was small, neat and brisk as a squirrel; with forked flowing whiskers, plentiful iron-gray hair and a long, straight nose. Eyes boring from behind gold-mounted spectacles, the lawyer arose, gravely offering a plump, well-manicured hand.

"Pray accept my most sincere condolences on your grievous loss, Mr. Hovey. May I say that I have never been privileged to advise a finer lady? Pray seat yourself." He indicated an old armchair mounted on white porcelain casters and upholstered in black horsehair. The lawyer's light gray eyes seemed suddenly to assume an opaque quality as they lingered upon this tall young client.

"Ha-arumph!" Mr. Stetson cleared his throat, then honked his nose on a blue bandanna handkerchief produced from the tail of a claw-hammer coat. Meanwhile he surveyed the sandy-haired figure sitting ramrod-straight and uncomfortable before him. "Presume you've called in regard to Mrs. Hovey's estate?"

"Yes. Dr. Larrabee told me you wrote my mother's will. I presume Dr. Larrabee has talked with you?" Had this brisk, young-old gentleman learned anything concerning Abigail Hovey's dying remarks?

The lawyer shook an iron-gray head and stroked his short, forked beard. "He merely forwarded a copy of your mother's death certificate. By the bye, it has been filed at the Court House." Mr. Stetson swung about in his cane-backed swivel chair until his face presented its profile. "Er, Matthew—Mr. Hovey, do you recall your mother's ever having made a statement concerning her past? I mean her life previous to the time she came to Dexter?"

Matt shifted uneasily on his seat. The broken horsehair upholstery had begun to penetrate even his thick, red, winter underwear. "No, sir. I can never recall her speaking about that. Of course I wondered and used to ask, but always she'd put me off."

"Um. Makes matters difficult. Difficult indeed." From an ink-spotted green desk blotter the lawyer lifted a fat brown envelope, revolved it absently between stubby fingers. It was secured by a bright red silk ribbon. He seemed not to hear a dog fight which broke out in the yard just below his window.

He attempted a new line. "Mr. Hovey, I gather your mother lay ill for quite a spell before her untimely demise. Please think back. Did she, at any time during her sickness, impart anything which might lend you some clue as to where she came from and—ah, harumph—the circumstances of her marriage?"

Color welled into Matthew's high, flat cheekbones. "Why—yes. Well, on the night of her—" he couldn't bring himself to say "death" and choked —"she was out of her head."

"What was it she said?" insisted Mr. Stetson still staring out of the window and fingering that fat Manila envelope.

"Why, it was nothing sensible, sir. She muttered something about 'South Paris.' She spoke several times to someone she called 'Joe.' "

"Did anyone else hear this?"

Matt's color deepened to the roots of his curly blond hair. "Why, yes. Dr. Larrabee and Rob Ashton—"

"He the one that's just joined the Army?"

"Yes. As a surgeon's assistant."

"Good." Mr. Stetson nodded. "Then he can be trusted not to talk, either."

A sharp uneasiness invaded Matt's mind, commenced to eat like an acid.

Mr. Stetson swung to face him. "What else did Mrs. Hovey say? Try to remember exactly her words."

"Then she mentioned a clergyman, the Reverend Adams, D. Adams she said, and—and—"

"Yes?" prompted the lawyer.

"She said something about her going to have a child."

"And then?"

"Of course she was out of her head, sir, and couldn't know what she was saying."

"Pray continue," insisted the inexorable voice. "It is most important that you should do so."

"Why, Mr. Stetson," Matt said in a low, anguished voice, "she cried out that she had sinned greatly." Angrily, he looked up. "As if she ever committed even a little sin during her whole life!"

"I know, I know. It's rather like imagining that the Angel Gabriel might betray the Gates of Heaven. Is that all?"

"About all, except that she said she hoped that Our Lord would have mercy on her." Matt bent well forward, hands pressed flat to the lawyer's desk. "Of course, Mr. Stetson, Mother couldn't know what she was saying. Dr. Larrabee and Rob Ashton will swear so. You understand that, don't you?"

The lawyer drew a slow breath, fiddled with the tapebound envelope again. "Mr. Hovey, I'd sooner be boiled in oil than tell you this—Mrs. Hovey was out of her mind—and yet *she wasn't.*"

The scream of the arriving northbound train's whistle impinged on Matt's consciousness; he wanted to scream, too. "She wasn't out of her mind?" He jumped up, suddenly white to the lips and stood glowering, big fists balled. "I won't believe it! You are contemptible, sir, to make such a statement concerning the noblest vessel Our Lord ever sent to grace His earth!"

Edwin Stetson's gray eyes gleamed suddenly behind their square-lensed spectacles and, sharply, he raised a hand; its highly starched cuff gleaming in the sunlight. "Pray hold your tongue, Matthew, and be seated. I have never, in over forty years of legal practice, been faced with a more painful duty than that which I must now undertake. You must believe me," he added quietly while untying the envelope's ribbon. "So please restrain your emotions whilst I read a statement prepared by your mother some fifteen years ago. This," he held up a single crisp sheet of neatly folded paper, "is her will. It is very simple; it bequeathes all her property to you."

Only by the summoning of considerable will-power was Matthew Hovey able to force his limbs into a trembling obedience; he sat rigid, eyes fixed unseeingly on "The Surrender at Yorktown." The chromo had become wetted at some time so there remained a brown, wavy line across one corner. Specks left by many a summer's flies dimmed its glass.

"Many years ago," Mr. Stetson went on, "when your mother was taken ill with the scarlet fever she sent for me and retained me both to take a deposition and to draw her will." To a crisp rustling sound Mr. Stetson's plump, well-tended hands smoothed two sheets of paper covered with writing executed in a beautiful Spencerian script. " 'I make this statement,' " he read, " 'in the consciousness that Our Lord may summon me before Him to stand in judgement before His Awful Throne. However, I speak with dire misgivings as to the wisdom of doing so, and so do only after having prayed long hours for guidance that this is the right manner in which to inform my son concerning the circumstances of his birth and of my unhappy past. The only reasons which prompt me to speak out is fear that he may seek to become ordained as a Minister of the Gospel and so compromise not only his soul but those of other innocent Christians. Also, I greatly fear further to wrong him.' "

On his lap Matt Hovey's big and capable hands tightened until their joints cracked softly. Mr. Stetson glanced over his spectacles, said quietly, "You must now summon considerable fortitude, my boy, and listen to what I must read."

Matt wanted to speak but could only nod. Overwhelming was his confusion at this shattering departure from the secure, peaceful and even tempo of the only life he had known up until four days ago.

" 'I was born in the village of South Paris, in Oxford County, Maine, where my father was Pastor of the Congregational Church. I was his only child for, in giving me birth, my adored mother suffered some injury which prevented her from giving me brothers or sisters. My name was, and is to this day, Abigail Everett. To the name of Hovey I have no legal right having adopted it in my desperate necessity. It is that of a favorite schoolmate who was lost at sea.'

" 'Suffice it to say that, in the spring of the year 1839, I travelled with my father to Portsmouth, New Hampshire, where he was attending a synod of Congregational pastors. It was there that I met Josiah Cosby. He was young and intensely ambitious. He attracted me greatly.' "

Matt blinked. Josiah? Joe? Of course!

Evenly, Mr. Stetson's dry voice continued, " 'Whilst I spent the summer there with my Aunt Judith and cousins, Mr. Cosby paid me earnest, flattering and impetuous court. "Impetuous" I say because he persuaded me to elope with him to Portland in the State of Maine where I believed we were duly married by a rector of the Presbyterian denomination, D. Adams by name, and in the presence of two witnesses, both persons residing at our hotel.'

" 'Mr. Cosby then took me to the town of Belfast in this State, where he owned an interest in a sawmill. There we set up housekeeping and lived very happily because I had written home and had secured my parents' blessing. Mr. Cosby proved to be as tender and affectionate a husband as any female could desire and his affairs, which were exceedingly varied, prospered so greatly that I wanted for nothing. However, he had much occasion to travel, so often I was left solitary for days and sometimes weeks on end.'

" 'Nevertheless I would have been blissfully happy had I not discovered that Mr. Cosby could be utterly ruthless towards any who opposed him, that he would do anything, no matter how unethical, to advance his career socially or financially; in fact, Success was his god. I should not have been as surprised as I was at his later inhuman treatment of me since I, being practically penniless, could give him nothing save love and devotion.'

"'All the same, when it became apparent that our union was to be blessed with issue I was delighted beyond all expression for I greatly loved Mr. Cosby and truly believed him to reciprocate my tender affection.'"

Mr. Stetson broke off to fumble in the envelope and presently produce two clippings, yellowed with age and frayed about their edges. He placed them on the desk before his tight-lipped client.

"'I shall never forget that dreadful spring day when, in April of 1840, a letter came, together with these cuttings from the *Portland Post* and supported by the *Portsmouth Herald.*'"

Edwin Stetson broke off. "Perhaps," he suggested, "you had better read these for yourself— Immediately I received them I corresponded with the editors of both newspapers. These publishers verified that such articles did appear in their issues of March 12, 1840, and unfortunately were perfectly genuine."

Swallowing hard, Matthew picked up the first of the yellowed and brittle clippings which were about one and a half inches long. One was distinguished by a small headline:

BOGUS PASTOR EXPOSED

Portland, March 12, 1840. Today a clever and plausible rascal who has been masquerading about this city for nearly two years as the "Reverend" D. Adams has been exposed as an unordained impostor. Last week he absconded from this city together with the funds of two Missionary Societies which had been entrusted to his care. It is feared that many embarrassing legal problems will arise due to this shameless fellow's long presence and impersonation in Portland.

By telegram this newspaper has ascertained that no one bearing the name of D. Adams has ever been graduated from the Theological Seminary at Hartford, Connecticut.

Consternation and embarrassment have descended upon various respectable young couples who believed themselves to be lawfully married by this unordained and utterly conscienceless rogue.

The clipping escaped from Matthew's calloused fingers and fluttered onto the big, ink-scarred green blotter covering most of Mr. Stetson's desk top. He made no effort to read the second cutting.

"No, there's small point perusing it since this piece from the *Portsmouth Herald* only substantiates the first," Stetson said kindly and tugged at his heavy mustache which innumerable cigars had stained yellow-brown. He retrieved Mrs. Hovey's statement.

"'Mr. Cosby had been absent for over a month. When he departed he explained that he intended to travel far up into the North woods in order to inspect and survey some timber lands he contemplated purchasing. It came as a thunderbolt when he directed my attention to the cuttings enclosed and pointed out that our marriage was not valid. He invited me to credit that he had not deceived me by intention; that this was merely an unfortunate mischance.'"

Mr. Stetson paused, cleared his throat. "Now we come to the really villainous part.

"'Mr. Cosby wrote, however, that since we were not actually wed, he felt constrained to inform me that recently he had conceived a deep attachment for a Miss Drusilla Nickerson, a well-born young lady *of considerable wealth;* a circumstance he deemed fortunate since she better could aid his callous climb to power and wealth than I.'

"'Oh, my son! My son! I hope you will never comprehend the depth of my despair when I read those dreadful words. I, Abigail Everett, the daughter of a respected Minister was at once unmarried and growing great with child! Mr. Cosby threatened that should I cause him the least embarrassment he would swear that we never participated in a marriage ceremony, which was possible since, so he said, the marriage license could not be produced, why, I don't know. So, my son, if I made an outcry it would only serve to advertise your illegitimacy to all the world and gain me nothing save opprobrium. Your father is ruthless, half mad in his pursuit of riches.'"

Out in the Main Central railway yard bells clanged and whistles screamed again as the southbound and the northbound trains pulled out simultaneously. Matthew, however, kept his eyes fixed on a circle of stars on a flag depicted in "The Surrender at Yorktown."

"'Mr. Cosby, by way of alternative, offered me an annual stipend of nine hundred dollars provided I retire to some remote village and never breathe a word concerning our invalid marriage.'"

The sound of Matt's breath, rushing in as if he had run a hard race, filled the little office.

"There is really very little more to tell you," continued Edwin Stetson. "You can deduce what followed. Your poor, sweet and overtrusting mother, dreading to visit disgrace upon her family and fearful of affixing the stigma of bastardy upon you, accepted the worthy Mr. Cosby's offer and so severed all connection with her family and past life."

So this was why, unlike all the other children, he had never heard of uncles, aunts, cousins or grandparents. This explained the absence of family portraits, heirlooms, keepsakes and gifts at Christmas. What was this neat old man saying?

"I well recall when your mother first appeared here in Newport, a pale, frightened young thing, and you but an infant in arms. At first she took in sewing and gave out to the neighbors that her husband came from Georgia of a family that had been all but exterminated by the yellow fever. Mr. Hovey, she sighed, had been lost at sea. She herself, she averred, had been an orphan reared by an aged relative long since dead. In short, she and her child had not a single surviving relative. We all felt mighty sorry for the poor pretty little thing.

"Well, pretty soon the railroad's spur was built up to Dexter and the lumber camp grew into a village, so soon they built a school and began looking about for a decent female to teach there. Your mother immediately won the appointment and, as you know, taught there ever since. Certainly that gentle lady became one of the most beloved and respected citizens in all Penobscot County."

"Illegitimate. *Illegitimate!* ILLEGITIMATE! You are a bastard!" The words beat in Matt's brain like the roar of a rapids.

So Josiah Cosby and his vaulting ambition had done him and his mother this unforgivable wrong. Josiah Cosby? Vaguely he recognized and then identified the name. Why, wasn't it Josiah Cosby who owned several sawmills and lumber yards along the Penobscot River? Wasn't he often mentioned in the Bangor and Portland newspapers as a very important shipbuilder, timberland owner and manufacturer of wagons? No wonder Abigail Hovey—no, her name really was Abigail Everett—had scanned the newspapers so avidly.

Josiah Cosby had been one of the first State Senators ever sent to Augusta from Penobscot County. Why, not a year ago he'd read in the Bangor *Whig & Courier* about an elaborate housewarming given at the splendid new mansion Cosby had built out on Old Town road near that city. Pretentiously enough, Cosby had named his place Sachem Hill.

Mr. Stetson's dry voice obtruded upon his recollections. "Here is your mother's will. As I said, she has bequeathed everything to you."

"Everything?" growled Matthew. "A frame house, five acres and no name!"

"Easy on, Mr. Hovey." The lawyer spoke sharply; anything to dispel that misery in this tall young fellow's eyes. "You're in for some more surprises—this time pleasant ones."

"To the—the deuce with them!"

"No. Listen. Your mother, because she spent very little of her annuity, saved and invested and so has left far more than you or anyone else imagines," the lawyer continued. "Your mother owns a half interest in a box and barrel factory at Brewer, she owns outright, although under a fictitious name, that new planing mill which was built out on the Garland road last fall. She further owns ten square miles of a very fine hardwood forest up in Piscataquis County. True, this tract is not yet to be reached by a railroad, but it soon will be. In addition she also owns fifty shares in the Merchant's Bank of Bangor. It's a good one—Charlie Stetson, my first cousin, is cashier there. No, Mr. Hovey, you are a long way from being penniless."

Matt surged to his feet, features contorted and gone scarlet again. "Maybe not penniless, but still without a name of my own." His mind boiled like a pothole in a river when the spring freshets were running. A succession of cruel passages from the Old Testament occurred to him. He caught up his foxskin cap.

"Hold on! Hold on!" Mr. Stetson cried jumping up. "Think of your inheritance. There are legal formalities to be—"

"To hell with an inheritance bought through Mother's shame and suffering. To hell with it, I say!" It was the first time Matthew Hovey had ever cursed.

"Now, now, Mr. Hovey! Do calm down," the lawyer begged. "Of course it was a horrible, unfair thing your father did to your mother—and to you. But," he held up a monitory forefinger, "no one remembers, *or knows* about it. Only you and I are aware of this terrible secret—"

"Isn't it enough that *I* know?" growled Matt in choked and quivering accent. "Besides, you're wrong. Josiah Cosby knows the truth. Probably his lawyers, too. Being the sort he is, he must long ago have taken steps to make positive that neither Mother nor I could ever cause him trouble. I'm right about that, aren't I?"

"I fear so, but nonetheless I am convinced that, without provocation, Mr. Cosby will never alter the *status quo*." Mr. Stetson picked up Abigail Hovey's will and nervously readjusted his spectacles. "I shall read the will. It is very brief."

"Don't!" Matthew's voice rose until it filled the whole little pine-lined office. "I don't give a damn what you do with that property."

"'Damn?'" Mr. Stetson's whiskers quivered and he looked definitely shocked.

"Sell it! Give it away! I want no part of it." Matt glared about like some cornered animal then burst out, "I am the instrument of the Lord's vengeance. Let the guilty beware!"

Mr. Stetson hurried forward in anxious agitation. "Mr. Hovey! Matthew, my boy! Stop and reflect. You mustn't do anything rash. Of course I realize what a horrible, stunning blow this has been, yet—"

That bright but transparent crimson curtain which more than once before had lowered itself before Matt's eyes commenced again to descend, to tint the world crimson. It had been like this that time he'd almost beaten to death a drunken trapper he had caught hammering his poor, chained dog with an ax handle.

"Matthew! Pray calm yourself! Reason with yourself and remember that the ways of God are inscrutable and that vengeance is His!" The little lawyer might just as well not have spoken for Matthew thundered on.

"I am become a vessel of wrath. I am the Lord's sword and I will seek out Josiah Cosby and the 'Reverend' Adams and lay them even with the dust."

He whirled, plunged towards the office door ignoring Mr. Stetson's frantic "Wait! For God's sake wait, boy! What you plan is madness!"

Matt descended the stairs three at a time, pounded out into the glare of winter sunlight and across the road to where a train of empty lumber trucks was gathering speed for a trip up to Dexter.

V PROFESSIONAL ETHICS

A FAINT JINGLING of sleigh bells in the still, icy air caused Mrs. Larrabee to wince and to glance anxiously across her well-supplied table even though the doctor was murmuring Grace over the first full meal he had consumed at home in three days. A small sigh escaped her when he said, "Amen" and glanced out towards the road.

"Oh, Henry, not again!" His wife's eyes narrowed in the lamplight. "You simply must not go out tonight! You—you're dead on your feet." She employed a more telling argument. "Besides, your horse is exhausted."

He smiled over a steaming tureen of Irish stew. "Now don't you fret, Betrag. Of course I don't want to go out and maybe I won't have to." He took a big mouthful of stew, then speared a piece of butter from its dish and spread it on a crisp biscuit but all the same cocked an attentive ear to that silvery tinkle of bells drawing inexorably closer.

"Now, Henry, just you eat your victuals. I'll go answer the door. If you don't get some hot food into that big body of yours you'll need doctoring yourself."

Dr. Larrabee settled back in his chair. Dear God, how tired he was, and hungry. So very tired. Why did so many folks take to having the lung fever and babies in such weather? While helping himself to some boiled cabbage and dried-squash pudding he heard the jangle of bells fade, then saw his wife open the inner door. She had flung her old green tartan shawl about her shoulders. Although it had crossed the Atlantic with her mother from Argyll a generation ago yet it remained wonderfully light and warm.

Who could have come for him? Mrs. Trumbull? Certainly she had grown big as a house this last week. Or had the Edmund's little girl taken a bad turn? Hardly. She was a sturdy piece and her whooping cough had been coming on fine.

While sectioning a particularly succulent lump of mutton, the doctor strained his hearing but, to his surprise, the voice sounded quite unfamiliar. A draught of cold air came blustering into the kitchen before the front door banged shut.

"I beg your pardon, Mrs. Larrabee, for thus intruding at mealtime," the stranger was apologizing in brisk accents, "but, alas, trains don't often run up here."

Still gulping his supper Henry Larrabee made a quick calculation. His caller must have ridden the train up from Newport Junction. Napkin in hand he sought a side window and saw a blanketed horse standing to the new, cast-iron hitching post he'd bought last summer. It was Tom Barker's livery-stable cutter all right. Tom himself sat waiting in the sleigh. Presently Mrs. Larrabee appeared conducting a small bright-eyed individual whose features above a neat forked gray beard shone scarlet with cold.

"Henry, this is Mr. Stetson from Newport Junction."

Still chewing, Larrabee arose and pulled the napkin's end out of his collar.

"Oh, yes, I'm acquainted with Mr. Stetson. We attended the Republican rally down to Augusta together last year. Come in, sir, come in. Pray remove your overcoat and make yourself comfortable. Betrag, my dear, pray lay another place and open the parlor door. I'll kindle a fire there in a moment."

"I deplore intruding upon you like this," Stetson said, blinking behind his spectacles in the kerosene lamp's mellow radiance, "but I—well, Doctor, I felt I've no choice in the matter." He commenced to undo a row of hickory toggles securing his shaggy overcoat. "It is of utmost importance."

"Don't apologize, sir. That is why I am in practice." He pushed a chair up to the table. "Someone has been taken critically ill, I take it?"

The lawyer hesitated, held his hands to the pot-crowded stove. "I might say so, Doctor, but in this case the illness is not of the body, but rather of the mind or soul."

Dr. Larrabee shot the newcomer a penetrating glance and somehow guessed the nature of the other's mission. Mrs. Hovey had mentioned him on several occasions as her lawyer. "Do I take it there's no necessity to be up and out immediately?"

"I hardly believe such a step to be required. But we'll have to have a talk—and go calling here in Dexter later on."

"Betrag!" Larrabee called to his wife, busy in the pantry. "Mr. Stetson is staying the night, so send Tom Barker home if he won't take a cup of coffee first. Tell him to come for Mr. Stetson for the train tomorrow morning."

Mr. Stetson offered no objections. There was no earthly way of his getting back to Newport before morning—except by the use of snowshoes.

Once the hired cutter had tinkled off down the primitive road towards Dexter, Mr. Stetson applied himself with considerable gusto to Mrs. Larrabee's cooking—especially the scones for which she was famous. Her plain red features brightened at the way he sailed into her mince pie and the damson preserve hurriedly fetched from the jam closet. The coffee, too, was dark, oily, fragrant and stronger than a bear trap.

"Suppose, Mr. Stetson, we seek the parlor?" Larrabee smiled. "It's my consulting room, too."

Daintily, Edwin Stetson cleaned his short whiskers, belched and apologized, then stood up with gold watch chain dully agleam across a braid-bound waistcoat of brown tabby velvet.

Once seated before a brilliant fire in the doctor's tiny parlor both men filled pipes from a jar of birchbark ornamented with dyed porcupine quills and sat puffing in silent enjoyment a long moment. Presently Stetson undid his waistcoat and Dr. Larrabee shed his country coat of thick black wool. Impaled now and then by crimson rays from the fireplace, their tobacco smoke curled upwards.

"Doctor, have you any idea why I've looked you up?" Stetson inquired abruptly.

"Might have, might not. But I think I've a pretty good notion as to why you're here. Still, I'd prefer you to state your business." He sighed, stretched long booted legs out to the glow. "After all, you *did* come to seek me."

Pipe poised, the lawyer bent forward and addressed the flames. "I find myself, Doctor, in an unprecedented and, I might add, an awkward quandary."

"A lawyer in a 'quandary'?" smiled Larrabee. "Thought there 'weren't no such an animal.'"

A bleak smile flitted over Stetson's pink features. "There is. Like you medical men, we lawyers are hampered by professional ethics although you'll find precious few folk who'll credit that fact. I have come to you only because I have been searching my soul since this morning, as a clergyman would put it. You see, Doctor, I'm convinced that you are one of the few, the very few people who can help advise the son of a deceased client—who was one of God's noblest creatures."

Dr. Larrabee's curved pipe ceased giving off little bubbling noises as, without taking his eyes off the stove, he nodded several times. "I take your meaning, Mr. Stetson, and I'm glad you came. Professional ethics, like the law, I've come to learn, should be tempered with reason and justice." He elevated a massive, grizzled eyebrow. "You're concerned about Matthew Hovey?"

The lawyer nodded. "I am. Gravely so."

"You are concerned about his—his present state of mind?"

The lawyer nodded. "Dr. Larrabee you enjoy a fine reputation in this part of Penobscot County so I ask you to believe that I would not for one instant invite you to betray a confidence that might not benefit the young man in question."

"Mr. Stetson, I appreciate your sentiments. Now what is it you would learn?"

A silence ensued during which a large gray-and-white Persian cat insinuated itself through the hall door and, with plumed tail gracefully undulating, advanced to a warm spot before the fire where it crouched and, without glancing at either man, made muffs of its forepaws.

"You have known Matthew Hovey since babyhood, or at least for a good many years?"

"I have. I've doctored him through the croup, mumps and the measles, but I came close to losing him through scarlet fever." He nodded his big, unkempt head to himself. "Yes, I allow I might say I know Matt Hovey tolerably well."

The lawyer arose, selected a paper spill from a Mason jar on the mantelpiece, and rekindled his pipe before turning to face his host. "What is your considered estimate of Matt's nature? Of course, we both know he's honest, well-mannered and a good Christian and uncommon intelligent. Tell me, Doctor, what's your opinion of his character as it's likely to become on being confronted with an ugly, and unprecedented, problem?" While awaiting a reply the spare little man fixed unseeing eyes upon the gray cat now blinking and quite motionless except for an all but imperceptible switching of its tail's tip.

Dr. Larrabee deliberated while tugging at flowing side whiskers. The homely sounds of dishes being washed and pans being cleaned floated in from the kitchen. The cat yawned. "That's not easy to predict. Perhaps you've noted that while Matthew's a whole man—and a handsome, powerful one—he remains in many ways oddly immature, sadly inexperienced in the ways of the world, all of which can be explained by his rearing and education. He never went further away to school than to Mr.

Benton's Academy down in Newport Junction." The big man smiled. "There isn't a great deal happens around Dexter except that folks get born, get married and finally die. Did you know Matt has never seen a town other than Newport or travelled anywhere save in the woods?"

"That I didn't. Now I begin to comprehend." Mr. Stetson pursed pale pink lips and stared into the fire.

"Again, Abigail Hovey's boy—well, he has been all his life deprived of those relationships which normally prevail in a family," Larrabee broke off, raised quizzical brows then stated evenly. "I have often wondered why."

Stetson straightened on his tall, barrel-back rocker. "I suspect, Doctor, that you know better how to answer that question than anyone else alive—*excepting one*. If you think it justified I shall waive what we term 'professional ethics' and tell you—if you wish."

The doctor quickly raised a blunt-fingered hand. "Thank you. There's no need to—just yet. I would much rather not have confirmed certain sad facts which at present I only suspect. But you were asking me my opinion concerning Matthew's character? Well, I tell you quite simply that at present young Hovey is an intelligent, sensitive and headstrong young animal."

"Animal?" Stetson looked his surprise. "Did you say 'animal,' Doctor?"

"Yes. He's full-blooded and terribly vital. He's inclined to respond strongly towards his natural impulses. His mother was aware of this and labored hard to teach him self-control, but she only partially succeeded."

In the woods beyond the snow-spattered windows the bitter frost cracked a bough, causing a report as loud as a musket's. Both men jumped, then grinned a little shamefacedly.

Edwin Stetson arose, crossed to rest one elbow on the plain mantelpiece of pine. "Then you believe he could become violent, even capable of fatal actions based on impulse rather than on reason?"

A series of blue cloudlets rose from the doctor's charred blackthorn pipe before he said, "Yes. And since you are one of the few people who has ever suspected this, I'll tell you that when Matt was twelve he just failed of murdering a schoolmate—some insult to his mother, I believe—he was pulled off just when young Martin was about to die of strangulation."

"But he seems so mild, so Christian—"

"As a rule, yes. There's no one kinder or more peaceable; but on another occasion he half killed a trapper who tormented his dog. I know. God help the man who rouses him and God help Matt Hovey if he doesn't learn to control himself—if he doesn't, he'll hang or go to prison."

The eyes of the two men met, lingered soberly. Then Stetson heaved a sigh and commenced to run his heavy gold watch chain back and forth between his fingers.

"That, Doctor, is just what I came hoping not to hear. He was at my office this morning and learned certain facts I had no choice but to reveal. He took the matter so hard I fear that he is about to ruin himself and also his mother's good name. Do you know what I am talking about?"

"Yes. As I've said before, I *know* nothing, Mr. Stetson, but I can guess all too well," Dr. Larrabee replied heavily. "Abigail Hovey was one of the noblest women I've ever seen or even heard of. Were I to talk from now till dawn I couldn't commence to describe her wonderful unselfishness, her generosity, her tolerance and her—her sheer goodness.

"Because I have been her physician all these years I have deduced bit by bit that something unspeakably terrible *must* have happened to her before she came to Dexter. How else is one to explain her dreadful fear of the outside world? Her complete lack of family connections? Her silence as to her origins? And what of those letters which come every three months containing only money?"

Springs groaned under Larrabee's weight when he sank onto a worn leather armchair.

"All of this is true," the lawyer asserted and, reaching into the tail of his frock coat, produced a handkerchief with which he polished his spectacles.

"Matthew learned today that he is illegitimate," Dr. Larrabee said. "That's it, isn't it?"

"Yes, that's it. Tell me, do you think—?"

The big doctor arose and confronted the neat figure in black and brown. "What you're trying to learn is whether I think that Matt will attempt to kill his mother's—well, I suppose we should say, 'betrayer'?"

"Yes."

"I do. Matt worshipped the ground his mother walked on. He was devoted, perhaps too devoted, to her because she was all the family he had ever known. Yes, I think quite conceivably he will kill this man. Does he know his father's name?"

"Yes."

"Did you have to tell him that?"

Edwin Stetson stiffened, spoke succinctly, "I had no choice but to carry out my client's instructions."

Dr. Larrabee crossed over to the wood box, deliberately tapped cold ashes from his pipe then strode out into the hall and called to the back of his house.

"I am sorry, my dear, it appears I will have to go out after all."

"Oh, Heavens! Henry, must you? It's so cold out. I hope you're not going far."

"No, it's not far. Just over to the Hovey place."

"But Henry," she said anxiously studying her husband as, wearily, he pulled on his fur coat, "you speak just as if this were a matter of life or death."

"Maybe it is," her husband replied, winding a muffler about his neck.

VI EVASION

PHOEBE WHIDDEN, ALTHOUGH handsome, serene and possessing a figure that was well developed, was only nineteen years of age. Like most young people in the neighborhood she had experienced only the life usual to Penobscot County. Of course by now she had attended several funerals and weddings, and once even had assisted intimately when Bertha Newell's pains had quickened too fast for Dr. Larrabee to get there. She had not, like Matt Hovey, studiously read the Portland and Bangor papers which afforded at least a vicarious familiarity with the great, fearful and challenging world beyond Newport Junction.

Benjie, her half collie dog, commenced to bark out in the farmyard. Then, in answer to a furtive knocking at her father's back door, Phoebe raised a kerosene lamp and peered out into the chilly gloom.

"Why–why, Matt!" she gasped. "Whatever fetches you here at this hour?"

He stared at her with a curious fierce intensity which suddenly she recognized from the time years ago at school when he had fought–and licked–Elmer Winslow for pulling her hair and making her cry.

"Why–Phoebe, I–well, I'll linger but a few minutes," he said and stooped swiftly to cast loose rawhide thongs securing bearpaw snowshoes. In rising bewilderment Phoebe noticed that Matt shouldered a woodsman's pack with his best serge overcoat strapped onto its top.

Matt tramped in without kicking the loose snow from his boots. "Your folks–where are they?"

Phoebe fell back a step, drying her hands on a gingham apron–she had been doing the supper dishes when Benjie had set up such a furious alarm. Mercy! What a tense, wholly unfamiliar look Matt wore. Obviously he'd walked a long way and hadn't shaved recently–which was unusual unless he'd been timber cruising the woods.

"Why–why–Matt, Ma's been ailing; caught a little cold at the funeral I expect. Pa, he's driven in to Dexter for his Lodge meeting." She smiled brightly. "Mercy, Matt, I'm that pleased to see you. Cold out. How about some coffee? There's some I was saving for Pa."

He shoved the rough door shut behind him, stood with yellow hair all but brushing the ceiling—the Whiddens' house was old, with the low ceilings of Dexter's early days.

"Mercy me!" Phoebe repeated. "What ails you, Matt? Stop acting so queer. You scare me."

"Can't help it," he replied in a monotone. "I—I—" he broke off and crossed to the burnished kitchen stove. Well fed, it glowed and feathers of steam drifted from the spout of a copper teakettle. Nancy Whidden always had prided herself on her copperware.

"Please, Matt, give me your cap and coat and rest yourself. What's wrong?" Mechanically, he took off his foxskin cap and great bearskin coat. At his wooden expression her dark blue eyes widened in real alarm. She had been aware of Matt Hovey for nearly fifteen years. Childishly at first, then soberly, shyly and tenderly. Privately she was convinced that someday they would marry.

"Better have some coffee," she urged. "You look cold." Her long straight skirt of coarse brown wool and a pair of linsey-woolsey petticoats beneath it swung rythmically as she started over to the cupboard.

Harsh and unfamiliar, his voice checked her. "No, Phoebe. No! I tell you I can bide here only a minute." He towered there beside the stove, yellow hair tinted deep gold by the lamplight; his dark brown eyes appeared much smaller than usual, but shone brightly.

"Well, Mr. Matthew," Phoebe burst out in irritation, "so long as you intend to act unfriendly, why did you come calling on me?"

He took a half step towards her, big hands extended. "Oh, Phoebe, don't scold. Please. I came because I'm going away."

"*Away?* You're going to enlist?" Phoebe advanced, her smooth features suddenly drained of color.

His shadow magnified by the lamp mimicked and magnified the curt shake of his head. "Not now, anyhow."

"But why?"

"I can't tell you," he burst out. "It's only that I've got to leave Dexter and never come back."

"Not come back? Matt Hovey! Have you taken leave of your wits?" She was gravely concerned now. Dark red lips parted in incredulity, she hurried forward. "Have you taken a fever? Shouldn't wonder but you have, what with all this grief and affliction. Please—dear." There now, she'd said it, although it wasn't modest. "Sit down and let's talk. Haven't we always been trustful of one another?"

He pushed aside the hand she would have placed upon his forehead. "No, Phoebe, let me be! I'm not fit to be touched by you; I'm not fit to mingle with decent folk!"

Incredulously she stared up at this tall, suddenly unfamiliar man she had known for so long. "Why, Matt Hovey. Whatever are you saying? Why, you talk as if you'd done something dreadful!"

"I haven't—not yet. But soon I'm going to." He drew himself up, glared into the oval of her slightly freckled face.

"Matt—you—you really talk crazy-like! If you've done nothing, then why can't you touch me? Why can't you—" Eyes suddenly swimming, she flung herself forward. It pierced her being to see Matt standing like this, so grim, miserable and with that dangerous gleam in his eyes. "You must tell me what's wrong. Please!" she implored.

"Why?"

"Aren't—aren't we—aren't I—" in her alarm Phoebe became desperately forward, "aren't—aren't we—aren't I your—your real true friend? Aren't I your—" Despite her distress she couldn't find courage to say "intended."

For a moment Matt remained rigid, permitted her to clasp her arms around his neck and press her warm and smooth cheek against his stiff, chilled one.

Slowly he unlocked her hands, lowered them. "Don't ask me to explain, Phoebe," he cried brokenly, "but we can never marry. Believe me, there's a terrible reason why not." He framed her features between big work-roughened hands, stared into her drowned eyes. "Just remember this, Phoebe—I want nobody else in all the world for my wife, but I'm too shameful a person ever to marry!" he cried in so loud a voice that Mrs. Whidden called from upstairs to know who was there.

"You? *Shameful?* I don't believe it!" Phoebe cried in desperation. "Never was a better, more devoted son nor a more God-fearing and useful member of this township. Somebody has lied."

"No, they haven't, so I'm leaving Dexter." His voice was flat, toneless. "Best for you to forget I ever existed." His hand groped for the wrought-iron latch of a kitchen door defaced by the scratchings of Benjie and several generations of outward-bound dogs.

Phoebe went scarlet and rage such as he had never before seen contorted her usually placid, well-loved features. "I've listened to your nonsense," she blazed. "Now just you heed me, you great numskull! If you fancy I've dreamed and prayed and hoped for our happiness all these years in vain, you've another think coming. Since you admit, as you have just now, that you love only me, I *will not* let you go like this. No! No!

For Heaven's sake wait, listen to me!" He was struggling to open the door. Mrs. Whidden began calling out in alarm.

"What's wrong, daughter—isn't that Matt down there?"

"Stop it, Phoebe!" he ordered roughly. "It's bad enough to be going away like this, so don't—"

"Very well," she choked, staunching her tears on a blue gingham apron, "but remember this. If you run away as—as you seem bound, and try leaving me behind I—" her long-lashed dark blue eyes grew terribly intense—"I swear I'll follow, n-no matter where or how f-far you go, because, right now, you act as if your wits are addled and you n-need help and c-comfort. And d-don't think for a moment I'm not going to f-follow you. If you do enlist I'll join the Sanitary Commission and nurse our poor fellows just to be near you. I won't be left behind. I love you, Matt."

"No. You'll do no such a thing," he protested while lifting the door latch. "All sorts of terrible things could happen to you. No. Just you bide here and take up with Fred Thatcher. Heard tell he'll soon come into his uncle's sawmill over to Garland." Almost roughly he pushed her aside, jumped out into the darkness and, without delaying to tie on his snowshoes, tucked them under his arm, ran slipping and floundering off towards the woods.

Phoebe started out into the back yard and felt a chill blast bite at her face and hands. The snow climbed to her knees, hampered her heavy skirts until she fell headlong into a drift. "Matt! Matt!" she sobbed. "Come back! You must come back or I'll follow you to the ends of the earth, if need be." But she could see him running lightly across a stump lot towards the brook.

She lingered where she was long enough to see his tall, broad-shouldered figure halt. Hope sang in her heart until she became aware that he had only stopped to secure his snowshoes and heave on his woodsman's pack. Once his oval-shaped bearpaw snowshoes were secured he hesitated, turned and must have seen her forlorn figure standing there at the edge of the farmyard for he raised an arm in silent farewell, then with the ease of the born woodsman, Matt trotted off into a birch thicket and became lost among shadows created by the blazing starlight.

Characteristically, Phoebe Whidden didn't weep any more. It would have accomplished nothing. Her chief reaction was bewilderment, mingled with exasperation and anger. What *could* be ailing Matt for him to act like this? Certainly something pretty awful must have chanced. But what? Around Dexter nothing like that ever happened.

She started at the faint sound of sleigh bells on the pike. "Papa! He must have come home early," she whispered and commenced brushing the snow from her clothes. Then she recognized an unfamiliar timbre to those bells and hurried back into the farmhouse. No, it wasn't Papa. She stamped ankle-high black laced shoes free of snow and again dusted her heavy wool skirt and petticoats. Glory, how cold it was tonight! The chill crept right up her legs despite the ankle-length drawers she wore. Who could be calling at this hour?

The strange sleigh went right around to the back of the farmhouse. Like the foundations, the front door had been heavily banked with fir boughs and so remained unused from first frost until late in April.

A heavy, familiar figure came creaking over the snow into the range of the lantern Phoebe brought out to the back porch.

"Why, Dr. Larrabee! There's nobody sick—Mamma's got over her little sniffle."

He shot her a penetrating glance, wiped frost from his beard. "Has Matt Hovey been here?"

"Why, yes, sir. He left only a moment ago. Come inside, won't you? It's fit to freeze the flippers off a seal tonight. Never did see it so cold so early in the year."

"Nor I, Phoebe. This gentleman is Lawyer Stetson from Newport Junction."

"How do you do?" Phoebe bobbed a rudimentary curtsy.

"Tolerably," Edwin Stetson sighed, looked sharply about. Um. Azel Whidden must be winning more than moderate bread these days—if that new stove, banjo clock, copper kettle meant anything.

Dr. Larrabee noted the tear stains and the half-melted snow on her garments. "Where did Matt go?"

"I don't know, Dr. Larrabee," Phoebe said miserably. "I wish I did."

"Pray, er, Miss Whidden, confide in us," urged Mr. Stetson and wiped fog from his spectacles. "I—er, perceive that you are distraught."

Phoebe wailed, her features crumpling, "Matt—he only said he was going away and wouldn't ever come back."

"He didn't say where he was headed?" the doctor prompted.

Phoebe blinked at this strangely assorted pair—noted that they held only anxiety in common. They, too, were worried over Matt.

"No. Matt only said that he was—was shameful—that he was going away and that he'd never come back. Oh, Dr. Larrabee! Please—please tell me. What's happened to Matt?" She clutched at the shaggy forearm of his moth-eaten coat.

"I don't know," Dr. Larrabee told her, truthfully enough. "I don't know for sure; but Mr. Stetson and I are trying to come up with Matt before—before he might do something terribly wicked."

Phoebe's bright upper lip became clenched between her teeth. "Oh,

Doctor, he came bursting in like a wild creature—he wouldn't listen to me. He set off on snowshoes down towards the brook."

The two men exchanged helpless glances.

"We regret to have pestered you, Miss Whidden," the lawyer said. "Come on, Doctor. Obviously we cannot further our purpose here."

Dr. Larrabee nodded. "Please give my respects to your parents. Your mother's cold is better?"

"Oh, much better. Won't you let me brew you some coffee?" Phoebe tried to smile. "Look, the kettle's on the boil. Won't take a minute." Desperately she wanted to learn what these two wise and respected men knew. To her infinite chagrin the callers excused themselves and tramped back out into the sparkling night where the snow crunched crisply under their boots before they got back into the cutter.

"What's to be done?" Dr. Larrabee inquired, for once quite helpless.

"Blessed if I know for sure," the lawyer returned, tucked the fur robe carefully about his shins. "But soon as we reach Dexter I intend to dispatch a telegram to Bangor if I have to haul Lem Potter out of bed to send it. That boy is on his way to commit a murder."

VII BANGOR

HAD HE NOT been so consumed by a sense of outrage and grief Matthew Hovey would have derived deep interest on viewing, for the first time, the myriad-seeming steeples and roofs of what to him constituted a vast metropolis. Think of it! Bangor, now looming into ever plainer view beyond a bend in the Penobscot & Aroostook right-of-way, boasted a population of nearly twenty thousand souls. From prints carefully studied over the years he recognized instantly a number of landmarks in this town sprawled on hilly ground at the confluence of the mighty Penobscot and the lesser Kenduskeag.

He was well aware that this neat, pretty little town was expanding rapidly. He knew that the Federal Government maintained a Court House and a Customs House here, that President Lincoln's Vice-President, Hannibal Hamlin, hailed from this place, and that Bangor boasted extensive steam sawmills, cooperages and shipyards.

In fact, he had read repeatedly in the *Daily Whig & Courier* that Bangor was becoming the most important lumber center in all New England, if not in the whole of the United States. Matt even had learned the principal streets of the city, the location of important public buildings and the names of all the churches. His church, were he to live here, would be the First Congregational, situated at that corner of Maine and Union Streets. And here in Bangor was located the Theological Seminary which once he had hoped to attend. The celebrated Enoch Pond was its President and Professor of Ecclesiastical History.

But it was not until he found a discarded newspaper on his seat in the cars that he had learned the name of a gunsmith. There were apparently only two such in business: Charles V. Ramsdell in East Market Square and Macomb Long whose shop was in the west side of Granite Block.

Once the railway coach's trucks commenced to clank and bump over a series of switchpoints Matt carefully folded the newspaper cutting and put it into his pocket. During the long, twenty-seven-mile ride down from Newport Junction he had had time to figure things out, to plan his next moves very carefully, to foresee all manner of contingencies. He had not the least intention of making a botch of the task he had set himself. From the railroad station he would board an omnibus and ride over to the Hatch House—one of Bangor's smaller hotels.

"I'll give out I'm up from Portland—on business," he told himself. "The lumber trade." That should be an easy role to portray. While working at the furniture factory, he'd met numbers of dealers and had learned the names of half a dozen firms with headquarters in or near Portland.

Once established in his hotel he would make casual inquiries concerning Josiah Cosby. Already he knew that his father was one of the richest men in the State; that he controlled enormous interests in timber lands, various railways and even owned a line of steamboats which, when the river was open, ran from Bangor to Portland by way of Belfast and Rockland.

Momentarily Matt forgot his burning indignation. Criminently! Bangor was a mighty big place, easily twenty times the size of Newport. Beyond the car's frosty windows loomed a series of factories, warehouses and then a long succession of snowy streets lined on both sides by modest but neat white-painted clapboard houses over which blue wood smoke hung in the windless air in a series of delicate strata.

When at last the train clattered to a halt under a long, smoky shed, Matt remained seated watching the brakemen set their brake wheels at each end of the car while his fellow passengers pushed eagerly out, as passengers invariably will.

Only a tired-looking young soldier who had fallen asleep and a couple of half-drunken woodsmen lingering to adjust leather muzzles upon their double-bitted axes, remained. Carefully Matt lifted down his pack from the rack and slipped its arm loops into place. To his infinite relief the railway station proved to be far from crowded. In it loitered only a party of soldiers in long-skirted and caped blue overcoats and a few travelling men in stovepipe hats who stood talking with backs to a huge cylindrical stove. No one paid the tall young countryman the least attention.

He found no omnibus but outside there were a couple of sleighs drawn by ribby-looking skates whose drivers offered, for a half dollar, to convey him anywhere in town.

Red-faced and diffident, he underwent the formality of registering at the Hatch House and in his confusion all but forgot to sign the name he had so recently adopted. After all "Matthew Everett" was the one name to which he felt in the least entitled. Like the rustic he was, Matt gaped about the lobby at some frayed potted palms and, wonder of wonders, upon the first gaslights he had ever beheld. Of course at this hour they weren't ignited but they looked all-fired strange.

For a small and none-too-cleanly room he insisted upon paying a dollar in advance, causing the desk clerk to cast him a curious glance. Once left to himself he eased his pack to the floor, hung up his new blue serge overcoat, and seated himself upon a white-painted iron bed. Its springs screeched faintly under his weight.

What with all these new sights, impressions and experiences crowding in so fast it proved quite difficult to think in orderly fashion, but at length Matt roused himself and went in search of Mr. Ramsdell, the gunsmith. He guessed he'd better stop by when there were likely to be a number of customers—he didn't want to be overly noticeable. The gunsmith's shop, however, proved to be deserted save for Mr. Ramsdell's clerk, a slick-haired, weedy youth wearing an obviously outgrown homespun jacket. He looked disconcertingly hard at Matt when he opened the door and so set to tinkling a bell bolted on to a spring.

"Yes sir?" He demanded briskly. "What'll it be? A skinning knife? You look like a woodsman to me. Lead? A can of gunpowder? Percussion caps? We have a few boxes left."

"No," Matt strove to keep his voice steady. "I want to buy a—a hand gun."

"Oh, a pistol, eh? Well, sir, what's your fancy? A revolver or maybe a derringer? What with this war and all they're mighty hard to come by."

"Why—why—I don't rightly know," Matt stammered. Of course he'd have had a ready reply in the matter of shotguns and rifles, such he had been handling ever since boyhood. In fact, locally, he was considered quite a tolerable marksman. But about revolvers and pistols he knew mighty little. No one ever carried hand guns about Dexter, or into the woods.

"Say, you ben't going away to the war, are you? If so, you'd best buy a revolver big enough to knock a hole clear through a Rebel. Now Colonel Varney and Cap'n Levi Emerson—he was the first man in Bangor to enlist after Sumter—bought themselves each a forty-four."

"No. I don't want a big pistol. Only a little one."

"Then I must know, sir," the clerk continued loftily, "is this hand gun to be worn in a holster or carried in the pocket—something small, like the soldiers try to hide in case they are captured?"

Matt wished the sweat would stop cascading down his cheeks from under his brimless fox fur cap. "Yes—that's the sort of a gun I want—the kind that you can hide."

The clerk turned to a row of drawers, spoke over his shoulder. "Then I expect what you need is a derringer—two barrels, eh? About thirty-four calibres? Like this." He held out his hand. In its palm lay a small, snub-nosed nickel-plated pistol with one barrel set above its fellow.

"Is—is that little thing heavy enough to kill a man?" Matt heard his voice inquiring.

"Kill a man?" the clerk stared hard at his customer. "My God, yes! Aim her right and she'll kill a horse. Say, you sure don't know much about hand guns do you?"

"Not much. How much is this one?"

Again the clerk ran his eyes with disconcerting attention over this tall, yellow-haired young fellow blushing so furiously across a counter loaded with canisters of powder, bullet moulds, powder flasks, cartridge boxes, reamers, rammers and all manner of shooting equipment.

Despite himself, Matt's gaze wavered to the glass-fronted case in which hung a gleaming row of single- or double-barrelled shotguns. All looked brand-new and there was one double-barrel which held his admiration, a beautiful, slim-looking piece the stock of which fairly glowed and displayed all manner of engraving about its lock and hammers.

"That there's an English-made gun," said the clerk following his gaze. "Last summer the cap'n of an English bark took her off a passenger who couldn't pay his fare. Real purty, ain't she?"

"It surely is," Matt agreed.

"Don't expect you could hardly buy her—she's priced at a hundred and fifty."

"Whew! I couldn't. But how much is, well, that derringer?"

"She'll stand you eighteen dollars, mister, plus two dollars for your bullet mould and twenty-five cents for a stick of lead. You're just in time; come another month prices will go up again. As it is we are about cleaned out right now, what with all our boys gone off to fight the Rebels. Thirty-two and twenty-eight calibres is our most popular derringer.

Thirty-four is a leetle mite hefty for most folks who aim to stow their firearm in a weskit pocket."

"Eighteen dollars!" Matt gulped. In his furious headlong flight from Dexter he had taken along only the money contained in that last accursed letter from Josiah Cosby.

"Well, d'you want her or don't you?" The clerk tapped the wicked little weapon.

"Maybe you've got a single barrel?"

"Yep," replied the youth, patently disappointed. "Here's a thirty-four single shot for only eight-fifty. 'Tain't much, but it'll do to kill a man."

"Kill a man!" The words resounded in Matt's imagination like the clashing of cymbals. Kill a man? Execute him, rather.

"Thanks," said Matt, "I'll buy it and I'll want a dozen percussion caps too, and I—well—I don't think I'll require the mould if you can let me have a few bullets. I—I've a friend who has a thirty-four." He guessed he could teach himself how to load this pistol which nestled so snugly into the palm of his hand. He didn't want further to rouse this pimply-faced youth's curiosity.

Once back out in the street, Matt, to quiet himself, tramped down Market Street towards the Penobscot River until he entered a district where towering piles of logs and stacks of sawed lumber lined both sides of frozen, manure-splashed streets. From the high river bank he could see several boats, huge lumber rafts, barges and ships which had been trapped and frozen in by that early blizzard of last week. Nearer at hand several steam saw and planing mills were hard at work with buzz saws screeching and whining like mad.

When various whistles sounded noon they fell instantly silent and soon gangs of workmen in clumsy boots, knitted or fur caps and heavy red blanket coats appeared on their way towards various bars and eating houses. Those of the better sort, Matt noticed, patronized a place displaying a spandy-new signboard which announced that one Charles Dolan was prepared to serve meals as well as liquor. It required all of Matt's sullen determination to approach such a den of iniquity as a saloon. Still, what difference did it make where he now went, or what company was kept by a nameless bastard?

From his slight experience he suspected that bastards inevitably drank, gambled and had to do with loose women—whatever "to do" implied. Yes. He *would* go into a saloon—and meet old Satan halfway.

He drew a deep breath, squared his shoulders and tramped over a splintered wooden sidewalk well coated with ice and ashes to Mr. Dolan's "Eagle Saloon." He lingered diffidently just inside, for the bar was crowded with workmen and there wasn't a seat to be had at any of the long, oilcloth-covered tables. The air was heavy with the odors of cabbage, stale beer and rank tobacco. Yes. He'd have to learn to smoke, too, Matt decided.

To his astonishment the Great Rebellion against the Union was hardly ever mentioned. The drinkers and diners seemed far more concerned over the future price of lumber and how many millions of running feet might be received into the booms once the ice went out next April.

At length Matt plucked up sufficient courage to order a large mug of beer for which he paid five cents. Now that he was lifting this foaming glass surely the Devil had begun breathing down his neck! His lips curled away from the bitter tasting suds and he recalled Jim Clifford, the town drunkard, and William Little Eagle, the old Penobscot trapper who got roaring drunk every time he had the price and could bribe someone into selling him a bottle.

"To Tunket with it!" In a defiant gesture he drained his mug and, copying his fellow tipplers, wiped his mouth on the back of his hand. Just then he heard someone behind him say, "My God, don't try telling me Joe Cosby ain't smarter'n a whole den of foxes. Heard tell he's dickering with a Portland firm, Alexander Edmonds I think, for a prime hardwood tract down below Searsport." Turning, Matt saw that the speaker was a dumpy, well-dressed little man lurking behind a huge bushy beard.

"He'll get it away from the Chapins—no matter what the price," returned the little man's companion. "Once Joe Cosby sets out to get a thing, he gets it, and God help thems what gets in the way."

The two rattled on over huge helpings of corned beef and cabbage. Josiah Cosby, it appeared, must be a mighty big frog in that puddle called Bangor.

The two were pushing away their chairs when Matt tramped over. "Beg pardon," said he, "but I couldn't help overhearing you talking about Mr. Cosby."

"Yep," admitted the little man while picking his teeth with a grimy forefinger. "What's it to you?"

"Only that I—I—" There again was that wretched weakness about fabricating a story. "Well, I got some timber land for sale, first-class spruce and fir. I was wondering whether Mr. Cosby might be in town or not."

"What about it, Bill?"

"Think he is. Heard someone tell he's spendin' a lot of time up at that new mill he's built on the road to Old Town. Know how to locate his place, bub? That is, if he ain't to his office, which is in the Granite Block Building."

"Why—why no, sir. I would be obliged if you'd inform me." Lord! How his pulses had begun to throb. Cosby was in town and unaware that every tick of the clock brought nearer the end of his days.

"Well, ye'd best hire yourself a rig at some livery stable lest you aim to tramp above two miles upriver. He's built himself a fancy place overlooking the river, so you've only to follow the Old Town road till you come to it."

VIII SACHEM HILL (I)

MATTHEW EVERETT HAD hardly pulled in a tolerably handsome bay gelding hired from Vickery & Sargent's Livery Stable when a manservant in a queer-looking black-and-white suit—he was foreign by the look of him—opened Sachem Hill's fancy storm door and peered out on to the driveway. This being the first private servant Matt had ever beheld he gaped, then wondered what such a fellow might do when it came to a pinch. This plump, red-faced apparition appeared to be somewhat taken aback on perceiving the back-country cut of Matt's black bearskin coat and round foxskin cap. Yet he was impressed by the well-groomed livery horse and the red-and-black cutter.

Matt guessed maybe he had been clever, after all, in squandering an extra dollar for the hire of this really handsome sleigh with its curved, patent-leather dashboard and a row of highly polished brass bells tinkling merrily along each of its shafts.

"Yes, sor, and shall I order yer baste put into the stable, sor?"

Matt hesitated, ended by shaking his head. Lord! How his heart had begun to hammer. "No. It's a warm afternoon. I'll just tie him to this hitching post. Is Mr. Cosby to home?"

Before Matt descended to secure a halter rein loosely to a cast-iron hitching post, he couldn't help testing for the dozenth time that slight bulge in the right-hand side pocket of his blue serge Sunday jacket.

"No, sor, but I'm after expecting the Master any minute. And will yez be coming in?" The butler lingered inside the storm door, his little blue eyes veiled by his breath vapor.

"Yes. I've come a long way to see Mr. Cosby." Matt felt reassured over the even way his voice was sounding. "I'll wait for him."

"And who, sor, might yez be?" queried the formidable figure in the doorway.

"I am Mr. Johnson from Portland—representing Fernald and Pettigrew." All the way out along the frozen road Matt had rehearsed his story. "I'm in the timber trade."

"Mrs. Cosby's in. Shall I announce you to her, sor?"

"God above, no!" Matt thought but only said uneasily, "No. I'll not trouble her. My business is with your boss."

After blanketing the livery-stable horse, Matt ascended broad stone steps sheathed in wooden treads to enter quite the most imposing residence he had ever beheld. Built of white clapboards and boasting bright green shutters, Josiah Cosby's home had four tall chimneys, and elaborate cornices running all the way around the house. Flanking the main entrance were four Ionic pilasters. A wide white front door was adorned by a Federal eagle knocker of highly polished brass; on it in bold letters was engraved the name "Cosby."

From the road Matt had glimpsed not only a large cow barn but also a long stable capable of accommodating a dozen or more horses. Off on a knoll to one side stood a circular gazebo which commanded a fine view of the now white and silent Penobscot.

The butler vented a slight sniff after aiding the caller out of his shaggy, horse-scented overcoat. Clearly, he was less than impressed by Matt's clumsy cowhide boots and the backwoods cut to his apparel. Matt was frantic for fear the manservant might notice that ominous outline in his pocket and the way it dragged at the serge.

"This way," the foreigner said—this time without any "sor"—and pushed open a door to the right of the entrance. It had been fashioned of some richly gleaming dark wood and, in swinging back, disclosed what was evidently Josiah Cosby's office and library—if rows of matched and obviously unused books so indicated.

Matt had taken only a couple of steps towards it when a brisk rustling of skirts sounded on a wide "welcoming-arms" staircase carpeted in dark turkey-red. Involuntarily the caller halted, his yellow blond hair agleam in late sunlight reflected off the snow; he looked up and noticed a girl of perhaps seventeen or eighteen halted on the main landing. She paused there with wide, blue silk skirt gently a-sway and affording a glimpse of frothy petticoats. She was of medium height, with elaborately braided dark hair coiled about a small and gracefully carried head. High color glowed in rather pointed features. She lingered on the landing, then proceeded deliberately down into the hallway.

"No," she turned and called back over her shoulder. "No, Mamma, I told you it wasn't Father!" Then to the butler, but with large sherry-brown eyes fixed on the tall figure hesitating so awkwardly below, "Who is this?"

The butler coughed and bowed. "Why, Miss Flavia, 'tis some gintleman is come on a business matter with Mr. Cosby."

"Business?" The girl's small and brilliant mouth tightened, then she cried sharply, "What in the world ails you, Timothy? Haven't you been told twenty times not to admit tradespeople by the front door?" Her voice sounded a trifle shrill as she swept down the rest of the stairs with her gaze still fixed on that country-clad figure lingering before the office entrance.

"What do you want?" she demanded and slightly raised her chin. "And just what do you mean by using the front door?"

At her tone Matt stiffened. "Who I am is no concern of yours, miss, nor is the nature of my business."

Had he slapped her on both cheeks this girl in navy blue silk could not have flushed more furiously or have appeared more outraged. "Timothy! Show this—this fellow to the servants' hall and tell him to wait there for my father."

"But—but, Miss Flavia. This gintleman is—"

"He is no gentleman," she snapped. "Just a common timberjack afflicted with outrageous effrontery."

Flavia Cosby advanced until she stood at a short distance with color high and lips flattened. This must be his half-sister, Matt suddenly realized with a start. Handsome all right, but with a mean temper it seemed.

She actually stamped a small foot encased in a black balmoral boot. "You, whoever you are, go to the back of the house, where you belong!"

Within Matthew's being there commenced to stir the fiery currents which had begun to seethe yesterday morning in Mr. Edwin Stetson's office.

The butler wavered. He looked big enough, all right, to enforce the Cosby girl's command, but Timothy must have found that in this caller's manner which gave him pause.

The man Timothy turned very red and looked anxious. He mumbled, "Please, Miss Flavia, your father's orders were to conduct anyone calling on business—not tradespeople—into his office. Mr. Johnson, this gintleman, has travelled, so he says, all the way from Portland."

Her chin rose a fraction of an inch higher and beneath a white challis shawl gently sloping shoulders could be seen to quiver. "How dare you argue with me? Show this fellow out to the servants' hall immediately or I promise you'll be given the sack and with no references."

Matt was about to speak right out when from somewhere down the hall sounded the *click* of a door lock and out into the spacious hallway sauntered into view an elegant, languid-appearing fellow of approximately Matt's age.

"God's love!" he complained. "Why can't a man be allowed to study in peace?" He came striding forward, a tall but slight figure clad in smartly cut gray broadcloth, a yellow silk-brocade waistcoat, frilled shirt and standing collar secured by a black silk cravat.

"Be quiet, 'Gustus, and don't you dare to interfere!"

"That will be all, Timothy," the new arrival remarked and paid the angry girl no more attention than a mischievous kitten.

The two young men stood regarding each other and Matthew suddenly became overwhelmed with the realization that all at once he was being confronted by another of his own father's children; he who had never even heard of, let alone seen, a distant relative. To his vast astonishment the other suddenly smiled and strode forward with hand outstretched.

"I'm Augustus Cosby," he announced casually. "Please pay no attention to my sister Flavia's rudeness. She's been in a swivet all day because George Thaxter is beau-ing somebody else to Belle Chapman's dance."

Although it required quite an effort to grasp his half-brother's hand, Matthew managed it. Lord! Who could have foreseen these complications?

"You're being simply hateful, 'Gustus. Mean and low!" blazed Flavia Cosby. "Just you wait and see. You'll be sorry. I shall tell Henrietta all about your kissing that silly Nancy Bigelow."

To a furious swishing of dark blue skirts Flavia Cosby spun about and almost ran down the hall to disappear through a door to the right.

"Well, Mr. Johnson," grinned Augustus, fingering the weak beginnings of reddish brown sideburns, "now you've gained some idea what life can be like in Sachem Hill."

Matt's long features composed themselves, for all that he was again fervently aware of a deadly weight in his jacket pocket. "I'm sorry, Mr. Cosby, to have caused all this to-do but, well, you see I am not—I am not used to calling in houses even half as grand as yours."

"It's too grand, if you ask me," muttered the elegant young fellow. "Well, come in, Mr. Johnson, I expect Pa will come along directly, but I'm afraid you won't find him in a very good humor."

"Say something," Matt urged himself. "He'll get suspicious if you stand there like a dumblock."

Aloud he asked, "What could have upset your father?"

"It's my young brother, Decius. He's got Blanche Lamont, daughter of the foreman of Pa's Old Town mill, in trouble and there's the deuce to pay. The foreman's valuable—best Pa's got." Augustus laughed mirthlessly and toyed at a big agate watch fob, then sauntered to Josiah Cosby's bureau. The butler reappeared carrying a telegram in a pale pink envelope on a silver tray. Augustus picked it up and turned it idly over before flipping it onto a wide, flat-topped desk covered with a profusion of papers impaled on spindles.

" 'Tis for Mr. Cosby, sor," the butler said. "Shall you require anything, Mr. Augustus?"

"Why, Timothy, I do believe so." He cast the wind-reddened caller a glance. "Bring us a decanter of sherry—out of the barrel that came last week." Again he flashed that curiously winning smile of his. "I guess it wasn't any too warm driving up from Bangor?"

"Why no, sir," Matt said and silently cursed himself for adding the "sir." Confound it he couldn't help liking this handsome half-brother. And he mustn't; not with what he had to do.

"Oh, yes, Timothy. You can fetch us some water biscuits too. They go well together," he added to the broad-shouldered figure in shiny blue serge and gray kersey pants tucked into clumsy country boots.

Again aware of that weight relentlessly dragging at his right coat pocket, Matt advanced over the office's thick, bottle-green carpet and pretended to examine several bookshelves and their unread contents.

"For seventeen years of age my brother Decius has acquired quite an eye for the girls," Augustus was commenting, "but not a jot of sense. That Lamont girl, well, a man's only to take two steps in her direction and she heads straightaway for the hayloft. So, Mr. Johnson, let's hope your business will prove of a pleasing nature because it will likely cost Pa near fifty dollars to square matters; and Pa, as you may have heard, is mighty near with his money."

Augustus Cosby again picked up the telegram envelope and started to slip a thumbnail under its flap, but shook his head and put it down. "It can wait. Pa should show up any minute." Suddenly he fixed a penetrating glance upon the caller. "D'you know, Mr. Johnson, just now I got the oddest feeling that we—oh, I know we've not met before, but I seem somehow to know you. Absurd, isn't it? Oh, here's the worthy Timothy."

The butler fetched in a handsome cut-glass carafe and the two slimmest, most graceful glasses Matt had ever beheld. While the amber-red liquid was being decanted, Matt in desperation for fear that Augustus might resume his speculations, indicated a daguerreotype standing on a nearby bookcase.

"Who is that?"

"Pa. Makes him mad every time he sees it. Some fancy photographer down to Portsmouth wheedled him into a sitting. Pa keeps it around just to get his money's worth, I expect."

So this powerful, big-jawed man was his father? Odd. Although he'd seen his mother nearly every day this was the first notion he'd received concerning his father's appearance. Matt had an impression of overpowering determination, shrewdness and, curiously, something of Augustus' charm. Josiah Cosby, he saw, was powerfully built, with massive jaws that jutted out from between flowing side whiskers like the prow of a battleship, a shock of bristly hair, craggy brows and a short, thick nose. The eyes were large, but in attempting to look stern succeeded only in appearing sly. *So this* was the man he had come to kill?

"And what, Mr. Johnson, is your opinion about this war we're having? Not going too well, is it? Seems they've got the better officers—from the Regular Army; although I hear our Navy came out ahead in their case. Do you think it will end next year?"

"Why—why, we don't hear much war news around Dex—" he caught himself barely in time. "Nobody pays the war much attention except to hunt for big, fat contracts. Plenty of folks are making a mint of money out of this war." God in Heaven, *when would* Josiah Cosby appear?

"I may be crazy," the other commented soberly staring into his sherry glass, "but I don't think the war will end next year—or the next. I am studying for a commission in the Navy. Pa thinks I'm crazy, swears he can get me elected to a captaincy in the State Militia. But, my God, Mr. Johnson," his clear dark blue eyes hardened suddenly, "I'm damned if I want to have happen to me what happened to those tinsel heroes who went swaggering off to Bull Run breathing death and destruction at the Rebels only to come slinking back with their tails between their legs because they didn't know 'come here' from 'sic-'em' about soldiering.

"No," he announced slowly, "I intend to serve in the Union Navy 'though Pa's dead-set against it. I am going down to Boston and apply for examination and appointment as a sub-lieutenant, if I can cram enough mathematics into my thick head." Augustus frowned, drew a deep breath. "Guess it'll surprise a lot of people who know Pa, but I aim tc fight in this war the way Great-Grandpa Bancroft did in the Revolution and my Granduncle Elijah did in the War of 1812. You see, Mr. Johnson, I really believe in the Union—we'll go to pieces without it."

It seemed odd to be putting so elementary a question concerning his own father, but Matt inquired, keeping one eye on the drive all crimson now with sunset, "Does your family hail from hereabouts?"

Augustus Cosby savored his sherry. "Lord no! Mother's from Portland. Perhaps you'll have heard of her folks, the Nickersons? They own an iron foundry down there."

"It's not likely," Matt muttered. "You see I'm not originally from Portland."

"Really. Where then?"

"An upcountry place called South Paris." Why that name should have popped into his mind Matt could never explain. Hurriedly he countered, "And where does your father come from?"

"Pa's from New York. Not the City, I'm told, but a little town upstate, a place called Amsterdam. Most of his relatives must be dead. We never seem to hear from any of them."

Silence ensued in which the snapping of the birch logs in the office fireplace directed wavelets of fragrant bluish smoke out into the room. Curse it! What *could be* keeping Josiah Cosby? It was hard on one's composure to wait so long to kill a man—gave one time to think—but every time he started to cool off he thought about his mother—her long years of exile, loneliness and hidden shame. He forced a stiff smile, ignored his sherry beyond a perfunctory sip. He never had touched wine or spirits in all his life.

"Then I take it you are not overly interested in the lumber business, Mr. Cosby?"

"Lord no, Mr. Johnson," he laughed quietly. "When this stupid war ends I intend to practice law, then maybe go into politics. Did you know that Vice-President Hamlin comes from Bangor?" Augustus Cosby sauntered over to peer out of that same window through which Matt had been glancing so restlessly.

"Hah! There comes Pa." Into a driveway nearly quarter of a mile long and edged by new little spruce trees had turned a large red sleigh driven by a coachman and drawn by two horses.

The afternoon sun was about to dip behind a row of hardwood-crowned hills to the westwards and so drew vivid flashes of fire from the brasswork adorning the harness of the pair of powerful blacks which, scenting the nearness of their stables, broke into a canter which set sleigh bells to jangling importantly. The livery-stable horse raised its head, stared, then whinnied softly.

A moment later the tintinnabulation outside faded away. The butler hurried out, with Augustus following, and banged back the storm door. Heavy feet tramped into the hallway. "God damn that silly idiot Decius!" Cosby was growling. "By God, I'll cut him down to size and in a hurry. If he's got to go philandering why does he have to tumble the daughter of the best mill foreman I've ever had? Whose rig's that out there?"

"It's a Mr. Johnson, Pa," drawled Augustus. "Young chap—nice-looking."

"What do I care about his looks? What's he want?"

"He's come up from Portland, represents Fernald and Pettigrew's, I think."

"You *think?* Damn it, why don't you *know?* Why is nobody ever sure of anything around here except me? Where is this fellow?"

"Waiting in your office. Oh, by the bye, Pa, there's a telegram just come for you."

"All right, all in good time," the deep voice rumbled. "Timothy, fetch me a hot buttered rum. It's getting perjured cold out."

"I'm going back to my study," Augustus announced. "Call out if you want me."

Sleigh bells jangled softly towards the back of Sachem Hill and, as heavy footsteps drew near, a humming like that of a nest of wasps commenced to sound in Matthew Everett's ears. All at once he stopped trembling; his hand dropped into his pocket to draw back the derringer's hammer and cause its lock to *cluck* softly. He then drew himself erect and balanced himself on the balls of his feet, as if he were about to fight somebody.

Wearing a brown frock coat bound in black braid Josiah Cosby surged into his office. He walked with head outthrust as if to impale opposition on invisible horns and directed at his tall, ruddy-faced visitor only a careless glance before, on sturdy, square-toed shoes, he tramped over to his desk.

"Well, who are you?" he snapped, chin whiskers a-quiver.

"My name might be of interest," Matt heard his voice saying thickly —not at all as he had intended. "My business—"

"Wait a minute." Cosby snatched up the pink telegram envelope, made a small snarling noise in ripping off its end. "What's your business?" he demanded while unfolding the message. Squinting like a man who has only recently become shortsighted he commenced to read.

Matt, poised in a far corner of the office, watched his father stiffen, saw color drain from his full cheeks and emphasize the ginger color of his sideburns. Cosby let the telegram fall, stared round-eyed, incredulous, on his visitor.

"My business has to do with Abigail Everett!" Matt burst out, then levelled the derringer and without a tremor sighted in line with a brass button securing the center of Josiah Cosby's black velvet waistcoat.

The telegram fluttered floorwards and Cosby extended both hands palms outwards, bright blue eyes round and intense. "Don't! Hold on! If you are Matthew Hovey I've something to say to you."

"No. I am Matthew *Everett!* Damn your cruel soul!"

Matt pulled hard, forgetting just to squeeze the pistol's trigger which, as an experienced rifleman, he should have done. A report flat and stunningly loud preceded a spurt of whitish gray smoke from the pocket pistol's muzzle. Through it Matt saw Josiah Cosby's hulking, brown-clad figure recoil behind the desk as under an invisible blow. The big man's breath escaped in a grunt, then his head snapped forward even as his hands clutched convulsively at his chest.

Matt watched his father sway, jerk forward, then claw futilely at his desk top and upset his inkwell.

As if incredulous of this thing which had happened to him Cosby straightened long enough to glare furiously upon that tall figure still levelling his pistol. Suddenly Cosby commenced to cough, then coughed harder and harder until his massive shoulders violently hunched themselves and a fine crimson spray burst from his mouth to stain papers scattered across his desk.

"You—you bastard!" choked Josiah Cosby. Then his knees gave way and he fell forward.

IX CONTRACTORS

Only a few instants were required to unsnap the livery-stable boy's halter strap, to jump into the cutter and lash the beast into a frightened run. Halfway down the drive leading from Sachem Hill the horse blanket came loose, slipped under the runners and briefly slowed the fugitive before it was left behind, a dark blue splotch on the crisp clean snow. Once on the River Road leading to Bangor the hired cutter slewed violently from side to side behind the straining horse. Spurts of powdery snow flew like spray over the dashboard of patent leather, stung Matt Everett's eyes and nose.

"Get away! You must get away! Get away quickly, quickly! As far as you can from that which you have done." Frantically, cruelly Matthew Everett applied a buggy whip to the bay hack's rump. Terrified at this mad lashing the beast pounded along with head far outthrust and nostrils flaring scarlet.

Matt needed to leave behind a demonic voice that commenced to howl in ears that still rang with that thunderous report in Josiah Cosby's office. "'*Thou shalt not kill!*'" shrieked the inner voice. "'THOU SHALT NOT KILL!' You're a parricide!"

Etched clear as a series of engravings came recollections of Josiah Cosby fingering the telegram, his incredulous stare dissolving into an expression of stark fear. Again Matt saw that sturdy, brown-clad figure recoil under the impact of his bullet, saw Josiah Cosby's leonine countenance convulsed as his body jerked forward. There were his father's bright blue eyes rolling upwards as he clutched his desk top with fumbling fingers and commenced to cough blood over papers impaled on those rows of bayonet-like spindles.

A sudden chill caused Matt to realize that he had abandoned his cap and bearskin coat at Sachem Hill. It would cost a pretty penny to replace them—if he got away. And he must. He'd no intention of hanging for the killing of Abigail Everett's betrayer. Locking his jaws he fought down his panic, set about controlling the maddened animal he was driving. Was it possible that his father's soul in the next world might encounter the gentle spirit of the woman who had died less than a week earlier?

"What I did was right!" he panted into the icy wind. "It was only just that Josiah Cosby should suffer death."

As, gradually, the horse responded to his savage reining, Matt sobered. What now might be happening at Sachem Hill? Probably a hurried saddling of gallopers to be dispatched in search of a doctor, for a clergyman. Flavia likely would be shedding dramatic, futile tears; Augustus would be administering the crisis and Mrs. Cosby bending over a husband who certainly must be dead or dying. That shot had struck hard—in the center of the body.

How quickly could a hue and cry be raised? In a gesture forever characteristic of the hunted, Matt glanced back over his shoulder up the long, winding and spotlessly white River Road. Worse luck, this highway was characterized by a succession of gentle dips and rises. Two rises away and perhaps a mile behind him he watched a black speck appear and head in his direction. Again he urged on his hired horse but guided it along the center of the road.

The cutter sped along incredibly smoothly and fast, until, among a scattering of shingled houses on the outskirts of Bangor, the fugitive took care to rein in lest passersby take note of his hatless and coatless condition on such a frigid evening. Also his hackney was gasping and steaming between the shafts. He turned into Main Street, then drove along trying to comb his hair with rigid, half-frozen fingers. Were people noticing him? To his surprise he became able to think, plan his most immediate steps. He pulled the horse to a walk down the slippery length of Main Street hill. It being well after five o'clock, darkness had descended and from various windows lights glowed warmly.

First he must return to the hotel quietly, secure his pack and knitted cap and the spare overcoat. Then it behooved him to quit Bangor at the earliest possible moment; the town was much too small to afford concealment for the great Josiah Cosby's murderer.

Half frozen and with teeth chattering like an angry squirrel's he drove the hired cutter into the Hatch House's well-trampled stableyard.

"Whew, mister! You must ha' come from somewhere's in a tearing hurry," observed a thin-faced stable boy who came clumping up to catch Matt's reins.

"Yes. I was." And before Matt realized what he was saying he added hurriedly, "Here's a half dollar for you. See that he's cooled out careful-like. He's a good horse."

The boy's red-rimmed eyes glittered once the silver coin was produced from Matt's worn, snap-catch purse. "Whew! Say, mister, I sure thank you. Will I unhitch your horse and put him up?" Apparently this youth was unaware that this was a hired rig.

Matt jumped down and commenced to flail his arms. "You'd better. Shan't want him till morning."

Because he'd had the foresight to pay for his lodging in advance Matt had only quietly to proceed up the stairs, which were deeply pitted by lumbermen's hobnails and calks, and vacate his room. He figured he must have traversed the dimly lit lobby almost unobserved since most of the Hatch House's patrons were at supper.

Five minutes later he reappeared with his woods pack slung over his best Sunday-go-to-meeting serge overcoat and wearing a dark blue knitted wool cap over his collar-length sandy yellow hair. Fortunately the clerk on duty appeared entirely occupied in calling down an overly pert Irish chambermaid. Thus Matt was enabled to regain the gloom of the street all but convinced that his hurried departure had gone unnoticed. But had he really escaped observation? By now a sleigh from Sachem Hill must have reached town to spread the momentous news. What would Phoebe think when the story trickled into Dexter? Mr. Stetson, for one, shouldn't be astonished. All the same it now appeared that he might get clean away from Bangor—if not from that terribly graphic impression of Josiah Cosby's mortal agony.

Easing the well-oiled leather of the pack's shoulder straps, he struck off down Exchange Street for the river, walking warily because of icy patches on the wooden sidewalk. He wished he had brought along his bearpaw snowshoes. With them he could cross over the Penobscot to Brewer and travel north towards New Brunswick and Canada. He guessed that this would be the least likely direction the authorities would figure he might take.

Without knowing when the trains departed he didn't dare seek the railway station which might prove to be practically empty. Lacking a crowd, people would be bound to notice his presence. Didn't he stand considerably above average height? Just under six feet? What with this oddly assorted lumberman's pack and Sunday coat someone would be bound to notice.

A group of roughly garbed men singing in loud conviviality debouched into Exchange Street and came weaving along, slipping and cursing all the while. About twenty in number they obviously were well on the route towards a high old time.

"Hey, bub!" bellowed a towering, black-bearded individual. "Chance of a lifetime. Be you minded to do a mite o' travellin'?"

From the shadows of the doorway to an empty house Matt grinned. "Shouldn't wonder. What's up?"

"We're on our way to make our tarnation fortune," belched Black Beard. "Better come along."

"Guess so. Where to?"

"Hey, Big Pig!" Another stalwart hailed one of the swaying bearded figures. "Here's a young dimwit says he might join up with this here band o' hope and glory."

The whole party—they now numbered nearly thirty—halted in the street and stood swaying and swigging when they weren't trying to sing.

"Where's this feller?" One of the biggest men Matt had ever beheld came striding forward. As Mr. Whidden used to say, he'd the map of Ireland written all over his broad, flat face which was dominated by an upturned nose and short chin whiskers red as copper. His upper lip looked longer than a day without bread.

"Lay off the horseplay, you Cullies," boomed the giant, "an' let this foine young feller speak up. Do yez really want to travel? Och! I see by yer pack that yez do."

"Aye. Where to?" Matt emerged from the shadows but stood ready to counter any overt action.

"Out west—to Ohio or further mebbe. How's that?"

"It's all right with me," Matt said, relieved that so many men were crowding all about, hiding him from occasional passersby.

"Me name's Callahan, Temus Callahan, called 'Big Pig' by me friends. Ye handy with yer dukes?"

"I suppose so. I can dress most any kind of wood and when I worked in Bell's joinery I guess I was considered pretty able." Matt glanced uneasily about. He was always uneasy in the presence of drunken men, had witnessed too much violence on their part.

Callahan elbowed his way to a patch of light cast on the manure-sprinkled snow from a near-by dwelling. "I'm thinking ye'll do, Mr.—?"

"Everett—Matt Everett," he replied before he realized his error.

"Good. Well, mister, I'm recrootin' a company of mechanics and carpenters to go out to Cincinnati. 'Tis some place out west, I'm told, where Mr. Lincoln is after buildin' some river warships. Of what sort they be I don't give a poop. All I knows the contractors out there is paying top wages to shipbuilders, carpenters, mechanics and ironworkers."

Matt's native caution asserted itself. "And what do you call top wages?"

"Ten dollars a week and found, at the least, and me and partner will pay yer way out."

"Grub on the way?"

"Grub, too. Ye'll eat sound once ye've signed yer contract wid Callahan and Grogan."

"You're labor contractors then?"

"The bhoys call us such when they feel polite. We've a special car coupled to the night freight down to Portland. Come along then, yez can sign up once we get on board. It's all right with me."

Callahan's ham-like hand suddenly shot out and closed vise-like on Matt's shoulder and his battered face loomed near. "Ye'd best remember wan thing, young feller; once ye've signed up there'll be no beggin' out o' yer contract. Be Jesus, me and Fats Grogan has undertook to deliver wan hundred mechanics and artisans in Cincinnati and we'll do it, by grabs."

The night train to Portland, sure enough, was waiting in the Exchange Street Station, with locomotive hissing, panting, softly, rhythmically while giving off occasional cloudlets of oily steam. A special coach for the construction gang had been coupled on behind the down train's only other passenger car and in front of a chunky little caboose. By now more than half of the company had become noisily or belligerently drunk, kept passing bottles back and forth, lurching about and trying to start fights which were promptly put down by Big Pig Callahan and his almost equally enormous partner, Fats Grogan.

Stoves glowed redly, too efficiently for the moment, at either end of the car while overhead a trio of gloomy kerosene lamps smoked and created a dim amber radiance to reveal the hard wooden benches and dirty floor. The scheduled hour of departure was to have been seven-thirty but many minutes dragged by and still there came no premonitory "A-all aboard" from the conductor who could be seen tramping disgustedly along the snowy platform.

Criminently! Why wouldn't this train move out? By now the alarm for Josiah Cosby's assassin must be spreading far and wide. Surely one of the first places the constable's men would search would be the railroad station. Lord! Why hadn't he kept those snowshoes?

"What t'hell ails this here chug wagon?" hiccoughed a black-bearded mechanic shoving a canvas sack of tools under his seat. "Engineer drunk or bedded down wi' a fast woman?"

Eight o'clock sounded clear and resonantly from some belfry near the station and still the train lingered while the increasing cold sketched delicate silvery designs outside the steam car's grimy windows.

Matt pretended to sleep after drawing his knitted wool cap as low over his face as he dared. Could news of the murder have spread so rapidly? Were the police and the sheriff holding this train for a search? He realized that he felt sick, sour inside.

Despite himself he saw his father coughing blood all over those papers on his desk. If only he could rid himself of that terrible incredulous expression he'd read on Josiah Cosby's whiskered countenance. How could Cosby have recognized him? "Matt Hovey!" he'd shouted. Over the strident singing of a party of shipwrights at the far end of the car, Matt kept on wondering. Did he so greatly favor his mother? Certainly Cosby never before had beheld his by-blow son. Then a plausible explanation dawned. That telegram. *That* was it! Lawyer Stetson must have telegraphed a warning—received too late.

The malodorous mechanic in a scarlet blanket coat who was sharing his seat roused suddenly and produced half a pint of whiskey from his hip pocket. " 'Pears like we're going to bide on in Bangor a while. Help yourself, friend, it's going to git cold in this car before long."

"Thanks." Matt forced a smile. "I—well, I guess I'm not much of a drinker."

But because several artisans occupying near-by benches had commenced to take an interest, Matt ended by raising the bottle. On impulse he took a generous mouthful of this flaming hot liquor, swallowed, immediately all but strangled. He coughed so long and so hard that tears commenced streaming down his cheeks and his head swam. The onlookers roared with laughter.

"My Gawd! He don't know good likker."

"Look at that whiskey starting out'n his ears."

"Jeezus! He's smokin' like a frame house a-fire!"

The lumberjack grinned a trifle shamefaced. "Sorry, friend, but that there red liquor sorts the boys out from the men. King of strong, I guess, but it's a long way to Ohio and this ain't exactly a palace car we're ridin'."

Matt summoned a watery smile. "Went down my Sunday throat, I guess. Gee, mister, that booze sure scratches like a cornered bobcat."

Thus Abigail Everett's son was introduced to hard liquor. Presently he didn't think badly of it for it warmed his stomach, made him forget his present fears; in fact it began to make him feel like a quite a fellow. "Say, mister," he said, "mind if I try it again? Cussed if I'll choke this time."

"Sure, help yourself." To his own great surprise Matt this time didn't choke and, blessedly, his fears commenced to abate. Filled with a strange, uncomfortable courage he looked calmly on when a portly blue-clad figure wearing brass buttons on his long overcoat appeared on the platform and stood conferring at length with the conductor.

By nine o'clock the atmosphere within the passenger car could readily have been cut with a dull spade, so hot, so thick and so foul it was, what with the acrid reek of cheap tobacco, the smell of sweaty wool and chewing tobacco squirted on the floor and the all-pervading odor of whiskey. Not until half past nine did the door next to the caboose open and a lean, bittern-beaked conductor appear.

"Listen all!" he called out. "Sorry, but there's been a tolerable big snowslide block the line nigh to Etna. There's a crew workin' on it, but this-here train won't pull out till round seven tomorrey."

A chunkily built carpenter jumped into the air and cracked his heels. "Hurray! Me, I'm headin' back to Ma Boudreau's parlor and buy me another tumble with that black-eyed dolly she's fetched down from Queebec!"

"Like hell ye are!" roared Callahan, closing the door behind him and scowling the length of the car. "Ain't a single one of ye lop-eared jackasses quittin' this car!"

"Like hell we ain't!" A trio of stalwart mechanics in heavy pea-jackets surged forward. "Stand aside, you goddam' bog-trotter!" But when they tried to push past Callahan the labor contractor punched the foremost on the nose so hard that he reeled and his blood sprayed the littered aisle. The second he knocked senseless and bore menacingly down on the third but that worthy fled before he could be hit.

"Grogan!" Big Pig yelled casting loose his jacket's buttons. "Block that other door and if ye favor yer front teeth ye'll allow niver a one o' these whoresons outside."

"Sure and I'll not!" bellowed back Callahan's beetle-browed partner.

Both stoves then were stoked until the heat became all but unbearable and the stench of bodies long-unwashed assaulted the nostrils. A few artisans attempted to play tonk or euchre, fewer still tried to read by the dim lamps but the most part fell to brawling or bragging of recent amatory experiences. As for Matt, he swallowed another huge drink from someone's bottle, then with head buzzing pleasantly, commenced loudly to recount purely imaginary conquests among the girls of Penobscot County. Oaths and foul words overheard about the logging camps escaped him so fluently that respect commenced to dawn in the eyes of various listeners.

"Ah-h-yer a damn' liar. You ain't bedded nothin' but yer pa's calf."

"Who said that?" shouted Matt. "I'll knock his teeth in."

"Sit down, bub." McMasters, the mechanic who shared his seat, pulled him down. "You're drunker nor any hooty owl. Any one of these hellions could gouge yer eyes out or beat you inter a pulp."

Largely because he had eaten nothing beyond a single plate of pork and beans at midday, Matt grinned foolishly, collapsed and dropped soundly asleep.

When he awoke it was to discover his stomach queasy and his head throbbing as if all the fiends in hell were hammering upon his skull with red-hot sledge hammers. His mouth tasted like a logger's sock at the end of a hard winter. Only gradually did he become aware that the train was in motion and bumping along a long, snow-mantled valley.

"Where—where are we?" he demanded thickly, knuckling hot and swollen eyelids.

"Dunno. We must ha' pulled out o' Bangor 'bout an hour gone."

From his pocket McMasters produced an apple and advised not unkindly, "Here, bub, eat this—should clear some of that goat's taste outen yer mouth."

Body yielding to the coach's lurching he crunched and sucked eagerly at the apple. After awhile he noted with a start of fear that across the aisle one of his companions was scanning a copy of the Bangor *Whig & Courier*. From the newspaper's fresh condition he judged it must have come aboard the train just before it pulled out. Cautiously he scanned a single column leader. It read:

MYSTERIOUS ATTACK UPON PROMINENT CITIZEN
JOSIAH COSBY AT DEATH'S DOOR.

The newspaper owner noted his interest. "Pretty bad," he said, "when a citizen can't set in his own home lest somebody come in and shoot him down. Don't know what the country's comin' to, what with this war and all that nonsense."

"What does—what else does it say?" Matt inquired.

"Nothing much. This Cosby feller was unconscious straight off, but the family give out a description. Seems like the assassin was young, a young feller, name of Johnson. Ah, to hell with it! Looks like the Rebs have whipped us again, place called Occoquan Creek. My God! Why can't we find us some generals who know their business?"

It seemed hardly a moment before familiar hills loomed beyond the rime-coated windows. The train clattered over a trestle, entered a hardwood forest. When it emerged Matt knew that Newport Junction would lie down the track a little over a mile ahead. Newport. Home. Peace and security. He wondered what Phoebe might be doing right now? Probably milking the cow or feeding the hens—poor Phoebe! He couldn't remember much from that anguished fog in which he had departed. Well, likely she'd do as he told her, forget all about him and take up with that Fred

Thatcher. A nice fellow, Fred, and keen as mustard. They'd probably marry and, like most young folks, move either to Portland or Bangor.

Once the train bumped onto the siding, Matt pretended to go to sleep, pulled the wool hat low over his nose, but he could still see out of the corner of his eyes. There was Appleton's grocery shop and Dean's hardware store. It being nearly ten of the morning, quite a few people were abroad. Thank goodness, there wouldn't be any of those passengers waiting on the platform come into this special coach. Besides, Messrs. Callahan and Grogan, each gripping a pick handle, waited doggedly by each of the exits.

When the train ground to a halt, Stetson & Stetson's offices lay almost directly opposite Matt's window. A host of confused and wretched recollections came flooding back. Yonder he'd heard his future blasted, his whole scheme of life uprooted. Edwin Stetson certainly had taken a lot on himself to send such a telegram. Well, maybe there wouldn't be a Stetson around when he came up with the "Reverend" D. Adams, that wretched fraud, who, after all, was the secondary cause of his present misery. Yes, surely he'd come up with Adams some day, somehow.

The engine whistled sharply, twice, three times, its blasts echoing resonantly among the surrounding hills. At that moment the door to Messrs. Stetson & Stetson's office opened and Phoebe Whidden appeared. She lingered on the threshold obviously accustoming her eyes to the glare of the sun off the snow.

She glanced uninterestedly at the string of boxcars and the two passenger cars commencing to move off behind the steam-clouded locomotive, then turned and trudged off down Main Street to C. W. Coffin's dry goods and notion store.

Presently the engineer sounded his whistle, opened wider his throttle and speeded his train on its delayed journey to Portland.

X SOUTHBOUND LOCAL

PHOEBE CONDUCTED THE purchase of a pattern for a new blouse, a paper of pins and one and a half yards of cheesecloth because Pa's Jersey cow had come fresh again. Soon there ought to be plenty of cottage cheese and cream on hand at Azel Whidden's snug little farm. A dab of yeast and a ball of blue knitting yarn concluded her shopping list. While she was stowing her purchases in a hickory splint basket, the strident whistling of a locomotive showing two yellow flags to either side of its pilot attracted her attention. Normally no train was due to pass through the Junction at this hour.

She turned to gaze at the tracks and siding opposite Mr. Coffin's dry goods, hay, grain and feed store—he also did a little preaching on Sundays—and so caused her piquant profile to become sharply outlined against the windowpanes and a row of icicles dripping from the roof gutters. Proceeding under a great ball of smoke the southbound local clanked into sight around a bend. Because the Maine Central used wood for fuel the smoke was blue-gray—not black—and sparks soared high into the air as the train of freight cars and two dingy passenger cars, coupled just in front of the caboose, began to jerk and buck under an application of their brakes.

"Now that ain't today's down train," commented the dry-goods clerk. "She's last night's Portland local. Got held up in Bangor by a thumping big snowslide east of Etna. Lem Sparks 'lowed the crews didn't get the track cleared till near dawn."

With precision Phoebe Whidden closed the snap of a worn calfskin change purse and stowed it in her petticoat pocket after modestly stepping behind a barrel of potatoes. Basket on arm she watched the train take on a couple of sacks of mail, drop a bundle of newspapers, then sigh and chuff off. Gradually the delayed local gathered speed. Absently Phoebe noticed that there was an extra car attached to the long line of freight cars, lumber flats and the regular passenger car. On the caboose's rear platform a brakeman in a shabby gray jacket was stuffing a pair of faded red flags into iron sockets.

Since the train up to Dexter wouldn't be ready for at least another twenty minutes Phoebe decided to stay in Mr. Coffin's warm store and dropped into a rocker seat situated in comfortable proximity to the big pot-bellied stove. Presently she smiled and began to play with a very young and fuzzy puppy that came waddling, bright-eyed, up to her. Lost in thought she caressed the pup which on climbing onto her lap proved embarrassingly eager to stuff its cold little nose deep into the front of her well-worn rabbitskin coat.

A boy wearing a muffler up to his eyes came shuffling over from the railway station bearing a packet of newspapers under his arm.

"Here's yer paper, Mr. Coffin," he called cheerfully. "Oh, hello, Phoebe. How air ye?"

"All right, I allow," the girl replied absently. In her mind's eye she was reviewing a conversation she'd had with Lawyer Stetson. For all that he'd sworn up and down he knew nothing concerning Matthew's whereabouts and claimed he'd not laid eyes on that young man since before he and

Dr. Larrabee had made their mysterious call, she felt convinced he knew something.

Abstractedly, Phoebe tucked a short, pleasantly curved upper lip between her teeth. Mr. Stetson *had* appeared to be speaking the truth and yet–and yet– The newsboy returned from the rear of the store to pat the puppy's mother. He came shuffling up on damp, copper-toed boots.

"Say, Phoeb, saw a friend of yours just now, a kinder extry-special friend." He grinned, winked clumsily. Everyone in and about Newport and Dexter was aware that Matt Hovey had been sweet on Phoebe Whidden and she on him ever since they'd been gangling, long-legged and inarticulate adolescents.

"That so?" Phoebe's long, strong fingers continued to smooth the puppy's orange-and-black fur. "Who was it?"

"Yep. Bet you couldn't ever guess who it was?"

"No, Mark, guess I couldn't."

"I just seen your feller. You know, Matt Hovey."

"Matt Hovey!" Phoebe sat up so abruptly she spilled the puppy squeaking onto the floor. She grabbed the boy's arm. "Did you say you saw Matt Hovey?"

"Sure, but there's no call to snap a body's head off over it."

"Oh, Mark, are you absolutely sure?"

"Why, sure."

"Where is he?"

At her vehemence the boy looked definitely startled and Mr. Coffin began peering over the tops of his steel-rimmed spectacles.

"He was aboard that Portland train just pulled out. Saw him in that extry car when I went on it to pick up my papers."

The girl's dark blue eyes widened and her fingers closed desperately over Mark's lumpy homespun sleeve. "Did you *really* see Matt on that train? Please don't tease me. It's terribly important."

"It's the Gospel truth, Phoeb. Not bein' blind as a bat I guess I know Matt Hovey when I see him."

So Matt had just passed within a few dozen yards of her and had made no effort to catch the Dexter train now screeching up to the little log-built station and pushing a long string of empty lumber cars before it.

She blinked several times and from the corner of her eye watched the dry-goods merchant unroll and smooth his copy of the *Whig & Courier* on the counter.

"You said Matt was riding in that special car?"

"Yep, with a lot of rough-lookin' workin' fellers, labor gang headed fer Portland in a special car. There was tool bags, muzzled adzes and carpenters' chests all over the place. A whole bunch of 'em."

"Whose men were they?" the girl queried sharply.

"Brakeman said they were hired by fellas called Callahan and Grogan, I think."

Phoebe rushed to the door. Off to the southward a blue haze still hovered over the Maine Central's right-of-way. She swallowed hard, caught up the shopping bag and hurried out into the thawing mud in the street.

"Say, Mr. Coffin, what ails Phoeb today?" demanded Mark. "Reckon her and Matt have had a fight?"

"There's no understanding females, Mark, as someday you'll learn," commented the old man. "Don't seem likely they've had a spat, though. Him and her both are uncommon steady for young folks."

Unseeing, Phoebe started for the station. Whatever could have gone so terribly wrong with Matt? Why should he be on a train from Bangor and not get off at Newport Junction? She wheeled sharply and almost dropped her basket when a voice called out, "Miss Whidden! Phoebe Whidden! Step over here a minute, will you?"

To her astonishment Edwin Stetson was standing in the middle of the street clad in his shirt sleeves and clutching a newspaper. At the lawyer's agitated expression she experienced a curious sinking sensation.

"Yes, Mr. Stetson. What is it?"

"I think you'd better return to my office," he said with his breath-vapor forming a gray halo about neat pink features. "I guess you'll miss your train but I, well, I have just read something which you're bound to hear about sooner or later."

Once upstairs and the plain pine door closed upon them, the lawyer thrust forward his newspaper. "Read that." After setting her splint basket of purchases on the floor and with coat still buttoned and muffler in place, Phoebe obeyed.

MYSTERIOUS ATTACK UPON PROMINENT CITIZEN
JOSIAH COSBY AT DEATH'S DOOR.

She looked her bewilderment. "I have heard of Josiah Cosby, of course. Who hasn't? He owns that big timber tract north of Papa's property over to Sebec Lake."

"Keep on reading," Stetson directed.

Bangor, Nov. 9, 1861. Late yesterday afternoon our eminent fellow citizen and that pillar of the community, Mr. Josiah Cosby, was the victim of a mysterious and dastardly attack delivered by a young man who gave his name as Johnson.

The would-be assassin gained entrance to Sachem Hill, Mr. Cosby's elegant new mansion on the River Road, by representing himself to be a lumber dealer from Portland.

Deadly Assault

Mr. Cosby returned from an inspection of his extensive mills at Orono to find the stranger awaiting him in his office. According to Mr. Augustus Cosby, the man Johnson immediately drew a pocket pistol and fired. His bullet took effect in Mr. Cosby's right lung causing a succession of hemorrhages which cause this great and good man's life to be despaired of by his grieving wife and distracted family.

Mr. Cosby's Only Words

Just before he lapsed into unconsciousness Timothy O'Hara, Mr. Cosby's butler, rushed in to his master to hear him mutter, "Matthew Everett."

"But what has this got to do with me? I don't know anybody named Johnson or Matthew Everett."

"But you do. Pray continue to read."

Commencing to tremble, Phoebe obeyed.

Both Miss Flavia Cosby and her brother, who had had conversation with their father's assailant, describe him as being of about twenty-three years of age, standing nearly six feet tall, with a ruddy complexion, curly yellow hair and dark brown eyes. Miss Flavia further recalled that Mr. Johnson bore a crescent-shaped scar on the back of his left hand–

"Oh-h. They can't– You don't mean it was–?" she turned deadly pale and got swaying to her feet.

Mr. Stetson's steel-colored chin whiskers descended in a nod.

"Do you mean to tell me that Matt Hovey and this Johnson man who attacked Mr. Cosby are one and the same?"

Again the lawyer inclined his head.

"But–but–I don't, I won't believe it! But why should he do so–so terrible a thing?"

"I know, but I cannot tell you. I'm dreadfully sorry, but I can't," Stetson said choosing his words with care. "I tried to prevent him but I failed, alas. It's only because you are–well–I presume you are promised to Matt and so have a right to know, that I have revealed these dreadful facts so that you may do anything you can to aid or protect him."

Phoebe sat down as suddenly as she had risen, stared unseeingly at a frayed place in the faded green carpet.

"Please, Mr. Stetson, don't say anything for a minute," she begged. "Please—I'm trying to think—to think back."

She recalled Matt's grim aspect the night he had gone rushing out of her mother's kitchen, his incomprehensible decision to leave Dexter immediately, permanently. What was it he muttered about being "unworthy" to touch her? And then he had gone rushing off into the dark. She lifted clear blue eyes, met the lawyer's even gray ones peering out from beneath shaggy brows.

"You knew Matt was going to do—this?" She pointed at the newspaper at her feet.

"I didn't know for sure," he replied precisely. "I was only guessing at what Matt had in mind."

She leaned forward with color commencing to return to her handsome features. "And that was why you and Dr. Larrabee tried to find him that night?"

"That's about the size of it," the lawyer admitted and, pulling out a pair of small, blunt-ended silver scissors from a waistcoat pocket, commenced with absurd concentration to trim his fingernails. "I was terribly distressed that we couldn't come up with him."

Red-gold hair agleam under her knitted gray wool toque she walked over to the desk. "But *why*, Mr. Stetson? Why should dear, straightforward Matt Hovey have decided to kill Josiah Cosby? What wrong could Mr. Cosby ever have done him?"

The lawyer flicked a sprinkling of nail parings off his lap then looked her full in the face. "I fear, my dear Miss Whidden, that I am not at liberty to disclose the reason, although I *can* say that Matt had what a young man of his temperament would consider a valid excuse for his action."

Her strained pink-and-white features loomed near and she extended an entreating red-mittened hand. "Please! Oh, please, Mr. Stetson. I won't ever breathe a word, truly I won't. Won't you give me the least notion what all this terrible business is about?"

"Can't and won't," he announced succinctly. "I haven't observed professional ethics for near twenty years to abandon them today. Suppose now, Phoebe, you were to come to me as a client and entrust me with a mighty important secret? What would you think of me if I betrayed it?"

"Please," she begged on the verge of tears. "I know you're right b-but I—I'm so miserable and w-worried." She commenced to cry softly at first then louder until she broke into great, rending sobs.

"I'm sorry, Phoebe, indeed I am. Perhaps you can help him. Now if you don't hurry," said he gently, "you'll likely miss your train up to Dexter."

XI PASTURES NEW

WHEN PHOEBE WHIDDEN returned to Dexter she begged a ride out to her home with Fred Colwill's wife, who had been doing the week's marketing, and then set about getting dinner exactly as she had during the past twelve years. Mrs. Whidden was still bed-bound in that same wide black walnut fourposter in which Phoebe had been conceived and born, but Mamma looked quite spry in her best frilled nightcap and a frogged, Lincoln green bed jacket over a nightdress of heavy gray flannel.

"Well," demanded the invalid smoothing the Jacob's Ladder quilt, "and how was everything down to Newport?" She cast her daughter a penetrating glance. "Hear any word about that scamp Matt Hovey? I do declare, daughter, I never did hear of anything so tomfoolish as his rushing away from Dexter like—like a bee-stung colt. Natural enough he should grieve sore over poor dear Mrs. Hovey's untimely death, but that's no excuse for abandoning his property and leaving you flatter than any flounder." Never waiting for a reply, Mrs. Whidden rattled on. "Did you bring a newspaper?"

"No, Mamma. Sorry, I—I forgot." Phoebe occupied herself by mending the sea-coal fire in the grate.

"How does that war down South progress? Have the Rebels beat us again?"

"No, Mamma, at least I didn't see anything in the paper about any battles. I expect the armies must have gone into their winter quarters, just as Papa said." Hurriedly she added, "Guess I'd better empty your slop jar."

She removed the chamber pot and having disposed of its contents carefully replaced its lid guarded by a crocheted "husher." Once safely downstairs she delayed long enough to throw a saucepanful of shelled corn to her mother's flock of fat Plymouth Rock hens. Next she poured cream into a small patented hand churn and set about making some butter. Vaguely she wondered as the churn rocked back and forth who would tend to these chores once she had departed. Most likely it would be poor Abner, Pa's overworked hired hand—if he didn't go piking off to the war like so many other youths under the notion that life in the Army would prove easier than working on a farm on the edge of the wilderness. Maybe it was. Phoebe had no way of telling.

Mechanically she mended the fire in the big, cast-iron kitchen stove and added a couple of seasoned oak sticks. One thing was Gospel sure. Papa certainly knew how to select firewood. One never caught him using green or quick-burning wood.

After coddling a pair of eggs for her mother's dinner and brewing a big pot of tea, she made toast; then, from the jam closet, selected a jar of that blackberry preserve over which Nancy Whidden justifiably set considerable store. Just how, Phoebe pondered, could she let Mamma learn about the unalterable decision she had taken without unduly putting her back up?

While waiting for the tea to steep she stared unseeing at the preserve closet door. Recently a rat had begun to gnaw off a corner of it—the yellow wood shone clearly in the neat gray paint. She mustn't feed Hortense so much. Cats too well-fed were apt to prove lazy. Then in surprise she recalled that, after tonight, she wouldn't be feeding Hortense any more.

The loaded tray she placed on a small table beside her mother's bed, sank onto a rush-seated rocker and commenced a description of styles she'd noticed in a catalog at Mr. Coffin's. Apparently in 1862 ladies' skirts would be nowhere near as full and all the modes less elaborate.

"That will be on account of the war," Mrs. Whidden observed. Her night bonnet was waggling in cadence with the motion of her chewing because a ribbon of faded pink had been knotted beneath her jaws.

Carefully Phoebe considered her mother's short and wiry figure and her angular but kindly features. "The Butterick people claim that this year bonnets will be smaller than ever and showing mostly gray and brown ribbons." She leaned forward. "I—I think I'd like to take up millinery—there's a sight of money in it, they say."

Her mother stopped chewing, stared. "Heavens to Betsy! Don't try to tell me, Phoebe Whidden, that all of a sudden you've been took with an interest in hat making!"

Phoebe picked up a wooden needle which had escaped her mother's knitting bag and replaced it. "Well," she admitted, flushing, but with sweeping, reddish brown brows immobile, "I—I've been thinking of it. Do you remember last fall Aunt Margaret wrote something about my going down to Portland and helping her in her shop?"

"Humph. Come to think of it, Maggie *did* say something about your learning to become a milliner." Mrs. Whidden's deep-set, shrewd gray-blue eyes fixed themselves upon her daughter's smooth, healthily pink features, then she said quietly, "My dear, I can only guess what you're up to, but you don't deceive me a bit. You're no more interested in millinery than—than Hortense there." She pointed to the tortoise-shell cat asleep on her bed.

"But, Mama, I am. Really and truly I am."

"Stuff and nonsense, daughter. Since you were knee-high to a grasshopper you've never been able to pull wool over my eyes," said Mrs. Whidden and loudly blew her nose. Kindly, she considered the slender yet sturdy brown-clad figure of her only child.

"But, Mama, I–"

Mrs. Whidden put down her handkerchief. "Phoebe dear, do you really deem me a perfect numskull just because we live on a little stony farm in the heart of Maine? Look at me, dear. Shall I tell you what's your real thought?"

Her daughter's wide, dark red mouth contracted and she dropped her gaze.

"You want to clear out of Dexter on account of poor Matt Hovey. You can't abide not having him around and want to go where you won't be forever minded of him."

"Oh–yes! Yes!" Phoebe rushed over and flung herself sobbing on the bed. "Oh, Mother, I do love him so terribly–even if we're not even promised." She said nothing concerning the awful news from Bangor, nor of her determination to find him, to console him in this fearful hour and to marry him. She was amazed at herself that she didn't blush.

"Well, daughter, since you're free, white and nineteen years of age, you've achieved the right to shape your own life. I'll write to Aunt Margaret in the morning, but I hope your pa won't be too deeply grieved or get the notion that you're going down to Portland to escape gossip –about Matt's leaving Dexter so suddenly."

"Dear Heavens!" Phoebe thought. "What will happen when Mamma learns that Matt most likely has murdered a man?" When would she hear? Still sniffling a little, she picked up Hortense and cuddled that sleek feline to her breast in a desperate effort to regain composure. Edwin Stetson would keep his mouth shut, she was sure of that, and Dr. Larrabee would not talk, either, although she'd no notion of just how much he knew about this miserable, mysterious business. Only one fact remained crystal clear–*she must get away at the very first instant* and come up with, or trace, Callahan and Grogan's labor gang.

Her mother's voice impinged upon her thoughts. "And when, daughter, do you propose to leave? Some day next week, I presume? That'll allow me time to finish that new gown for you."

"No, Mamma," Phoebe controlled her expression, tried to remain calm. "I want to leave Dexter quickly. I think I'll pack and take the afternoon train to Portland tomorrow."

"Tomorrow!" For the first time an edge appeared in Mrs. Whidden's voice. "Young lady, you will do no such a crazy thing! Heavens, girl, I must write to your Aunt Margaret and tell her you're coming. She'll have to be given time to find a suitable place for you to board. You just can't go flying down to a great city like Portland on a moment's notice. Besides," she announced firmly, "I must write to the Reverend Mr. Staples, Pastor of the Second Congregational Church. His wife, Clara, is an old schoolmate. She'll see that you meet some nice respectable young people."

"But, Mother, I've *got* to go tomorrow." The Lord only knew how soon that party of laborers would be shipped out—Heavens knew where. The longer she waited, the harder it would be to find out.

"*Got* to?" Mrs. Whidden's gaunt figure sat bolt upright and her eyes became piercing. "Just what do you mean by '*got* to'? You and Matt haven't been—trifling?"

"Mercy no! Why, Matt's only kissed me three times in all," Phoebe declared, her cheeks blazing.

"Well, then," snapped the invalid, "don't talk like such a dratted ninny-hammer. You'll go next week and that's that—three days at the earliest." She smiled suddenly. "I suppose I could telegraph your aunt."

Phoebe swallowed hard on nothing but met her mother's eye. Three days? Dear Heavens! Matt would have left Portland by that time and likely she'd never learn where he'd gone.

To make such a sharp break with all that she had ever known hadn't come easy to Phoebe. Of course she had travelled down to Portland once before on a visit to her grandmother—since dead—and her Aunt Maggie whom she remembered as being as skinny, lean as a bittern and with a tongue that stung like a swipe from a juniper branch. By peering out of a very dirty window, she could glimpse the white church spires of Portland looming in the distance. Another ten minutes ought to see the train into the depot. She hoped Aunt Maggie had received her mother's telegram all right because no acknowledgment of it had been received. How terrifying it would be to arrive alone in a big city like Portland.

Poor Pa! Although he had attempted mighty hard to understand her sudden decision he'd fallen far short of doing so, probably because he'd been so dog-tired, what with hauling felled timber off his northeast section and trying to get a real day's work out of his little crew of lazy, half-breed Indians. One couldn't get anything better now that practically all young men were drifting away to enlist. Men were being called for to replace those "ninety-day heroes" who had rushed off to war in response to the President's call for volunteers last summer and had got their bellies full of soldiering at Bull Run.

For the dozenth time in as many minutes Phoebe smoothed her skirts and pressed her ankles against either side of her green-and-brown carpet bag to make sure it hadn't been stolen. Papa had said one couldn't be too careful on the steam cars, especially these days with all manner of riff-raff on the move.

Stitched into her best blue flannel petticoat pocket was her entire capital of eighty-two dollars—carefully banked throughout the years when on Christmas and on her birthday, Papa invariably had presented her with five silver dollars. Another three, to meet immediate expense, rested in her change purse. Although she had attempted to appear as unconcerned as if she'd made this trip alone many times, she guessed she wasn't fooling many people, especially the kind gray-haired woman who had offered to share her seat with this pretty young woman.

Mrs. Sewell proved to be a godsend to Phoebe's diffidence. A resident of Portland, she spoke at length about Portland's fine prospects, how war orders had set business to booming, how many shipyards were working day and night to build ships of war for the Union. Secretary of the Navy Gideon Welles, it seemed, was in a tearing hurry to enforce his blockade, so hang the expense!

It was only towards the end of the trip that Phoebe learned that Mrs. Sewell's youngest son, despite poor eyesight, had enlisted in the Fifth New Hampshire Volunteers only to die of the typhoid fever before his regiment even started south.

"Dear me!" Mrs. Sewell had remarked, rearranging a thick white shawl over her black silk gown. "It's not all peaches and cream, though. Insurance rates are climbing clear out of sight what with those awful commerce raiders the Rebels have set loose. Why, one of them—the *Sumter* I think, captured *six* of our ships in one day. Mr. Sewell's in shipping, so I hear all about it. Our other two boys went away to fight last autumn. Thank Heavens they're serving in the Navy. They'll be safe." The prim, black-clad figure smiled in a pathetic attempt at confidence.

"Have you heard from them recently, ma'am?"

"Mercy no! The mails from below New York are gone all whopper-jaw nowadays. Last we heard from Louis he was on duty at some place in Virginia, Fortress Monroe, I believe. Andrew is supposed to be aboard the *Weehawken* and the good Lord alone knows where she is now. She's a converted New York Harbor ferry boat. Seems the Government's setting up some kind of a catch-as-catch-can fleet," Mrs. Sewell sniffed, "trying to enforce an embargo on all the Rebel ports because dear Queen Victoria's Government won't respect a paper blockade." Suddenly she laughed a little. "Now to be honest, my dear, Lord Russell is entirely within his rights in saying he'll respect only a blockade in being so we are sure enough 'hoist by our own petard,' as Mister Shakespeare would put it."

"Why, ma'am, I fear I don't follow you," Phoebe admitted.

"Well, I'm not surprised. I wouldn't either, except for my grandfather. He served back in the War of 1812 and was captured in the *President*, frigate. Seems that old Boney and the British were solemnly declaring the other's ports blockaded—which they weren't, especially on the French Emperor's part. Did you know, my dear, that if the English Prime Minister back in 1812 had been only a little smarter and politer, why, we would very likely have fought on England's side against Napoleon?"

"No, ma'am, I didn't. But—but, Mrs. Sewell, didn't the French come to help us during our Revolution?"

This bird-like old lady folded neatly mittened hands upon her lap. "Yes, but 'twas only to further their own designs against England and not for any love for American liberties. That's the truth, my dear, although I know that's not what the fashionable General Lafayette preached. Heavens alone knows what nonsense isn't being taught nowadays. And what are you going to do?"

While nibbling a cold chicken pie bought from a vendor—it tasted a bit high but maybe that was due to foreign seasoning—Phoebe said, "Why—why, I mean to apprentice in the millinery trade under my aunt, Miss Margaret Hunter. She keeps a shop in Temple Street."

"Oh, are you Miss Maggie's niece?" Mrs. Sewell considered her fair, red-haired young companion with fresh interest. "Why, I've purchased many a bonnet at her shop. Pray let me look at you again, my dear. No, you don't resemble your aunt the least bit—which if you'll pardon me, is just as well, though, like the singed cat, she's better than she looks. Well, I declare, there's no accounting for families. And where did you get that lovely golden red hair?"

Phoebe laughed, but wished her stomach wouldn't keep reminding her of that soggy chicken pie which had cost all of fifteen cents. "Why—why, I guess from Papa's side. His mother was redhaired. But tell me about my Aunt Maggie. I've not seen her in seven years."

"Well, I'll vouch that Miss Hunter knows her own mind. I've heard tell that she's a mite hard on apprentices, but of course being her niece would make a difference. Isn't this a dreary dress? I wonder whether we ought to keep on wearing black? Of course it's one way of showing respect for the departed, but Billy was always such a merry lad I wonder if he'd approve?"

"I'm ever so sorry about your son Billy," said Phoebe softly. "It must be dreadful sad to bring a boy all the way to manhood and then lose him."

"It is," Mrs. Sewell admitted. "But I'd have never been able to bring him and his brothers up the way they were if a lot of other mothers hadn't sent their sons to war for Freedom." The sprightly little woman in black silk compressed thin, violet-tinted lips and looked quickly out a frozen river upon which great rafts of logs lay imprisoned. "I could only wish, Miss Whidden, that my Billy would be the last boy to be lost before this terrible war ends, but quite a few of my friends have suffered losses. Alas, from what I hear the Rebels are determined, brave, and well led. Ah! We will reach Portland in a very few moments now."

Rows of dull, badly painted boxcars flashed by, then several strings of passenger coaches. While fighting down a sudden queasiness Phoebe strained her eyes. Might Matt's train be among these desolate-looking cars? Was he still in Portland? How long would be required to ship a party of contract workmen out of town?

"You *are* excited, aren't you, my dear?" Mrs. Sewell smiled while adjusting her bonnet. "Who, beside your aunt, might you be expecting to see?"

"Why—why, whatever would make you think that? As I told you I'm going to work for my aunt."

"Tush, Miss Whidden, a girl doesn't fidget as you have the past half hour over a homely old aunt. You're quite flushed."

Phoebe shrugged and swallowed hard. That boughten pie certainly wasn't sitting any too well on her stomach. "Oh, I expect it's just because this car's so dreadfully hot."

The engineer whistled for brakes, doors banged as brakemen hurried out onto the icy platforms and commenced to spin their wheels. The train slowed, bumped, clanked and came to a shuddering halt beside a long, smoke-stained shed.

Suddenly Phoebe commenced silently to pray that her Aunt Maggie wouldn't be on hand right away; she needed time to dash into the dispatcher's office and learn whether he, the passenger agent or whoever, could say what had befallen the occupants of that special car which had come from Bangor three days ago.

When she had helped Mrs. Sewell down onto the platform and fetched out her own carpetbag the first person she beheld was Aunt Maggie, walking ramrod-straight and with penetrating eyes questing like those of a ranging hawk. She deliberated an evasion by descending the far side of the coach's steps but unfortunately Mrs. Sewell called out:

"Ah, there Miss Hunter! I've had such a nice trip down with your pretty niece. Here she is, safe and sound as a dollar. Good-bye, Miss Whidden." She waved a black-mittened hand. "You must come and see me very soon. Your aunt knows where I bide."

Phoebe sighed and wondered why she had begun sweating so hard—all over, too. It was cold on the platform, "cold as Christian Charity with a deficit," as the Reverend Mr. Holcombe was fond of saying. A curious buzzing sensation suddenly weakened her knees.

"Mercy!" she thought. "I just can't get sick at this time."

But she did. Next morning a lugubrious physician informed her aunt, "She must have et something spoiled on that train. The hucksters are always selling stale pies and such. There ought to be a law."

XII THE WORKMEN

To Matthew Everett's acute disappointment Messrs. Callahan & Grogan's company of workmen were kept in Portland only overnight, so he was afforded no opportunity at all to explore that fabled, prosperous town and visit its three Presbyterian churches. Surely someone, somewhere, could, under judicious questioning, give him some information concerning that so-called "Reverend" Mr. D. Adams, who had contributed so much towards ruining his mother's peace of mind and establishing his own illegitimacy. By God, he wouldn't rest till he'd come up with that impostor and beat him into a pulp.

He and his unkempt, unshaven and increasingly ill-smelling companions were held as veritable prisoners in a baggage shed of the Boston and Maine Railroad. They were, however, fed enormous meals of split-pea soup, steak, baked beans and cabbage.

At ten o'clock of the morning after they had reached Portland a similar draft of artisans from up the coast appeared. They were shepherded by a detachment of very disgusted and foul-mouthed Navy bluejackets who, under the command of a crotchety old lieutenant out of the Regular Establishment, were also on their way out to the western rivers. Loud and sulphurous were these veterans' curses at being ordered inland, away from salt water, tall ships and familiar routine. Confidently, they expected at the end of a few days to find themselves deposited in a howling wilderness peopled by painted savages and scarcely less barbarous frontiersmen.

"And what kind of hell ships are they going to assign us aboard of?" demanded a bearded petty officer in a wrinkled dark blue uniform at the side of which swung a big, brass-guarded regulation cutlass. All the naval party wore side arms of some sort and carried their belongings in sausage-shaped sea bags.

Observed another well-tattooed veteran, "I seen some o' them river boats onct when we put in to N'Orleans. My God! They're the most reediculous craft you ever seen since Noah's Ark put to sea."

"Ships on the Great Lakes aren't so different," put in a younger man, heaving his sea bag onto a broad shoulder. "My pa's been out there, says they got regular steamers just like on salt water—only they're flat bottomed and built o' soft woods."

"But we aren't headed fer the Great Lakes, you great numskulls," called out one of the civilians, "we're agoin' to a place called Cincinnati."

"Where the hell's that?"

"Dunno. It's on some river called the Ohio."

"Sweet Jesus!" grunted the boatswain. "So we got to fight on *rivers?*"

"That you are," growled the ancient lieutenant in command. "Now look alive, men, and see that none of these contract men run out."

So that was why the naval party wore heavy pistols or brass-hilted cutlasses? A special train came bumping up through the cold Sunday sunlight. Another group of contract workmen had preceded Matt's party aboard and these stuck shaggy, blear-eyed heads out of the windows to call obscene greetings and derisively wave liquor bottles. They had managed to break several windows, Matt noticed, and would be sorry for it once the bitter wind came streaming in.

"All right, you hellions. Git into yonder palace cars!" Big Pig bellowed, indicating a pair of ancient passenger coaches to the straggling column of men bent beneath tool boxes, bags and bundles. "And ye'd best ease off the booze or you'll run dry before we git even halfway to Cincinnati."

Matt shouldered his pack. Never in his life had he been so thoroughly unwashed and unkempt. He had attempted to shave in the freight shed but made a miserable job of it. Twice he had cut his chin because his hand was shaking violently as a result of drinking most of the night. His stomach, too, felt queasy through trying to digest the mess of corned beef and cabbage he had managed to choke down a while back.

At each end of the car, detachments of surly bluejackets deposited their sea bags in the racks, but maintained their side arms. After this these big, brown-faced fellows, for the most part heavily bearded, occupied benches reserved for them. They bit off huge chews of tobacco, spat on the floor of the car and, in lurid detail, expressed their deep disgust with the war, the Navy Department in general and their Middle Western assignment in particular.

One leather-faced boatswain wearing an extra neatly pressed uniform growled, "T'hell with these contract bastards, coining money while we fight. Me, I didn't sign on to act as no jailer over a bunch of lousy civilians."

Because he had been among the last to board the train, Matt found himself forced to enter a coach largely filled by men from the other parties. Chiefly because the man who occupied the other half of a narrow wooden bench was one of the smallest men he had ever beheld, Matt heaved his grease-stained pack up onto the luggage rack, then lowered himself onto the seat. The other, clad in a too-tight shirt of heavily checked silk and a mottled duroy waistcoat, sat up, cast him a suspicious glance.

"My name's Everett," Matt explained. "Guess I'll have to crowd in here with you."

The other whose hirsute adornments consisted of a scraggly black goatee and two long and limp mustachios offered a hand embellished by no less than three rings set with suspiciously huge diamonds. His complexion was so coppery and his cheekbones so pronounced that Matt suspected this stranger must be a considerable part Indian. The little man's smile however was quite engaging and his manner the embodiment of courtesy.

"Press the flesh with Philo Daingerfield who, sir, is honored by your company," he said in mellifluous tones. "I am indeed happy, sir, and proud to make your acquaintance." From his speech Mr. Daingerfield obviously hailed from no part of New England. "Yes, sir, ere long I venture that you will congratulate yourself on chancing to seat yourself alongside of Philo Daingerfield, explorer, river pilot and steamboat engineer. My card, sir." He fumbled into his food-spotted waistcoat of crimson velour and produced a dingy, dog-eared calling card. It read, "Mr. Philo Daingerfield, M.A., B.S. and M.S., Master Engineer and Licensed Pilot." In the left-hand corner was printed "Paducah, Kentucky."

Delicately the little man flicked some crumbs from his wrinkled black-and-brown checkered pantaloons, then cocked a speculative bright black eye at his companion. He reminded Matt of a robin prospecting for a worm.

"Your home still in Paducah?"

"No, brother. I don't live there any more and that's a fact. Last summer a passel of Rebel sympathizers wrecked my business and I had to skedaddle, fast, else I'd have been rid out of town on a hick'ry rail and wearing a brand-new coat of tar and feathers. Yes, sir, these days partisan feeling runs mighty high over in Kentucky." He cocked his head at this tall, yellow-haired young man seated beside him. "What's your line, brother?" demanded the little man.

"Why—why, I guess I'm what you would call a lumberman and a carpenter-joiner. But I've always wanted to learn about steam engines. You see," Matt admitted carefully, "I haven't travelled very much." His hand crept inside his jacket of spotted blue serge to test an envelope pinned into its inner pocket. He surely wished he could come across a needle and thread and sew in those precious three hundred dollars.

He stared fixedly out of the window. Come to think of it, those same bills must have been handled by the man he had killed. Odd, how clearly he even now could recall every detail of his father's massive, powerful figure, strong, ruddy features and flowing brown side whiskers. Why, he even remembered the diamond that was set in a locket swinging from a thick, red-gold watch chain draped across that unforgettable black velvet waistcoat and the brass buttons winking on it. Had any kind of a chase or search for him been organized? Would anyone in Bangor remember seeing him among the recruited laborers? Someone might. If so, it would not be too hard for the police to trace the movements of Callahan & Grogan's party and at almost any station come stamping into the car. What then?

To his considerable surprise he had retained the fatal weapon and surreptitiously had reloaded it in a lavatory. But he didn't intend to use it again except in self-defense or maybe on the "Reverend" D. Adams. Better than half of the men in this construction party carried pistols more or less openly; others wore Bowie knives strapped about them, some were armed with both knife and pistol. He stole a glance at Philo Daingerfield's waistcoat and recognized the outline of a small derringer beneath the stained velour.

The little man was saying, "Yes, sir, they chased me out o' Paducah and I sure was lucky to catch a river boat two spits and a jump ahead o' a passel of smokin'-hot Rebels." Daingerfield produced a penknife and commenced to remove dirt from beneath singularly well-manicured fingernails. "Yes, brother, you could do a lot worse than to tie up with Philo Daingerfield. I can turn my hand to 'most anything. It's wise to have a side-kick at a time like this." He grinned and looked up, bird-like again. "You play cards?"

Cards? Matt stared. Why, cards were "the Devil's handmaidens," as he had been told ever since he could remember. "Why, I guess not," he returned, flushing. "Where I come from card playing is sort of frowned on. But I wouldn't mind learning." This was the snapping of another tie with Dexter and the past. Matt Hovey never had drunk spirits, played cards or employed curse words, but that didn't mean that Matt Everett wasn't going to. After all, had not Society played him an evil and unjust turn by branding him illegitimate and so unfit to associate with respectable people?

His companion sighed, looked disgustedly about at his companions sprawled all over the benches or snoring uncomfortably on the floor as they lay propped against their luggage. "Well, now ain't that a pity? I figgured mebbe to pass the time in a sociable leetle game of cribbage. I've got a board in my bundle." Stooping, the small man produced a curious oblong of wood drilled with many little holes. "This here's a cribbage board to keep score on. It's a mighty fine two-handed game," he explained over the interminable *clickty-clack* of car wheels. "Piquet's even better. Now *there's* a real game of skill which was taught to me by a Frenchy when I was piloting the old *Bulletin No. 2*, back in 1858. He came up from New Orleans, he did, but got run off the Ohio without his ears for bein' lucky just a leetle too often. Don't pay to win all the time."

Rapidly the train passed among a succession of steep, hardwood-covered hills all gleaming with snow. Here and there little groups of farm buildings dotted the landscape. For the most part they were painted white and had a red barn standing behind. How very similar to the farms Matt had seen all his life: that one was just like the one Phoebe's father owned. How long would it be before he beheld it again? Probably never.

Before his mind's eye reappeared that little group of neighbors waiting for the burial service to begin behind the severe white outline of the Meeting House at Dexter. He saw again fir branches hiding the raw earth so dark upon the trampled snow, familiar, grief-stricken faces all about; and there stood Phoebe Whidden, Phoebe of the rich, red-gold tresses and with so much sympathy and tenderness showing in her clear, dark blue eyes.

He found himself wondering whether anyone in Dexter had as yet associated Abigail Hovey's son with Josiah Cosby's murderer? He shivered, whereupon Philo Daingerfield reached into a pocket in the tail of his claw-hammer coat and produced a whiskey bottle.

"Why don't that damn' lazy brakeman come and stoke the stove?" he complained. "It's getting colder in here than a well-digger's butt. Here, brother, take a swaller of this." He winked. "You'll find it's smoother than the rot-gut the rest are swilling. I'm persnickety 'bout what I drink. Don't want my hands to start trembling. Wouldn't do at all and that's a fact."

To Matt's surprise he was able to drink Philo's liquor without coughing and choking as usual. Criminently! It was wonderful how these spirits spread out and warmed his vitals. Almost immediately they banished those haunting recollections.

"Suppose you try a hand of cribbage?" The little man glanced up, bright black eyes narrowed.

"Don't mind if I do, but I can't give you much competition," Matt flushed down to the dirty collar of his red woodsman's shirt. "I don't really know the names of the cards."

"You don't *what?*" The Kentuckian's jaw dropped wide open.

"No, I don't know those different kinds—what the spots mean—or the ones with the pictures."

"Well, may I be dipped in dung!" Philo stared incredulously at his broad-shouldered companion. "You really can't tell a jack from a king?"

"No."

"Jesus! It's sure time you learned. Where we're headed you damn' well better know a deuce from a ace."

Steadily, the special train clanked, bumped and rattled its way down to Boston where the construction party would be fed before changing cars. There Callahan relaxed his vigilance. He had become resigned to the fact that the naval detachment were too disgusted at being sent out west or had grown too drunk to care what their civilian companions did, or possibly the big Irishman realized that his laborers no longer intended to desert him. Most of them now were penniless and far from home. They must inevitably go hungry if they slipped away.

About an hour before the special was due to arrive in the "Athens of America," Philo drained the last of his pint and tossed the bottle onto the floor. "I reckon I've just about time to pick up a leetle change before we reach Bean Town. We'll be wanting further consolation for that damned long trip out to Ohio so you look on, real attentive, bub, and ye'll learn a little about how the great game o' draw poker is played. You need to understand poker just like you need yer pants."

The chipper little Kentuckian—if indeed he did hail from that State—selected for his opponents such fellow travellers as seemed to be still in the possession of funds. A cardboard telescope bag was pressed into service and for quite a spell Matt sat perched on a bench arm across the aisle trying to familiarize himself with various terms and the method of play. Darkness having set in most of the near-by laborers had fallen asleep so only he watched the progress of the game and learned that this particular variety of poker was known as "Jacks or better." There was evident a certain grim earnestness about the play. Two tough-looking Irishmen wearing sheath knives in their belts hugged the greasy cards close to their scarlet woodsmen's shirts and talked hardly at all. Deftly Philo Daingerfield's grubby fingers shuffled and distributed the cards.

A lanky, lantern-jawed individual who had signed up as a steamfitter kept repeating, "Be sure to call your hands right, boys, and throw in yer discards, but remember to keep yer openers to show."

Stacks of silver coins, for all that such were growing scarce, fractional banknotes called "shinplasters" and some soiled bills appeared on the cardboard valise.

At length, Matt got tired of watching and settled down for a nap only to be roused by a sudden sharp, "Don't you touch that money, mister!"

"Why not?" demanded Daingerfield. "I won, didn't I?"

"You opened and now claim to win on a straight. You drew a card, didn't you?"

The other players stiffened and shifted positions to look hard at Daingerfield.

"Why," said he smiling, but with his eyes alert, "I'd a pair of queens to open but since I held a straight open at both ends—"

"Yeah?" snarled the lantern-jawed man, "but *where's that other queen?*"

"I discarded her."

"And you've since messed up the discards so there ain't no telling whether you really had openers. So you'll leave this pot where it is. It goes to the winner of the next hand."

To his vast surprise Matt heard his voice saying, "He had openers all right, fellows. I saw them. They were the queen of spades and the queen of diamonds."

Why he lied like this he had no notion, but although the other players cursed and grumbled, Philo chortled, "Thanks, stranger," and solemnly raked in his winnings. But as soon as the game came to an end the diminutive pilot removed his luggage from the rack and disappeared into another car.

Matt did not see him again until after the change of trains in Boston. A supper of greasy Irish stew supplemented by soggy dumplings and a wedge of apple pie was sitting heavily on Matt's stomach when Daingerfield's wiry little figure appeared swaying along the aisle.

"Thanks, brother," he said quickly and passed over a bottle of whiskey wrapped in a newspaper. "You sure saved my bacon and made me some handy money. Reckon I'd better not set down beside you lest them other fellers get to thinkin' mebbe we was in cahoots. This here's for you," he winked and pressed into Matt's hand a small roll of banknotes. "I won't be talkin' to you again till we get off the train and then I'll have plenty to say." He winked again. "I got holt of a smart idee—it'll fetch in plenty of greenbacks."

Matt said, "I don't want this money."

"Go on, take it and don't act crazy," Daingerfield insisted. Then added "If you don't want it, then keep it for me case I get cleaned out." He hesitated. "How come you saw that other queen? Thought you was asleep."

"I was, but you looked to be in bad trouble."

"You'd have been a shining wonder to have seen that queen," Philo revealed a gold tooth in a wide grin, "because she weren't ever there. So take yer share. Jee-sus! You sure do fool a body with that holier-than-thou and carry-me-off-to-Heaven look of yours. Fooled me even with all that guff about not knowin' one card from another. Yessir, brother, if ever I see a natural-borned gambler, you're him. Like I always say, the innocenter a feller appears, the better his chances. See you in Cincinnati," and he strutted off down the aisle with battered stovepipe hat canted rakishly to one side.

Whether it was this unaccustomed consumption of whiskey or whether the stew consumed in Boston had upset his stomach there was no telling but, in any case, Matthew Everett awoke on the verge of nausea. It must have been very early in the morning for this stuffy and smoky car's two tin-shaded kerosene lamps had been turned down and all the passengers save one appeared to be asleep in various contorted attitudes. A terrifying variety of snores sounded all about him and a few laborers were muttering querulously in their sleep. The train was proceeding quite smoothly for a change and frosty moonlight revealed low wooded hills rolling off into the distance.

It must be cold, bitter cold out there for despite the fact that the stoves at either end of the car had been fired until they glowed dull red it was chill in the car.

What appalling changes this week had wrought with his destiny, his character and way of life, Matt brooded after spreading his overcoat robe-like about him. Only seven days earlier Abigail Hovey's son had been a respected member of the Congregational Church, deeply conscientious and clean living—without being in the least priggish about it. He'd been self-dedicated to the ministry, admired by most of his neighbors and loved sweetly and profoundly by tall, golden-haired Phoebe whose devotion was not less because it remained unexpressed. Upon reflection he realized that he should have heard Mr. Stetson out—instead of rushing off like a cat with its fur afire. Take those holdings of his mother's—he recalled knowing nothing about them. Of course his mother's house wasn't much in itself but the thousands of acres of fine hardwoods in Piscataquis County were.

Grimacing with distaste he pulled out Daingerfield's present and took a big swallow which, sure enough, rid him of the queasiness and dispelled a troublesome sense of remorse. He soon achieved a sort of satisfaction in reviewing the thoroughness of his downfall. He was now a murderer and a fugitive from the law. He had twice gotten pretty drunk. He had lied about that queen and had cheated, too, because of course, he *had* cheated those other men in the poker game. He was unshaven, dirty and his linen smelled bad and no obscenity was too vile, too terrible for his use. Worst of all was the fact that every decent tenet, every ideal, every notion of service to his God and to mankind had been swept away and now he looked upon himself as utterly unprincipled, predatory and intent only on indulging as many vices as might interest him.

What lay ahead in this strange and turbulent country in which he had contracted to work for the next three months? He had heard little concerning the Northwestern States of Minnesota and Wisconsin, nor of Missouri and Kansas, and that little, in the case of the last two, had to do with savage border wars, Indian raids and lawlessness. Suppose, as Philo predicted, he did make a good gambler? He'd probably have to maim and possibly kill not a few men—if what was said about a gambler's life was true. What of it? Since now he was condemned, past all hope of redemption, he guessed he'd make a thorough job of insuring eternal damnation.

Unseeing, his eyes studied the black-and-white landscape as it rolled by and he was beginning to feel drowsy when he became aware of someone bending above him.

"I beg your pardon," the other said in a low and pleasant voice, "but I notice that you can't seem to sleep, either, so would you very much mind if I sit with you for a while?" In the gloom, teeth glinted in a brief smile. "Of course you may not, when you learn what I am."

Matt struggled up on his bench and pulled aside the skirts of his coat. "Sit down," he invited. "If you're unworthy to sit beside me you'd have to be a pretty low character."

The other sank onto the wooden bench. "I'm going to tell you straightaway who and what I am, though you may well not be interested. I come from New Haven, Connecticut. My name is Dent—Paul Dent and I'm an ex-junior at Yale College." Fine, dark eyes set somewhat too closely together bored anxiously through the half light. The stranger, Matt guessed, must be about his own age but it was hard to be sure because he wore a short and curly beard the shape of which could have been improved by trimming.

"I'm Matthew Everett, from 'way up in the center of Maine." Solemnly Matt offered his hand.

The other made no effort to take it. "Before we shake hands I must tell you that I—well, I'm a coward and a deserter from the Army. You have only to say the word and I'll leave at once."

When in sheer surprise Matt remained speechless Dent gathered his feet under him. "Sorry to have bothered you, but I couldn't sleep and when I noticed that you, too—"

Matt's hand shot out and closed over the other's wrist. "Please stay. I'm no one to cast the first stone."

"You? You, too, are in trouble?"

"Yes, and worse than yours because I'm a murderer—a parricide."

Wheels clacked and clattered during the several long moments in which the two men stared upon each other. Shadows wrought by the moonlight alternately darkened and brightened their unkempt heads and grimy features.

Suddenly Dent buried his face between his hands and his shoulders quivered. "You've no idea what a hell it was at Bull Run. No one can who wasn't there. I—I saw John Phelps, my roommate at Yale, disemboweled by a cannon ball and go reeling off screaming and trailing his guts after him. I saw other classmates—a lot of us volunteered in a body —falling dead or howling in their agony—fellows I'd grown up with and was fond of.

"Have you heard that horrible screech the Rebels raise? Then there was the crash of cannon, the rattle of muskets. Believe me, it was the noise that made me turn and run!" Dent's voice sank and shook so Matt could barely understand him. "Yes, I turned and I ran and I left my comrades to die, to be taken prisoner. Twice, I think, it may have been three times, I tried to stop and go back to face the enemy but, God help me, I couldn't.

"I haven't dared to go home," the anguished voice continued, "because my family settled in New Haven in 1695, long before the Revolution and members of it have fought honorably for our country ever since—" he broke off, said quietly, "that is why I signed up to go out west. I—I'm going to try, with God's help, to atone for my weakness."

And moved by this confession, Matt found it natural and vastly relieving to unburden himself at last—and to this young stranger.

XIII VARIOUS CONFERENCES

JOSIAH COSBY LAY on his wide, ornate and not-too-soft black walnut bed propped against a pile of bolsters and pillows. For the first time in ten days he had been shaved between his luxuriant side whiskers and so experienced a gratifying sense of self-confidence. He was attired in a nightcap of plum-colored flannel the tail of which terminated in a tassel of gold lace, and a dressing gown of claret-hued silk which effectively concealed the clumsy mass of bandages encircling his hairy and barrel-like chest.

To his disgust the Master of Sachem Hill observed that his freckle-mottled hand still trembled whenever he raised a glass of medicine, but his bold blue eyes were clear once more and penetrating when he considered the spruce, conservatively garbed lawyer seated bolt upright on his armchair and balancing a thin black dispatch case upon his knees.

Mr. Stetson's well-cut black gabardine coat fitted him to prefection, as did a waistcoat of magenta grosgrain bound in braid of black silk.

"It's good of you, Mr. Stetson, to travel all the way to Bangor at this time of year. I trust you received the money for your expenses?"

"Otherwise I should not be here," came the succinct response. Somehow as he spoke Edwin Stetson appeared much larger than he actually was.

He was thinking, "So *this* is the celebrated Josiah Cosby. Well, it's easy to see that what they say is so. He looks ruthless. I can believe that he's built his fortune on the necks of weaker men and women."

Surveying Mr. Cosby's massive jaw and arrogantly held head balanced upon a bull-like neck, he could understand how it could be entirely possible for this man to maltreat and dominate so gentle a person as Abigail Hovey.

What was the wounded man saying? Dear me, for Matt's sake I must pay attention. "I'm indebted to you, Mr. Stetson, for sending that telegram of warning, for all that it arrived too tardily to prevent this." He tapped his bandages.

"You needn't be," Mr. Stetson's manner was acid, precise. "I only sent it in the hope of preventing my late client's son from ruining his future."

Josiah Cosby frowned. Damn this country lawyer fellow, he wasn't acting in the least impressed. "It wasn't, er—young Hovey's fault that he failed in killing me. I'll never forget the way he looked down that pistol." Cosby winced as he braced his hands to shift his position against the mound of pillows supporting him. Then he spoke out, his eyes riveted on the lawyer's smooth pink-and-white features.

"You, I take it you were Miss Abigail Everett's lawyer?"

"I was Mrs. Hovey's lawyer," Edwin Stetson corrected and decided he'd be eternally damned if he'd let on just how much he knew concerning this overbearing fellow's scurvy record. Yet he must be cautious. This Josiah Cosby could be dangerous—because he'd grown powerful in the State government of Maine, what with his interests in so many various endeavors and his wife's family connections. Before driving out to Sachem Hill he'd taken the precaution of entering into a long and instructive conversation with his first cousin, Charlie Stetson, who, as cashier of the Merchant's Bank of Bangor, knew a thing or two about Bangor's more prominent citizens and not always to their credit.

A tinge of color crept into the powerful features framed by Cosby's ginger-colored side whiskers.

"In your legal capacity as Mrs. Hovey's adviser—we'll call her that if you insist—I presume you gained her entire confidence?"

"That, sir, is as may be," came the soft reply, "and is no concern of yours."

"Come, come, Stetson, let's quit beating about the bush," grunted the Master of Sachem Hill. "You're shrewd all right, so I'm prepared to pay handsomely to retain your services. I mean it. I'll meet any reasonable retainer—say anything up to five thousand dollars."

Despite himself, Edwin Stetson caught his breath. Five thousand dollars? Whew! that was far more than he could hope to earn in a full year of practice in Newport Junction and around Dexter, but his gold-mounted spectacles glinted to a single shake of his head.

"I'm sorry, Mr. Cosby, but my time is taken up for quite some time to come."

"Eight thousand dollars, then?"

Mr. Stetson arose, pink features rigid. "I fear you are being obtuse, Mr. Cosby. Cannot you understand that under no circumstances do I wish to be retained by you? To do so," he looked the invalid squarely in the eye, "would be disloyal to the memory of the finest, gentlest and most unselfish woman I have ever been privileged to meet, and to her son."

Devils looked out of Josiah Cosby's eyes. "Oh! Then that damned would-be murderer is your client, too?"

"He is," Stetson replied evenly for all this was, of course, a flat lie unless he chose to construe Matthew's instructions to administer Abigail Hovey's property tantamount to being retained.

A snort escaped the big prostrate figure. "Say, Stetson, aren't you acting pretty high and mighty for a backwoods lawyer? Funny, I'd have bet that the very mention of eight thousand dollars would set you to licking your chops like a hungry dog over a beef bone."

A bleak and mirthless smile flitted across the lawyer's thin, pale pink lips. "Your simile and your reasoning do you justice, Mr. Cosby. I fear you must excuse me. I have important consultations awaiting me in Bangor." He started for the door.

"No! No! Please don't be angry, Mr. Stetson," Cosby pleaded. "Of course I shouldn't have said that. You obviously are that rare thing, a lawyer with integrity. Please tarry here a little longer and tell me how much you know about my er—part in Miss—Mrs. Hovey's past?"

"I am not at liberty to disclose that." Dear God! How could so insensitive a fellow have climbed so high?

"But you *must* know something?" insisted the Master of Sachem Hill, "else you'd never have sent me that telegram."

Edwin Stetson lingered, with one hand resting on the well-polished brass doorknob, the other gripping his dispatch case and merely raised his brows.

"Since you seem to be my bastard son's lawyer," rasped Josiah Cosby, "I'm astonished you haven't tried to find out whether I intend to prosecute that young brute for attempted murder."

"I have not been concerned, Mr. Cosby, for two reasons: first I doubt whether you dare to bring into the public eye certain discreditable, if not downright dishonorable, acts of yours. I am convinced that this community *and* your family would not relish hearing about them."

Cosby struggled to restrain his temper. Obviously this rural sharper must have learned all about his illegal marriage with Abigail Everett and its consequences.

"And what's the other reason I won't prosecute?"

"Because, although I expect you'll deny it, you are very much afraid my client will return to complete the job he has bungled. Good day, sir."

"You are wrong, damned wrong on both counts!" roared Cosby and actually shook his fist. "I intend to make that young villain pay dearly for his crime. I've the means and, by God, I'll have him hunted out and I'll crush him, no matter where he tries to hide. I'll ruin him and send him to prison; I've broken no law, Stetson, whatever you may think."

"Except that of elementary decency," observed Edwin Stetson. He ignored the taurine bellowings from within the sickroom and stepped out into the hall so quickly that he all but collided with Flavia Cosby. The girl managed, amid a frantic whirl of skirts, to avoid a collision as she gasped, "Mercy! You really needn't knock a body over."

The neatly clad lawyer treated this lithely handsome young woman who, beyond question, had been eavesdropping, to a single penetrating glance, then bowed stiffly and, ignoring the butler's assistance, struggled into his overcoat. He swung sharply to a sound of sleigh bells nearing the front door to Sachem Hill.

"Goddamn you, Stetson, you come back here!" Cosby was shouting in a hoarse voice. "Come back here else I'll ruin your practice, I'll see you run out of Penobscot County!"

Firmly Edwin Stetson settled an old-fashioned bell-crowned beaver hat and disposed a two-yard-long muffler with a deliberation admired by Flavia hesitating further down the hall, with full, crimson-hued skirts a-sway. Her vivid dark eyes had grown very round indeed. She could feel her heart hammering over what she had just overheard. That dialogue between her father and this calm stranger from Newport Junction, Maine, would furnish much food for thought. Inordinately, it pleased her to realize that now she knew more about her father's nearly fatal wounding than Augustus, Decius or her own shrewdly thoughtful mother.

Timothy, the butler, meanwhile had opened the door to admit a red-faced individual distinguished by a huge red mustache, blue pop-eyes and a bulbous nose veined in magenta. While he lingered in the vestibule to kick snow from his boots he noticed the country lawyer's spare, erect figure.

"Why, God bless my soul, if it isn't Edwin Stetson! What're you doing 'way out here?" he boomed jovially. "Thought I was Josh Cosby's legal adviser."

"You were—and are," Stetson reassured him.

"But you aren't leaving? Can't have that, Ed. It's years since I've seen you."

"But I am, Mr. Leach. I have concluded my business with Mr. Cosby."

"Come back here, you damned dog-leg lawyer," Cosby's voice sounded perceptibly weaker. Undoubtedly his wound must be beginning to hurt.

"But—but—" boomed the new arrival slipping out of a handsome wolf-skin coat, "Josh told me to drive out for a—a conference."

Mr. Stetson replied briskly, "Perhaps he did, but your client was mistaken. Good day, sir." He bowed, then pushed firmly past Tobias Leach's portly figure and trotted briskly down ash-sprinkled steps, and disappeared towards the stable because his horse wasn't to have been readied for another half hour.

Once he was driving down towards the River Road and his cutter had begun sliding smoothly, silently over powdery snow, Mr. Stetson actually cracked his whip. By God, it wasn't every day you turned down an eight-thousand-dollar retainer for a matter of principle. He grinned wryly because lawyers, of course, were reputed to have none. If only he knew whither poor, tortured Matt Everett had betaken himself he could inform the boy that only narrowly had he failed in his intent. Most likely his deeply distraught client had gone to enlist under an assumed name and so lose his identity—and possibly his life when, in the spring, the conflict again would begin to rage. Certainly the whole country was being plunged into an increasing turmoil.

Once his horse broke into a fine, swinging pace along the River Road paralleling the frozen Penobscot, Stetson became impatient to talk matters over with Dr. Larrabee. Certainly *he* must suspect why Phoebe Whidden had so very suddenly departed for Portland. Um. 'Twas more than probable she might know where Abigail Hovey's son was hiding.

What a mighty lucky thing it was, mused Stetson, that Matt's bullet had squarely struck a big brass waistcoat button and so had become sufficiently deflected to preserve Josiah Cosby's existence.

Augustus Cosby returned from Bangor that evening somewhat later than he had intended and found his mother waiting up for him. She remained spare, ramrod-straight and still handsome despite graying prongs that divided the glossy black of her elaborate coiffure.

"Land sakes, 'Gustus!" she demanded sharply. "Why *did* you have to be so tardy? Your father's been in the most terrible fret all afternoon—never have heard him use such language."

"Concerning the Johnson affair?"

Nervously Mrs. Cosby snapped and unsnapped the cover to a gold watch dangling from her belt. "I expect so. Mr. Leach and a strange lawyer called Stetson were here. I've no idea what chanced but this Mr. Stetson—he comes from Newport Junction—marched out all of a sudden and left your father in a towering rage." She smiled wanly on her eldest son, then sighed. "Oh, dear! What a dreadful mystery all this is. Come, dear, I have some coffee brewing and Flavia is—"

"Plague take Flavia!" he snapped and flung his muffler onto the hat rack of elk horns. "That snippet's too nosy for words and what a shameless gossip!" He flung apart exasperated hands. "Really, Mother, why did Flavia have to spread that scandal about Decius and the Lamont girl all over Miss Boutelle's Seminary?"

"Flavia *didn't!*" Drusilla Cosby drew herself up to her full five feet five inches, and the six yards of bombazine composing her skirt rustled, betrayed her deep agitation. "She couldn't do such a silly thing."

"Oh, but she did. She must have. No one else knew except Blanche and her family and they're not likely to talk." Augustus produced a comb and restored order in dark wavy hair that fell to the top of his green velvet collar. "Grace Archer told her brother Dan that Flavia was spreading the story; apparently my dear sister thought it almighty funny that Decius should seduce one of father's employees' daughters and a Frenchie at that."

Mrs. Cosby's vivid blue eyes hardened. "If that's true, I'll attend to that Miss so she'll wish she had kept her lip buttoned!" She checked herself, raised a Paisley shawl higher over fashionably sloping shoulders. "By the bye, did you call on Colonel Varney of the Second Volunteer Regiment?"

Deliberately Augustus brushed a speck of dandruff from the bottle-green grosgrain of his jacket. "No. I went nowhere near Colonel Varney," said he quietly. "We'll talk about that later, Mother, if you wish. But now—" he grimaced, "I have—well—I've got to speak with Father and give him some unpleasant news."

The black velvet ribbon supporting a gold locket over Mrs. Cosby's slender throat moved convulsively and her fingers, sparkling with gems, darted forward to rest on her eldest son's forearm. "Oh, 'Gustus, please don't! I don't know what's happened, but your father's worked himself into a fine fury. Poor Mr. Leach slunk out as if he'd been whipped. That Mr. Stetson must have brought ill tidings."

Young Augustus straightened a flowing canary-colored cravat. "Well, he's in for some more. Mother, do please try to keep that little sneak Flavia from eavesdropping."

"Eavesdropping? What a horrible thing to say!"

A little impatiently Augustus considered his mother's erect, black-clad figure. "Where she's concerned, you certainly are surprisingly blind sometimes. Don't you know *why* she's all of a tizzy to find out about this Mr. Johnson?"

"What is odd about that? It's entirely natural that a daughter should try to bring her father's attempted assassin to justice."

Augustus' finger crept up to test the tentative appearance of a mustache. "I declare, Mother, I sometimes wonder how you can be so clever in some ways."

"Just what do you mean, young man?" She spoke just as she had when he'd committed some adolescent folly.

"That silly chit's gone silly over this fellow," said he in grim amusement. "Why, I couldn't begin to imagine, but she has. Why, it's as plain as the nose on your face." An unfortunate simile that, because Drusilla Cosby's nose was thin and quite long.

"Really, Augustus, you must be daft! To imagine that Flavia could be —be—well, interested in a cowardly villain who so nearly murdered her father?"

"You don't think so? Ask her." Lightly he kissed his parent, then strode off down the hallway's gleaming length towards the sickroom into which the bureau had been transformed—Cosby's doctor positively had forbidden the least transportation of his critically wounded patient.

When Augustus arrived at the sickroom, Josiah Cosby was still digesting a bit of pertinent information, almost the only result of Mr. Leach's extensive investigations in and about Bangor. All his researches added up to the fact that young Hovey—or as he now seemed to call himself, Everett—had arrived in Bangor the same day he had made his attempt, had stopped at the Hatch House and had rented his sleigh from Vickery & Sargent's Livery Stable.

"The Devil take it!" Cosby had roared at his big-bellied lawyer. "What in Tunket do I care where he stayed or what he did before he tried to murder me, it is where he went afterwards that counts."

Mr. Leach had flushed, looked most embarrassed. "I've only learned that someone answering to young Everett's description was seen aboard a train headed for Portland. Apparently he'd signed up with a labor contractor by the name of Callahan."

The Master of Sachem Hill had actually grinned, albeit grimly. "Good! Now we're getting somewhere. Where was this Callahan fellow taking his roughnecks? To Boston? To New York?"

"To neither," the lawyer informed him, "but somewhere out in the Northwest."

"Somewhere?" Cosby had snapped. "'Somewhere'? Is that the kind of information I'm paying good money for? Dammit, Leach, the Western States are vast! Wisconsin, Minnesota, Missouri, Kansas and the rest."

"Please restrain yourself, Mr. Cosby. You'll injure yourself shouting like that. I have already sent an investigator down to Portland. He shouldn't find much trouble in tracing Callahan's labor company, but a search will prove expensive."

"Plague take expense!" the wounded man roared, then had winced for, as Leach had predicted, sharp pains commenced shooting through his injured side. God, how he loathed being incapacitated like this and at the mercy of his wife's all-too-efficient nursing. Then, too, he was annoyed by Flavia's covert but insistent snooping, probing about. What could she be after? At the thought that the rest of the family and the public might learn that he had sired an illegitimate son, he went cold.

Exactly what was he going to do about Abigail's bastard? Despite long cogitation on his bed of pain he hadn't quite made up his mind. Certainly he must find some way of shutting Matthew's mouth forever; perhaps in the same way he'd silenced a shipbuilder, an independent young fellow down to Rockland, who wouldn't sell his yard. And while he was about it he intended to show that dog-leg lawyer from Newport Junction who was what in Penobscot County.

A brisk knocking at the door terminated his reflections.

"Who's there?"

"Augustus, sir."

"Good! Good! Come in boy, I'm uncommon glad to see you. This has been a very trying afternoon for your old father." For the first time it struck him that more than a passing resemblance existed between Abigail Everett's son and his principal heir. Although Augustus wasn't nearly as solidly built, their features were surprisingly similar. *Could* Flavia have noticed this? Possibly. It seemed the chit had had quite a conversation with "Mr. Johnson."

"Sit down, 'Gustus, and tell me how you made out with Colonel Varney?"

Augustus remained standing, steadily regarding his father's massive form and pallid features. "I didn't make out at all."

Incredulity narrowed Josiah Cosby's eyes. "Didn't he get you a captain's commission in the Second Maine Volunteers *and* an appointment to Major-General Butler's staff?"

"Don't blame Colonel Varney, Father," Augustus' voice sounded strained. "I never even went near his office."

"You didn't!" rasped the wounded man. "And why not? I went to a mort of trouble to arrange that interview. Varney's a busy man and a hard one to please."

A slowly drawn breath preluded Augustus' next words while in the pockets of his modish green tartan pantaloons his fingers clenched themselves. But he spoke evenly. "I fear you will be annoyed, sir, but I do not intend to trade on your standing and influence. I have been examined and have accepted a commission in the Navy."

Josiah Cosby's jaw sagged open, then snapped like a sprung trap. "In what grade and serving under whom?"

Augustus flushed to the roots of his curly dark brown hair. "Why—why—as a sub-lieutenant. I think I'm in the Naval Volunteer Force. I really didn't notice and I've no notion where I'll be sent or whom I'm to serve under."

"You're a shortsighted, blundering idiot!" In a flaming rage Cosby from his mound of bolsters glowered upon his eldest son and wanted to shout but couldn't manage to; his wound was throbbing far too much. "You'll do nothing of the sort!" he rasped. "You'll accept that major's commission on General Ben Butler's staff. I have your Uncle Theodore's promise you'll get not only the appointment but also rapid promotion."

The line of Augustus' jaw hardened. "But, Father, I—"

"Be still! You will do as I say. Now clear out of here. I—I am very tired."

Augustus was aware there was no use in attempting to argue. He also knew that he would never accept an Army commission because he had no knowledge whatever about soldiering while, on the other hand, he knew quite a lot concerning ships and their engines. He even had made three cruises to the West Indies aboard his father's vessels.

"Very well, sir," came his noncommittal assent. He bowed slightly and swung the massive mahogany door shut behind him. As usual, he discovered Flavia pretending to rearrange coats on the elk-horn hanger.

He cast his handsome, dark-complexioned sister no second look but stalked upstairs and, on entering his room, opened the door to its closet and stood there deliberating. What should he take along? Not much. After all, when he got to Boston he'd be forced to buy all manner of uniforms. Um. What would it be like to be subservient to the orders of someone other than his father? It might prove a rather pleasant experience.

XIV "A LITTLE FROLIC"

All through supper Augustus sat bolt upright and remained silent, only half listening to his mother's not very subtle conversation concerning the political situation in Washington and what an influential part there was played by her brother, the Honorable Theodore Nickerson, Republican Congressman from New Hampshire.

Decius, who already resembled his father to an absurd degree, crouched over the table and stolidly devoured a huge meal. He ate enough to nourish three boys but Flavia merely toyed with her food and continued to regard her elder brother with a wise little smile.

There was little to be gained, Augustus decided, in announcing his determination to refuse Colonel Varney's or Uncle Theodore's patronage. Now that his father was definitely on the mend he felt it not undutiful to leave for the war at once.

Directly after the man Timothy, pink, plump and pompous, and a parlor maid had cleared away mounds of side dishes and dinner plates and had served a dessert of Nesselrode pudding, Augustus sought his room and began packing. He was including certain volumes on seamanship and navigation when a brief knock sounded and without waiting for invitation Flavia rustled in. A modish gown of canary-yellow brocade set off by an emerald-green silk shawl emphasized her cool, classic and delicately formed features. Despite himself, Augustus could not but admire the patrician quality of her budding beauty. How smoothly that glossy brown-black hair was parted in the middle and swept back over small ears recently punctured to admit small pearl earrings presented by her Aunt Janice in Boston.

"Well, and what can I do for you?" demanded Augustus sharply, while slipping out of a chocolate-brown lounging jacket. "I'm busy."

"Oh, it's nothing much, 'Gustus," she said eyeing the portmanteau lying half filled on his bureau. "Only I've learned something that might interest your high and mightiness."

"Small wonder, the way you're forever eavesdropping."

"I don't either!"

"You do so."

"No more than Papa, and he says it pays big dividends to keep well-informed." Skirts whispering, Flavia drifted over to a bookcase, idly inspected textbooks concerning steam engines and their management. Ever since he'd been a small boy 'Gustus had always been fascinated by them.

"Maybe you wouldn't be interested," she murmured without turning her small sleek head, "but I've learned that Mr. Johnson's *real* name—and where he's from."

Augustus straightened abruptly. "You did? How?"

"There was a lawyer here today, a Mr. Stetson, who came up from Newport Junction—it's a little village west of here, I think. He and Father had *quite* an interesting talk."

"You eavesdropped?"

Flavia dropped her gaze then defiantly raised her rounded chin. "Don't be a prig. It didn't do the least harm; besides, I was curious." She turned about, dark red lips parted in a little smile. "You see, dear brother, I already knew that Mr. Stetson's visit would have to do with that attempt on Papa's life."

A look of wonderment crept over Augustus' long ruddy features. "You do beat all, Flavia," said he. "Damned if you don't. Who is this Johnson man? Who is he, really?"

Flavia turned aside and pretended deep interest in a ship model. "His name? Oh, I've forgotten. You're above listening to the results of eavesdropping." She smiled sweetly and started for his bedroom door.

"Don't be more of a pest than usual, Flavia. Of course I want to know why that Johnson fellow, who seemed such a decent sort, tried to kill our father. What *is* his right name? Odd, but he reminded me of someone and I can't recall who."

Exasperatingly Flavia delayed and, while her brother winced, ran fingers over the model's delicate yards. "His first name is Matthew and his second name—" she hesitated, ivory-smooth brow wrinkling—"is either Hovey or Everett. I couldn't quite make out which it really is, because Father spoke of him as 'Everett' and that lawyer—he was a shrewd little man and no mistake about it—kept referring to him as 'Hovey.' But that's not what was most significant." Flavia turned to face her brother, surveyed him steadily. "Father called someone by the name of Abigail '*Miss* Everett' and Mr. Stetson called her '*Mrs.* Hovey.' "

Augustus' hand crept up to tug at his budding mustache. "The Devil you say! And where does this mysterious fellow hail from?"

"Dexter. You know, it's that little logging village at the end of the north spur of Penobscot Railroad."

"How'd you learn that?"

"Remember that telegram Papa received just before Mr. Johnson shot him?"

"Yes. I was wondering what became of it?" Augustus said frowning.

"I took it," Flavia airily admitted. "It was from Mr. Stetson warning Papa that he stood in deadly danger because Abigail's son now knew what had happened and was coming to exact vengeance. Now what do you make of all this?"

For a long instant brother and sister queried each other's eyes across an elaborate brass-headed bedstead dividing Augustus' disordered bedroom.

"I am sure I can't even guess," Augustus admitted slowly. "I don't understand that '*Miss* Everett' and '*Mrs.* Hovey' business."

"Why should this woman Abigail's son, whom Papa had never seen before, try to kill him?"

"That," he announced firmly, "is Father's affair. The main thing is that this Everett fellow, whom I confess I rather liked, did not succeed. I imagine Papa can look out for himself in this matter."

Carefully he folded a pair of long red woollen drawers into his portmanteau, wishing fervently that Flavia would clear out.

"Do you know, I'm certain there must be something pretty ugly behind all this that Papa doesn't want us to know about?"

"Why, then, there's an end to it."

"Not so far as I'm concerned," she replied and, picking up a penholder, began absently to tap her small and very white teeth with its tip. "What you said just now about liking Matthew Everett interests me, 'Gustus, because I seldom have seen a more manly-appearing fellow. Heavens! The way he carried himself, the way those fine dark eyes of his glistened, incidentally there's the same look about the eyes as yours and until just now I didn't remember that his hair is wavy, too. No, my dear, virtuous brother, I intend to find out a lot more about him and why he wanted to kill Papa." She smiled secretly. "Who knows but information on that point may prove useful sometime? Papa is so short-tempered and impulsive."

Augustus shrugged as if to relieve an itching between his shoulder blades. "True enough, but don't bother me about it. If I know Father, he'll decide, as I said before, what to do about this Matthew chap and will accomplish it, come Devil or high water."

Flavia made no effort to leave, but remained, a dainty figure in yellow and green, before the marble-fronted fireplace in which a grate of cannel coal was brightly sputtering.

"You'll make a serious mistake, 'Gustus," she warned, "if you don't get to the bottom of this matter. Do you think Papa's had an—an affair?"

"Oh, nonsense! Everett's likely the son of some woman Papa has tricked in a business deal. There must be plenty of such, God knows."

Many petticoats rustled as the dark-haired girl turned, nodded at the portmanteau and teased, "Do my eyes deceive me or is my big brother about to run away to sea?"

"Now look here–" Something of his father's violent temper flared in Augustus' dark eyes. "Open your mouth one word in that direction and I'll–"

"–Just what will you do?"

He was upon her in a flash and, before she could sense his intent he had pulled her slim figure over his knees. Despite Flavia's outraged squeals and wildly threshing legs he administered a sound spanking.

"You've had that coming a long time!" he panted. Then he stood up and pushed her away. "And you'll get more of the same the next time you stick that impudent nose of yours into my affairs."

"I hate you! Oh, how I hate you! You'll pay dear for this!" blazed Flavia. "I'll tell Papa. You'll rue the day you went against Papa's will. I'll make you pay for this. Just you wait and see."

He started for her again, warning grimly, "You'll not, if you know what's good for you."

From below Mrs. Cosby's level voice called, "What in the world is going on up there?"

"Nothing, Mamma, really," Flavia's voice became so miraculously calm and controlled that Augustus was astonished. " 'Gustus and I were just having a little frolic. I teased him and he got angry." So saying, Flavia flounced out into the upper hall and, darting past a row of handsome walnut balusters, disappeared into her room.

BOOK TWO

The Western Flotilla

I SPECIAL TRAIN NUMBER FORTY-SEVEN

That the Ohio & Mississippi's special train Number Forty-seven was gradually entering a theatre of conflict became increasingly evident once it had departed from Cincinnati, which, after all, proved not to be the destination of Callahan & Grogan's contract workmen. Several cars jam-packed with raucous, blue-clad troops were added to Number Forty-seven at several towns of importance. For the most part these troops proved to be replacements destined for regiments already guarding various strategic points along the Ohio River and in southern Illinois.

In Cincinnati Big Pig Callahan's company had stared round-eyed from across the platform when a company of wounded, many of them legless or lacking arms, had descended from a hospital train. This visual testimony that a war was actually in progress made a deep impression upon Matthew Everett while Paul Dent, who had shared his hardwood bench for two days and a night now, shivered, fell silent, then bit his lip and looked aside.

At almost every railway station groups of plump, plain and painfully cheerful women appeared, to present baskets of pies, doughnuts or equally indigestible provender. What the weary and unwashed travellers really relished was the coffee they produced. Invariably it was full of cream and sugar and wonderfully rich, strong and fragrant.

On practically every siding along the Ohio & Mississippi's track stood flatcars transporting forage wagons, caissons, gun limbers and an occasional ambulance or two. Just outside of Pittsburgh the Westbound Special had passed car after car loaded with snow-shrouded fieldpieces, slabs of armor plating and heavy ordnance which some wiseacre declared to be naval guns fresh from the forges and rolling mills that, night and day, glowed in and around Pittsburgh.

As Number Forty-seven rolled on and on fewer towns were to be seen along the right-of-way; lonely-looking farmhouses stood amid fields appearing incredibly huge and flat to a New Englander's eyes. Throughout western Pennsylvania and in Ohio it was unmistakable that the primeval forest which once had covered this region was still in the process of being cleared away for mile after mile of sere cornstalks fluttered and canted wearily between fire-blackened stumps. Here and there great numbers of felled trees were being burnt.

The further west the train progressed the rougher-dressed did people on various platforms appear. Most of the men wore square-toed, knee-high boots tucked into frieze or homespun trousers; peaked caps and flannel shirts under short-skirted coats of heavy wool or buffalo skin. Out here hoop skirts were a rarity and, almost without exception, the older women appeared to be gaunt, strong and weather-beaten.

Of these Paul Dent, an ardent sketcher, rendered impressions on a sketchpad he always kept by him.

"We ought to reach Odin Junction pretty soon if we don't get side-tracked for another troop train." The Yale man had produced a large, nickel-plated watch. During the last few hours several supply trains which had the right-of-way had caused Number Forty-seven to be shunted onto sidings while the passengers cursed and shivered in this unusually bitter winter of 1861–62.

Matt inspected his gray-tinted hands and was ready to swear he could not have bathed or shaved in months. When the heat went on, his shirt and long woollen underwear gave off a sour effluvium; and again felt stiff and clammy when the penetrating cold invaded this decrepit old coach.

Dent was stating, "I'll work out my three months' contract in whatever shipyard I'm assigned to and there do my best over a drawing board in some engineering office."

"And then?" Matt demanded while shuffling and reshuffling a deck of cards upon a length of pine board fetched from a passing freight. ("Dealing sharp takes practice and more practice," Philo Daingerfield had warned him during a hurried meal en route. "You've got to limber them fingers till they handle the pasteboards real delicate-like. A clumsy gambler gen'rally comes to a bad end.")

"I shall attempt to enlist in the naval forces I hear are being recruited at Cairo."

"You are going to go back into the fighting?"

"Oh, no, I wouldn't dare, even if I used a false name. As an engineer. . ."

"You miss my meaning," Matt said without looking up and still frowning at the greasy cards flying between his fingers. "Why do you want to get yourself wounded or killed? Even an engineer takes that risk. You know what it's like in battle and you've noticed those pale-faced cripples limping around the railway stations."

From their corners Dent's steady blue eyes considered his stalwart companion. "This war, doesn't it mean anything to you?"

"Nothing," Matt grunted. "This war means nothing except a fine opportunity to make money, lots of it, and to get ahead. What other course is open to a nameless bastard?"

The slighter figure turned to face his companion, grit-streaked features gentle with understanding. "Once in New Haven I heard a famous minister declare that no child is ever illegitimate—only its parents."

Matt flared right up. "My mother wasn't illegitimate!"

"I didn't mean that the way it sounded," Dent apologized softly. "I only meant that the stigma should not be placed upon the result of an unlawful union, but rather upon one or both of those responsible for it."

Up ahead the locomotive's bell commenced to clang for a crossroads. Because there had been a new fall of snow, the train's wheels, muffled thereby, clicked softly, almost harmoniously, on and on.

"What else can one do?" Dent presently inquired and his voice gathered in strength and depth. "Why not dedicate yourself to preserving that Union our forefathers created and so often died for? Why not bestow the God-given right of freedom upon those less fortunate than ourselves?"

Bitterly Matt shook his tangled yellow head and stared out over a seemingly endless snow-covered plain. "And who could be less fortunate than an illegitimate child?"

"What about the slaves? Hardly any of them are born in wedlock."

"My God, you're not an Abolitionist, are you?" jeered Matt and, ruffling his cards, noted with satisfaction that they now fell into place evenly and swiftly. "You talk like a preacher—funny, isn't it? Until last week I was going to study for the ministry."

"I wasn't preaching," Dent objected, flushing. "To begin with I was no Abolitionist. I answered the President's call for volunteers simply to help preserve the Union, but after what I heard and saw down in Maryland and Virginia—and slaves are supposed to be extra-well treated there—I became one."

A big mechanic across the aisle caught the word "Abolitionist" and rasped, "To hell with all niggers! Them black bastards ain't nothing but dirty competition for free labor. If I had my way every jigaboo in Amurica'd get kilt or shipped back to Africa."

"That's right!" half a dozen voices called. "On with the Union and to hell with the damn' niggers."

Just then Big Pig Callahan's burly form entered the car. He was waving a pink telegram obviously picked up at the last stop. "Shut up, bhoys, stow that goddam' gabbin' an' listen to me, or shall I be knockin' yer skulls together some more?" He swayed at the end of the aisle in sunlight reflected off a snowfield, his pug nose glowing fiery red and his small eyes agleam. "I've just received fresh orders from the War Department." Everyone fell silent and those workmen who had been dozing sat up and knuckled their eyes. "When we reach Odin Junction this here company will be divided in two."

"Eh, what's that? Split up?"

"Now listen well. When we get to Odin, two-thirds o' this company will change train for Cairo, which is somewheres down in Illinois; the rest will go on to St. Louie. Now listen well—and when yer monicker's called, stand up and holler 'Here'! Now these men is for Cairo." Over the soft clatter of wheels the big labor contractor bawled out name after name. "Paul Dent," was the only one that meant anything to Matt.

Presently Callahan came to the end of his list. "Thim's what is left will go to St. Louie with Mr. Grogan and mind yez don't go straying off at Odin Junction—the Provost Marshal there is meaner'n a singed wild-cat." From a seat down the car Philo Daingerfield, whose name had not been called, twisted about in his seat, grinned and tipped Matt an elaborate wink.

"Callahan proposes but the War Department disposes," observed Dent and commenced securing a very frayed carpetbag. "I assume the naval detachment will be sent to Cairo."

"What makes you think so?" Matt inquired.

"Why, in Pittsburgh I heard that while most of the gunboats have been, and are being constructed, in St. Louis a majority of them have been sent down to Cairo and Mound City to receive crews and armament. Cairo's been made a Naval Station, you know. It's the most important in the West." He fell silent when the locomotive's hysterical whistling indicated that Odin Junction must be near at hand. Matt put down the section of plank and restored Daingerfield's deck of cards to his pocket.

"And what do you intend to do, Matt? Will you really work at the Eads shipyards?"

The New Englander nodded. "For a while I expect I'll have to, but the first minute I can, I mean to buy up my contract. I hear there are pots of money in Government supply contracts, especially if you meet the right people and pay 'em enough."

"You don't mean to enlist or serve aboard the gunboats?"

"Hell, no. I'm no such a fool."

Dent hesitated, then pitched a stick he had been whittling into the car's nearly empty fuel box. "So say you now. However, I wonder—"

"You wonder what?"

"Matt, inside you're too decent to dodge your duty—to take up swindling the Government."

Stubborn lines appeared upon the New Englander's unshaven countenance and he shook his head.

"True, you have suffered unjustly and terribly but, nonetheless, you *do* have a man's murder on your conscience. Don't you feel that unselfish service on your part might go far to—"

"Shut up!" snarled Matt. "Who are you, a goddamn' coward and a deserter, to preach to me?"

Dent winced, stiffened, then rose to his feet swaying because brakes were being too hurriedly applied.

"Whatever my mistakes have been," said the man from Connecticut in a low and quivering voice, "I intend trying to atone for them. Good-bye, Matt, I wish you a swift change of heart."

Now the train was rattling past a series of snow-shrouded flatcars most of them bearing well-tarpaulined parts of steamboat engines, engines designed to propel fast river transports or those slow but deadly gunboats which John Rodgers, Samuel Pook and James B. Eads were producing in such a tearing hurry.

A brakeman in red wool stocking cap thrust his head in from the platform. "Odin! Odin Junction! Change trains for Centralia, Mound City and Cairo!"

II ILLINOISTOWN

FROM THE BLUFF on which was located the western terminus of the Ohio & Mississippi Railroad one could make out the dark loom of St. Louis across the Mississippi but none too clearly on a day like this. Snow squalls were chasing each other like playful puppies across this great, coffee-colored and floe-dotted river separating Illinois from Missouri.

"This wind sure must have been honed on the North Pole," Philo Daingerfield commented through chattering teeth and bent his frail figure against the wind. "Let's seek the lee o' yonder freight pile."

Matt shook his head. He was enjoying the icy blasts after the fetid atmosphere in the steam cars. Besides, it reminded him of home, although here there were no evergreens, no hills or mountains, only flat snowy expanses of farmland back of rowdy, busy little Illinoistown. "You go if you want to. Back in Maine we never see anything like this."

Although the wind whipped at his shabby jacket with its greasy rabbit-skin collar, Daingerfield lingered, pointed at the four-mile-long line St. Louis sketched along the opposite shore. "Look at all them steamboats tied up account o' the war—must be near a hundred of 'em. She's quite a town, ain't she? The St. Louie Directory claims there's above 170,000 people of all conditions livin' over yonder."

"Ever been there?"

"Nope, most o' my piloting's been done from Pittsburgh to Paducah. I know the Ohio like the working end o' a demijohn. But I know Ole Miss' from Cairo to Vicksburg pretty well, too." He tucked hands under armpits to warm them and directed eyes, rendered teary by the gale, back to the city. "They're prosperous and none too smart, except the Dutchmen."

"Dutchmen?"

"Yep. St. Louie crawls with what they call 'Dutchmen' who ain't Dutch at all but Germans, really. Heard tell they can drill and sing to beat the band. Iffen we like it yonder we'll visit their Turn Club sometime. Make damn' good soldiers but they're hard and cruel, so they say, and the rest o' St. Louie's scared stiff they'll get massacred some fine day."

Matt offered no comment, only studied the sprawling metropolis and suffered a presentiment that somehow St. Louis would figure large in the course of his career. His blue serge overcoat was proving quite as capable of foiling this damp and icy wind as it was in Maine. As Philo had said, the inevitable twin funnels, stacks or chimneys, as variously they were designated, of steamers and river craft of all sorts, tied up to the levee and to wharfs and slips, suggested a forest of long-dead trees fringing the river.

The larger steamboats, he perceived, predominately were sidewheelers, some of them much bigger than the coasters which ran from Bangor to Portland and Boston. Most of the lesser craft looked to be sternwheelers. These, so Philo explained, were used on small and shallow tributary rivers such as the Osage, the Kansas and the Illinois. The rest were freighters, tugs, snag boats and the like.

"Yes, Matt, they claim St. Louie's a live, wide-open town. Over there's as many gambling saloons, theatres and whorehouses as you'll come across outside o' N'Orleans. It's a rich town, too, or was, till the fighting broke out last summer. Right now, St. Louie is Gen'ral Henry Halleck's headquarters. He commands the whole Western Department. Now will you for God's sake come into the lee o' that lumber pile? The damn' ferry don't leave for a half hour yet and I'm colder'n a well-digger's eye teeth. You can look at St. Louie any time."

Matt started to follow his companion but checked himself because when the snow let up it seemed that some special occasion was being celebrated on the far bank. It looked as if some vessel were about to sail. From this distance one couldn't be sure whether or not there were bodies of troops drawn up on a long wharf, but certainly flags were fluttering above it. Presently he watched spurts of steam break from above the pilothouse of several big steamers but heard no whistles.

An individual in a long-skirted black overcoat sporting a collar of marten pelts and a shako-like cap of the same lustrous fur came tramping up, florid features set in a friendly grin. Said he in a hearty manner, "Heyo, boys. I see you're strangers and no doubt wondering what all the ruckus across the river is about."

Promptly Philo offered a slim and long-unwashed hand.

"Whew! Marten pelts," Matt was thinking. "This fellow must be rolling in money."

"Well, that there boat's the *Essex*," said he. "Another of them iron-clads Jim Eads has been buildin' for Uncle Abe. She's bigger than the first ones he built last fall," he added. "The *Benton* will be bigger still."

The stranger noted Matt's interested expression. "Yep, Jim Eads' been doing one mighty fine job. Built four gunboats under contract in just forty-five days and couple of 'em was launched with their engines already seated. Three others were constructed down to Mound City over in Illinois."

A booming of cannon sounded when, across the river, an ungainly vessel gradually pulled away from its slip with torrents of sooty smoke pouring from twin funnels.

The stranger beamed but his small, bright blue eyes were hard as agates as he observed, "Reckon you two boys must be contract ship-builders from the East?"

"Ye're sharp as a new Barlow knife, friend, that's just what we are," Daingerfield supplied quickly. "How's business these days in St. Louie?"

"Fine, fine," boomed the well-dressed stranger, "but not so brash since the President replaced that gold-spangled, wind-bag called John C. Frémont. Halleck's clamped down in jigtime." The speaker hesitated and, shiny red features a-glow, inquired hopefully, "Say, you boys don't happen to be contractors?"

Matt started to say "No," but Philo clutching wildly at his battered stovepipe under a sudden gust off the Mississippi, said diffidently, "Now, that's as may be. Why?"

The stranger treated him to a sidewise glance. "Iffen you could coax a trade permit out o' Halleck's Quartermaster I know where I can lay hands on plenty of second-grade wheat and corn—cheap, real cheap, enough to make a smart feller a hundred and fifty percent on the Government purchase price—more from, well, never mind where."

Matt followed the others back towards the siding where the Special still panted softly and the contract laborers were gathering to straggle down to the ferry slip.

"Why ask us?" was Matt's natural query. "Why offer to share such a profit with strangers?"

"I got my permit cancelled. It was one Major McKinstry wrote for me and I had to grant him a fifteen percent share."

The stranger halted beside a pontoon carrier and lingered there stamping his feet, sparse red chin whiskers tossing in the breeze.

"Since you're new from the East," said he briskly, "maybe I, or my friend Greenway, could help you land a contract, can't myself; 'Old Brains'—that's what they call Halleck—won't let any of his quartermasters have nawthin' to do with any of Frémont's contractors. See how it is?"

"Reckon I do." Philo grinned. "Permit me, sir, to offer my card." He produced another of those grimy pasteboards such as he had showed to Matt. The other squinted and moved his lips while reading the inscription. "Um. So yer a river pilot, among other things? Sounds interesting, 'specially you bein' a engineer and such."

"What's your name, friend?" Philo queried gently. "And where do you live?"

"Around St. Louie I'm called Quirk. I live over there in the Virginia Hotel, but I hail from downriver," he added.

"How far down?"

"We'll say Memphis."

Philo's bright, bird-like little eyes intensified their interest. "You've maybe still got a few friends down yonder?"

"Might and then I mightn't," the other evaded and produced an alligator-skin seegar case. "'Tain't healthy 'round here to own friends south of Cairo."

"You goin' across on the ferry, Mr. Quirk?"

"I don't aim to swim," the other grunted.

Matt glanced out over the great stream and noticed that several big floes had appeared from upstream, jagged and muddied by dirt. "Think she'll try to cross what with all that ice?"

"Oh, sure. Even drunk as he is right now Tom Bancroft can miss that much ice easy enough."

Straight out into midstream threshed the new gunboat *Essex*, sluggishly propelled by a single paddlewheel, her vitals concealed under a casing of armor that gleamed gray-brown in the morning sunlight. Long streamers of sooty smoke were whirled instantly away from the new gunboat's twin smokestacks set just abaft of what must be her wheelhouse. White puffs of steam from her exhaust pipes too, immediately were dissipated.

The *Essex's* armored sides, the New Englander noticed, were angled upwards and inwards from the water line at roughly forty degrees. From her stern streamed a big, brand-new National Flag.

Presently Matt made out the outlines of what must be gunports. "How many and what kind of guns might she mount?"

"She don't carry none at all, right now," replied Quirk pulling his martenskin cap lower over large, bat-like ears. "Likely they'll put her cannons aboard downriver at Cairo, or maybe Mound City."

Never, Matt was thinking, could a more ungainly vessel have been designed. There was no trace of fluidity in her lines such as would characterize a seagoing ship; she was all ugly, sharp angles and suggested nothing more than a gigantic bread pan mounted upside down on a pointed raft. Soon the current carried her downstream towards Cairo and the deadly Gray batteries lying in wait for her.

A shout from the direction of the railhead drew their attention. A Mr. Dykes, a yellow-eyed and lantern-jawed individual who was the St. Louis agent for Messers. Callahan & Grogan, was bellowing through cupped hands. "Get down to the water's edge, boys! Ferry leaves in ten minutes."

Presently the little party of mechanics, carpenters and steamfitters were guided down a very steep and muddy street to a ferry slip at which lay a good-sized three-decked sternwheeler called the *Pembina*. She presented a weary and battered appearance. All about her were ranged mounds upon mounds of assorted supplies awaiting shipment to Brigadier-General Curtis' troops near Rolla in southern Missouri and Brigadier-General Ulysses S. Grant's slowly gathering forces. Once she started her trip cakes of ice threateningly bumped along her hull and the muddy, dirty yellow current tried savagely to swing the *Pembina* downstream. However, her sternwheel splashed and her exhaust pipes sputtered so mightily that her correct course to the western shore was resumed.

The closer the ferry approached her destination the more numerous became the signs of war. On the levee above a great crenellated building, which was the Federal Arsenal, stood a big earthenwork fort and another on an island below it.

The atmosphere prevailing in St. Louis, Matt quickly discerned, was totally different from what he had experienced thus far. The city existed under martial law and seemed well aware of it. Grimly, Quirk related that when someone had asked the Provost Marshal what martial law could do, Major McKinstry had replied, "Martial law can do pretty much as it damn well pleases."

Smiles were few and people moved as if in a hurry to transact their business and then regain the security of home. Everywhere moved swarms of blue-clad troops under arms or off duty. Some of them were garbed in gay Militia uniforms or wore faded and antique Federal garments that might have been regulation during the war with Mexico.

Most Western units wore no uniform at all except big black slouch hats and white cross-belts over checked shirts and homespun jackets. For the most part these Kansans and men from Nebraska were big, fierce-looking fellows wearing uncombed hair dangling down to their shoulders. Even the younger men boasted long, drooping mustaches or chin whiskers grown in ragged profusion. Everyone carried a Bowie knife or a pair of private pistols in addition to their Government-issued weapons. Although in ranks, they steadily chewed tobacco and were forever staining the dirty snow with their spittle.

"Pick yer feet up, fellers," pleaded an officer in a fringed hunting shirt. "We ain't got much of a march down to the Arsenal. I've a train waiting at the Iron Mountain deppo that'll fetch you straight down to the shipyards at Carondelet."

Matt was reminded of practicalities when Mr. Dykes appeared at the ferry landing clutching a sheaf of yellow papers. "Come along, you Callahan and Grogan men."

"How far's it to Carondelet?" someone wanted to know.

"Why, 'tis a lovely little village sityated at the southmost end o' St. Louis," Dykes evaded. "Now follow me and stay close 'cause if you figger to go strayin' off, yer wrong. To move about this here city you've got to have a pass signed by the Provo' Marshal hisself. See? Otherwise ye'll end up in Myrtle Street or Gratiot Street Jail or mebbe in some stinking guardhouse."

Coughing, spitting and cursing, but nonetheless happy to have reached their destination, the labor party moved off along Main Street, which paralleled the river between rows and rows of huge, empty and gloomy-looking brick warehouses. Tied up at the far end of these lay dozens upon dozens of river steamers immobilized for lack of freight and passengers. Most of these showed rust on slender chimney stacks rising sometimes sixty feet tall, and otherwise betrayed neglect. Paint was peeling off ornate scrollwork, pilothouses and paddle-wheel housings which often were elaborately decorated with sunbursts, panoramas or patriotic devices. Snow had not even been cleaned off their decks or bulwarks so icicles hung in festoons from guards and railings.

"By God, if that ain't the old *Green Mount!*" suddenly said one of the party. "Many's the time I've rid her 'twixt Cincinnati and Memphis."

A half hour's train ride southward past the U.S. Arsenal which was the fountainhead of Union military strength in St. Louis, brought the one car special into the overcrowded and bustling village of Carondelet. Here loomed half a dozen long shiphouses. Easily a dozen ship's ways dominated the landscape amid a small forest of cranes and hoists. Over the main gate leading to the shipyard was a weathered sign reading "James B. Eads Salvage and Construction Co."

Philo Daingerfield stretched his scrawny neck in peering this way and that at various shabby buildings and up various muddy streets, much like a hungry sparrow in search of a meal.

"Je-sus, have we got to live and work in this godforsaken hole?" grunted a lanky New Englander. "Ain't nary a spruce or a fir in sight nowheres."

"Fer tonight you fellers will bunk at the Elkhorn House," Dykes announced. "'Tain't no deeloox hotel and you'll have company in bed I expect—six-legged, I mean. Haw! Haw! Ye'll find all kinds of boardin' places, but don't try puttin' up at no whorehouse," he cautioned seriously, "'cause the Provoo's men will put ye out and jail ye like as not. General Halleck don't figger ye've been brought near two thousand miles just to catch a dose o' clap so's you can't work. The War Department's mighty impatient for this yer *Benton* to get finished. They must be big doin's afoot below Cairo, else I miss my guess."

III THE U.S. ARMY GUNBOAT *BENTON*

As THE SATURNINE Mr. Dykes had predicted, the Elkhorn House proved no bargain; so old that its clapboards had become warped from many a fierce summer sun, its walls admitted cold air as freely as a sieve. Guests, the new arrivals from the East discovered, were expected to sleep three in a bed. There was exactly one water tap for each of the Elkhorn's four floors and a visit to the privies entailed a Spartan expedition out back of the stables.

In all public rooms the atmosphere was heavy with a persistent reek of stale sweat, tobacco juice and the odors of cabbage and various fried foods. Never a rug graced this hostelry's gritty floors, and its crude furniture had been patched and mended so often that a good half of it had been stacked, quite useless, on a wide verandah.

Contractors, armorers, steamfitters, draftsmen and a sprinkling of petty officers from some naval contingent comprised the bulk of the patronage. Whatever services were performed, and they were few and far between, were carried out by mournful, loose-jointed and very stupid Negro men.

"We give up hirin' wenches—even homely ones—'way back last spring," a gold-toothed and pimply desk clerk informed Philo. "Yessir, couldn't get no work out of 'em *at all.* They was spendin' all their time in bed.

When a feller's been campaignin' a couple o' months he ain't choosey—even officers."

"Now ain't that a pity?" Philo suddenly cocked his narrow head to one side, a mannerism of his, and grinned.

"Hell! Don't you fret none, brother," the clerk reassured him. "You kin get all you want along Water Street."

Matt surveyed the Elkhorn's grubby saloon. By now he knew that practically all the Pook and Isherwood-designed ironclads had been completed and long since had departed for Cairo. Only the gunboat *Benton* remained in Eads' shipyard and she was so nearly complete it was obvious that Messers. Callahan & Grogan would have done much better to have diverted their whole company to southern Illinois. He told Philo as much.

"Well, Matt," said the former pilot, gambler and *soi-disant* engineer, "I been kind of inquiring around. 'Pears like them gunboats *has* been mostly finished, but the sitooation hereabouts ain't half so poor as one might reckon. There's a wad o' money floating around loose."

A steamfitter who had travelled all the way from Bangor growled from across the lobby. "What ails this tomfool government in Washington? I'm mad clean through. Thought we'd come 'way out here to build a parcel of gunboats to whip them damn' pesky Rebels."

Philo tugged at his goatee and drawled, "Well, friend, you go get your hands blistered if you want. Me, I was ready and willin'; so was my friend Matt, here. But bein's how we've been sent out on a wild goose chase, what sense is there in settin' round, sucking yer thumb and howlin' like a hound dog at the full of the moon? That right, Matt?"

Matt frowned, twirled his pony of bourbon with care. After all, it had cost ten cents. "I *would* like to get in at least a lick of work on account of Callahan's put up good money to fetch us out here. Somehow, I can't just sit around doing nothing so I'm heading for the shipyard office tomorrow morning."

"Good idee," Philo agreed a trifle too readily. "Once we get our contracts endorsed by Eads' office we can draw passes from the Provoo and go take a look about St. Louie."

The winter of '61–'62 would remain memorable for years to come because of its frigid ferocity, so Matt and Philo had become blue-nosed and chilled through before they stood before a gaunt Indian-like sergeant wearing inverted scarlet chevrons on both dark blue sleeves. He never even looked up at these new applicants, only selected two squares of printed pink cardboard.

"You, the big man, name? Age? Color of eyes? Where from?"

"Matthew Everett, twenty-one years, dark brown. I hail from Portsmouth, New Hampshire."

"Uh. A real Yankee, eh?"

"Yes. I guess so."

"Abolitionist?"

"No."

"That's good. No use freeing the niggers, they'll become a public charge. Where you living hereabouts?"

"We don't know yet," put in Philo, "but, by God, we ain't staying at that Elkhorn rat-trap."

The sergeant's enormous black mustaches lifted as he stamped and shoved forward the passes. "Fill that in when you find a place. Take it to Lootenant Snell for endorsement, he's second door down the hall, iffen he ain't already hauled out to supper. If he's gone you'll have to come back 'round eight. Pass ain't no good 'thout his signatoor."

Fortunately Lieutenant Snell was still on duty. He proved to be a large, plump individual wearing a single-breasted tunic at least a size too small. He actually glanced up before scrawling his signature.

"Which of you is called Everett? You? You got kinfolk in Massachusetts?"

"No," Matt replied stonily. "I've no kinfolk—anywhere."

"Too bad," Lieutenant Snell said, his pen scratching over the cardboard. "I'm from Springfield and my Aunt Hephzibah 'bides near Lowell—thought you might know her." He straightened, surveyed the tall, broad-shouldered figure before him with disconcerting attention. "Mister, by what's written across this pass," said he, "you're a New Englander, so I'll offer you a word of advice. Never forget that out here the people are savages, damn' crude, treacherous and bloodthirsty savages, and that includes Missourians, Kansans, Kentuckians and those triple-dyed bastards down in Arkansas. If you trust 'em so far as you can throw a bull by the tail you'll rue it. Isn't a one but what will sell his sister to a half-breed, provided he gets his price."

Back in the street again Matt decided that Carondelet was not much of a place. It was composed mostly of one- or two-storey shacks of which about every third one was either a saloon or a sporting house.

Although true darkness had not yet defeated a yellow afterglow in the west, the tinkle of ill-tuned pianos, shouts and songs already began to resound.

"Well," said Philo buttoning his short overcoat, "now that we've got us our passes what say we go and look up this Greenway feller?"

"Who in hell's Greenway?"

"That friend of Mr. Quirk's."

"Quirk—who's he?"

"Who's he?" For the first time Philo Daingerfield sounded annoyed. "Look here, Matt, you damn' well *got* to learn to remember names, 'specially when yer in a strange city. Quirk was that well-dressed feller we met on the bluff over in Illinoistown. You still got them three hundred greenbacks?"

"You didn't notice me lose any in that faro game last night?"

"No, Matt, I didn't." The small man slapped his companion on the back, had to reach up to do so. "You sure catch on quick for a feller that couldn't call one card from the next a week ago. I'm right proud of you, Matt, and thankful too."

Caution entered the big New Englander's manner. "Why?"

"Well, on them steam cars I won above a hundred dollars. With what you got and I got, if we pool, we've got enough to make a good beginning, if we handle it right. Let's go find this Greenway feller."

"How'll you locate him?"

"That's easy." Philo grinned. "Just you wait and see."

The oddly assorted pair pushed their way along a narrow, unpaved street bucking a throng of workmen many of whom had been paid off and were speculating on what they might do next now that the two gunboats General Frémont had ordered personally during his incumbency as Commander-in-Chief of the Western District were just about completed.

In the Guiding Light Bar a mechanic drawled, "Me, I'm haulin' right out o' this sinkhole lessen old man Eads has got him a passel o' new contracts. Water front's dead as Kisley's hen when she was stuffed with onions. Figger on headin' fer Cincinnati or Youngstown; hear tell they're paying top wage at that ordnance works where they cast all them cannons fer the gunboats."

While sampling a glass of new, rank-tasting whiskey with Philo, Matt listened to the hum of conversation all about. Someone said, "I ain't in such an infernal lather to clear out of Carondelet. Heard tell there's to be another whole flotilla of gunboats to be built here come spring—bigger and heavier than them Forty-five-Day-Wonders we finished and sent off last month."

"Ah, the hell with that!" grunted a steamfitter in a red-and-green checked flannel shirt. "Credit all the gossip you can hear and there's to be a hundred ironclads and three hundred mortar boats built in St. Louie before spring comes."

By dint of weight and muscle Matt managed to pilot Philo into a corner of the teeming bar, a point of vantage from which they could view the changing panorama of clients. The bartender, a fat German, bald save for a crop of blond bristles rising rigidly from his pink and shiny scalp, drew near. "Vot vilt it be, poys? Order up or move on; customers iss vaiting."

"Two more o' the same," Philo ordered tossing a twenty-five-cent shinplaster on the sopping mahogany. "By the way, friend, you ever hear o' a feller named Greenway?"

"Phil Greenvay?" the bartender checked himself in the act of tilting a dark green demijohn. "You iss freunds by him?"

"Sure, old friends," the Kentuckian blandly asserted.

"So?" Swiftly the bartender recovered the two small glasses he had set out and replaced them with two larger ones. "On der house," he said, and reaching for a labelled bottle, filled them with rich red-brown bourbon. "Mr. Greenvay iss out back, second room on der right, same as usual."

"Thanks, friend," Philo said aloud, then hissed to his companion, in an undertone, "quick, slip me a four-bit shinplaster.

"There you are, my friend, that's just so's you remember Daingerfield, Everett and Company next time we show up."

"Dank you, Mr. Everett."

"Oh, no, I'm Daingerfield. This here is Mr. Matt Everett." As Philo drew himself up his preposterous resemblance to Jefferson Davis became so pronounced that several people stared, put their heads together and whispered.

"Dank you, Mr. Daingerfield. Best you go right now to talk mit Mr. Greenvay. Later on, ach! he gets so busy."

They discovered Mr. Greenway smoking a huge seegar and leaning upon a scarred wooden table in what must once have been a private dining room. The squalid bareness of this room was more than offset by the splendor of the speculator's attire. His enormously fat form was enclosed in a plum-colored claw-hammer coat, a waistcoat of vermilion velvet set off by a row of turquoise buttons leading down to pantaloons of a vivid blue striped in black.

Across Mr. Greenway's ample belly was draped a red-gold chain massive enough to anchor a towboat, as Daingerfield later commented. Further, he was clean-shaven, with a cherry-hued snub nose and slightly crossed eyes of the palest blue imaginable. About a heavily freckled scalp clung a woolly line of thin black locks.

In the act of taking their leave was a singular pair of visitors. One was an obvious Hebrew with beady black eyes, a long black beard ending in a fork and sombre clothes that were neither clean nor well-cut. The other stood as tall as the Jew was short and had a long sallow face dominated by a hawk-like nose and high cheekbones, one of which was diagonally traversed by a livid scar. He wore a big Bowie knife in a fringed sheath strapped to the front of a wide, brass-mounted belt. His eyes were yellow as any canary.

"These here gents are Mr. Rothstein and Mr. Callam," boomed Mr. Greenway when the four men hesitated just inside the doorway. "They're old friends of mine and now that I've got 'em their trade permits I reckon they'll do a land-office business."

Daingerfield bowed and made a flourish of his battered stovepipe hat that all but swept the floor. "Mr. Rothstein and Mr. Callam," he said.

"That's right," the Jew said quickly. "Pleased to meet you. Any friends of Mr. Greenway's are friends of mine."

"But we're not friends—yet," Matt protested. "We've never seen Mr. Greenway before now. This is Mr. Daingerfield and I'm called Matt Everett."

"Tut, tut!" came Greenway's genial protest, "let's say 'new friends.' I can see we're going to get along. I like honesty such as yours, sir," and he fixed his convergent eyes upon the big New Englander. "Come in, gentlemen, come in and state your business."

The callers then underwent a swift but thorough appraisal that included copper-skinned Daingerfield in his shabby, flashy garments and Matt still in his travel-stained and wrinkled Sunday-go-to-meeting clothes from Dexter.

"Grab a chair, gents," invited the speculator. "Here, try these—" He produced a leather case of seegars, two of which Daingerfield selected with alacrity.

"My friend don't smoke. Well, Mr. Greenway, we've just come in to St. Louie from the East—we've contracted to work on them ironclads, but that was only to win free transportation to this glorious golden West."

"You ain't the first to figger it that way," Greenway commented sourly, restoring the seegar case to his pocket, "nor will you be the last. You two got any ready cash?"

"Some," Matt admitted. He was sitting on the edge of a chair with a narrow-brimmed felt hat crushed between powerful hands.

"Enough," Daingerfield declared carefully, "to maybe do a mite of business."

"Now, now!" chuckled Greenway standing up to light his seegar at the lamp chimney. "You fellows ain't answering at all. How much you got? A thousand, maybe?"

"No, about half of that," Matt said before Philo could stop him.

The fat man's interest waned considerably. "Um, that ain't much, and that's a fact." He blew a great smoke ring. "Still it might do; depends on the kind of business you had in mind."

"Why—why, supplying the Government," said Philo. "A friend of ours says there's easy pelf to be made in that direction."

Mr. Greenway settled back on his armchair the cane bottom of which creaked under his weight, cocked his head to one side and surveyed his seegar. "And who might this friend be?"

"His name's Quirk—"

Interest suddenly gleamed in the other's eyes. "You ain't referring to Sam Quirk?"

"Why, to be sure. Sam's an old friend of mine."

The big man heaved himself to his feet. "Daingerfield—if that's really your name—I'm thinking you're not only a liar but a damn' clumsy one."

"Sir, I resent your implication!" Daingerfield's jaw shot forward and his short body quivered with outrage but all the same his always supple hands hung curiously loose by his sides. "Mister, I've killed a man for lesser insult."

"Have you?" Greenway said, shiny features suddenly frozen into an evil smile and it seemed that a pair of nickel-plated derringers abruptly sprouted from his well-manicured hands to be held unwaveringly in line with the Kentuckian's flat belly. "You are a liar, ain't you?"

Completely aghast, Matt looked first at Daingerfield's small taut figure, then at Greenway's towering form. Philo blinked at the two menacing black circles and summoned a sheepish grin. "Well, maybe I haven't known Sam Quirk so long at that."

"You bet you ain't," rasped the man in the red waistcoat. "On account your friend here 'pears honest, I'll tell you why I spotted you for a liar. Quirk's given name ain't Sam and never was, because it's Simon. He's my brother-in-law. Daingerfield," he barked, "just you clear out of here. This gent and I are going to talk."

Philo Daingerfield drew himself up with an amazing semblance of dignity. "A gentleman, sir, never lingers where he is not wanted. Matt, I now depart to hunt us up some living quarters. Meet me at the hotel."

As the door closed upon the little Kentuckian, Greenway, chuckling, replaced his derringers in the lower pockets of that garish waistcoat. "Now, Mr. Everett, just what had you in mind?"

Only after swallowing a couple of times did Matt find his voice. The sight of those derringers had sent wretched recollections flooding into his mind. "Well, sir, I aim to work for Mr. Eads just long enough to earn my freight but I see small sense in slaving over a lot of gunboats any longer than I have to."

"Why not buy up yer contract from Big Pig Callahan?"

"Might be a good idea," Matt admitted. "Will he sell?"

"Sure, if the price is right."

"I'll talk to him."

"Now that's real commendable, real honest," Greenway's fleshy fingers flexed themselves several times. "Me, I prefer dealing with honest men." He winked. "Of course, there's honest men and honest men, so give me a man who keeps his eye on the main chance but who plays fair. You got how much money of your own?"

Matt stood up, hat in hand, and said mournfully, "Only three hundred and eighteen dollars, so I guess I've got a lot of gall to take up your time. You wouldn't be interested in my little stake."

"Sit down, man, sit down," boomed the contractor and waved his seegar in an expansive gesture. "You're wrong, 'way wrong. Not a year ago, Mr. —what did you say's your name?"

"Everett."

"Mr. Everett, I crossed from over in Illinois bringing nawthin' more than a carving knife, hickory shirt, a pair of galluses, homespun pants and the boots I stood up in. Right now," he patted the great watch chain and his diamond-studded shirt front, "I reckon I must be worth a couple hundred thousand dollars, more or less, every cent of which was honest earned through the sale of goods under boney fide Government contracts, signed, sealed and delivered by Gen'l Frémont's Quartermaster. No, sir. No one can't ever rightly claim Tobias Greenway's commerce is crooked or illegal." He hunched over the table, small eyes intent. "Now, Mr. Everett, I'll speak right out. If I help you get a permission to trade and mebbe a contract or two, it'll not be just for love of them brown eyes of yours. I want ten percent of any profits you earn."

"*Ten percent!*" Matt burst out. "Why, good God, up in Maine three percent—"

"This ain't Maine," snapped Greenway, "and nowadays ain't ordinary times. Would you rightly kick at paying me ten percent if you was to clear, well, something like thirty, mebbe forty thousand dollars inside the next three months?"

Matt fairly goggled. "Thirty-forty—thousand dollars? That isn't possible."

"It is. But *only* if you hold a permit to trade and contracts issued by Gen'ral Halleck's Quartermaster. See? Since all agreements signed by Frémont's officers have been voided there are precious few permits valid these days. So them what has 'em can pile up the cash." And Greenway proceeded to supply Matt with some further details.

"All right," Matt's yellow head inclined decisively.

"Let's shake on it then," grinned Greenway. "And I'll see Callahan about buying your contract. I'll even advance you money if you need it

—at ten percent. May take a short while, though, so keep yer pants on."

"I will. When do I see you next?"

"Here, tomorrow evening, 'round six. Oh, one thing more, Mr. Everett. You'd better get rid of the big-talking weasel who came in with you. He'll queer a lot of deals for you. He's got card-sharp, liar and cheat, written over him in letters a foot high.

"Now, I'll just take a hundred dollars on account."

Heart hammering wildly at the thought of parting with so much money, Matt counted out that sum onto the table.

"Ninety, one hundred. Good. You'll never regret this," beamed Greenway. "If you can keep your mouth buttoned you'll go far."

IV THE MYRTLE HOTEL

To MATTHEW EVERETT'S considerable surprise, Philo Daingerfield appeared not the least bit downcast or angry when he found that diminutive individual busily writing in that cheerless bedroom they shared. "I'm sorry," Matt began awkwardly, "I suppose really I should have gone out when you did."

"Hell, no, Matt. I wasn't half so insulted by Mr. Greenway as I let on." Reaching into his battered carpetbag the Kentuckian produced a pint bottle. "Here, take a pull of this bust-head, it's still considerable cold and raw outside."

"Then you weren't really insulted?" Matt could not conceal his amazement.

"Hell, no! Fact he paid me the high compliment of admitting that my wits were sharper than his. I only hope," the little man observed while pouring water from a pitcher the lips of which someone had mended with lead, "that he didn't bamboozle you and get any cash away from you."

There was no need to admit that he had, Matt decided. He would remain miserably uneasy until his next interview with Greenway.

"While you were talking with Greenway I made some further acquaintances. They'll prove useful, and it was useful learning Mr. Quirk's first name is Simon." Cheerfully he waved a grimy hand. "Yes, sir, that Greenway cuss did us a real service when he gave out that fellow's correct name. Drink up, Matt, and tomorrow night let's move to better quarters. On the way over you can tell me about yer arrangement with Greenway, which," sharply he eyed his towering, fresh-faced companion, "I judge you've already concluded?"

"Yes. I have."

Philo angrily spat tobacco juice into a tin cuspidor. "Ye should have talked to me first," he complained. "Bet he's even charging you seven percent commission—"

A groan escaped the New Englander. "No, ten."

"My God, what you need is a nurse!"

To the hotelkeeper's chagrin they paid for their room with local scrip which had grown incredibly limp and dirty for all that such currency had been in circulation less than a month.

"Where are we headed?" demanded Matt, shouldering his woods pack.

"I hear there's a tidy little hotel on Hickory Street and not far from the Iron Mountain Railroad Station and," he winked, "close by the levee and water front."

"Why, that's right in St. Louis itself."

"Sure is—we want to be right handy to the center of things, as we ain't here in Carondelet. You see, we'll meet some almighty keen competition in this contracting business—a lot of big fellers have been in it since the start of the war like Quirk, Rothstein, Gus Krausmaier, yer friend Greenway and some others. Yep, we'll have to look sharp and act real smart."

Early next evening after finishing his work at Eads' boatyard, Matt sought out Tobias Greenway, resplendent this dull evening in a waistcoat of variable green-and-purple satin and wearing a dark blue clawhammer coat over his enormous belly.

"So you turned up?" He waved an affable greeting. "Figured you would."

In response to a gesture, Matt seated himself, cap on lap, and carefully eyed the gross figure behind the desk. "I make it a point to keep my word," said he shortly. "Now what is it you wanted to tell me?"

"As I've already told you, friend Everett, my license to trade with the Army was revoked by that Halleck bastard's Quartermaster-in-Chief. Means that although I still can buy," he winked ponderously, "and I know just where to find the hard-to-get merchandise—I can't nowise negotiate with the Army Purchasing Commission. So you, son, will have to carry on our dickering with Colonel Sherrod." He stared fixedly at the New Englander. "Know how to drive a hard bargain?"

A faint grin curved Matt's unshaven mouth. "There's scarce a soul in the State of Maine that isn't a born trader. A man doesn't amount to much up our way unless he can drive a bargain sharper than a woodsman's ax. We take real pleasure in trading or swapping." Phoebe's pa was famous for his skill in such matters.

Phoebe. A disquieting recollection recurred of her peering out of her mother's kitchen and calling out for him to come back. What was it she had said? "I won't be left behind. I love you, Matt." And, "I'll follow you to the ends of the earth if need be." Well, no matter how much Phoebe had meant it at the moment, most likely she'd gotten bravely over those heroics. Such were to be expected from a young female in the midst of a crisis.

All the same he wondered what had become of her, whether her red-gold hair still glistened as brightly in the sunlight and whether her smile was as quick as ever.

"Good." Greenway's voice brought him back to reality. "Now come over here, son, and lemme teach you arithmetic as she is learned in the Western Department!" He shuffled papers on his desk until he found several bills. He passed one over. "What do you read there?"

"Says H.B. and C.S. Blood, Commission Merchants, have sold Tobias Greenway two gross of horse collars and two gross of mule collars at six dollars and seventy-five cents each."

"What would you price 'em to Colonel Sherrod?"

"Eight dollars, maybe?"

Greenway's guffaws made the whole untidy "office" resound. "Ain't you the innocent?" he jeered. "Listen, Everett, us contractor fellers nowadays won't touch nothin' don't show a hundred-fifty percent profit!"

Matt's jaw sagged. He then did some rapid calculation. Four gross of horse and mule collars would come to five hundred seventy-six items. If a hundred and fifty percent profit were to be made on each of those collars—? At long last Matt came to bless those weary hours during which Mother endlessly had drilled him in mental arithmetic. Why, he'd have to charge sixteen dollars eighty-seven cents per collar! This, multiplied by four gross, would fetch a net of—he gasped—of $5,829.12!

A parabola of tobacco juice spurted from Greenway's loose lips onto the floor. "Makes you blink, don't it? Don't look so damn' startled. And that's the profit on only one little deal."

"But—but, Mr. Greenway, surely nobody in his right mind would pay such a price for horse collars?"

"Wouldn't they? Approach him right and Colonel Sherrod will. Remember, wagon trains, field artillery batteries and their ammunition wagons have *got* to be equipped." Greenway settled back and his spring chair creaked under his bulk. "Now when you deal in wheels, forage-wagon bodies, ambulances, limbers and caissons, a feller does a heap better." The contractor grinned. "Of course the real money's to be made in—" he went over to open the door into the hall and glanced out, then lowered his voice before he said, "in shipping certain kinds of supplies downriver —below Cairo."

Matt's broad features went scarlet. "You mean running contraband to Rebels?" He started to shake his head, and half rose from his chair so strongly it went against his grain to deal with the enemy. Then he remembered; for nearly a month now it had been a case of Matthew Everett versus the world.

"Us contractors don't talk such a way," sharply reproved the contractor. "Us fellers simply trade 'downriver.' Understand? Now come over here. I'll let you buy in your stake on a deal in anchor chain, then horse collars and a couple hundred rotten old tents. They've been forgotten in a warehouse since the war with Mexico till *I* found 'em. Yes, sir, soon's your Provost's license to trade shows up, and it should within forty-eight hours, you'll head for Colonel Sherrod's office; be bold and he won't put too many questions. I figger, son, you'll get the hang of things quick enough. Well, here's luck."

During fifteen minutes or so the contractor continued to hold forth, listing for his new associate the names of certain dealers, the commodities they dealt in and their general reputation.

Greenway's huge shoulders hunched themselves forward. "Got it? You'd better remember all this. Ain't you paying me ten percent for the money I'm advancing for you to buy the stuff on your own? And me, well, we're splitting the profits—until I get my license back. Now this here is merchandise that brings the best profit." Greenway reeled off, and Matt memorized, a brief list of those commodities in especially short supply.

When feet came tramping up the corridor Greenway offered a moist hand. Matt accepted it, but had to suppress a shiver of revulsion.

"You can't be squeamish, you poor bastard," he reminded himself as he tramped off down the street towards the horsecar terminal. Philo should be awaiting him there.

Suspiciously Matt eyed his diminutive, ever-restless companion.

"Say, just what kind of a place is this Myrtle Hotel?"

"Like I said—reasonable rates, clean and handy to the business district."

"Respectable?" Matt unslung his woodsman's pack, and settled it between his knees while directing a sympathetic glance at the two weary old nags that stood with gaunt heads held low to the manure-sprinkled slush. They really should have been given blankets for it was beginning to snow.

"It ain't no sporting house if that's what you're thinkin'," Philo announced, then grinned. "But I expect there might be a few females living there without their husbands. In wartime a lot of men go away or get themselves killed."

More than a little drunk, the bottle-nosed horsecar driver came lurching out of a saloon across the snow-covered road, climbed onto the horsecar's platform and cursed under his breath as he lashed his pitiful team into a jolting, stiff-kneed trot. A single kerosene lamp partially illuminated the interior of the car and revealed only a couple of tired-appearing mechanics who promptly fell asleep, a long-legged cavalry corporal wearing bright yellow chevrons and stripes down breeches of sky-blue, and a hard-faced young bawd. These last two, sublimely ignored Philo's obvious interest, embraced and fell to kissing noisily until the corporal's rakish dark blue képi, adorned by a pair of crossed brass sabres, fell onto the floor and he broke off to retrieve it.

Philo said, "Now then—just what kind of a deal did you make with fat-cat Greenway? For ten percent it ought to be a beauty."

Matt steadied himself against the horsecar's bumping lurches. "Well, he's going to get me—get what's called a 'permit to trade' from the Provost Marshal. It'll be made out in my name, but," he added quickly and with a reassuring smile, "you can trade under it as a silent partner and it'll cost you nothing."

By an effort Philo managed to suppress his sharp disappointment. "I suppose you'll have to pay through the nose for that permit?"

"I expect so. But then Mr. Greenway's going to put me in touch with Colonel Sherrod who lets considerable purchasing contracts for the Army. Next he's going to introduce me to a Mr. Bullwinkle here in town. He's from Memphis, Tennessee, and doesn't exactly go around talking about his sympathies in this war."

"God! Maybe you didn't get skinned so bad after all." Philo nodded with breath vapors drifting in silvery clouds about his head. "Now, and this is right important, just what does he figger the Army is keenest to buy and what might Mr. Bullwinkle especially be craving?"

Matt frowned, merging straight yellow brows into a single line. Somehow he still couldn't quite cotton to this business, for all that he had determined to win himself a tidy fortune before emigrating to the little town of Portland in Oregon. Many New Englanders had settled there, had stayed and had prospered. "Why, Colonel Sherrod needs mostly iron chain, blocks and tackles and hemp cable big enough to serve for breechings—whatever those are—on cannons."

"Good! Good!" Briskly Philo rubbed his well-tended hands together. "I'll start nosing around, Matt, and, holding a pilot's license like I do, I'll find what we want by way of a freight boat somewhere."

As the horsecar rattled on Philo canted his head towards Matt and murmured in an undertone, "Now don't you buy up Big Pig's contract in too big a hurry—iffen you work on the *Benton* a while you'll learn what's in short demand at the shipyard. I hear Jim Eads soon'll be layin' down five more gunboats. Yessir, pays to know what's needed bad and what's hard to come by."

"All right. I'll delay quitting and feel better for it."

"Course once we get set we ain't paying that damn' fat-cat Greenway any ten percent or even five percent. That feller's too smart for his own good. Imagine hooking a greenhorn so hard!"

"Hold on," Matt objected hotly. "I agreed to pay Mr. Greenway for six months and I shook hands on it." Speculatively he regarded the small, untidy figure beside him. "Somehow, Philo, I don't think I'd cross Mr. Greenway were I you. He knows this city like a book and he doesn't look to me like a man who'd take kindly to getting bilked."

"What if he doesn't?" The Kentuckian stiffened, and a curious deadly gleam shone in his small jet eyes. "My young friend, 'tis obvious you've a heap to learn; here in St. Louie we're all out for the main chance and it's a case of dog eat dog. I suppose you were impressed with the fat cat's trick with his derringers? Look!" In a movement so fast that it defied being followed Daingerfield produced a stiletto and levelled it in line with Matt's stomach. "Kinder surprised, ain't you? If I couldn't produce cutlery or artillery about twice as quick as yer friend Greenway, I wouldn't be living this minute. When I allowed I've killed more than one man I wasn't lying—for once."

All in an instant that slim, evil, blue-gray blade had disappeared—up Daingerfield's sleeve—and he laughed softly.

"Just let good old Philo Daingerfield in on that trading. Your permit'll come in a couple of days and we'll begin piling up coin. We'll go well together, see if we don't. Me, I got more faults than a dog has fleas, but I ain't forgot that time you backed me up on the train. Yessir, we'll be wearin' pearls in our shirtfronts six months from now."

"Unless, of course," Matt pointed out, "Greenway gets you done in."

"He won't," the Kentuckian assured. "I went out so peaceable-like 'cause I didn't want him to guess how much smarter I am than him." He fell silent and the car bumped onwards through ever-increasing snow.

The soldier had undertaken to explore his companion's soiled petticoats so boldly that eventually she slapped his hand away with an assumed air of outraged innocence.

"Park Street! Park Street!" The driver bawled without bothering to open the door. "Next stop's Hick'ry."

In lively curiosity Matt stared out into the street which, despite the falling snow, was busy. Drays, wagons, carriages and travellers on horseback appeared and became lost to sight in the storm. Numbers of soldiers, laborers, clerks and other civilians hurried along with heads bent against the wind. Saving Boston, of which he had seen practically nothing, this was the biggest city he had ever beheld. Did not St. Louis boast a population of approximately 170,000, exclusive of the troops stationed there?

They pushed aside the horsecar's sliding door, paid the somewhat sobered driver five cents in tiny scrip and descended onto the brick pavement to stand peering up at a snow-splashed sign reading, "Thos. Lynch. Slave Dealer & Auctioneer." It was affixed to a big grim structure the windows of which were heavily barred.

From a passerby Philo ascertained that the Myrtle Hotel was situated on Hickory Street between Valle and Ham Streets. Presently the lights of a three-storey building loomed ahead and a big black-and-yellow swing board proclaimed that here stood the Myrtle Hotel. From its architecture Matt judged that this must once have been an imposing private residence. Apparently encroaching business structures had driven the owner further westward, probably in the direction of Tower Grove Park.

Lamplights glowing within momentarily gilded the whirling snowflakes. Indoors someone was playing "Old Zip Coon" on a badly tuned piano and bursts of loud laughter indicated that this hostelry promised to be far from a dull place.

Behind the registration desk stood an individual so enormously fat that an ellipse had been sawed out of the desk's edge in order to accommodate his monumental belly. Monsieur Henriot's thinning black hair had been slicked down flat with pomade and the color in his blubbery cheek was so high that Philo afterwards commented that he was existing but a short jump removed from apoplexy.

Flanking the proprietor stood a hatchet-faced female clad in a black silk gown cut in the most conservative of styles. Her complexion was that of old ivory effectively emphasized by jet earrings and a jet necklace supporting a huge cross of the same sombre-hued stone. Her lips were thin and pale purple; and her nonexistent eyebrows had been supplanted by two thin lines of mascara.

"This elegant establishment was recommended to us by our good friend Tobias Greenway," Philo announced with a hint of patronage.

"*Alors*. Then you are *amis* of Monsieur Greenway?" boomed the proprietor.

"Yes," replied Daingerfield easily. "We shall each require a good-sized room with comfortable furniture and a big bed."

"You must be prepared to pay well for such."

"We are. We shall accept nothing but your best."

The proprietor's moon-like visage wreathed itself in smiles and his pudgy fingers closed over a penholder.

"One moment, Jacques," Mme. Henriot promptly placed a hand bearing an enormous red gold wedding band across the registry book. "First one must inspect your passes from the Provost Marshal." Meanwhile her eyes as small, black and bright as her jewellery, narrowly scanned Daingerfield's well-worn and rumpled finery, then with less disapproval viewed the tall, weather-beaten young fellow with the bold dark brown eyes, yellow hair and country-cut garments.

"Why, yes ma'am," Matt produced his pass, also his copy of the work contract with Callahan & Grogan. Madame Henriot's expression did not relax in the least as she scanned them.

"*Bigre*, a contract carpenter, hein?" She sniffed, returned the identifications. "You, the leetle one. I do not theenk Monsieur Greenway he would have sent me such a one. I shall ask heem. You, Monsieur Evairette, may have a room but your companion, *non pas*."

Whereupon Monsieur Henriot turned purple and exploded into staccato French wildly waving his arms. Finally he stood up, the better to rant on, until the woman in black shrugged so violently that a huge ring of keys at her belt softly jingled.

"Thees ees your property, Jacques, so have your way," hissed the *patronne*. "But you, the leetle one, do not forget that thees ees a respectable house so you weel not wear boots to bed. Neither weel you drink een your room nor weel you entertain women there. I repeat, thees ees a very respectable hotel."

As if to raise a question on that point, a door opened upstairs and released loud peals of feminine laughter and piano music. Then sounded a shrill squeal as if some girl's bottom had been soundly pinched.

"We'll give you no trouble, ma'am," Matt gravely reassured her. "We've so much work to do there'll be no time for nonsense."

A giggle prompted him to turn about and glance upwards. Peering through the banisters were a pair of merry gray-green eyes. He caught an impression, too, of full red lips, a heart-shaped face and black hair.

"*Zut!*" snapped Madame Henriot. "I must go upstairs. That Léonie must be neglecting her company."

V THE BOATYARD

JAMES B. EADS' YARD at Carondelet had been located along a low slope which descended to the Rivière des Pères, a minor tributary to the Mississippi, and consisted of six long shiphouses lying at right angles to the river. At the upper end of each shiphouse—which really was little more than a great shed—was situated a drafting and engineer office. At the moment five of the six ways were unoccupied save for timbers that would be used in the flat bottoms of the next gunboats to be built for the Army along Eads' designs.

Long since, Matt Everett had discovered that a most unusual situation at present prevailed along the Ohio and the Upper Mississippi. While all Federal gunboats had been ordered, designed and built by the War Department, their navigation and the serving of their guns were undertaken by the Navy Department. The Army, however, lately had begun to furnish small details of infantrymen to act as sharpshooters since the Rebels had taken to the distressing habit of masking fieldpieces and of lying in ambush in the narrower stretches or where some vagary of the channel forced a vessel close to the bank. Crack rifle shots from the Southwest also had taken to sniping gunboat crews at such times, as had been learned aboard the original two "timberclads" *Tyler* and *Lexington*, which had distinguished themselves in the first river action of the war—the Battle of Belmont.

"Yep," the boss carpenter observed while Matt checked the contents of a battered carpenters' chest. "The Navy does the navigating and handles them big cannons and it sure gravels the hell out of them brassbound webfoots that they have to take orders from the Commanding General of the district they serves in. 'Twas the Navy, though, sent Commander John Rodgers out here 'way back last summer to see what kind o' craft was needed. 'Twas him bought them timberclads which sure have proved mighty useful."

The boss carpenter spat a stream of yellow-brown tobacco juice silently, accurately at a knothole in the floor ringed and befouled by less experienced marksmen. "But then the War Department stepped in and, last August, contracted with Mr. James B. Eads—there's a real fine patriot for you—to build seven ironclads in forty-five days—four here at Carondelet and three at Mound City 'crost the River in Illinois. It was twenty-four hours a day and bonuses for extra work and we got 'em built.

"Eads got together with a feller named Isherwood and a feller named Samuel Pook who were loaned by the Navy, and together they designed what us fellers call 'turtles' 'count of, without their chimneys, they look just like that. Too bad you weren't here to see them gunboats set off for Cairo couple of weeks back."

"How were they called?" Expertly, Matt tested the temper of a chisel with a broad thumb. He really wasn't interested but he wanted to stand in with his boss.

"Well now, let's see. Right in this shipyard was built the *Carondelet*, of course," the boss said. "I worked mostly on her. Mighty useful piece of work even if she *is* slower'n molasses in January. Then there was *St. Louis, Louisville* and *Pittsburgh.*"

"What are the others, the ones built in Mound City, named?"

"*Mound City, Cincinnati* and *Cairo*; you kin bet your boots them gunboats are going to give them Rebs bad fits when they start to fight."

"I don't know much about boats," Matt admitted, "being as how I've all my life lived in the backwoods of New Hampshire. How long and how wide are they?"

The boss carpenter, whose name was Kniesche, substituted a new keyhole saw for one that was bent and about worn-out.

"I'll describe the *Carondelet* on account of I know her inside an' out. Well, let's see, she's a flat-bottomed sternwheeler—no ribs, just a frame. She's five hundred and twelve tons, she's a hundred and seventy-five feet long and fifty feet wide—"

"—in the beam, you mean," corrected a passing steamfitter. "Whyn't you use the right term? Navy boys don't like for you to speak of width."

"It'll always be 'width' to me," Kniesche replied seriously. "Now, Everett, like I was saying, these gunboats are fifty feet wide and draw six feet—account of all their armor."

"I wouldn't think six feet was so much," Matt commented.

"For these waters it's a hell of a lot. Noticed them big steamboats tied up along the levee? You won't believe it, being from the East, but there's plenty of 'em don't draw more than two foot and four inches."

Matt stared, then grinned. "Those great vessels draw just over two feet? Shucks, Mr. Kniesche, you're funning me."

"I ain't. Not a bit of it. Take the *Crystal Palace* what's laying right now to Greely and Gale's wharf; she can carry a hundred ton o' freight on less'n twenty-two inches of water." The boss carpenter chuckled as he returned a steel angle to the chest which was about to become Matt's responsibility. "Last year, heard tell of a steamboat built down on the Green River that drew only eight inches, so her owners tied a watering pot to her jackstaff so's she could slide over any bar that came up for air. Then there's the *Isaac Shelby*—I been on her myself—she draws only eleven inches and they say her cap'n keeps a keg o' beer mounted on her bow so's if the river goes dry he can keep going on the suds."

He chuckled and spat again. " 'Course you can believe that last or not as you please, but them drafts I mentioned is true. No sir, always to find six feet of water in most of these rivers is like finding virtue in a Government contractor—it may be there, and again it mayn't. Yes, Everett, we sent them four boats off into the River des Pères down yonder with their armor all bolted on."

"How thick is this armor?" Despite himself Matt was becoming interested.

"It's two and a half inches of plate iron at the bow and to either side of the engines; about one inch on the front of the pilothouse, or 'texas', as they call it here. Everything else is protected—if you can call it that—by boiler plate which will stop musket or minié balls, but nowthin' much bigger."

A sudden furious clanging of mauls seating red-hot rivets designed to secure plate armor in position caused the shiphouse to resound so loudly that what the boss carpenter was saying as he locked the tool chest and handed the new employee its key was drowned out.

When Matt could hear again the boss carpenter was saying, "Believe it or not, we built all four boats according to contract, mounted their engines and raised and guyed their smoke pipes in just forty-five days." A quiet pride characterized Kniesche's bearing and he pulled out a length of lumber. "What's this?"

"Yellow oak."

"And this?"

"Poplar."

"And this?"

"Cedar, of course."

"And this?"

"Um. Don't recognize it."

"You wouldn't. It's gum-maple. But you'll do. If you don't know, you say so. Let's go warm our bellies with some coffee at the cook shack."

Once they were picking their way between tall stacks of lumber and great baulks of timber, Kniesche resumed his dissertation. "I tell you Jim Eads is a shining wonder. You should have seen the stuff come piling in. Wood from Minnesota, plate armor from Pittsburgh, cannons from Youngstown, and ship carpenters from the East and all up and down the rivers, and machinery from Cincinnati, Pittsburgh and from right here in town.

"Yes, Everett, this here yard was a fair boiling all last fall and she'll boil again the minute Mr. Eads starts his next lot of ironclads. Hi, uncle!" He waved to an old colored man who came shuffling over to offer crullers from a cloth-draped basket. "Now these new gunboats, I hear, are to be considerable smaller, lighter but heavy armored and, *listen to this,* they'll draw only three and a half feet, which is more like it for the kind of fighting they'll be called on to do."

The thermometer, Matt sensed, certainly had risen and now hovered close around the freezing mark. There must have been a real thaw up in the Northwest for great chunks of ice had begun drifting down upon St.

Louis, ice created far up the Missouri, because, as Kniesche put it, it was dirty ice showing dark streaks of mud and gravel in it. "The Mississippi, risin' as she does in free territory, is clear—the Missouri's dirty, like the slave trade."

"You ought to find some friends in Shed Number Six," Kniesche predicted. "Most of the fellers Big Pig Callahan brought out are working on the *Benton*—she used to be Eads' own snag boat and was called *Submarine* 7 before they named her for the Senator."

They picked their way across a deep litter of timber ends, chips and the dung dropped by teams that hauled heavy lumber down to the yards from the end of the Iron Mountain Railroad tracks.

"Can you do real honest-to-God cabinetwork?"

"Tolerable well. At least they used to say so back home," Matt replied. Home. How incredible, how amazing that less than a month actually had elapsed since he had deserted Dexter to go to murder his father. He swallowed hard. Criminently! It was just a month ago today that he'd escorted Phoebe to the Woodruffs' corn husking bee and, having chanced on a red ear, had been privileged to buss her right in front of everybody. Godfreys, how they'd blushed and enjoyed it. Dear Phoebe, dear Phoebe of the sunset-colored hair and the steady, dark blue eyes.

"In that case I'll set you to work on the officers' wardroom aboard the *Benton*. She's the oddest craft you'll witness come a month of Sundays. Mr. Eads said she'd do fine for a gunboat and Commander Rodgers wanted to refit her but Isherwood, his Chief Engineer, turned her down."

Once they had gulped sour-tasting tin-cupfuls of stale but smoking hot coffee, he led the way up a catwalk treacherous with mud and melting ice. Under Shed Number Six lay the strangest-appearing craft Matt could ever have imagined. The former snag boat *Submarine* 7 was a big boat, a thousand tons in burden, and had been very powerfully built to uproot snags and deadheads from the river bottom. Even a landsman such as Matt Everett could appreciate her formidability.

"You can see," the boss pointed out, "she has twin hulls which Mr. Eads has bridged over. By grabs, she'll swallow the worst them Rebs can throw at her. Know what? The armorers is layin' on three-and-a-half inch armor and she'll mount sixteen cannons; three more than the *Carondelet* and the rest. Hi, Phil."

A big, red-haired man whose beard flared like an exploding shell peered down from a scaffold above that great rust-colored hulk reposing on the stocks. Sunlight streaming through a series of windows at the shed's top revealed a swarm of armorers, ironworkers and steamfitters hard at work on this ungainly vessel.

Derricks creaked and whined and the donkey engines which powered them chuffed self-importantly in fashioning this ungainly monster. How many men in the months to come would the *Benton's* broadsides slay, cripple or terrify into surrender? Fascinated, Matt gazed upon the new ironclad. What a vast and deadly engine of destruction this was, obedient to the will of her masters be they Northern or Southern. She could cause hundreds of thousands of dollars in damage, dress hundreds of women in black, sear and maim unguessable numbers of mankind.

"By God, Kniesche, I'll bet you fifty dollars I'm right!" the red-bearded man called out. Despite the dank and penetrating chill he was wiping a beading of sweat from his forehead. "Them engines they've got in her now will never push all this goddamn' iron they're layin' onto her at nine miles an hour, let alone upstream. Mark my words, no matter what Jim Eads claims, she'll prove clumsy as a mired hog."

"Can't nawthin hurt her in her guts though," pointed out a sallow-faced armorer at work on her well-armored and circular pilothouse mounted forward of the smokestacks—a new concept. "Rebels ain't got airy a gun can punch through them three and a half inches. If I was to fight, which I don't aim to do, I'd like to be inside this here *Benton.* None o' yer godamn' timberclads or boiler iron vessels for Joe Browne. Hey, you Jim! Get down there and tell them dunderheads to re-rig tackles on that for'ard plate."

Matt kept quiet, so utterly amazed was he by this extraordinary vista. This powerful, half-born ironclad's twin hulls appeared to be spaced some twenty feet apart but strongly joined above water. Aft, a long and powerful stern paddlewheel raised its buckets almost to the shed's roof supports. Upon them a multitude of sparrows twittered and fluttered. Now and then a slate-gray pigeon plummeted earthwards to retrieve crumbs from some workman's lunch.

Heart in mouth, Matt followed his boss up a narrow plank walk which shivered and swayed beneath their weight fit to give a man the fantods.

"Now this here will be the wardroom. Yonder's some yellow pine. You're to build double bunks with it to either side. Can you read drawings?"

"I guess so." Matt had to shout, so loud was the reverberation and deafening clangor of the mauls driving rabbets into the casemate. He tramped over to a pile of resinous, pitch-leaking boards. Godfreys! They were so roughly finished he'd have to spend long hours in planing to get them sufficiently smooth to pass inspection.

Here and there he recognized various men who had come west with him and noticed that most of them seemed to be working as if they'd their hearts in their work. Poor fools. How curious to hear how the Eastern shipbuilders referred to this or that part of the vessel by contrast with the unnautical phraseology employed by steamboat carpenters from western rivers or the Great Lakes. There could be no doubt whatever that any real shipbuilder from Maine, New Hampshire or Massachusetts had forgotten more about the fine art of constructing a vessel than any of these raw-boned Western Yahoos would ever learn.

It became a revelation for the New Englander to learn how intimate with war St. Louis had become. People in omnibuses, saloons and other public places still discussed the sanguinary Union defeat at Wilson's Creek last August the tenth, and the Rebel defeat at Springfield, Missouri, later on. Mingled among troops wearing every shade of blue were many women in black moving along Gratiot, Chouteau and Seventh Streets, many more than one would have encountered in Bangor, Portland or even in Boston.

Because a good third of St. Louis' population entertained violent Southern sympathies—the socially elect, well-to-do and powerful merchants in particular—the city seethed under the chilling administration of military law.

To Matt's complete amazement not a few of those actually engaged in the construction of the *Benton* talked, at least, like red-hot Rebels and gloried in how bitterly they hated—and feared—St. Louis' very sizable German population which they referred to contemptuously as "Black Republican Dutchmen." Several times following the outbreak of hostilities, and Nathaniel Lyon's capture of Camp Jackson where had collected a majority of local Secessionist fire-eaters, terrifying rumors circulated that these German-Americans were about to massacre anyone accused of the least Seccessionist sympathy. He had learned, too, much concerning Major-General Frémont's energetic but arrogant and often ill-advised administration of the then Department of the West.

Now it had been renamed the Missouri District. Not yet could the Union element in St. Louis perceive that flamboyant figure's many solid accomplishments in the face of enormous difficulties and a complete lack of support from Washington. They recalled only Frémont's spectacular manner, his luxurious tastes and usual inaccessibility, as well as his unauthorized expenditure on shady contracts.

Apparently this intrepid cartographer of the unexplored Far West and undoubted winner of California for the United States had offended local patriots by surrounding himself at his headquarters in the luxurious Brant house on Chouteau Street with such dashing foreigners as Captain Charles D'Armand, a Frenchman, the Hungarian Major Zagonyi and some Italian captains, Cottaves and Saccippi among them. How people had used to hoot the General's dazzling uniformed bodyguard. It had numbered thrice that protecting President Lincoln!

When, next day, Matt set to work on the officers' quarters aboard the *Benton*, he recaptured a degree of well-being such as had not been his since that dreadful interview in Edwin Stetson's office. All that week as he sawed, planed and joined he kept his ears open. Fortunes indeed were being made right and left, so great was the haste of Federal authorities to get a flotilla in being. At General Halleck's command they paid little heed to the prices, or to the terms of vast contracts being authorized and approved by their supply officers.

By Godfreys! he intended to share in this scramble for riches and in no small way, either. Every time he remembered Sachem Hill's lofty chimneys, handsome entrance and the rich panelling and spacious apartments within, he felt affronted. All this now undoubtedly belonged to the Widow Cosby, Augustus, Decius, and that young virago called Flavia.

To his great surprise he had to admit he wanted to see more of his handsome and whimsical half-brother; doubtless this was due to his lifelong yearning for kinfolk. The name Adams recurred in that connection. When, if ever, would he come up with the "Reverend" D. Adams—Josiah Cosby's partner in that monstrous deception and betrayal? The impostor might well be dead, but he intended to go on inquiring.

While nailing in place a length of moulding he found himself wondering about Phoebe Whidden. How terribly stricken the girl had appeared, so round-eyed and tight-lipped in her mother's kitchen. Of course Phoebe was much too level-headed to attempt anything so hare-brained as trying to find him. Still, it was mighty pleasing to realize that this lovely and steady girl had cared for him enough even to consider so mad a project.

Around four of the afternoon when light in the long, dank boat shed commenced to fail, coal-oil flares were ignited and work on this great, ungainly gunboat was resumed by a new shift of craftsmen.

While the New Englander was putting away his tools, Kniesche, the boss carpenter, appeared to inspect Matt's efforts and, to that thoroughly chilled individual's relief, pronounced his work better than satisfactory. "They must turn out real cabinetmakers where you hail from," said he, biting off a chew of tobacco. "That's as purty a piece of joinin' work as I've seen about this boatyard. Say, Everett, there's to be a big parade tomorrow. Some of our best regiments—the First Missouri Artillery, Birge's Sharpshooters, Colonel Woods' Thirteenth Infantry—hope that number don't prove unlucky—are boarding the transports and will shove off downriver. Heard tell this here Gen'ral Grant is fixing to take some forts the Rebs have thrown up along the Tennessee and Cumberland Rivers. Come along," he invited, "you'll enjoy watching them damned Dutchmen drill. Old Franz Sigel's Third Volunteers is something to see.

Colonel Hassendubel's been drillin' their tails off near two months so now they've got a snap to 'em like none of our Butternuts show."

Glowing under the old boss carpenter's approval Matt heaved his tool chest onto his shoulder and lugged it up a treacherous catwalk for stowage in the Eads & Nelson's Submarine Boat Company's storeroom.

He was pulling on his coat when Eads' chief mechanic came tramping over with long, unshaven jaws working steadily at a huge quid.

"Say, Everett, ain't you friends with a feller calls himself Philo Daingerfield? Come out here in the same gang?"

Matt caught his breath. "Why, yes. What of it?"

"Well, it's two days now that little bastard ain't showed up. You see him, you remind him he's still under contract. Iffen he don't turn up tomorrey, by God, I'll turn his name over to the Provost's men. Maybe yer friend would like to find himself playing tag with them rats they raise in Gratiot Street prison?" He frowned, wagged a blunt forefinger. "Me an' Mr. Eads, we don't tolerate no such trifling, being's we got to get this here *Benton* in the water 'fore the end o' next week."

"If I see him I'll tell him," Matt promised. He felt downright annoyed. No matter what bright plans loomed in the offing it wasn't right to undertake an agreement and not live up to it, at least for a while.

Gloomily he joined a trickle of laborers ascending a muddy road leading towards the end of the Iron Mountain's spur and waited among mounds of building materials, engine parts and rusting sheets of armor plate until the "General Winfield Scott," an ancient wood-burning locomotive, spouting veritable volcanoes of sparks from a bell-shaped stack, appeared pushing a pair of dilapidated passenger cars before it. On the front platform stood the diminutive figure of Philo Daingerfield smoking a larger seegar. The Kentuckian, no longer clad in sorry finery but resplendent in a fur-trimmed cloth overcoat, a round beaverskin hat, waved a cheerful greeting, then ducked back into the car which lacked glass in most of its windows.

"Well, Matt," he chuckled, when his companion dropped onto a wooden bench beside him, "reckon you can put a big red ring around this date. While you been hammering and sawing I been gettin' around St. Louie. Yes, sir. I've looked up our friend Simon Quirk." He directed an anxious glance at his big companion. "You've kept your money safe?"

"Sure. Belted on—the most of it."

"That's fine, finer than duck feathers, 'cause tonight," excitement lit his pinched and pointed features, "we're to be let in on a little deal which *ought* to turn us a pretty penny—yessir, a mighty pretty penny."

"What sort of a deal? Nothing crooked?"

"Crooked? Oh, no!" Philo looked positively pained. "Just a matter of selling the Government some sets of mule harness I've bought cheap that will clear us 'round a hundred and fifty percent. From the profits I'll buy some hospital cots I've located and make us another killing. Why, a week from today we should have cleared five thousand apiece."

"Five thousand?" Godfreys! That was near twice as much as 'most anybody around Dexter or Newport Junction could earn in a year. Good God, what couldn't be accomplished with a start of five thousand dollars? Silently he resolved to play this lucrative game for all it was worth, for as long as it lasted. Hadn't Josiah Cosby won himself a tidy fortune despite starting from scratch? Whether he liked it or not, he was still Cosby's own son. He paid close attention to Philo's discourse, conducted of course in such a low voice that no one could overhear.

"Very soon I reckon we'll have enough capital to charter a steamboat called the *Western Arrow* I've got my eye on. She's small, about one hundred and ninety tons, but fast as a scared cat and draws only eighteen inches. First, till we get to know the River real well, we'll haul troops and supplies down to Cairo. There's good money in that, by the way. Later—" he laid a forefinger beside his nose—"mebbe we'll slip on down the River a piece where *certain* kinds of supplies—" he emphasized the word ever so slightly—"will bring real fancy prices, say New Madrid or Columbia, for instance."

"But—but they're in Rebel territory!"

Philo considered his companion in mock surprise. "Now whoever said they weren't?" he demanded softly. "Good thing you got off early."

"Why?"

"Got a kind of a celebration party planned for tonight." He cocked his head to one side and winked. "There's a right pretty little girl living at the Myrtle and, well, she's noticed you about and aims to meet you. Don't frown like that, this Léonie's a pippin, full of ginger and pretty as a speckled pup." He sighed gustily and fell to smoothing the fur of his beaverskin hat. "You big, well set-up young fellers win all the breaks. Damned if you don't."

VI LÉONIE DULAC

The Myrtle Hotel's small but ornate private dining room glowed with light cast by candles supported by four German silver candelabras. In the well-heated atmosphere circulated the odors of rich sauces mingled with the smell of bourbon whiskey and the bluish fragrance of real Habana seegars. A few paper flowers of garish hue drooped upon the disordered table above a scattering of dirty dishes and half-emptied wine glasses of varying design.

Due to the heat Simon Quirk belched and, in order to close blunt fingers heavily tufted in black hair about a champagne glass, slightly unbalanced a plump blonde perched upon his lap. She giggled shrilly. Long since the contractor had undone a thick black silk cravat permitting his collar points to thrust like misplaced horns from either side of his bull neck.

Raising his glass a trifle unsteadily, he nodded to his guests. "Well, boys, here's wishing the *Western Arrow* a quick, safe and goddamn' prosperous trip south—*and* back."

"And sky-high prices at New Madrid," amended Philo Daingerfield in drunken gravity. Because the Kentuckian's bold-eyed and frizzle-haired companion loomed almost twice his size she was not occupying Philo's lap much of the time but sat beside him with a plump arm twined about his scrawny neck. "What say, Matt?"

He might not have spoken for all the attention Matt paid him, so absorbed was the New Englander in gazing into the slightly slanting gray-green eyes of the slim young woman known about the Myrtle Hotel as Léonie Dulac.

"Hi, Matt, wake up," complained Philo. "Friend Simon's offerin' us a toast. He's drinkin' to a venture that should set us on the road towards gilded halls and silken couches." He winked at his well-upholstered companion and patted her bosom. "Gilded halls. That's pretty good, ain't it?"

"Now, Philo, you're shorely gettin' drunk," giggled the big brunette and noisily kissed the top of Philo's semi-bald head.

Matt remained completely oblivious. He was far too occupied in attempting to steady the uneasy rocking of the room and to focus his gaze upon those fascinating, long-lashed eyes peering so trustingly up into his own. Godfreys! How those candle flames dipped and swayed. Yessiree. For all that this champagne wine tasted innocent, it packed a blow like a logger's ax, especially when poured onto several jiggers of prime Kentucky bourbon. He was only aware of the nearness of Léonie. Her bright, neatly delineated lips curved ever so gracefully, invitingly, and her bosom glistened as white as snow on those little stump lot fields back of Dexter.

"My, Leenie, you're wonderfully pretty!" he mumbled, annoyed that his tongue should have grown so clumsy and his lips so slack. "No, you're more than pretty. You're lovely as an angel come straight down from Heaven."

She bent close and a tiny gold locket suspended from a black velvet band about her throat gleamed briefly as she peered eagerly into his face. "Oh, Monsieur Matt! Must you mock a poor, plain girl like me?"

"I mean it. I'll lick anybody says you're not pretty as an angel," mumbled Matt staring about in muddled belligerence.

Fortunately Quirk and Philo were too intimately absorbed with their companions to notice. Quickly Mademoiselle Léonie poured champagne and treated him to a deliberate, almost langorous smile. "Then I thank you, Monsieur Matt, from the bottom of my heart. To be so admired by such a—a strong and handsome gentleman is too much an honor. Come, let us drink to the mending of poor little Léonie's fortunes."

Owlishly Matt regarded her piquant, pink-white features and the carefully arranged ringlets of a lustrous, raven's-wing black. "What's gone wrong with your fortunes?" he demanded over the strident laughter of Philo's buxom companion.

"One would not wish to sadden so happy, so beautiful a dinner."

"Tell me, please, because I—I like you a lot, Leenie," which was as close as he could come to pronouncing her name. "Trust me; I can understand. I've had a hard time lately, too."

The weary-looking blonde called Vera smiled loosely over a shoulder bared by Simon Quirk's insistence. "Go ahead, Leenie dearie, tell him the sad, sad story of your life. The ten-dollar one."

Léonie spat something in French, then her shapely hand, adorned by several rings of doubtful quality, crept out to caress Matt's.

"So you've been in hard luck?" he insisted heavily.

"Ah, yes, yes." Fringe-like lashes fluttered downwards. "It was only last year."

Philo sat back, draped an arm about his massive companion's now completely revealed bosom and winked at the host in his usual bird-like fashion.

"Sure, speak up, sis," drawled Mr. Quirk. "Le's hear the story of your downfall."

"I am not downfallen!" blazed Léonie, gray-green eyes suddenly narrowed and glittering with rage. "I am good girl!"

Quirk bellowed with laughter. "Good? Who said you ain't? Hell, you're wonderful! All the boys say so."

"I resent that!" Matt tried to gain his feet, but instantly Léonie's hand closed over his wrist.

"No! Let there be no fighting. I hate it," she pleaded and hurriedly touched her glass to his. "He is a coarse one, your friend Monsieur Simon, so it is no wonder his jokes are the same."

Because he had become occupied in the audible enjoyment of a lingering kiss, Quirk missed hearing the observation. Léonie, a lovely, black-haired girl whose great, wide eyes seemed to be forever viewing the world in trustful innocence, leaned over the table so far that most of a pair of pale, gently swelling bosoms became exposed by a daringly décolleté gown of yellow-and-black brocade.

"Oh, Matt," she murmured brushing his ear with full, shiny and dark red lips, "one so easily can tell you have the heart of a good and generous gentleman. One sees also that you too have suffer'! I will tell you that, until last year, my papa was important sugarcane planter in Avoyelles Parish. He owned Beau Sejour, a plantation near Hambourg on the River. But then Papa's enemies, of which he owned many because he was so proud, so honorable, plotted his ruin." Léonie's luscious mouth quivered as she delved hastily into the front of her canary-yellow-and-black gown and produced a frothy bit of handkerchief with which she dabbed carefully at first one eye and then the other.

Philo stroked his now neatly trimmed goatee and settled back, obviously prepared to enjoy Léonie's discourse to the fullest.

"Oh, it was the mos' unfair, mos' cruel, how those villains combined to bankrupt my poor papa." Tears brimmed in the girl's eyes. "Then *poof!* everything was gone—our lands, our slaves, our house. A proud Dulac could never support a shame so great, so he—he—"

"He what?" Matt queried quietly.

"He shoot himself!" Léonie's small white hand aimed its forefinger at lustrous blue-black ringlets trembling above her temple. She commenced delicately to sniff. "As if this were not enough sorrow, when Maman, my two little brother' and I seek refuge in New Orléans, the *coup-de-bar*, called by the American 'yellow fever,' spread all through that city. It was bad that summer. They all die and now lie buried in Cemetery of St. Honoré."

Matt placed an arm about the girl's narrow and sloping white shoulders, gently kissed her forehead. "You poor little soul. What dreadful experiences you must have had!"

As Léonie's arms slipped upwards to join hands behind his neck, he became aware of a scent, delicate, yet undoubtedly titillating to the senses. How very white her skin appeared by contrast to her raven tresses!

"It was mos' terrible. For me there was nothing. Papa's enemies remained without mercy and I could not stay in New Orléans so I sell the last of poor Maman's jewels and come upriver two months ago, just before the Confederate and Union armies stop traffic upon the Mississippi."

"Oh, for God's sake, Leenie. Get your story straight," grunted Quirk. "River's been closed for six months."

Léonie glared at the interrupter but continued in piteous, tragic tones, "And so—I come to St. Louis. In vain have I seek employment as a governess, as an instructress in French but now that this war, this so-terrible war is fought none have money for such purposes. And so–" Léonie's slim and pearly white shoulders rose in a forlorn shrug–"and so Monsieur Matt, if in two days I do not find a position–" her intriguingly dimpled chin trembled pitifully "–I shall do as my poor dear papa."

"Good God!" cried Matt, completely aghast. "Why, that's too awful to even think about!"

"For we Dulacs, death is nothing to be feared," she declared in a low voice. "Yes, I think I will throw myself into the River. I have heard drowning is not an unpleasant sensation, besides, water so cold should kill me quickly."

Léonie now commenced to weep softly, like the wind in a spruce grove.

"Look here, you simply mustn't do such a dreadful thing," Matt protested, and fumbled in his pocket. "How much money would you need to keep on hunting a job for another week?"

"Oh, no, Monsieur Matt!" She rolled genuinely wet eyes up at him. "You are so kind, so noble, but, *hélas*, I cannot allow you."

"Why not?"

"A Dulac cannot accept money from strangers."

Lord, but she looked lovely in her distress, and that perfume she wore was so delicious–almost intoxicating. "Léonie, you must listen to me. Maybe you haven't known me extra-long, but I'm not a stranger, and I intend to get to know you better, a great deal better. How much does your room here in the hotel cost you?"

"Seven dollars a week," Léonie informed shyly. "But indeed, Monsieur Matt, really, I cannot permit–"

From the slender remains of his roll of banknotes, Matt stripped a ten-dollar bill. "Here. Oblige me and accept this. You can pay me back if you want when you land a position."

At the picture of Léonie's ever repaying any amount of money Philo and Quirk exchanged derisive glances and grinned like horse collars.

"Oh, Monsieur Matt, you are too generous."

"No! No! I mean it!"

Léonie flung herself onto his lap, twined arms about his neck and fervently pressed her soft and brilliant mouth to his. "Oh, Monsieur Matt! In very truth you have save' my life!"

VII TRAIN NUMBER FIFTY-SEVEN

THE STATION MASTER at Odin Junction, where the Ohio & Mississippi Railroad crossed the Illinois Central, was a big, moon-faced German who wore a red-and-white "Dutch blanket" overcoat. He nodded heavily. "*Ja.* Dot train I remember. Here it vas Big Pig Callahan his party in two split; vun gompany for Cairo, vun to St. Louis."

"I—I presume you've no idea about which of his men went where?" pled Phoebe Whidden peering up from under a travelling bonnet of dark green grosgrain lined in black ruffles. "Please try to remember. It's—it's, oh, so important."

"*Fräulein!* Gladly I vould help, but how could I know their names? *Nein! Unmöglich.*"

"Oh, dear!" Phoebe wrung mittened hands in an access of helplessness. How exasperating successfully to have traced Callahan and Grogan's labor party thus far only to come up against this dreadful dilemma. She had no idea whether she should purchase a ticket for Cairo or for Illinoistown; she only retained sufficient money to reach one destination.

From behind gleaming, steel-rimmed spectacles the station master feasted his eyes upon this straight-backed and clear-eyed young woman. She was beautiful in a serene sort of way; her red-gold hair was so neat, tidy-looking and somehow she had remained clean despite the smoke and grime and scant toilet facilities. Twenty-four hours she must have spent travelling westwards from Cincinnati!

"*Bitte, Fräulein.* Me, I vould look first for this Herr Everett in St. Louis; *ja,* because much easier it is to buy passage on a steamboat bound from St. Louis to Cairo than in the other direction."

"And why, pray?" demanded Phoebe in desperate perplexity.

"Because alvays from St. Louis supplies, guns and troops keep moving towards Kentucky und Tennessee."

Biting her lip Phoebe gazed out over a level expanse of fields so limitless that they stretched all the way to the horizon. Not at all did they resemble the tiny, two-and-three-acre fields so laboriously hacked out from the forest around home. "Thank you, sir. I will go to St. Louis."

"You in a sleeping car should ride, *Fräulein,*" the station master advised. "From here on vest most passengers are rough and drunk and are soldiers everywhere. You, so pretty, are not to be pestered in a day-coach. *Ja.* There is vun ladies' sleeping car on Number Fifty-seven."

When he mentioned the price Phoebe realized, with a sinking heart, that she now retained exactly eight dollars and seventy-five cents. God send she could quickly come up with Callahan and Grogan's men in St. Louis! This kindly, gold-bearded German must have sensed the acuteness of her distress for after he had written out a ticket entitling her to a built-in bunk, a mattress, two blankets and a coverless pillow, he scribbled further.

"*Fräulein*," said he, "here iss name of *mein* sister, Mrs. Gussie Schmieler. Her *mann*, a *Dumkopf*, off to var has gone leaving her with seven *kinder*, but she a big heart has. Ask her advice. Maybe she with her vill let you stay until you your *mann* Everett find." The station master's pale blue eyes widened. "He iss vun lucky *Kerl* so pretty a young lady to run after him."

Phoebe long since had discovered that Matt, for some unfathomable reason, no longer was using the name of Hovey. "Oh, thank you! You have been so very kind. I'll never know how to reward you save in my prayers." She read the written name and address until she had memorized them; slips of paper had such an annoying way of getting lost.

"*Nun*," the station master grunted through the wicket, "if you vant to vash come around through that door. In *mein* private office is kettle on the stove. Maybe on the vashstand a basin, soap and a not-so dirty towel are."

What a strange and unfamiliar world! Ohio, Indiana and now Illinois appeared incredibly flat and treeless to one reared among the rugged hills and mountains of New England. Here you never saw a hill, let alone a mountain. The Ohio and Missouri's Train Number Fifty-seven clicked evenly along over an endless succession of yellow-brown grain fields—a warm spell had melted away all snow except in drifts or where there were hollows.

To Phoebe the sheer immensity of these vistas was terrifying; often the train would rattle on for minutes on end without sighting a single human habitation. Several times, though, the engineer had to slow and shriek his whistle to discourage cattle from browsing upon sere hay-grass sprouting between the crossties.

"Gol-dern critters!" growled the conductor. "They'll be the death of us yet; always on the right-of-way, especially wintertime. Ought to be a law to make these damned stupid Polacks and Dutchmen fence them in."

This sleeping car, Phoebe noticed, differed decidedly from those she had seen in the East. Bunks were built solidly along both sides of the car except at its ends where benches accommodated passengers in daytime. Each bunk, she perceived, was equipped with a grimy canvas curtain, a pillow, two shoddy blankets and a single sheet which appeared to be far from pristine.

Many of her fellow passengers in the ladies' car were clad in black. A brakeman explained to the girl in the gray travelling cape that these ladies were journeying west to bring back the remains of their menfolk who had fallen in battle or, more frequently, had perished of disease. By contrast there sat in this car two gay and radiantly happy young women on their way to marry the men of their choice on duty in St. Louis. Also included among the voyagers in the ladies' sleeping car was a trio of handsomely garbed, but haughty and aloof refugees from the border State of Maryland. Resentful and tight-lipped, these three ladies kept to themselves breathing hatred and contempt upon anyone who evinced even the slightest of sympathy for the Union cause.

The person who interested Phoebe most was a flighty but kindly appearing old lady wearing a sacque of plum-colored silk shot with green. Under a bonnet of purple velvet, trimmed in bengaline and blonde lace, two red roses were revealed next to the wearer's plump features. Her hair had been dressed into innumerable tight little ringlets and her lips were surprisingly pink for a woman of her years. When she turned to smile across the aisle at Phoebe, the latter noted that around her neck was secured a black velvet ribbon garnished by a handsome cameo.

"Ah, my dear, I perceive that you travel alone," she volunteered in a pleasing voice. "That's bad; it's even dangerous for a pretty young female in these distressing times. Permit me to present myself. I am Mrs. Wilber, a widow, alas, these past ten years."

"Oh, I'm not afraid," Phoebe assured her, smiling steadily. "I'm stronger than most girls and used to putting up a pretty good fight at school."

"You–*fight?* Dear me!" The lady in the plum-colored sacque raised neatly mitted hands in horror and so attracted the attention of three lively and extraordinarily pretty young females who appeared to be travelling under her aegis. Phoebe judged them to range in age from eighteen to about twenty.

These, Mrs. Wilber presently explained, were young ladies from distinguished families in the East on their way to attend a seminary she maintained for genteel young women in St. Louis. There they would receive instruction in advanced French, polite conversation and social deportment.

"Is dancing taught?" Phoebe inquired eagerly, aware of the other's covert but intense inspection of her person and clothes.

Mrs. Wilber again raised pudgy little hands in horror. "The schottische, polka and the quadrille to be sure, but certainly not that vulgar dance called the waltz, of which dear Queen Victoria so highly disapproves."

Phoebe, of course, had been aware for some time now that her garments, purchased in Portland under Aunt Margaret's dour supervision, were hopelessly uninspired, if not downright dowdy, but so far she had never been particularly concerned over that discovery. By the light of rattling, acrid car lamps, she surveyed the truly elegant attire of Mrs. Wilber's charges. Why, their flounced and tiered gowns looked quite as lovely as those depicted in *Godey's Ladies' Book*.

Phoebe presently became conscious that the young ladies on the seats opposite were whispering about her and giggling among themselves. Mercy! What lovely little boots one of them wore. They were brave with mother-of-pearl buttons and tassels of silver thread. Another wore Congress gaiters of gray kid showing insets of black elastic on either side.

"What might you be called, my dear?" Mrs. Wilber queried, gray curls trembling to the train's violent jolting. "Miss Whidden? Ah, there's a fine old New England name—and will you be stopping with friends in St. Louis?"

Phoebe's wide, dark red brows climbed a trifle. "No. I haven't any friends there. I—I'll admit I'm just a little frightened." A vast understatement. "I—I'm travelling out to," she raised her chin and levelled her voice, "marry a gentleman from home."

"Mercy! How very romantic!" Mrs. Wilber fluttered and tilted her cheek to one side against hands clasped in gentle enthusiasm. "I'm sure your intended must be handsome. He'd have to be to win the hand of so lovely a girl as you."

Phoebe blushed furiously and her honest laugh rang down the car, momentarily drowning out the monotonous clicking of wheels over rails. "Oh, Matt's not handsome, but he *is* nice-looking."

From a reticule of petit-point Mrs. Wilber produced a twist of paper and offered a peppermint ball. "And where is he?"

"Why, I—I really don't know."

"You don't *know?*" Mrs. Wilber's small eyes, black and shiny as those of a canary, narrowed, became thoughtful. "With what regiment does he serve? St. Louis is jammed-packed with all kinds of soldiers these days."

"He's not in the Army, as near as I know," Phoebe replied, dropping her gaze. "That's what worries me about finding him."

The artificial "French flowers" beneath Mrs. Wilber's bonnet fluttered to a sharp reaction of some sort. "You mean you actually don't have his add—" She broke off suddenly. "I notice that you carry no food parcel. Perhaps you would care to join my young ladies and me in a sandwich, and a morsel of fried chicken?"

Would she? For some time now Phoebe's healthy young body had been craving sustenance but, because her funds were so low, she had purchased only a soggy apple tart for supper. Never again would she buy anything with meat in it around a railroad, not after her agonized arrival in Portland.

"Oh, I really couldn't!"

"Nonsense, my dear," Mrs. Wilber sounded firm and determined to be friendly. "I want you to meet the girls—I mean my protégés. Pray come over here, young ladies, I wish to present you to Miss Whidden. This," she beamed upon a tall, slender, black-haired girl, pert and vivacious in dark red turban decorated with a long and drooping white ostrich feather, "is Miss Loretta Bentalou. Her papa is a very important—er—official of the Jersey Central Railway. And this is Miss Clairette Vansant. Her's is one of the oldest and most distinguished families in Maryland."

"How do?" drawled Miss Vansant, a petite blonde with bangs showing under a fashionable new "Jockey" hat.

"Cha'med I'm sure," declared Miss Lola May Askins. She was a big, curvaceous girl possessed of huge and melting black eyes that reminded Phoebe of nothing so much as Belle, Pa's prize Jersey cow.

"And now let us sup, young ladies," beamed Mrs. Wilber and spread a cloth over her lap. "Have a chicken leg, do, my dear."

Mrs. Wilber's charges fell-to with such gusto, giggling and grabbing of victuals that the refugee ladies sniffed disapprovingly and stared out of the car's dirty windows.

With considerable relish Phoebe was consuming a hard-boiled egg when, suddenly, the locomotive's whistle commenced to shriek hysterically, frantically for brakes. Brakemen rushed onto the platforms but hardly had they reached their posts when the cars of Number Fifty-seven commenced to buck and jolt like wasp-stung colts. There sounded such a grinding, snapping, crackling turmoil it seemed as though a crew of lumbermen were felling a hundred trees.

The last thing that Phoebe Whidden would remember for a very long time was the jangling noise of glass being splintered, fearful screams and a sensation of being hurled violently through space.

By a wavering yellow-red glare created by burning passenger coaches—glowing coals from the stoves had been spewed into jagged masses of splinters and other combustibles—Mrs. Wilber dashed disordered ringlets from her eyes. After glancing carefully about she then threw some stranger's mantle over Phoebe Whidden's limp form. The girl lay quite unconscious in a cornfield bordering the right-of-way. Blood had commenced to streak features still lovely in colorless repose.

Survivors crouched among withered stalks trying not to notice the soul-shaking shrieks and cries arising from the blazing wreck of Number Fifty-seven.

"Oh, God!" the girl known as Clairette Vansant was wailing, "I've one hell of a big rent in my brand-new Chicago gown and my hoops are bent. Christ alone knows what's happened to my hat."

Train Number Fifty-seven's fourteen cars had degenerated into a wildly heaped and shapeless line of wreckage. Its locomotive, the "General Ambrose," lay on its side in the ditch oozing steam and smoke among the carcasses of several heavy steers which, invisible around a bend, had caused the derailment. For some reason the "General Ambrose's" cow-catcher had failed miserably to function. Survivors of the herd stood about bawling out their terror or staring at flames which, with each moment, were spreading in frightful rapidity.

That car in which Phoebe and Mrs. Wilber's party had ridden could be seen reared up, like an amorous bull, over the end of the coach preceding it. For a miracle it had not yet caught fire.

"Damn' lucky thing," laughed Clairette, tying a handkerchief about a small gash in her arm, "our car was so near the train's end else we'd have got our hair curled for nothing."

Uninjured male passengers directed by soldiers on leave risked their lives to haul shrieking victims from the splintered and brightly burning cars. Surviving members of the train crew secured axes and crowbars from less damaged coaches and worked frantically to prise apart riven timbers while crackling flames were commencing to spiral a hundred feet into the air.

In a water-filled ditch beside the track, workers struggled to extinguish the flaming garments of shrieking, hysterical women whose voluminous hoopskirts afforded dreadfully ready fuel.

"Oh, God! Make them stop that. Stop!" wailed Loretta Bentalou. In a sitting position in the mud she commenced to rock to and fro. She was holding her hands, one of them bleeding from a cut across its back, over her ears.

"Shut up, you noisy little bitch!" rasped Mrs. Wilber. But the girl kept swaying back and forth, all the while uttering little whining noises. More and more smoking figures, some writhing, some significantly limp, were lugged up onto the cornfield and placed on rough mats fashioned of cornstalks ripped from convenient shooks.

Exasperated, Mrs. Wilber arose, strode over to Loretta, hoisted her own ripped skirt and fetched her pretty protégée a shrewd kick on the behind. "Shut up, you damn' silly slut! You ain't hurt. Get over there and help Clairette and Lola May care for them poor, scorched folk. I'll 'tend to this girl myself."

As if the horror was not yet sufficient, rifle ammunition packed in one of the freight cars coupled ahead of the passenger coaches commenced to explode, sending bullets keening viciously through smoke and firelight.

Although no dwelling was visible within miles of the wreck, a farm cart presently appeared and a pair of moon-faced Germans stolidly commenced to herd away the cattle. They paid little or no attention to the wrecked train, answered all queries in guttural and incomprehensible *Platt Deutsch*.

"You sure suffered a nasty knock, dearie," Amy Wilber informed her unconscious companion. This was no exaggeration. By parting lustrous hair glowing copper-red in the firelight, Mrs. Wilber noticed a long gash, which proved shallow, in the strange girl's scalp. It was bleeding freely, as was also a large lump on the side of her head.

"Good thing her looks ain't spoilt," muttered Mrs. Wilber. "Ain't felt such a skin in years. And them eyes of her'n. Any gent in St. Louie would go crazy. Damn! Must stop her bleeding to death." To create a compress and bandage Mrs. Wilber ripped some flounces from her skirt; might just as well, her dress was ripped and muddied beyond repair.

While searching for something to cover the red-haired girl, Mrs. Wilber noticed a flash of light and swiftly retrieved from the trampled earth a man's gold watch and a fat wallet lying near. She actually commenced to grin when she came across a well-filled carpetbag—whose it was she had no idea—and propped Phoebe's bloodied head upon it.

BOOK THREE

The Water War

I JIM EADS' IRONCLADS

By the end of January, 1862, that crusty yet energetic and clear-sighted commander, Flag Officer Andrew Hull Foote, had collected at the mouth of the Ohio River a flotilla of the ungainliest and weirdest-appearing men-of-war ever to fly the Stars and Stripes. Swinging to their anchors or tied up to the bank above Cairo, Illinois, lay three ten-gun "timberclads": *Conestoga, Tyler* and *Lexington*. They were so nicknamed because they carried no armor, only a protective sheathing of five-inch oak.

Like nearly all steamers navigating western rivers these former Ohio River boats carried two very tall smoke pipes, or "chimneys" as the local people called them, set approximately amidships. These served engines which had been lowered from the main deck into the hold for better protection against shot and shell.

Foote also commanded the huge thousand-ton *Essex*, which like *Benton* had been a snag boat. Although recently painted a dark gray she was already showing rust on her plates because there had been so much rain this winter. Not that the rivermen complained about these icy deluges; operations along the Upper Mississippi and its twenty or more navigable tributaries were strictly limited by the stage of the waters. Come a sudden fall and an inexperienced pilot might leave a powerful gunboat indefinitely imprisoned in some backwater or bend from which she might emerge only when the ever-capricious waters rose again. Hence rain was no enemy to rivermen.

As Paul Dent had ascertained shortly after reaching Cairo, low water was generally to be expected at two periods of the year: in the dead of winter when ice formed and choked that all-important flow from the tributaries, and again in midsummer when the blazing Middle Western sun dried up countless creeks and lesser streams. Small wonder that among those who wrung a hard living from the rivers, a licensed pilot stood in lordly isolation at the top of the social and economic ladder; a "close-fit" pilot might earn as much as four hundred dollars a month and found. On his infinitely detailed knowledge of currents and the exact locations of reefs, mud banks and a multitude of snags and wrecks, depended the very life of those imposing, but weakly constructed, steamboats which, until last summer, had plied that vast network of rivers opening up the West and Northwest Territories. Not yet had the remorseless tentacles of the railroads extended their trackage sufficiently to offer steamboat owners more than nuisance competition.

It was in Cairo's least noxious bars and hotels that numerous out-of-work pilots congregated to talk politics, fight, drink and curse the Federal Government for offering the humiliating pittance of two hundred and fifty a month to licensed senior pilots! Dent often proceeded to such a rendezvous to sit and listen, once his day's work as a draftsman was done.

Should he tonight patronize the Mudcat Bar or the Bald Eagle Tavern? Standing on the bottom of an inverted scow, Dent deliberated the question. Because of Cairo's miserable situation and vulnerability to sudden flooding many houses and cabins near the Ohio's edge had been constructed on old scows, barges or ancient keelboats. For that matter the United States Naval Station here was in reality a floating town in which Captain A. M. Pennock, U.S.N., toiled doggedly and successfully to arm and man Jim Eads' homely ironclads. Locally they had become known as Sam Pook's turtles—after the Eastern engineer who had designed them.

On this raw afternoon of January 29, 1862, no less than four of James B. Eads' gunboats lay at Cairo, alike as matches from the same box except for differently colored bands of paint decorating their smokestacks. All of them mounted thirteen rifled guns and had their low and too lightly armored pilothouses mounted just forward of the funnels—a Pook innovation since the typical river steamboat almost invariably carried her "texas" aft of her smokestacks. Each carried four small boats slung to davits located just forward of a great sternwheel which, theoretically at least, was protected from shot and shell by a housing of boiler iron.

Like Commander Henry J. Walke, U.S.N., of the *Carondelet,* Dent was observant and whenever opportunity offered was given to sketching whatever might challenge his interest. On impulse he pulled from his back pocket a sketchpad and commenced a swift rendering of the U.S. Army Gunboat *Carondelet*—chiefly because she lay nearest at hand and in a good light. She was charging ammunition and supplies and a swarm of black laborers were chanting as they lugged aboard powder chests and cases of shot.

Awaiting its turn alongside lay a coal flat, low in the water, under a mound of coal in bushel baskets—the standard of measure on western rivers. Apparently *St. Louis* and her sister ships *Mound City* and *Pittsburgh* as well as *Cincinnati,* Andy Foote's present flag steamer, had completed charging. These, the most powerful units in local waters, Dent deduced, must constitute the Federal main line of battle. Certainly a major campaign must be projected in the near future, otherwise why had taciturn Brigadier-General U.S. Grant and his staff come over the

Ohio from Paducah to spend long hours in conference with Flag Officer Foote aboard *Cincinnati?*

How ludicrous that an Army general should be able to issue positive orders to naval officers commanding these gunboats, even if Army-owned.

Seated upon a worn-out punt, Dent guided his pencil's point so deftly that soon *Carondelet* assumed form and detail. With her design and interior plan Dent was entirely familiar through shamelessly having curried favor with her assistant pilot, Mr. Daniel Weaver, a whimsical, slow-spoken Tennessean who, for some reason, appreciated the Yale man's rapt interest in the esoteric art of piloting. In fact that jolly individual had gone out of his way to encourage and befriend this dark and lonely man with the haunted eyes.

A small sigh escaped the sketcher. What foul luck that his contract with Callahan and Grogan must run another week to completion! Until then, he could not, in all honesty, volunteer for service in the Navy. Even out here he was resolved not to attempt enlistment in any of those regiments which nowadays came swarming down from Wisconsin, Illinois and Ohio to swell the Blue Armies of the West.

A stiff gust of wind off the river suddenly snatched away his round felt hat so he put away his sketchbook. Later he intended to draw two spans of magnificent oxen laboriously hauling a mud sled bearing a heavy sixty-four rifle gun towards the river's edge. Apparently this piece of ordnance was intended to arm *Benton*, an incredibly ugly ship-of-war recently arrived from St. Louis.

When he stepped into raw yellow mud in order to retrieve his hat he discovered that this mire had been churned so long by incessent traffic that he was forced to struggle hard each time he freed a foot.

A sudden sound of band music, briskly played, attracted his attention to a familiar scene. From a crude, temporary railway station built on high ground was descending yet another column of infantry in dark blue overcoats. Sight of the National Colors indicated the presence of a whole regiment, but if one counted the generous number of such standards already fluttering down on the levee few regiments could have numbered more than two or three hundred effectives.

Waiting to receive these newly arrived units lay the faded-looking *Kate Cassel*, one of innumerable river boats purchased by the Army for transport duty.

Because there remained little else to do until it came time to consume a wretched supper at some tavern, Paul Dent slogged down to watch the troops file aboard. They wore rakish képis and white cross-belts over warm overcoats equipped with red-lined capes. These tall Middle Westerners of the 12th Illinois Volunteers splashed along in a column of twos carrying single-shot, long-barrelled Springfield rifles. They were further equipped with a slender French-type bayonet slung over the left hip, a round blue canteen over the right and a patent-leather cartridge box between them.

As they squelched down towards the *Kate Cassel* they began to sing and shout as if embarking on a summer excursion. A majority of them were big young fellows walking in that shambling, loose-kneed fashion which suggested that they had recently been recruited off some farm.

A tightening sensation manifested itself in Dent's stomach and his eyes filled. Except for a handful, most of these youths could not yet have seen their twentieth birthday. How pitifully inadequate they appeared under those tall packs, full-skirted overcoats and long-barrelled rifles. His regiment must have looked and behaved almost exactly like this during that blistering march down into Virginia last year. As usual a pack of mascot dogs cavorted about the muddied legs of their masters.

When he noticed a lanky youth of seventeen trudging by singing "Buffalo Gals" at the top of his lungs and lugging an umbrella under one arm, Dent had to turn aside a quivering face. How little did that lad and his companion realize what lay ahead: the deadly whine of minié balls, the eerie screech of passing shells, the awful, stunning crash of their explosion and the resultant screams and cries of agony. They, too, were to hear the bewildered and hysterical shouting of inexperienced officers and the futile cursing of noncoms who only wore their stripes because of popularity. Across this coffee-colored river, in Kentucky and further down in Tennessee, they'd learn what a bursting shell could accomplish, in an instant, in the way of blinding, maiming, killing or, even worse, of dooming some previously healthy young fellow to the life of a querulous invalid.

"Hip, hip, hooray! Nashville City we're on our way!" chanted the 12th Illinois Volunteers though they appeared disappointed that none of Cairo's townsfolk had turned out to speed them on their way except a black-clad pastor who, with his wife and half-grown daughters, stood on a pile of lumber to wave little Union flags. The clergyman kept calling out endlessly, "God bless you, boys! Be strong and keep pure in your fight for the Right."

Two by two, the muddied infantrymen squelched down the slope towards the *Kate Cassel's* landing stage. Many, obviously from inland, stared in wide-eyed curiosity upon the transport as she lay with huge side wheel turning very slowly and her funnels raising twin columns of sooty smoke.

A little distance out on the Ohio another transport, the *Altona*, kept backing her paddlewheels while waiting her turn at the wharf. Another regiment, the 15th Wisconsin, singing beautifully in German, appeared on the bluff and commenced to file past the bloated carcass of a mule which had become mired and died in the bottomless mud of a lane. This unit, swinging smartly along under fixed bayonets, started down towards the river after their fat little colonel who, for all the world, resembled nothing so much as a mallard drake improbably garbed in blue with brass buttons; the scarlet lining of his overcoat's cape kept flaring in a wind off the river.

"Keep step, poys, und hold your heads up," he called over a rattle of drums and and the shrilling of fifes. "Py Gott, I vant this burg should the Fifteenth Visconsin remember."

Suddenly a shaft of light from the setting sun broke through and drew a ripple of red sparks from the bayonet points.

A pair of naval officers on their way to mess commented, "Poor bastards! Imagine trying to keep step in this muck. Wait till they set foot in Kentucky and see what quagmires pass for roads over yonder."

The rasping bark of a sergeant drilling some men on a comparatively dry piece of ground attracted Dent's attention. He wandered over to gaze with sympathetic and pitying eyes on a rank of the rawest-appearing recruits he had ever beheld. They were shaggy, dirty and undoubtedly the culls of some regiment raised in the farm country.

"Right, *turn!*" roared the red-faced sergeant. Half of the awkward squad promptly turned left. "God Almighty! That ain't right! That's left—like I told you fifty times! What have I done that I should be condemned to drill a bunch of dim-witted club-footed twerps like you? Johnson," he said, "raise your right arm." A gangling, buck-toothed youth hesitated, then raised his left arm.

"Jesus Christ!" Wildly the sergeant looked about, then his gaze fell upon a mound of supplies protected by a tarpaulin.

"Stand where you are or I'll skin you alive!" he snarled and went striding over to a pile of baled straw. From it he ripped a double handful of straw, then swung over to a pile of hay. He passed along the line of recruits. "You dumb farmers may not know right from left, but I reckon you can tell hay from straw. Here! Put that straw in your right boot—yes, that one! Put some hay in your left boot."

While Dent looked on convulsed in silent laughter, the recruits did as they were bidden.

"Now!" said the sergeant, "when I say 'Forward march!' you start off with your hay foot. Understand?"

Delighted smiles shone along the rank.

"Now then—hay foot—straw foot—hay foot—straw foot!"

A passing soldier added, "And belly full of rot gut!"

"Sing it, you bastards! Sing it!"

Grinning delightedly, the recruits moved off singing, "Hay foot—straw foot—belly full of rot-gut."

The drill sergeant shrugged, removed his képi and sighed his relief.

After attending evensong in a ramshackle chapel where he prayed long and earnestly for strength and the courage to redeem himself, Paul Dent picked his way across a succession of mud-covered duckboards over to the Quartermaster's wharf. Having no desire to return to the construction gang's barracks' stuffy air and foul, generally witless, conversation, he picked a course between lofty piles of supplies awaiting transportation to wherever General Halleck decreed they should go.

On obtaining a clear view of the river Dent's attention was attracted to a small, black-painted sternwheeler apparently inbound from the Mississippi. She had commenced to whistle for roustabouts who presently came slouching out from various saloons and eating houses.

Seated comfortably enough upon a pile of tents, Dent pulled out his sketchpad again and, despite gathering darkness, quickly recorded an impression of this swift-appearing sternwheeler now threshing importantly towards the shore. Bluish wood smoke streamed from jagged sheet-iron crowns capping her smoke pipes and curled about the spreader bars joining them.

Presently the draftsman was able to distinguish that this freighter carried a deckload of forage wagons and that a number of mules were waving long ears on her foredeck. Of course the inevitable blue-clad figures lounged about the hurricane or topmost deck or had perched upon the freight. Rapidly Dent's pencil filled in the name *Western Arrow* painted in gold letters around her texas. Expertly her pilot guided his craft around a big floe of ice building up about a drifting tree.

To continual strident screams from her whistle and a mad clanging of bells the steamboat was urged gently up to the wharf, then lines were sent snaking ashore to be made fast by roustabouts. Presently the new arrival's tackles screeched and a broad, sturdily-constructed landing stage was lowered onto the wharf's splintered surface.

Apparently the *Western Arrow's* captain was in no great hurry to depart from Cairo for at once his engineer blew off steam in great thuttering blasts, then smoke eddied in diminished quantities from the chimneys. In leisurely fashion a crew of ragged Negroes coaxed or hauled ashore the mules, then manhandled seven or eight forage wagons across the landing stage. Finally, a half company of grinning and gawping infantry straggled ashore lugging their packs and muskets any whichway.

Darkness had set in by the time the last bales and cases consigned for

Cairo had been toted into a Government warehouse by roustabouts who sang: "I kin sing Dora, I kin sing hit fine, I kin sing Dora, Well as Coonjintin' Jine," "Run here, dog, and git yo' bone," or "Show me which shoulder to lay it on."

Somewhat stiffly because of a cold wind which had begun to blow, Paul Dent put away his sketch, descended from his perch and wandered over to inspect the *Western Arrow* now taking on cordwood from a flatboat that was poled alongside. Just as he reached the freighter's side a tall figure elegant in a bottle-green greatcoat and a glossy, stovepipe hat descended a staircase and started across the emptied foredeck and into the glare created by pine knots flaring in a pair of iron torch baskets.

Dent started, called out, "Is that really you, Matt Everett?"

"Sure is." Grinning, the big figure hurried forward with hand outstretched. "Thought it was you, Paul. Saw you from the wheelhouse. What wonderful luck! Wait here, will you, while I leave this bill of lading at the Quartermaster's office. Won't be gone a minute."

He returned promptly, plainly eager to renew their acquaintance, and invited his friend aboard the *Western Arrow*.

In patent pride he showed Dent about; to the engine room where the machinery glistened and boilers hissed softly.

"This is Tim O'Hara," said he, "the hottest damn' engineer on the River. He can get up steam in two shakes of a lamb's tail. Tell Mr. Dent about our engines, Tim."

That burly, gap-toothed individual complied without hesitation and at length.

"Now these here are the pilot's signal bells—this here's the reversing gear, there's the steam drum and that's the cam-gear rod. This here's the poppet valve and that's the relief, or safety valve."

He moved about the hot, lantern-lit engine room his dirty red flannel shirt aglow.

"Now these here are two mighty fine engines, built last year up to Cincinnati. Their boilers will carry pressures up to a hundred and fifty pounds to the square inch and are non-condensers. In each o' my four boilers are four two-inch flues. With this here lever I can send escape steam up the chimneys to blow out soot and to increase the draft."

He patted one of the boilers. "Stout cast-iron, mister, so we don't fear blowing out a boiler head. Yonder cylinders are thirty-inch diameter and have a ten-inch stroke. It can drive." He showed a gold tooth in a wide grin. "Yessir, if Cap'n Everett here says the word I can drive this boat upstream at better'n eight mile an hour on an average stage of water, or twelve downriver." He winked. "Which, in our business comes in mighty useful sometimes."

At length Matt, heavier of build and older-looking than the man Dent had encountered on the train, broke in. "Guess you've confused Mr. Dent enough, Tim. Sure you've got plenty of wood? We'll likely have to do some fast running tonight."

For answer the engineer pointed to cord upon cord of wood stacked around the engines.

"Come along, Paul, let's slip up to my cabin and I'll treat you to a shot of prime old red-eye."

"Quite a cabin you have here," Dent presently observed while savoring a glass of red-brown bourbon that tasted as good as it looked. The Connecticuter settled himself upon a deep armchair upholstered in brown corduroy and quite openly inspected Matt's quarters.

The first thing he noted was a terra-cotta figurine of a voluptuously modelled nymph wearing a fetching smile and nothing else. To the walls were hung prints of such famous steamboats as the *Eclipse*, the *New Uncle Sam* and the ill-fated *Pennsylvania* aboard which two hundred persons had lost their lives when she blew up in 1859. Obviously several staterooms must have been consolidated to form this single spacious cabin furnished in the usual lavish style of a Western steamboat. Kerosene lamps in bright brass gimbals boasted hand-painted shades of frosted glass and a light green carpet was both deep and lustrous. No bunk at all but a big, highly ornate brass bed, occupied one end of Matt's quarters. A washstand, two deep armchairs, a wide sofa and several hassocks completed the furniture, but that which especially attracted Dent's attention was the pair of frilly and gaily decorated ladies' garters which had been slung over one of the bedposts.

"The *Western Arrow's* no beauty," Everett was saying, "but she's sound and new and, best of all, she draws only sixteen inches and can go like a scared cat when it's necessary. And, as Tim said, just now speed is sometimes damn' necessary for us."

His friend, Dent was deciding, certainly had filled out and his yellow-blond side whiskers had become considerably more than the promise they had been on the train. Undoubtedly he had prospered if that heavy chain of what appeared to be real gold, traversing an elegant waistcoat of red-and-yellow brocade, was any indication. On a hand which no longer looked chapped or rough sparkled a diamond as large as the pearl securing his cravat.

For his part Matt quietly surveyed the slightly built deserter, from mud-caked, knee-high boots to heavy black duroy trousers, navy blue flannel shirt and a heavy serge jacket. Dent's long and sensitive features appeared weather-beaten and somewhat thinner than of yore, which emphasized the fine modelling of his rather wide jaw, straight, thin nose and broad forehead. His blue eyes, however, had lost a certain furtive aspect which had been quite noticeable some weeks earlier.

"Well, you certainly seem to have done mighty well for yourself, Matt," Dent observed accepting a seegar from a handsome calfskin case trimmed in gold. "You couldn't have stuck very long under Callahan's contract."

"No, I didn't and that's a fact." Matt sent a cloud of seegar smoke whirling over to soar up from the lamp chimney. "I bought up my contract within a short time. You should have done the same."

"I didn't have that kind of money," the Yale man explained simply, but did not add that he would not have bought out even had he possessed the necessary funds. After all, Jim Eads' gunboats had needed to be armed and outfitted. Suppose everyone had bought up his contract? Then *Carondelet* and her sister ships would not now be ready to support the impending Federal campaign into western Kentucky nor could they meet, if necessary, the threat presented by the existence of the powerful Confederate flotilla reported to be concentrating in the vicinity of Memphis. No one knew much about this flotilla except that daily it was being augmented under the command of some of the ablest officers ever to graduate from Annapolis.

A small sigh escaped the host as he raised his glass to squint at the rich, mahogany-hued bourbon it contained. "Paul, since we parted I've often thought about you—and me—and I'm sorry to see you in no better case than you seem to be. So long as you haven't re-enlisted, I'd like to see you do better for yourself. Would you like to come along with me in the *Western Arrow?*"

He leaned forward, both elbows on knees, hands cupped about his glass. "You'd be wise to, because there are fortunes, great fortunes, to be made by the use of ordinary shrewdness and foresight. Look at me. Since I last saw you towards the end of November I've rid myself of a pack of damn' fool idealistic notions. Then I'd just over three hundred dollars capital. Today I'm half owner of this steamer and am about to buy one of my own—the *North Star*." When feet tramped along the main deck's passageway he lowered his voice. "I've ten thousand salted away in the bank and I own a warehouse and wharf in St. Louis. If all goes as well with this trip as I expect, I'll clear forty thousand dollars. Think of that!"

"But you *have* completed your trip," Dent commented through a haze of tobacco smoke. "Or haven't you?"

"Not by a jugful," returned the New Englander. "Didn't you notice all that freight still on my main deck? Why did you suppose we didn't shove off as soon as I'd unloaded?"

"I was wondering about that."

"Well, it's because now that I'm rid of those heroes in blue and their wagons and jackasses, around midnight I'm heading back out into the Mississippi," he paused, "then my pilot will head south—not north."

Dent put down his glass. "But, Matt, how can you steer south? The Rebels have forts at Columbus, Belmont and not to mention a great fort on Island Number Ten."

Matt took a sip of his whiskey and settled back intently eyeing his friend. "I have here on board a very useful gentleman," he confided, "an associate who knows just when and where to show blue and red lights arranged in a certain order. They will prevent either a Federal or a Rebel battery from opening fire upon the *Western Arrow*. Sometime tomorrow I will put into Columbus for a third time."

"My God!" Dent gasped and his long features suddenly contracted themselves. "Do you really intend to trade with the enemy?"

"Most assuredly I'll trade with certain Southern merchants. You've no notion the prices they'll pay for such items as medicines, percussion caps, boots and shoes. Anyone in this er—business, who doesn't make a three hundred percent profit is a great ninny. Paul," said he earnestly, "I'm offering you a job aboard this boat and a chance to coin money hand over fist."

"Thanks, but I'd rather not."

Matt flushed and his mouth hardened. "Don't be so damned quick about turning me down. Won't you face facts? Way you're headed you'll have never a dollar to show when this lovely war's ended. More likely you'll wind up with a bullet through your guts."

Quietly Paul Dent got to his feet, stood looking down at the powerful figure across the stateroom. "You never in the world could understand my reasoning. I thank you for your well-intentioned offer, but as it is, Matthew Everett, I can only pity you—and bid you good night."

II UP THE TENNESSEE

JUST BEFORE DAWN on February 2, 1862, Daniel Weaver, Second Pilot on the U.S. Army Gunboat *Carondelet*, thrust a hand into Paul Dent's bunk and prodded the Connecticuter into a groggy state of consciousness.

"Rouse up," he instructed quietly, "and come with me." At once Dent pulled on mud-caked boots which, despite the thick wool socks he had worn to bed, felt stiff and clammy. Puzzled, he followed Weaver's short, plump figure over to the dining shack in which a quartet of black cooks sleepily were preparing the workers' usual breakfast of eggs, fried potatoes, bacon, ham and coffee strong enough to drive a rivet.

"What's up?" yawned the draftsman.

Gleams of excitement shone in Weaver's jet eyes and the Indian-like pilot's thin mouth was a tight line. "You've allus claimed you hankered to try your hand at piloting?"

"That's entirely correct. Do you really mean it?" Dent burst out. "Do you?"

"Well, Ed Barnsby—me and Billy Hinton's relief pilot—claims he's got real bad bellyache cramps that won't let up." Weaver sniffed. "I reckon them cramps is the kind some folks get when there's fighting ahead. I can't bear a coward. Can you?"

Paul Dent winced. "I've no respect for such. Did you say there's to be some fighting soon?"

"Yep. Old man Foote's hull damned flotilla's due to shove off this mornin' account of that there Gen'ral Grant who came visitin' here last week is fixin' to tackle a big fort the Rebs have built somewheres up the Tennessee River."

Fighting! Small, icy shivers commenced to course down Paul Dent's spine and his throat contracted convulsively once or twice—just as it had that awful summer's day at Bull Run.

Weaver stroked short, stiff-standing, blue-black hair. "Billy Hinton and me have ranged all Cairo and there's not a cub pilot available what with the Army chartering so many transports and manning their gunboats. Iffen you really aim to come along I'll get you signed on as my cub. Bein' as you're eddicated I reckon you could learn quick enough to spell me and Hinton on easy reaches or when we have only to follow the *Cincinnati's* course; she's to be flag steamer, heard tell."

"But—but what about my Callahan and Grogan contract? It's got a week to run." Despite everything he now found himself fervently hoping that by this excuse he might avoid acceptance of the Second Pilot's invitation.

"Oh, don't you worry none 'bout *that,*" the other returned while accepting a tin cup of steaming coffee from a grinning Negro. "Billy Hinton already dropped a word to Grogan and he says he won't object to yer quittin' early, says your work at Naval Station's about finished anyways."

A stifled sigh escaped the Connecticuter. "Oh, did he?"

Daniel Weaver's little black eyes narrowed suddenly. "Well, what about it? Thought you was mustard-keen to handle a gunboat's wheel and to get in some licks 'gainst the Rebs."

"Oh, I am, I am, make no mistake about that!" The words came out with a rush lest his mounting fears choke them off. "When do I report and where?"

"Now you're talking more like it," Daniel Weaver offered him a small brown hand. "Just throw your gear into a bag and show up on Number Two landing inside a half hour." He grinned. "Me and Billy have talked things over and I don't figure you'll get rattled or scared in a pinch. Billy ain't so sure, but he's willin' to try you." His Adam's apple worked twice, thrice ere he finished his coffee, then he wiped his mouth on the cuff of a bright green flannel shirt. "Now don't you dast be late. Cap'n Walke's a stickler for discipline, for all he's a funny feller and likes to draw pitchers, same's you."

Amid blinding rain more violent than any that Dent had hitherto witnessed even in soggy, mildewed Cairo, Flag Officer Foote's flotilla got under way and left behind the Naval Station's receiving ship *Maria Denning*, the muddied walks, ramshackle barracks, warehouses and floating armories. His command consisted of four Eads-built gunboats, the largest of which, and the slowest, was *Essex* under command of Lieutenant William D. Porter, U.S.N.; *Carondelet*, commanded by Commander Henry Walke, U.S.N.; *St. Louis*, Lieutenant Leonard Paulding, U.S.N.; and *Cincinnati*, the flag steamer, her commander Lieutenant R. N. Stembel, U.S.N.

In company with these ugly, turtle-like craft steamed those ungainly but very useful timberclads, *Tyler*, *Lexington* and *Conestoga*. All the gunboats raised clouds of sooty black smoke which instantly were snatched away by a bitter wind lashing the Ohio's turgid waters into a frothing turmoil.

From his post in *Carondelet's* all-too-thinly-plated wheelhouse Paul Dent could see flags flown by the other vessels standing from their staffs stiff as though cut out of cardboard. He saw a puff of steam escape from *Cincinnati's* whistle whereupon Chief Pilot Hinton pulled a cord swinging to the right of his head. Bells jangled deep in *Carondelet's* bowels as her Chief Engineer, William H. Faulkner, eased open his throttles and set the ironclad's ponderous stern wheel to threshing more rapidly.

For the first time both Chief Pilot Hinton and his assistant, Daniel Weaver, had donned uniforms which were similar to those of an Army officer, but their gold-rimmed black velvet straps were blank, devoid of insignia of rank. Indeed, a contract pilot occupied a painfully anomalous position. Although legally civilian these individuals nonetheless were subject to Army discipline. However, they exercised no authority beyond that necessary safely to pilot the Union's gunboats through treacherous channels, chutes and bends.

Commander Henry Walke stood slightly forward of the wheel with hands tucked for warmth under the coattails of his long-skirted naval tunic and peered intermittently through a slit let into the pilothouse's forward side.

Under bushy, wide eyebrows Henry Walke had shrewd, penetrating gray eyes. He was tall, thin and clean-shaven save for the sparse chin whiskers typical of a New England farmer and his hair receded almost half the length of his cranium. As became an officer of the Regular Navy he held himself ramrod-straight except when he took to sketching—a pastime he indulged whenever opportunity offered.

"Why *would* they assign me the slowest of these damned floating barns of Eads'?" Dent heard Walke growl. "Confounded scow can't turn up better than seven knots, no matter how the draughts are forced."

Along the willow-crowned bluffs above Cairo had collected a dark throng of laborers, mechanics and townsfolk come to bid farewell to these grim ironclads on which they had labored so long. From the direction of Camp Defiance, situated upon a peninsula dominating the confluence of the Ohio and the Mississippi Rivers, sounded the faint thud of salutes being fired.

Time and again lashing rain and whirling mists blotted out all sight of *Carondelet's* consorts even as that vessel's fabric commenced to vibrate under increased impulses from her engines. From the exhaust pipes sounded an unending series of staccato, cracking reports characteristic of almost every steamboat navigating western waters.

In time with the splashings of the great sternwheel Chief Pilot William Hinton's gray-whiskered jaws commenced to work upon a chew of tobacco while expertly he whirled the six-foot wheel guiding this ungainly ironclad into the Ohio's main channel.

From below sounded a rumbling of gun carriage wheels handled in practice by crews of hard-bitten seamen out of the Regular Navy.

Carondelet's First, Second, Third and Fourth Masters, all civilians, were busy superintending the shifting of gear and ammunition to satisfy Chief Engineer Faulkner, that worthy having insisted that *Carondelet* must float on an absolutely even keel; he'd be damned if he'd tolerate a list which might leave certain boiler tubes so short of water that they could burn out or blow up when too much steam was developed in them.

Relentlessly, rain came beating in through eye-slits let into the wheelhouse's walls; these sloped inwards at a forty-degree angle, the better to deflect shot and musket balls. Soon a regular gale sprang up and set *Carondelet's* four small boats to rocking slowly from their davits. Big chunks of ice and even an occasional floe came drifting downstream, but these were not heavy enough to constitute a hazard.

"Must be one hell of a big rise some'eres," commented Weaver when a huge tree went drifting by and caused the *Essex's* pilot to swerve sharply.

By afternoon the Union flotilla, on its course towards the entrance to the Tennessee River, had become strung out in a straggling column nearly a mile in length. Around three the rain let up sufficiently to permit all manner of floating debris and snags to become clearly visible. Only then did the Indian-like Assistant Pilot beckon Dent. "Now, Paul, just you keep our jackstaff in line with the *St. Louis*' wheelhouse like I said t'other day. That jackstaff ain't been put there just to fly pennons and flags; she's more of a front sight, like on a rifle."

Pushing a cap with a battered patent-leather peak back on his head, Dent stepped up onto a grating traversed by a series of cleats designed to assure a pilot secure footing when there was need to cramp over the wheel in a hurry. He nodded, gripped the wheel handles and experienced a lifting sensation at this assumption of control over the ironclad. For a little while he experimented until he could gauge the exact pressure necessary to turn *Carondelet* and gradually got the "feel" of the vessel's four rudders—sternwheelers necessarily were so equipped. Commander Walke long ago had disappeared below to watch his gun crews at loading and firing practice.

By now even the newest member of the civilian engine room crew had learned that *Carondelet's* First Division armament consisted of two old forty-two pound rifled guns which could throw shells of eighty-four pounds weight, and an ancient sixty-four pounder, all three mounted to fire ahead. Her Second Division, or broadside batteries, were composed of four guns each: two rifled forty-two pounders, two sixty-four pounders and four light thirty-two pounders. The ironclad's Third Division or stern battery, consisted merely of two light thirty-two pound smoothbores. Of the thirteen guns aboard, at least six could hurl shot and shell better than two miles—and with extraordinary precision when handled by such veterans as were now sweating and cursing below.

No matter how diligently the stokers fed her fireboxes *Carondelet*—she always had been slightly slower than the other Eads-built ships—could not do better than five knots upstream.

Dent strained his eyes upstream. It seemed as if every passing minute brought more and more debris down the storm-lashed Ohio. He was more than ready to surrender the wheel towards dusk.

"Yep. There's a flood stage up the Tennessee or I'm a Dutchman," Weaver grunted. Flotsam of all description came so thick and fast that now it could not be completely avoided. Because *Carondelet's* free-board was less than three feet, branches and small snags presently commenced to ride up over her prow and lodge themselves on the gunboat's foredeck. Finally night closed in and proved so dark that Flag Officer Foote signalled his flotilla to pull under the lee of the Ohio's northern bank and there anchor for the night.

In the gray of the next day's dawn, bugles blew and bells clanged briskly aboard the Union flotilla, augmented now by a scattering of coal boats and several river steamers converted into Army transports. As daylight broadened, *Carondelet's* crew made out the half-submerged and muddied wreckage of a steamboat lying not two hundred yards distant. She evidently had broken her back on a sandbar. One of the *Henry J. Cass'* smokestacks had fallen and lay like a rusty log across her hurricane deck, but the other still rose forlornly above the surface.

"We'll be seein' plenty of wrecks, but not all of 'em show much above the surface; that's one thing you'll have to watch out sharp for," Weaver predicted as he appeared in the pilothouse showing a splash of egg on his bushy black beard. "Ain't all of 'em shows even something above water, specially when the river's in high stage as it's gettin' to be now. All you can see is an eddy or boil with streamers behind it—like that one yonder." The pilot pulled a plug of tobacco from his back pocket, cut off a chew with his clasp knife and with meticulous attention studied the turbulent entrance to the Tennessee.

"Nope. Ain't much changed from last year," he grunted. "Now, Paul, I'll sing out the marks to steer by and you memorize them. Take the wheel and make for the inside of that next bend—closer in than Sam MacBride is takin' the *St. Louis*. Always remember this. A pilot travelling downstream holds to the *outside* o' the bend where he can profit best from the depth and current; but steaming upstream cramp over to the *inner* shore and you'll find slack water as a rule. And remember this, too, goin' upstream you can 'weave,' as we call it, back and forth across the channel in a counter-direction—this will save wear and fuel and so make you popular with the owners."

In growing confidence Paul Dent steered with his jackstaff lined up on "the mark," an outcrop of rock.

"Lucky the river's deep here so we don't need to get out the lead lines or sounding poles. There!" he exclaimed. "Feel that?"

"Yes. The boat seemed to slow up for a minute."

"She did. We passed over a shallow place and it 'dragged' at our bottom—no, we didn't touch, so relax." Weaver spat through an eye-slit. "Better ring the engine room for a better head of steam. We're droppin' back from the *Cincinnati*."

That the rest of the flotilla, too, was firing up to fight the furious current was attested by dense clouds of black coal smoke beginning to rise vertically through the drizzle. Presently Commander Walke appeared in company with Chief Pilot Hinton.

Walke's craggy brows merged into a single line. "Devilish lot of debris out there—more than I've ever noticed." Recognizable were sections of fence, privies, water-logged small boats and, most threatening of all, whole trees which, having stood on a bank undermined by the current, had tumbled into the river.

"Cuss it!" growled Weaver when the Chief Pilot took over, "yonder's the makin's of a heap o' sawyers and deadheads."

At Dent's puzzled expression he explained in an undertone, "A deadhead is nawthin' but a log lodged just fur enough below the surface so's you can't spy it in a bad light. A big enough deadhead will stove in a steamboat's bottom or smash her paddle buckets quicker'n a deck hand will grab a whiskey bottle. But it's a sawyer that will do the worst damage."

"Sawyer?"

"Yep. See yonder oak tree floatin' by? Notice how its top points downstream? That's because there's still a lot of clay and stones still clinging to its roots. Comes the moment when the current don't move that tree fast enough its roots will sink to the bottom, generally after most of the branches have been broken off. Damned thing a'ways settles so's its roots dig into the river bottom and its top points downstream."

Keeping an eye on the naval officer, Weaver silently, accurately spat out of an eye-slit, then returned to his discourse. "Well, that old log's all right so long as the river's low and you can sight him, but when the water's high and fast like now, there's no tellin' where such a damn' thing lies. Worst of it is that-there hidden log keeps a-sawin' back and forth, mebbe twenty degrees. If a pilot's luck is out, that-there sawyer will punch right through his boat's bottom and plenty of times ram clean through to the engine room and cause the boilers to blow up."

"But how can you tell if there's a sawyer ahead?"

"You can't always tell, but mebbe if it's not too rough there'll be a little boil show on the surface." He broke off, his attention attracted to *Cincinnati*. A blue-and-white checkered flag was rising to her signal mast situated directly forward of her stern wheel's housing. "Looks like old Andy Foote aims to get this column to close up."

A dense flock of mallards came winging downstream. "Keerist! Wisht I had me a shotgun. Them birds is damn' sight better'n eating that sowbelly and beans we got for break—"

"Look!" Dent cried suddenly. "Over on the east bank!"

"What do you see?" Commander Walke called sharply and snatched up binoculars he carried slung about his long neck.

"Sir, there's a party of horsemen looking at us."

Immediately *Carondelet's* commander trained his field glasses. "You're right. That's cavalry and Rebel cavalry, too. Look at 'em go! Guess they're headed for their nearest semaphore station."

Quite clearly Dent could discern the brown-clad riders, six or eight of them, as they spurred hell-for-leather along a track which, for a distance, paralleled the Tennessee. Undoubtedly Brigadier-General Lloyd Tilghman, commanding at Fort Henry, would soon be apprised that a powerful Union flotilla was steaming to attack him.

Walke strode over to where Dent sat, with a sketchpad balanced on knee, sharpening a pencil. He viewed the slender, dark-haired young man with interest. "What's your name, mister?"

"Dent, sir. Paul Dent."

"You are a licensed pilot? We're only supposed to have two aboard."

"No, sir. I'm only an apprentice of Mr. Weaver's."

"Well, Mr. Dent, I'll say you've uncommon good eyesight. Nobody else noticed those Rebel scouts." He nodded at the sketchpad. "I see you're partial to sketching also."

"Yes, sir. Thought those other gunboats trailing their smoke downstream were worth an impression."

Henry Walke's long and craggy yet subtly humorous features relaxed their customary critical aspect. "Good enough. Come to the wardroom sometime and show me your work." He started to turn away, then checked himself and addressed Weaver. "Good idea that, of bringing aboard an apprentice—teach him your trade as fast as you can." His smile faded. "Every time I look at that silly, quarter-inch armor they've put on this pilothouse I get the notion that things are going to get damnably messy in here if ever Rebel batteries find our range."

III FIRST PROBINGS

ON THE FOURTH of February, 1862, Flag Officer Foote's flotilla dropped anchors some six miles below the Confederate stronghold known as Fort Henry. On the fifth, *Essex*, while on reconnaissance duty, ventured too near the enemy's earthworks and so was struck by a solid shot which crashed through her pantry, shattered the port officers' quarters and finally came to lodge in the former snag boat's steerage. Incredibly, not a single person was hurt so the ungainly craft churned back to her anchorage proud of having fired the first shots at the enemy and of having sustained the first damage—which caused the flotilla's carpenters to work all night long on repairs.

Next day, while the gunboats, under the pressure of flood waters, sawed and tugged savagely at their anchors and while their crews frequently cleared away debris that kept on riding up on the gunboats' low bows, Flag Officer Foote ordered out his barge and had himself rowed from one vessel to the next. Paul Dent would always remember the thrill he experienced when that stumpy individual with the grizzled hair and beard and piercing blue eyes came stalking over *Carondelet's* stern deck to be received by Commander Walke, erect and very spruce in a double-breasted coat bearing two rows of gold buttons, gold sleeve braid and gold-trimmed shoulder straps.

Gravely, the frosty old man handled his sword and saluted the big Stars and Stripes snapping smartly in an icy wind, then stepped through a stern gunport into the semi-darkness of the casemate where, in geometric patterns, naval officers and seamen waited at rigid attention beside their guns.

Carondelet's civilian complement of stokers, oilers, engineers and pilots, meanwhile stood in a silent cluster to one side. Paul Dent more than ever felt miserable in his shapeless civilian clothes.

In a silence disturbed only by the lazy hiss of steam from *Carondelet's* escape valves and the dull *bump-bumping* of flotsam along her hull, Andrew Hull Foote's heels clicked briskly across the gun deck. The Navy gun crews, mostly mature men wearing full beards, stood rigid in neat, dark blue uniforms. Light was admitted only through half a dozen gunports, the lid covers of which had been hoisted to afford ventilation for, whenever all were closed, it became insufferably hot within the casemate despite the presence of a quartet of iron ventilators badly mounted just forward of the ironclad's paddlewheel box.

Not a speck of mud, not a chip, not even a thread marred the gun deck's spotlessness. Even the long, brown-black tubes of *Carondelet's* guns shone dully. Every article of brass glistened, every tackle rope had been neatly coiled, every ammunition locker was full and opened for inspection.

Twice Foote paused to address some petty officer remembered from earlier service. After he and Commander Walke had inspected the gun crews the Flag Officer halted just forward of Number Two gun and whipped off his flat-topped, straight-visored officer's cap. He tucked it under his left arm.

"Men," said he, "I am about to invite you to join in a brief supplication to our Creator." He joined his hands and, as the whole company followed his example, Foote cried, in earnest and reverent tones, that struck deep into Paul Dent's soul, "Holy Father and Supreme Arbiter of our destinies, encourage us all that we may face the dangers which lie before us. Sustain us, we pray You, in the coming battle, make strong our hearts and so favor our cause that we may, without faltering, fight our best for this, our beloved Country and for that Union which was born of the suffering and courage of our forefathers. Amen."

During the afternoon even greater masses of tangled debris came whirling down the dark and foggy Tennessee presently to foul the Western Flotilla's anchor chains and cast upon their bows dripping masses of muddied snags and driftwood. Soon the gunboat's bows became so weighted that water commenced to boil over their foredecks, whereupon their crews used axes to slash free these encumbrances. Despite use of both of her anchors *Carondelet* at length was forced to use her sternwheel at half speed to avoid being pushed downstream.

Everyone aboard became mystified by a series of muffled reports, rather like that of a big gun being fired at varying distances upstream. What could the Rebels be up to?

Eyes wearied through an over-conscientious scrutiny of Sam Cummings' *The Western Navigator* and a recent edition of *The New River Guide* by one George Conclin of Cincinnati, Paul Dent volunteered to join the work party. Theirs proved to be the laborious task of hacking, levering and sawing.

"My God! What's that?" A startled voice demanded from a small boat occupied on towing away a deadhead.

Dent glanced down in time to watch a white, cylindrical object perhaps five feet long go whirling by parallel to the ironclad's beam. A naval officer standing amidships on the starboard guard rapped out a horrified oath. "My God! That's a torpedo! If that thing hit us right it would have blown our whole damn' bottom out!"

When he got a good look at this deadly engine a sickening sensation constricted Dent's throat. The torpedo had been equipped with a hinged iron arm ending in two sharp prongs. These points were designed to lodge themselves in a boat's wooden bottom and so activate the arm which, in turn, detonated a simple firing mechanism. Good God! He had escaped death by a distance of three short feet.

"So *that's* what caused them explosions we been hearin'!" grunted a gunner. "Thought it didn't sound quite like cannon fire."

Through the fog Walke at once hailed his nearest consort to apprise her of this hidden menace.

Before another fifteen minutes had passed another torpedo or floating mine apparently uprooted by a small dead pinetree, appeared heading straight for *Carondelet*. The mine might well have sunk her had not the gunboat's yawl towed it aside just in time.

Although no other gunboat was visible amid this silvery mist Dent guessed that by now they, too, had sent out boat crews. Desperately he attempted to concentrate on the work in hand yet could not conquer a soul-withering fear that, at any instant, there might sound a deafening, deadly explosion; trickles of sweat began coursing down his back, soaking his shirt and drawers.

"Damn' good thing this river's at flood. These here snags must have torn a heap of them Reb torpedoes from their moorings," commented First Master Richard Wade. "But sure as shootin' we'll run onto some of them when we close in on the fort."

All night long the Connecticuter lay rigid, praying for courage, strained and sweating in a hammock slung just outside the wardroom. Every time some floating object went bumping, scraping along the gunboat's length hairs on the back of his neck lifted.

Through sheer exhaustion Dent eventually sank into a profound slumber from which he was aroused by an insistent, querulous shrilling of the boatswain's pipe. Only a suggestion of gray light shone through the gunports but by it one could note that the fog had lifted, that the rain had ceased. February the sixth promised to prove a fine and cheerful winter's day.

Shortly after sunup a gig came pulling over from *Cincinnati* bearing a jaunty young naval lieutenant who promptly sought the Captain's cabin. A seaman on guard outside of the door could hear Walke's incisive voice snapping, "It goes without saying, mister, that I will do as the Flag Officer directs, but I must observe that this is the God-damndest manner of fighting gunboats I've ever heard of."

Later it turned out that the cause of Henry Walke's bitter complaint was certain of Officer Foote's instructions. Because the river immediately below Fort Henry narrowed so greatly there would be small room for maneuver; therefore *Carondelet* and *St. Louis* were to be lashed side-by-side.

"Which means," explained Second Master John Dorety, "we'll have to tackle the fort with only our bow guns."

"Still, Johnny, that ain't so bad an idea," Chief Gunner Richard Adams observed. "Our armor's thickest forward. I'd hate like hell to risk my life behind that quarter-inch boiler iron we carry aft of the engine room. Cussed if *I* see why Eads didn't call for real armor on the pilothouse. That place is bound to become a slaughter pen; every Rebel battery will try to hit it."

At twenty minutes past ten *Cincinnati* hoisted a signal to get under way and so sent the Western Flotilla threshing laboriously upstream with its crews praying that no torpedoes would be encountered. It cast anchor again at Panther Island lying approximately two miles below Fort Henry, in a position sheltered from the raging currents.

At eleven thirty-five of the morning the four ironclads steamed into a line abreast, with *Essex* on the extreme right, *Cincinnati* next to her, then *Carondelet* and *St. Louis* lashed firmly together. At a safe distance behind the Eads ironclads cruised those extremely vulnerable but very useful and swift timberclads, *Tyler, Lexington* and *Conestoga.*

In the pilothouse Paul Dent watched Weaver who "knew" this river in addition to the Ohio—Chief Pilot Hinton was more familiar with the Cumberland and Ohio—attempt to concert his vessel's steering with that of *St. Louis.* Considerable shouting back and forth became necessary.

Soon the Tennessee narrowed, hemmed in between high banks upon which dark hardwood forests advanced right to the water's edge; in fact several undermined trees hung canted crazily out over the furious, clay-colored waters.

Chiefly because Commander Walke, taut and observant, was present very little talk took place in the wheelhouse. In the casemate below, gun crews of the First or Forward Division stood at battle stations but offered obscene comment when civilian deck hands appeared and began scattering sand upon the wheel-scarred decking lest feet slip on bloodied places. From *Carondelet's* engine room sounded a continuous rasp and ring of coal shovels hard at work and the clang of fire doors being opened and shut. Soon various escape valves crackled louder than ever and great billows of sooty smoke commenced to gush from the flotilla's smokestacks.

It was almost high noon when Weaver guiding *Carondelet* around a bend suddenly called out in a voice that was not as calm as usual, "Well, sir, there she be; over yonder on the west bank."

"Yes. I see it. Thank God the forts are not on such high ground as I'd feared. Um. We'll suffer from little or no plunging fire."

Gradually the yellow-red glacis of Fort Henry became more visible beneath a ship-rigged flagstaff from which flapped the Confederate ensign. At this distance it appeared all but undistinguishable from the Stars and Stripes—a circumstance which would ere long prove costly to both sides until the Stars and Bars with its readily distinguishable red field was evolved. (Curiously, this banner under which the Confederacy fought for almost three years never was officially adopted by the Government at Richmond.)

As Commander Walke levelled his field glass a small muscle in his cheek commenced to work from time to time. Hinton, too, was anxious,

Dent observed in some relief, while the four gray-black gunboats churned steadily upstream all the while spouting flame and sparks from their smokestacks. Gradually embrasures in the red, raw earth of the various salients composing Fort Henry's earthworks could be seen in greater detail.

"The enemy are standing to their guns, sir," First Master Wade called up a short, steep companionway leading down into the casemate.

When the range had decreased to approximately a mile Dent distinctly heard the voices of the gun captains of the three bow guns—located immediately beneath his feet—order a correction in elevation. Still not a single shot was fired from the Confederate defenses; Fort Henry might have been deserted for all visible activity.

At length Commander Walke strode over to the companionway and called down into the casemate. "You will not open fire under any conditions until the flagship fires—then fire at will and aim—" He got no further for from *Cincinnati's* bow gushed a dazzling blast of flame and a cloud of gray-white smoke. Then the whole river resounded to a crashing, thunderous report. Instantly Paul Dent's mouth went dry, his stomach muscles contracted convulsively and his fingertips commenced to grow numb, just as they had at Bull Run.

Boom! Boom! *Cincinnati's* two other bow guns were discharged. Then, as Dent clung to a stanchion and gulped for air, the whole deck quivered beneath his feet. With a deafening report, *Carondelet's* sixty-four pound rifled gun had let fly and was followed in swift succession by the two forty-two pound rifles. Momentarily all view of the Tennessee and of the fort became concealed behind a whirling bellows of hot, choking and evil-smelling burnt powder. A fearful ear-shattering uproar ensued once *Essex* and *St. Louis* also opened fire. From below sounded the rumbling of *Carondelet's* gun carriages being hauled back amid excited curses and panted commands from various gun captains.

Fourth Master H. A. Walke—no relation to the Commander—appeared and waited on the companion ready to relay orders if the cannonade grew too deafening for the Captain's orders, shouted through a little speaking trumpet, to be heard.

Wishing someone would assign him a duty Dent gripped a railing and clung desperately to it for fear that, in an access of terror, he might lurch down the companion in search of safety in the gunboat's armored casemate.

When a shell from the fort burst with a deafening report squarely between *St. Louis* and *Carondelet* Dent became aware of a warm trickle descending his leg and only by making a violent effort did he succeed in preventing a further escape of urine. Scarlet with shame he stole a glance at Weaver, noticed that his lean jaws now were working to a more rapid tempo. Walke and the Chief Pilot seemed wholly occupied in watching the fort towards which the Western Flotilla was drawing inexorably nearer.

When a rumbling of carriage wheels warned that the ironclad's bow guns were about to be run out again Commander Walke imperturbably turned to his namesake. "Instruct the Captain of Number Two gun to elevate three degrees. He's firing into the bluff."

The Fourth Master had just disappeared when a terrific *clang!* caused *Carondelet's* whole fabric to shudder—the Confederates had got home the first of the thirty-odd hits she was about to suffer. Even as the ironclad's bow guns fired for a second time something went screaming *aoouw!* close over the wheelhouse. Again and again shells from the fort—evidently they had some excellent gunners up there—glanced off *Carondelet's* casemate.

Peering in dazed fashion out of an eye-slit Dent watched *St. Louis'* port chimney suddenly collapse about halfway up its length and topple over amid a serpentine tangle of severed guy wires to dangle, still smoking a little, over her side. Oily tongues of flame and smoke escaped from a series of gashes in the steamboat's remaining funnel.

To his great surprise Dent was able to command his voice sufficiently to speak. "Commander Walke, sir, that last shell has cut us free of the *St. Louis.*"

"That's good. Nevertheless, Mr. Weaver, I want us kept pressed close to the *St. Louis,*" Walke directed in an ordinary tone. "It steadies us both."

For the first time since leaving Panther Island Weaver spoke. "Praise God them snags was swept away with them torpedoes yesterday." He winked at Dent standing, great-eyed and white as cornstarch, a step behind him. "We don't wear even boiler iron on our bottom."

Again and yet again Confederate projectiles ranged the four gunboats or raised angry columns of spray from the river's surface, but *Essex* and *Cincinnati* now could take advantage of a broad reach of water opposite the fort and steam further apart.

All at once geyser-like waterspouts commenced to rise between fort and flotilla to betray miserably poor gunnery aboard the timberclads. These were firing hopelessly short of their target.

Thanks to a brisk slant of wind the battle smoke abruptly was cleared away and revealed telling hits the Federals were scoring all over Fort Henry. Plainly to be seen were sudden white puffs caused by bursting shells; also shattered timbers and clouds of dirt flung high into the air.

For some reason Dent suddenly became extremely conscious of the monotonous cracking noises caused by the engines' exhausts. Now that his initial terrors had become relieved the Connecticuter watched *Essex*, ever a sluggish boat, lumbering two lengths ahead and bearing steadily down upon the smoke-clouded fort. Fort Henry lay on a low bluff not a quarter of a mile distant amid a semi-circle of burning huts, tents and barracks. He could even see how, occasionally, the Rebel flag was blown against the wind by the concussion of a bursting shell.

"It's a cold day," Pilot Hinton commented with a wry grin, "but I'll wager them Secesh bastards think it pretty damn' hot."

"Yep. Glad I ain't ashore right now," Weaver agreed and deftly steered *Carondelet* out of the course taken by a giant oak which, with spidery black roots barely projecting above the surface, came drifting down upon the line of gunboats.

"Don't 'pear their shells can penetrate our armor," said the Assistant Pilot.

Commander Walke's head snapped about, threw his aquiline profile into silhouette. "Silence in the wheelhouse! When I desire comments I will request them. Can you steer two points to port, Mr. Hinton? I wish all three of my bow guns brought to bear. Firing in excessive traverse is hard on their crews."

By now Dent's ears had become so accustomed to this outrageous and confusing din that he could distinctly hear Matthew Arthur, Captain of Number One gun, order his big sixty-four pounder run out.

At this moment the range had been closed to a quarter of a mile, so the Western Flotilla's shells burst ever more accurately over Fort Henry. Conversely, the clanging rap of shell fragments smashing against the casemate grew more noticeable. An officer from the Second Division appeared in the pilothouse.

"Captain, sir—"

"Well, Mr. Gray, speak up. I can't hear you." Walke directed sharply.

"Sir! That damn' boiler iron we carry aft is beginning to split like walnut shells; big sections of it are coming loose and dropping overboard every time we suffer a solid hit."

"How interesting," Walke returned coolly. "Substantiates what I've said from the beginning. Need real armor everywhere. Now, Mr. Gray, pray return to your division and order your crews to relieve those serving the bow guns."

"Aye, aye, sir."

Suddenly Walke stiffened and his hands clamped themselves convulsively upon his binoculars. "My God! Look! What can have gone wrong aboard the *Essex?*"

Presently it became unmistakable that big, ungainly *Essex* must have received a shot in her vitals because her stern wheel had stopped. Further, furious clouds of woolly-looking steam began spurting out of her gunports and pilothouse.

"Christ!" gasped Weaver. "She's been hit in her boilers! God help Sam MacBride and Marshall Ford if they're in that wheelhouse."

Dent tried to speak, but couldn't find his voice. Beyond a doubt any man occupying *Essex's* pilothouse must now be dead or dying in the most ghastly pain.

What were the ultimate sensations of a man in the act of perishing? What lay beyond? All that the preachers promised for the godly—or simple oblivion? It was this mystery in which his cowardice was rooted.

Even over the thunder of the battle the horrified shouts of *Carondelet's* starboard broadside gun crews, who had witnessed the disaster, could be heard.

Like ants from a damaged hill, faltering, crippled figures struggled out of the hurt ironclad's gunports and dropped into the icy river. Most of these never reappeared but a few arose to fight the raging current and cling to the helpless gunboat's guards. Later it became known that Lieutenant Porter, wounded and badly scalded, had, by force of the explosion, been blown bodily out of the casemate. He would have perished then and there had not a blue jacket of the Regular Navy dived in and caught his semi-conscious superior; he then grabbed a line trailing from a bent and empty davit and had held on.

Dent saw Daniel Weaver's gaze flicker sidewise to Walke's long and impassive countenance. "Do we rescue, Cap'n?"

"No. The enemy is still firing, keep on."

Chills chased each other the length of Paul Dent's spine. Had he been ashore he knew he would most certainly have taken to his heels, just as he had at Bull Run; now, fortunately perhaps, nothing remained for him to do save to grab a hand hold and stand there, shaking like a colt which scents a bear, and watch a shell burst squarely between *Cincinnati's* smokestacks. The explosion shore her starboard funnel off close to the ironclad's hurricane deck and thereby reduced her engines' draughts so that she dropped rapidly astern of *Carondelet* and *St. Louis*. The remaining two gunboats kept on, all the while maintaining so accurate a fire that enemy artillerymen commenced to desert certain of their batteries.

"Pilot, maintain our present course. With luck in a few minutes we'll be able to enfilade the fort," snapped Walke and went below to correct *Carondelet's* fire.

Weaver dashed sweat from eyes grown hollow with fatigue. "Take over, Billy, I'm plumb wore out. Just keep our jackstaff lined up with that-there fort."

He grinned at Dent. "Wonder why them Rebs have left a steamboat tied up to their wharf?" He broke off when a hospital flag suddenly was run up. "Damn' Confeds should have flown that from the start."

On threshed the diminished flotilla, on until their crews could see not only a series of battered and crumbling salients but also the muzzles of overturned cannon pointed helplessly skywards.

"They'll have to holler quits pretty soon, now." William Hinton was speaking more to himself than anyone else. "If the Rebels reckon Andy Foote is going to haul out, they're plumb mistaken."

A few moments later a flash of white cloth glimmered upon the shattered parapets and stayed there until *Cincinnati* raised a cease-fire signal. Long since, the fort's signal mast had been shattered, had vanished.

Walke reappeared, his blue uniform jacket ripped open enough to expose the blue-and-white checkered shirt he wore beneath it. "They've quit, gentlemen. By God, the Rebels have surrendered. Reduce speed," he barked at Hinton.

Perhaps one hundred and fifty yards offshore, *Carondelet*, unable sufficiently to check her momentum, went hard aground just as clouds of jet smoke suddenly mounted into the sky upstream. A couple of enemy steamboats were attempting escape, their huge paddlewheels spewing spray and froth in frantic haste.

Apparently Flag Officer Foote had no intention of being deprived of the full fruits of victory so a string of brightly colored flags dispatched the timberclads, swift former river racers, surging in pursuit. *Cincinnati's* only remaining yawl was lowered and, a few minutes later, an officer appeared aboard *Carondelet* and saluted smartly.

"Flag Officer Foote's compliments, Commander Walke. Will you immediately proceed ashore to receive the enemy's capitulation?"

But even before *Carondelet's* barge could be lowered a gig flying a white flag appeared from that same wharf at which lay the Confederate hospital ship. She was bringing Brigadier-General Lloyd Tilghman, C.S.A., in person to surrender Fort Henry.

And thus it came about that a fort, defended solely by land forces, surrendered to a naval flotilla totally unsupported by troops. The weather had been so vile, the roads such quagmires that Grant had been unable to come up in time to cut off the retreat of a vast majority of the garrison. As a result, there fell into Union hands only the Commanding General, his staff, and seventy-eight artillerymen plus some sixteen invalids lying aboard the hospital boat.

The remainder of the garrison, some twenty-six hundred in strength, had been seen hurriedly retreating over a miserable road in the direction of much stronger Fort Donelson. It lay twelve-odd miles to the eastward upon the Cumberland River and barred a Federal attack upon Nashville.

IV MRS. WILBER'S "ACADEMY"

LORETTA BENTALOU AWOKE reluctantly when Cleodene, a slim octoroon recently assigned as personal maid to Lola May Askins and herself, pushed open a latticed blind. Immediately sunlight sketched an irregular pattern of black-and-gold bars across a pink silk counterpane covering Loretta's huge brass bed.

The girl yawned and, in stretching luxuriously, caused the deep lace collar of her lawn nightrobe to slip downwards until perfectly rounded breasts neatly pointed in coral became exposed. Still without fully opening her eyes Loretta tugged her gown back into position.

Despite the ornate gilt and brocaded French furniture and many mirrors Mrs. Wilber had insisted upon installing, the apartment's proportions, the chandeliers of cut-glass, its trim and wallpaper betrayed the original owner's good taste. Mrs. Wilber, who was a lot smarter than most people suspected, had purchased for a song this big, tastefully designed mansion of red brick. It boasted no less than four Corinthian columns before its porte-cochere. Most of its furnishings remained because, immediately following the capture of Camp Jackson and the consequent wholesale arrest of Southern sympathizers, Theodore Wilmer and his family had packed up in a great hurry and departed for Natchez.

A graceful mahogany washstand supported a pitcher, a basin and a soap dish of pale blue French china all adorned with a profusion of small pink roses. Even the slop-jar matched. The window hangings were of green brocade trimmed with tiny balls of dark green plush. The undercurtains were of real Irish lace and the floor covered by a thick pink-and-gray Aubusson rug that harmonized effectively with those green window curtains of which Mrs. Wilber so highly approved.

In a gesture Cleodene had come to expect, Loretta pressed fingertips to her forehead and stared unseeing before her. In the act of hanging up a pair of lace-trimmed drawers the octoroon glanced sympathetically over her shoulder and inquired. "You recallin' last night?"

Loretta's full red lips formed a wry grin. "Guess I must have drunk more champagne than I realized. The General was very insistent." She sighed as Cleodene gently massaged her forehead. "How is Phoebe today?"

The maid's Caucasian features assumed concern—she had grown truly fond of that mysterious girl whose head had got hurt so bad in the wreck and she offered her more than just the polite service she rendered Lola May, Clairette and the rest of Mrs. Wilber's pretty, but often ill-tempered protégées.

Cleodene clucked softly and carried an armful of Miss Loretta's generously frilled and flounced petticoats into a closet. It sure beat all about Miss Phoebe. The poor soul, she could recall nothing at all about her life before her arrival and long convalescence at the "Academy." Laws! She reckoned she never would forget that day Miz Wilber had showed up with all them high-steppin' young whore-ladies she'd fotched out from the East. Miz Wilber was the smart one, and lucky, too. Not one of those girls had suffered any real hurt in that awful train wreck—except Miss Phoebe and she wasn't really one of the girls—not yet, at least. Her poor head had kept on hurting and she kept on having dizzy spells any time at all.

My, my, she still could recall Miss Phoebe's funny-looking country clothes, all splotched with traces of blood that couldn't be washed out and her dazed way of walking and talking. Ten whole days passed before Miss Phoebe's scalp had healed and that bodacious big knot on the side of her head had begun to disappear. Some piece of wreckage sure had fetched her one mighty mean lick.

Of course Miss Phoebe wasn't even a bit crazy, but it sure seemed mighty strange she couldn't even remember her own name, even when it was told her—Miz Wilber had salvaged her purse from the wreck. Cleodene reappeared and smoothed out the green ball gown's billowing skirt, retrieved its crinoline and various undergarments such as a short-sleeved corset cover, canary-yellow silk stockings and a corset garnished by delicate blue bows descending its front. Them fancy French stays must a-cost Miz Wilber a pretty penny.

Ambrosia, the freed girl who cared for Miss Clairette and Miss Lola May, had been more than a little right when she'd sniffed, "Miz Wilber mus' be addled spendin' all dat doctor money on Miss Phoebe. That red-haid gal won't *never* pay off. She's too frozen-like and hard-bodied fo' most gent'mens. Besides, her hands is rough like she's wuked on a farm or sumpin'."

Miss Loretta, anyhow, was riding high these days. The Eastern girl's patrons always departed highly pleased and the next time paid a considerably larger fee for her favors. As it was, Miz Wilber was sharply curtailing the number of Miss Loretta's "callers" and proportionately increased her charges until finally only General Mixer could meet the tariff.

All the same, Miss Loretta sure was worth every cent Miz Wilber had

had to spend on fancy clothes. She was *sumpin'* to look at when she got herself all prettied up in a green or a black party dress. No wonder Major-General Mixer was takin' up all the time Miz Wilber allowed him, no matter what the cost. For a fact, only him and Colonel Buttons ever got to see Miss Loretta any more.

In all her fourteen years of working about spo'tin' houses Cleodene never had come across a gal so really full of fun, so warm-hearted and generous. Whenever possible she visited with poor, sick Miss Phoebe and brought her little presents and candy now and then. The other girls ignored her, even made fun of her dazed manner. Most likely they were scared of Miss Phoebe's beauty—when she "went to work" she'd surely make a formidable rival.

While Loretta Bentalou breakfasted with hearty enjoyment her maid dragged a tin bathtub from one of three enormous closets opening off this big, high-ceilinged bedroom and placed it before the fireplace.

"Tell me, who was at de pa'ty las' night?"

"Mostly all Army officers, friends of the General's, but there also were a few contractors and a real live Congressman."

The yellow girl chuckled. "Comes the day you git you a Congressman, Miz Loretta, I reckon you sho has reached the top of sassiety."

"You surprise me, Cleodene," Loretta observed. "Contractors make a lot more money. I suppose you've heard that some of them have piled up riches in only a few months?"

"Who ain't?"

"Have you heard about the one named Everett? He's made quite a fortune in only a few weeks."

The maid produced a huge bathtowel, a sponge and a bottle of Florida water. "Ah has, honey. Misto' Everett, dey sez, is de most up-and-comin'est man 'round dis town. Ambrosia she wuz sayin' she seen him drivin' along Walnut Street wid a pretty l'il lady frien' in a gre't big green-an'-black cutter. She wearin' a beaverskin coat. Dat Miss Léonie's sho pretty," Cleodene said, "but she ain't a patch on you, honey, 'deed she ain't; 'sides she acts common as pig tracks, so they say, when she drinks even a little bit. Ambrosia she sez dis Misto' Everett is *real* handsome; he a gre't big man wid yaller hair and side whiskers."

"Tonight I will see him myself; they say he's a great friend of General Mixer's."

Only when the tub was steaming and fragrant with a scent of violets did Loretta Bentalou swing long legs out of bed and walk over to a cheval glass.

When Cleodene started to remove Loretta's nightgown the latter waved her aside and with a flash of marble-white limbs whirled the gown over her head to stand fully revealed before the cheval glass.

Once her waist-long mass of lustrous black tresses had been twisted into a chignon Loretta stepped into the slipper tub, sat down and promptly sank back allowing her arms to float, supported by bathwater.

"Tonight," she smiled, "you must do your very best with my hair, Cleodene. General Mixer is escorting me to a small dinner Senator Blount Mason is tendering in honor of some naval officers who have come to take over that new gunboat—I think it's called *Benton*, or something like that. I've heard that this Mr. Everett will be present." Loretta raised a slender foot above the bath's surface and scrubbed it with unnecessary vigor. "You said he's handsome?"

The yellow bandanna securing Cleodene's black curls inclined. "Dat what Ambrosia she say; he got de handsomest haid she ever did see. What you fixin' to wear, Mis Loretta?"

"I'll leave that up to you," laughed the black-haired girl and squeezed the sponge to send a rivulet of soapy water cascading down the *val* between her bosoms. "Shall it be the black velvet or my sapphire-blue satin?"

"You best wear dat new black velvet gown. It sho' off yo' purty hair and complexion bestest of all. An' don't go wearin' no jewellery 'ceptin' de General's bracelet and mebbee dem diamond earbobs dat boatbuilder give yo'."

Loretta stepped out of the tub and immediately became swathed in the bathtowel's voluminous folds. She stood glowing, motionless while the maid dried her and then dusted her with sachet powder.

"What you thinkin' 'bout, honey?"

"About that poor Phoebe. Give me my dressing gown and let's go visit with her."

They found the convalescent in a tiny, bare room which certainly must have housed one of the Wilmers' servants in days gone by. Clad in a neat and simple gingham dress, she was bending over a sewing basket. Seated in the sunlight her rich red-gold hair gleamed like a polished copper pot set in the firelight.

Smiling, Phoebe got to her feet. "How are you, Loretta? Did you sleep well?"

"Wonderfully, as usual, honey."

"Did your Army admirer come in last night?"

"Yes."

Cleodene closed the door and departed on her duties, relieved that a little more color was visible in the hurt girl's sweetly oval face.

"When are you going to announce your engagement?"

"In good time," laughed Loretta, dropping onto a rocker and, crossing her legs to a rustle of flounces, arched delicate eyebrows.

"And how is your head this morning? Can you remember anything more than yesterday?"

"I'm afraid not. I try and I try to remember but I just don't seem able to catch hold of anything."

"But you remember everything that has happened since you were brought here?"

"After about the first two or three days," Phoebe said quietly, "and I'll always remember how awfully good you and Mrs. Wilber were to me." She picked up her needle and started to hem a new blouse, a very elaborate affair that would eventually grace the lovely form of Clairette. "It's so good of Mrs. Wilber to let me stay here as seamstress."

"You are mighty handy with that needle," drawled Loretta. "Mrs. Wilber said so. Does your head hurt the way it did?"

"Sometimes I get really sharp pains, then I just can't seem to see straight enough to do my sewing, but I don't get those spells as often as I used to."

"That's good." Idly Loretta rumpled her generously long black locks. "What do you think about the 'Academy'?" she demanded quite suddenly.

Phoebe's large dark blue eyes swung upwards. "I don't let myself think, Loretta. I can't afford to. I haven't a penny in the world and here I have a roof over my head, good food and decent employment and I have a true friend in you; even if the others are hateful sometimes." She arose and, crossing to a bureau, lifted out a bolt of cambric, then selected a pattern from a pile.

Glory! thought Loretta, viewing the mysterious girl's long straight legs, erect carriage and finely formed head. If she were to doll herself up in a ball gown, fix her hair and use a little paint—not that she needed much with that fine, clear complexion of hers—she'd surely command a lot of attention from the sporting element.

"You don't blame us for our way of—well—our way of life?"

"'Judge not, that ye be not judged,'" quoted Phoebe and tucked half a dozen pins between her lips.

Again and again she had reminded herself that this must be her attitude. Of course when she got strong enough and her head stopped hurting she would pull right out of here, find employment elsewhere. It was terrible not being able to remember why she was in St. Louis or from whence she had come. For a space she had really despaired when the effects of the concussion had been at their worst and she had almost always thrown up whatever she had eaten. Of course she must have had some reason for heading out west. Mrs. Wilber had said that they had met aboard a train heading from Chicago to Illinoistown and St. Louis.

If only Mrs. Wilber hadn't thrown away the clothes she had been wearing, she might have obtained a clue, but undoubtedly they had been too torn and blood-stained to be preserved. It was a pity, too, that Mrs. Wilber had discarded her purse which she claimed had contained only a few dollars and a religious tract addressed simply to Miss Phoebe Whidden. Sometimes, when she repeated her name, she felt on the verge of remembering something, but if she tried too hard to recollect that pain in the side of her head would commence.

The doorknob turned and Mrs. Wilber fluttered in, in her usual gown of black silk and with gray curls bobbing agitatedly.

"Well, well, how are we today, my dear?" she paused on the threshold.

Phoebe removed the pins from her mouth. "I'm fine, thank you, ma'm, and feeling a lot stronger. I will have that blouse ready tomorrow afternoon," she added and flushed under Mrs. Wilber's suddenly penetrating gaze.

"Turn around, dearie, and let me see you in profile. Hum-m. It's best from the left, which is lucky. Gentlemen generally escort a lady from that side. Hum-m. Nice legs, hasn't she?" she demanded of Loretta.

"Prettiest I've seen in a good while," drawled the other.

"You haven't had any dizzy spells recently?"

"No, ma'm, not in three days."

"Good! Good! You must be just about recovered. Dr. Ashby says that except for your loss of memory you're about as good as new." The madam waddled into the room, circled about Phoebe with much the air of a horse trader inspecting a likely filly.

"Yes, I expect you'll do. When you've finished, Loretta dear, please come to my room. I would like to consult with you."

A quarter of an hour later, Mrs. Wilber pointed to a green satin ball gown, inquired of Loretta, "With that red hair of hers, don't you think this should be real fetching?"

Loretta nodded, lips compressed into a straight red line.

"And I expect those lovely limbs will look even better in black silk."

Loretta again inclined her head.

"Come on, speak up. I want suggestions from you, Loretta. You got real good taste."

"So you're fixing to put Phoebe to work tonight?"

"Now's as good a time as any. Clairette's sick and Lola's come down with a streaming cold."

Loretta arose, went over to inspect herself in the mirror, said, "You know, ma'm, I wouldn't wonder but Phoebe's a virgin."

"What of it? So were we all once."

"Well, for all she can't remember who or what she was, I don't think you're going to get much profit out of her. If a girl's heart isn't in her work or if she isn't lazy, like me, the men won't cotton to her."

Mrs. Wilber's bright black eyes hardened. "You trying to tell me my business? I tell you that girl's going to be the best, except perhaps you, dearie, I have ever had. My God! Those legs of hers alone would make a stone saint jump, and did you notice her bust? It's just like one of them scandalous Greek statues I saw in Washington, puts me in mind of 'The Greek Slave.' She'll take to this business like a duck to water, mind my words. A girl isn't given a face and a body like that just to teach Sunday School."

"Maybe you're right, ma'm. You know more about it than I do. I'm no judge on account of I like this life, but I still say I don't think that Phoebe would. Goodness sticks out all over her."

To a sibilant hiss of silk petticoats Mrs. Wilber crossed to a black walnut chiffonier, pawed in one of its drawers and produced a rhinestone necklace and a pair of earbobs to match.

"These will go well," she announced, "and, come to think of it, there is an old rooster here in town who'll pay a mighty fancy price to break in a virgin." She backed off admiring the dress and the jewellery she had tossed onto it. "Now run along, dearie, and get some rest. General Mixer's coming for you tonight and mind you have Cleodene set those curls at the back of your head tighter than she did the last time."

V THE STREETS OF ST. LOUIS

THE AFTERNOON HAD deteriorated from a pleasant, wintry day into a raw and foggy twilight. A warm wind beating up the Mississippi had poured over the still-frozen plains creating a stifling miasma rendered dirty and noxious by coal smoke from thousands of chimneys.

Already Cleodene and Ambrosia were hurrying about igniting gas jets with long tin lighters from which a thin cord of waxed string flared.

Loretta Bentalou, in a wrapper of pink silk, advanced furtively along the corridor outside her room, then on tiptoe ascended a stair leading to the third floor and the room occupied by Phoebe Whidden. She didn't want to have George, the big ex-prizefighter who masqueraded as butler of the Academy, catch her. Actually he was there to handle obstreperous patrons and administer discipline to Mrs. Wilber's charges.

Daylight having failed, Phoebe Whidden lay upon her little iron bed planning the finishing touches on Miss Clairette's blouse. If she really had been asleep she would never have heard that faintest imaginable tap at her door. She half roused and then sat straight up when Loretta Bentalou whisked herself inside and reclosed the door behind her.

In the half light the girl's eyes seemed enormous.

"Listen, honey," she whispered, "you've got to get out of here—quickly! Quickly!"

"Tonight?"

"My God, yes, tonight! Just as fast as you can."

"But—but, why? Where would I go?"

"I don't know where you would go, but if you value your chastity, get out of here. Quick!"

Phoebe blinked, trying to pull her wits together. "But—but Loretta, what in the world?"

"Never mind!" muttered the other. "You're a good girl and I would give my half interest in hell to be just like you, but it's too late." Her voice changed and she spoke crisply. "Look, honey, in about half an hour by my reckoning, Mrs. Wilber and George will come up here. You are to be moved to a room downstairs. There will be a green ball gown in it, pretty shoes, silk stockings, even a necklace."

A cold flood seemed to engulf Phoebe. "But, but Loretta, where can I go?"

"I don't know, silly; that's for you to find out. Anywhere is better than here. Look!" She held out her hand, smiled a quick flashing smile. "Here's ten dollars cash and a little ring you can sell. Believe me, honey, do as I say—get out of here." Strange, Loretta thought, I should risk this, for all I'm content with the way things are.

Phoebe was saying, "But I've no cloak, no street clothes."

"Here is a dress isn't too flashy and I," she grimaced, "borrowed this cloak of Clairette's. She's tired of it."

In that bemused manner which had been hers during the past weeks, Phoebe tucked the bill and the ring into the neck of her dress. Then she flung both arms around Loretta's neck. She couldn't find anything to say, which was just as well because footsteps were advancing along the corridor, paused before the door then hurried on.

"Take care of yourself, honey," breathed Loretta, "and sometime if you think of it, remember that I tried to help you. Reckon I may need a little fire insurance someday. Good-bye, dearie, and good luck."

Thanks to Cleodene's guidance and the timing of her departure, Phoebe slipped out of the Academy's side door quite unobserved.

"God bless you, Cleodene," she whispered. "I will never forget your kindness."

"And de Lawd watch over you, Miss Phoebe. I hate to see you out on de street like dis."

"Can you suggest any place I could go?" Voices from inside the house caused Cleodene's eyes to widen and instantly she closed the door.

Clairette's mantel was too small Phoebe realized as she hurried off down the brick sidewalk stumbling now and then because the fog had so shrouded the already-inadequate street lamps it was difficult to keep one's footing. If only she had some idea where to go! But she hadn't, not having set foot outside of the Academy since her arrival in town. She shrank into a doorway to avoid being accosted by a pair of drunken soldiers, then blundered on up a side street along which clattered a succession of carriages and mounted officers. It seemed she must be heading in the right direction for shops, most of them shuttered for the night, became more numerous. She guessed she must be paralleling the river since off to her left was sounding the mournful tooting of some fog-blinded steamboats.

"I *won't* panic!" she told herself. "I won't because I mustn't."

Phoebe hurried along, not at the brisk pace customary with her but somewhat uncertainly; her strength obviously had not been completely restored. She looked about for a policeman but saw nobody answering that description.

A party of rivermen bursting suddenly out of a bar confronted her.

"Give us a kiss, Sis," one of them invited and flung an arm about her shoulder.

"Oh no! Please! Please! I'm on my way to meet my fiancé," she lied in desperation. "He will be here any minute."

Surprisingly, the riverman let her go with a mumbled apology and hurried after his companions.

At the end of another ten minutes' walking she found herself on the verge of a run-down residential district where the houses most certainly had seen better days. Presently a sign: "Mrs. Mallory's Genteel Boarding House" struck her eye.

Breathing a silent prayer that this establishment might live up to its pretentions she tugged at the bell pull, heard a tiny jangling from the depths of the house. A hatchet-faced woman with gray hair skinned back into a tight bun at the nape of her neck opened the door on a chain and demanded her business.

"I—I've got to find a room," Phoebe faltered. "Do you have any rooms to rent?"

"Might and I might not. Come in."

Phoebe found herself in a narrow hallway that reeked of stale cooking but otherwise seemed clean enough. She underwent the landlady's critical inspection with an uncertain smile on her lips.

"You look decent enough, Miss—?"

"Miss Whidden."

"Where's your luggage?"

"I—I lost it on the train. I expect it was stolen."

"Huh! Where you from?"

"The East."

"What are you doing here?"

"I—I am looking for employment. I am a seamstress."

"Got any money?"

"A little," Phoebe was cautious.

"Can you pay three dollars a week for your room and breakfast?"

"Why—why yes. Yes, I can."

"Let's see the color of your money." Critically the boardinghouse keeper inspected Loretta's ten-dollar bill by the hall light then sniffed it. "Perfumed money is new to me," she grunted, then made change from a purse strapped to her belt. "I reckon you can have the room, young lady. What are your sympathies? North or South?"

"North, I guess."

"That's good. I got driven out of Kansas by a parcel of Rebels; killed my father and my husband so I don't want any Southern sympathizers in this place."

She put foot to the staircase and, talking all the while over her shoulder, led upwards. "Now this is a respectable establishment so I won't stand for you entertaining gentlemen in your room; the front door is locked for the night after ten so don't go carousing about town."

Before an ill-painted door she hesitated. "Got any nightclothes?"

"No, I am afraid not. Everything I had was in my valise." This was true enough; her bag *had* been lost or stolen, Phoebe reassured herself.

"Well, you and my daughter are about of a size. Maybe she can spare you a nightshift."

From a ring jangling beside her purse, she detached a key, pushed back the door. The furniture consisted of a plain cast-iron bed much like that back at Mrs. Wilber's, a stand with a cracked washbasin and pitcher and a plain, straight-backed chair. There was not even a mirror, just a plain chest of drawers and a couple of pegs driven into the wall. The landlady set down a kerosene lamp with a metal reflector.

"This gets filled twice a week," she announced, "and no oftener, so don't go wasting coal oil. Good night."

VI THE STEAMBOAT *WESTERN ARROW*

PHILO DAINGERFIELD CAME slipping into the Western Arrow Contracting & Supply Company's offices bearing disturbing news: a change in command over the Confederate garrison on Island Number Ten was imminent. Therefore it would be impossible for Matt Everett to attend Major-General Mixer's banquet in honor of Congressman Blount Mason.

"Ain't no two ways about it, Matt. Either we've got to round up our crew and shove off tonight or wait maybe a couple o' months till Mr. Bullwinkle can arrange us a new set of recognition signals. We'd sure lose a mint of money by waiting."

Matt bit off the end of a seegar and glowered across his office at a long row of prints depicting various celebrated steamboats. He and Philo occupied unusually spacious and well-appointed offices in a warehouse they had purchased. It was on the levee at the foot of Washington Street.

"Damnation! Of course we must leave tonight, but Léonie surely will want to lay me out in lavender. She bought a new gown just for old Mixer's banquet." He laughed shortly. "I've bet Charley Buttons a thousand that Mixer's new fancy can't even hold a candle to my Léonie. Would have been fun to watch those two hussies tangle, in a polite way, of course."

Philo's slight figure dropped wearily onto a cane-bottomed rocker. "Maybe you're saving money at that, Matt. Hear tell this Loretta Bentalou's got black hair, big, dark blue eyes and the prettiest figger this side o' New York."

Matt's expression softened. "I used to know a girl with red hair."

"Did you? Where?"

"Oh, hell, that's neither here nor there."

After scribbling an excuse to Léonie, Matt rang a bell to summon a gangling Negro youth. "You know where Miss Dulac lives?"

The boy grinned. "Yas, sur! 'Deed Ah do. Ah kin git to Numbah Twenty Lucas Street 'side of ten minutes."

A twenty-five-cent shinplaster sailed over to be caught by the messenger's eager hand. "Present Miss Léonie my compliments and tell her

I'm very sorry to have to disappoint her. Tell her I'll fetch her back a nice present."

Once the door closed, he turned to Philo. "Cargo's all stowed?"

"Yep, and the boat's trimmed right. I don't want the water uneven in our boilers—may need every pound of pressure they can raise before this trip's done. Only items we're lackin' are the percussion caps and medicines, but Greenway swore they'll be on our dock by ten o'clock."

"They'd better be." Matt raised sandy eyebrows. "How's the River?"

"In good stage for wintertime and the ice ain't too bad right now. There's been a cold spell up the Missouri so all the creeks and little rivers up there is locked tighter than a duck's foot in the mud."

"What about Cairo? Is our friend Major Bridges still on duty at Camp Defiance?"

"Yes. Bullwinkle got a telegram from him yesterday." Philo commenced to tug at his slender black goatee. "It's below Cairo that the River's got me worried. Bullwinkle heard from Colonel Hazeltine that he's to be relieved three days from now; maybe sooner. That's why we dassent delay a minute. Rebs are rumored to have sent a new Commanding General down to New Madrid."

Matt scowled at a big brass cuspidor beside his desk. Damn! He'd anticipated parading Léonie in her new gray merlino pelisse; that, and her coat of prime marten skins had cost him a pretty penny but Simon Quirk's predictions concerning the astronomical profits to be won in certain government contracts had made possible such extravagances. Godfreys! It didn't seem possible but, even after all expenditures had been paid, there remained deposited to his credit better than one hundred thousand dollars in the Exchange Bank of St. Louis.

Although the *Western Arrow* could carry only ninety tons of cargo, she had proved uncommonly swift and handy and could navigate over a scant sixteen inches of water. Matt would never dream of replacing her. Somewhere Philo had learned of a device which minimized the loud cracking noise invariably caused by the steamboat's exhausts. Also, by a judicious relocation of the *Western Arrow's* rudders—she carried four in all—two to a side and located just forward of the sternwheel—she responded very readily to her helm.

Shortly after Everett and his partner had purchased the steamboat they had, in order to reduce her silhouette and resistance to the wind, caused all cabins to be razed from the hurricane deck. Further, all but a quartet of staterooms on the main deck had been demolished in the interests of cargo capacity.

On Philo's advice Matt had caused his vessel to be hauled out at the end of December in order to equip the contraband runner with a double bow and a "snag chamber" which should prevent the steamboat from sinking were she to run onto a snag bar, reef or sawyer at speed.

Thus the *Western Arrow* had ample freight room, was handy and unobtrusive and could outrun almost anything on the western rivers, except some of the big, sidewheel tugs.

Matt Everett began to breathe easier and gave over his taut pacing about the totally darkened wheelhouse now that the batteries of Camp Defiance lay astern smothered in darkness. Only a faint glow against a bitter winter sky indicated the existence of Cairo, Illinois. Jaws rhythmically at work on a quid, Philo nodded to Charley Brebner, the relief pilot, and himself took the wheel. He appeared dwarfed by its enormous diameter.

Once the contraband runner had steamed around the first bend below Cairo Philo observed, "Matt, I reckon we'd best run at full speed all night. I aim for dawn to find us off the water batteries on Island Number Ten. We can always loaf about if we get there too soon."

Matt peered into the gloom. "Damned if I see how you know where you are. All looks the same to me."

"It will if you don't *know* yer river like a real close-fit pilot has to," came the Kentuckian's voice out of the gloom. "Can't you see yonder bank with the big trees along it?"

"No. I can't."

"Well, I can; so can Charley Brebner. There's other ways of telling where you are. By the sound a bell's echo makes against the shore. Then again you can learn a lot from the run of the boat; for instance, we'll be passing over Scuffletown bar come a few minutes—you'll notice we dragged water two-three times? Now *I* know we'll find mark twain water this side and mark three water on the far side of it."

"What's a mark?"

"Same's a fathom—six feet. So 'mark twain' means twelve foot of water. 'Quarter-twain' is thirteen an' a half feet and so on."

"It's still a shining miracle to me how you can find your way through darkness like this. Well, I'm going below and tell Parker to make his stokers hump themselves."

Philo tapped the engine room bell three times to alert the engineer, then Matt, jamming a seegar into a corner of his mouth, swung down the companion hatch and out of the pilothouse's sable chill. Right now he was conscious of an uneasiness not associated with previous expeditions. Why? Well, there was that wholly unexpected and impending relief from duty of Lieutenant-Colonel Hazeltine. Suppose that venal gentleman *already* had been supplanted by some patriotic hot-head who believed in shooting first and talking later? What if Hazeltine, for some reason, had been unable to warn his successor that because the *Western Arrow* was bringing downriver supplies sorely needed by the Confederacy his batteries must under no circumstances fire upon a freighter showing a red, a blue and then a red light at her masthead?

Since the *Western Arrow* steamed quite unprotected even a light cannon ball could riddle her sides, puncture her steam chest, boiler or sever one of the several steamlines supplying the cylinders. In such an event all aboard would very likely perish; by drowning if they were lucky, amid blasts of live steam that stripped flesh right off the bone, if they were not.

Outside the engine room door Matt paused, aware that it had begun to sleet. He deliberated ordering the anchors dropped, but time and again Philo had proved himself intimately familiar with this particular stretch of the Mississippi. On several occasions *Western Arrow's* guards actually had grazed the shattered hull of some wreck or, at the last moment, had skirted an all but invisible sandbar. But could even so expert a pilot as Daingerfield find his way through this stinging, hissing darkness? Uneasily, Matt tramped aft past tarpaulin-protected bales of blankets and big cases of harness and shoes.

Briefly a small voice pled, "These goods you are fetching South will help to kill Maine boys like Thad Tyler, Billy Hildridge, Harry Watson, Phil Babcock and many more you've never known."

"To hell with it!" he grunted. "They knew the chances they were taking when they enlisted. Besides, if I don't benefit from this trade Quirk, Greenway, Feldman and the rest will." He tramped aft circling the main deck to make certain no crack of light was escaping to betray his speeding steamer's presence.

Damned lucky, he ruminated, that the entire Western Flotilla right now either was under repair or concentrating along the Cumberland in preparation for an assault upon Fort Donelson. Reliable reports stated that this fortification was infinitely more powerful and better manned than had been Fort Henry; probably because of its supremely strategic importance.

He lingered staring into the frigid dark and listening to the monotonous hissing splash of the sternwheel's buckets. Good thing such a strong wind was blowing; it muffled that betraying staccato *pop-pop!* caused by the exhaust valves.

Easing the buttons of the naval pea jacket he had picked up in some second-hand store, Matt Everett entered the engine room and shut the door as Chief Engineer Parker roared, "Close that door, you damn' dunderhead! Want us to git blowed clear out o' the river?"

The sweating and oil-smeared engineer promptly relaxed when the New Englander's big, familiar form came swinging across the floor plates.

"What's it doin' outside, sor?" called the red-faced chief fireman.

"It's sleeting and blowing hard, MacGuire, and blacker than a black cat in a dark cellar that isn't there." He watched his Irish coal-heavers bend to their scoops. Matt never signed a Negro aboard his vessel. Slaves were expensive to replace in case of death or maiming or capture. These Irish when sober were dependable and courageous above the average.

"What pressure are we carrying?" Matt presently demanded of his grizzled Chief Engineer. In a dirty checkered flannel shirt and baggy homespun pants he was squinting at a row of brightly polished gauges.

"One hundred pounds even," he returned, but I kin give him a hundert and twenty in two shakes. We need to make time right now."

"We're entering a tricky stretch of the River," Matt explained.

"Say, Mr. Everett," MacGuire wanted to know while the glow of an opened fire door dyed his whisker-framed face a bright orange, "what if them Reb batteries on the Kentucky shore spot the flame from our funnels?"

"They're mostly out of range," replied the owner with an assurance he was far from feeling. "Besides, they don't know we're not one of their own gunboats."

From above the signal cord sounded three short taps, then two *clangs*. Instantly more bags of coal were dumped onto the floor plates to be fed into the insatiable firedoors.

The ringing scrape of scoops over plating immediately before the *Western Arrow's* four firedoors drowned out the sibilant hiss of a leaky connection, the monotonous threshing of the sternwheel. Perceptibly the thrust of cast-iron pistons accelerated, while the pressure gauge's needle wavered upwards towards a red line marking the safety limit.

"Try to keep her up to one hundred and twenty pounds till Philo signals to slow down," Matt directed. "I don't want fire showing from the smoke pipes."

"Shall I cut them exhausts into the chimbleys then? It'll reduce our speed."

"Guess you'd better. We've been making mighty good time," said Matt, then sought the wheelhouse wondering whether it was time to show his recognition signals. For the life of him he couldn't guess how close they steamed to Island Number Ten. Worst of it was, irregular or independent

Confederate State units were forever throwing up small, unauthorized batteries here and there.

Right now Matt wished he had learned to enjoy the chewing of tobacco. To work his jaws might grant his overpowering apprehensions some relief.

Supposing Lieutenant-Colonel Hazeltine's friend in the Confederate Quartermaster Corps did not appear? Suppose that funds to pay for the shipment had not yet arrived and in the media agreed upon, gold, silver or captured Union banknotes?

As usual the wheelhouse remained pitch-dark even with its forward windows opened. Thus exposed, the pilot suffered from sleet that stung at his eyes like voracious insects. A snow flurry earlier had frosted Philo Daingerfield's muffler, goatee, shoulder-long hair, eyebrows and visored leather cap.

"Damned if I see how in the world you find your way!" Matt wondered again, through chattering teeth.

"River's right wide here," the Kentuckian admitted modestly. "We'll be all right 'lessen we run onto a new wreck, a snag or a big bank of ice. After the next bend is when Charley Brebner and I'll have to look real sharp. Down there I've got to cross the current and ride the deep water 'round its outer edge. On one side—the Missouri shore—there's the wreck of the *Nightingale* and over in Tennessee lies old *Emperor Number Two*. She rests just about opposite Reelfort Lake and its marshes."

Suddenly Philo glanced over his shoulder and to his alarm noticed tongues of flame six yards long commencing to stream out of the wrought-iron crowns surmounting the *Western Arrow's* twin smokestacks. "Say, Matt, for God's sake tell Parker to close down his drafts or we'll sure enough get shot at."

On his way back to the wheelhouse Matt paused before the door to the stateroom occupied by lean and saturnine Mr. Cassius Bullwinkle. The Tennessean, surprisingly, was awake and poring over a sheaf of invoices. A half-emptied pint of bourbon stood at his elbow. He stood up, waved to a seat.

"Howdy, Matt. 'Pears like Philo's snakin' us right along." He pointed to a tumbler fairly jumping to the vessel's violent vibration.

"He wants to reach the upper end of Island Number Ten just at dawn."

"At this rate, he shore will," predicted the Southerner.

"When do you figure we ought to show our recognition lights?"

"Lemme talk to Philo first," Bullwinkle tilted back in his cane-bottomed armchair, jet eyes peering out from cavernous sockets. "Only one thing I'm worried about," he confessed. "We'll be fine as silk if some dern Home Guard outfit hain't throwed up a dinky little battery above the Island. They're always doin' that, dern 'em. They're as independent as hawgs on ice and will blast away at anything they see." Bullwinkle filled a jigger of whiskey and passed it over. "Dern fools sank a Confederate tug last week that way."

"Well, then, I guess we'd better go up to the wheelhouse. It's nigh on five o'clock. You've readied your signal rockets?"

"Shore have," the Southerner reassured him. "I been in this business a good while, you know."

"All right, come along," Matt tossed the bourbon off, nodded his thanks and, after rebuttoning his pea jacket, stepped out into the chill darkness to discover that although sleet still fell it was not driving nearly so hard as before. Bits of ice kept bumping alongside but they remained small and therefore presented no real menace.

In the wheelhouse he found Charley Brebner, Philo's relief, at the wheel. The latter was crouched on the pilot's bench and peering attentively out into the night.

While awaiting Cassius Bullwinkle's arrival, Matt, for some inexplicable reason, got to thinking about Dexter. How had various neighbors reacted to his abrupt and unexplained departure? What had Mr. Stetson done about his mother's legacy? Twice Matt had sat down to write—but never had written. What of Phoebe Whidden? Most likely she must long since have pretty well forgotten about him. Maybe she was taking up with Fred Thatcher? On the other hand he doubted it. There, in her mother's kitchen, so much feeling had been evident in Phoebe's glorious dark eyes. What had she said? Something nonsensical about following him no matter what. Of course that had been only an excited young girl's talk when her emotions were out of kilter.

In the pilothouse's gloom he gnawed briefly on his lower lip. Why should he have taken to wondering about Phoebe of late? Why, continually, was he recalling her quick, bright smile, the trick she had of raising one brow slightly higher than its mate when she was amused, and the rich, red-gold gleam of her lustrous hair? Bitterly, he cautioned himself against any further moonings of this kind since he'd not the least intention of ever returning East. Too risky. Somebody would recognize and denounce him as Josiah Cosby's murderer.

On through the opaque and wind-filled dark threshed the *Western Arrow*, once more under Philo's expert guidance. What an amazing man. Certain it was that Daingerfield once had ridden as a jockey, had worked Western steamboats as a gambler, and had been a peddler of shady land-company shares somewhere in the East. Of course, now there could be not the least doubt that he had been—and still was—a "close-fit" pilot along the lower Ohio and knew intimately the Mississippi's peculiarities as far down as Memphis. When one considered the innumerable bars and other obstacles to navigation which must be remembered, in addition to an infinite variety of landmarks, it was no wonder that few pilots were familiar with more than certain stretches of given rivers.

All at once aware of a quickening vibration beneath his boot soles Matt peered helplessly into that wall of gloom beyond the wheelhouse's open windows. Godfreys! It had grown mighty thick out there!

"*Ha!* There it is—" Perceptibly the contraband runner's easy progress slackened while she passed over a bar and felt the tug of the bottom. The vibration also became briefly intensified, then decreased as the *Western Arrow* re-entered deep water.

What sort of reception would they be accorded at New Madrid? The Confederate's commander, especially if he were new on this station, might still be smarting over the loss of Fort Henry and so confiscate the *Western Arrow* and imprison her crew. It went without saying that the Southerners must also be anxious over the outcome of that big fight shaping up around strategically vital Fort Donelson. In Cairo, Generals Grant, Smith and McClernand had been reported to be closing in on that fortress like the jaws of a vise.

He was aroused from his speculations by Philo's voice drawling, "Must be close to five, Matt. I'm telling Parker to reduce speed."

Thrice he pulled a signal bell cord with the result that presently little tongues of flame no longer curled through the smokepipe's iron crowns and the *Western Arrow's* paddle wheel slowed.

"Reckon you'd best warn Bullwinkle to rig our signal lanterns," Philo drawled, but just then the swift little freighter became illumined by a series of blindingly bright flashes off to starboard. Then a roundshot and some shells screamed by sickeningly close to the wheelhouse. Something struck the contraband runner aft, heeled her over and caused a sharp, cracking noise.

"Keerist! Must be some wildcat battery on Nigger Head Island!" gasped Philo. With the help of his relief pilot he cramped the wheel down hard a-larboard and so presented a diminished target to the maverick guns. Bullwinkle came pounding up from below cursing wildly.

"Goddam' hayseed milishy's got no business there. Can we get clear before those lunkheads reload?"

"Dunno," panted Philo. "Better show them signal lamps."

But even as the red-blue-red lanterns were run up the independent battery's guns fired for a second time. Luckily this time it scored no hits.

VII CONTRABAND

THANK TO A PREVIOUS visit to New Madrid, Matt knew what ought to be expected once they left behind the frowning but mercifully silent batteries of Island Number Ten. New Madrid was a thriving River town. Situated on dangerously low ground it now was crowded beyond belief by the approach of fighting. Its sun-bleached, unpainted and uninspired buildings rose upon the Missouri shore, sprawled untidily away from behind its levee and a row of warehouses. The Court House, modelled on the usual Greek temple, was the only important building in evidence. Still, New Madrid remained a pretty place backed by tall woods and dotted with towering live oaks trailing ghostly gray beards of Spanish moss from gnarled branches.

Profound indeed had been the relief of everyone aboard the *Western Arrow* when, beyond a single challenging gun to which Mr. Bullwinkle had responded with his recognition signals, those long rows of batteries had remained silent. Matt decided that if Union gunboats ever steamed this far south they would be in for a very hot fight; at this point the Mississippi turned almost back upon its course, forcing traffic to hug the Eastern shore.

A surprising number of steamboats lay tied up along New Madrid's waterfront. The vessels most noticeable amid the huddle of transports, freighters and tugs, were two ironclad Confederate gunboats: *General Van Dorn* and *General Jeff Thompson*. Both were single-funnelled sidewheelers and undoubtedly much faster than any Eads ironclads Matt had ever beheld. Protected by casemates made of railroad rails bolted together, these small men-of-war appeared grimly efficient. Silently their crews tramped out on deck to watch this low, dull-black-painted sternwheeler come nosing cautiously into the levee.

Undoubtedly the white flag fluttering at the jackstaff where the Stars and Stripes previously had been shown, must have aroused curiosity, for numbers of Confederate soldiers, mostly clad in butternut-tinted uniforms or parts thereof, came shambling along the streets of New Madrid to loaf about the levee and gape at what they recognized to be a contraband runner. There were also a good many rag-clad Negroes in evidence but practically no civilians. Probably it was too early in the day. Sleet had given way to rain which lashed at the *Western Arrow's* superstructure and the wide guards running along her sides.

No sooner had the steamboat's landing stage been lowered than Matt, Cassius Bullwinkle and Philo Daingerfield tramped ashore and sought a small group of civilians wearing ponchos and stovepipe hats. Significantly, only a single military figure was on hand, a stout, red-bearded fellow wearing a wrinkled gray tunic which bore the braid of a major curling up its sleeves. His trousers, muddied to the knees, however, were of checkered wool and tucked into clumsy cowhide boots. He wore a black slouch hat with brim turned down to ward off the rain—képis evidently were not popular—or, more probably, unobtainable in this theatre of the war.

Matt, splashing through mire and horse droppings towards the group waiting under a rickety shed, reflected on what he had just seen about New Madrid. Very considerable improvements had been made and new batteries added at Fort Bankhead, situated on a bluff immediately upriver, and in Fort Thompson a little way downstream. Many more troops were in evidence. That the Confederate High Command intended to hold this strategically important town of New Madrid in force was evinced by the fact that on a near-by levee cannon of heavy calibre were being craned out of a pair of barges which must have been towed up from Memphis and Vicksburg.

Matt recognized several individuals standing in dripping raincapes and ponchos. Among them he was relieved to note Lieutenant-Colonel Hazeltine's corpulent figure, cadaverous Tom Jennings and dignified-appearing Mr. Luke Pender who resembled a deacon, but who could offer the subtlest of bribes. He was reputed to drive the sharpest bargains and to negotiate the crookedest agreements along the Upper Mississippi. Fat little Major Holmes of the Confederate Quartermaster Corps, Mat reflected, was in for a hard morning, whether he knew it or not. Presently he would shake his head, blow out his florid cheeks and agitatedly stroke at his ginger-colored beard in despair over the prices he must pay when he and the Southern civilian contractors sat down with Bullwinkle, Daingerfield and the master of the *Western Arrow*.

They all assembled on the second floor of New Madrid's dingy, white-columned Post Office to wrangle over and eventually settle upon prices and terms.

"My God, gentlemen, have you lost your wits? How dare you ask four dollars gold for a single pair of Army boots?" growled Deacon Pender. "Damn it, Bullwinkle, you know we just can't pay such prices; and three dollars for a blanket. Good God! On your last trip they weren't half that price."

Bullwinkle nodded equably. "I know, but prices are rising in St. Louis something fierce. You ain't heard nothin' yet; just you wait till you hear what quinine, epecac, ether and arnica will stand you; let alone a set of surgical instruments."

"Ah must protest," rumbled Lieutenant-Colonel Hazeltine, looking very anxious. "We cain't even think to pay such prices; 'specially for the medicines." Waving plump hands, he turned to confront Matt. "Sho'ly, suh, you wouldn't jack yo' prices on articles of mercy which will mend the sick and ease the sufferin' of the wounded?"

Matt drew a deep puff off the long seegar Tom Jennings had presented and replied steadily, "I am not, and never have been, particularly interested in the humanitarian aspects of this traffic with you. I know only that Mr. Daingerfield and I have risked our fortunes and a good many lives to fetch these supplies down to you."

"What else can you expect of a pack of damnyankees?" snarled Major Holmes, very red-faced in his faded gray uniform. "They'd sell their sisters into a whorehouse for a profit."

Angry color surged above Matt's collar. He cast a contemptuous glance at Pender and Jennings and another civilian contractor. "You can drop that kind of talk. Business is business. These gentlemen have ordered certain goods run through the Federal blockade. I have delivered them as agreed. I am not dealing with you, Major Holmes, and I guess you'd better get out of this place before I lose my temper." He turned to Jennings. "I didn't come down here to haggle with your Army."

"That's entirely correct," Bullwinkle agreed quickly. "I'm afraid you gentlemen will have to leave."

"By God, suh!" thundered Major Holmes, "I've half a mind to confiscate your boat and cargo and send you all down to Memphis in chains! How dare you so shamelessly bleed an Army fightin' fo' its home and rights?"

"Just you try confiscating our boat," Daingerfield's voice cut in incisively, "and when the word gets out you'll never receive another chest of percussion caps, case of harness, or another bolt of woollen cloth or—"

"—Why, damn your greedy guts, are you threatening us?"

Colonel Hazeltine spoke up. "That'll do, Major. Pender and Jennings are to negotiate the purchase. Reckon we'd better move on and let them negotiate with our Yankee friends."

The bicker ended with the two Confederate officers pulling on damp black slouch hats and stalking out, Major Holmes still breathing fire.

"Friends, let's get down to business," purred Mr. Pender. "But first—" He clapped his hands to summon a sad-faced Negro.

"Yas, suh, Misto' Pender?"

"Just you trot over to the Jackson House, Julius, and fetch back hot toddies all around and don't take all day. Br-r. It must have been infernal cold out on the River."

"It was until some addle-headed battery fired on us," grunted Bullwinkle. "Hazeltine didn't do a thorough job."

During the strained silence which ensued Matt surveyed his surroundings. If anyone had attempted to clean this office in over a year it didn't show it. Cobwebs, mud-wasp nests and mould defaced walls of ochre-tinted plaster and the floor was foul with dried mud, cigar ends and splashes of chewing tobacco. Unobtrusively he surveyed Pender and read beneath his benign expression the predatory and calculating lines. Mr. Jennings, however, radiated cordiality.

Philo demanded while tearing off a chew of tobacco, "Now what in the world ailed you fellers to bring in them Army officers before our private deal's completed?"

"Couldn't stop 'em," grunted Pender. "When Holmes saw your steamer heading inshore he came piking right over. Hazeltine came to—er—quiet him down, like he did."

Julius, the Negro, appeared bearing a tray of pungently steaming toddies, then stirred the fire in a cast-iron stove. Matt, still drawing upon his seegar, tried to recall what he'd seen during his progress through Jennings' warehouse on the way to Pender's office. Although plenty of cotton bales had been in evidence not one trace of Northern goods had he noted. Apparently the *Western Arrow's* last consignment, and certain others he knew about, had been reshipped to equip the armies of Generals Pillow, Floyd and Albert Sidney Johnson. What with the inexorable tightening of the Federal blockade, Messrs. Pender and Jennings must be very hard up for fresh stock.

Matt said, "I didn't particularly relish Major Holmes' threats."

"Don't take him seriously," Jennings reassured quickly. "Hazeltine will handle him. He won't dare touch the *Western Arrow* or anything aboard. You've noticed we've got plenty of cotton on hand for your return trip?"

"At how much?"

"Forty dollars the bale."

The New Englander burst into peals of laughter. "Forty dollars? My God, Jennings, are you crazy? Now that your President has clamped an embargo upon the export of cotton I can pick up bales for half that price at almost any landing below Cairo."

"Don't be too hard on us," pleaded Pender, a note of desperation in his tone. "What I'm offering is prime, long-staple cotton you can sell North for seventy-five dollars a bale and up."

"—If I don't get caught at it," the New Englander countered. "Since

Frenchy Frémont got relieved in the Western Department and your people have begun throwing up wild-cat batteries, running contraband's become a mighty risky business."

Presently the last hot toddy had been drained and serious dickering commenced. For Philo Daingerfield it remained astonishing to witness that down-East shrewdness with which Matt met the Southern contractors' every argument or objection with well-taken counter-objections.

"Better meet my prices," he warned them. "I know they're stiff but this consignment is top quality and it's dollars-to-doughnuts this may well be the last trip anybody will dare to risk. Once Foote's gunboats enter the Mississippi contraband running will be a thing of the past.

"Now just you take those ten surgeons' kits–" Matt's eyes narrowed –"they were manufactured in Sheffield, England, of the very best steel procurable. If you really want to help your people, this is likely your last chance. Once Donelson's taken, the gunboats–"

Unexpectedly Luke Pender spoke. "You're trying to cozen us, Mr. Everett! Fort Donelson *won't* be taken! There's a mighty powerful fort, mounting seventeen heavy cannons. *I know*. And six light batteries manned by the best blood of the Southwest."

"How d'you know so sure?" Philo tugged at his scraggly black goatee.

"Never mind," Pender replied, "but I'm certain on it. Besides, Generals Pillow, Floyd and Buckner have forgotten more about commanding troops than your drunken General Grant will ever learn."

"About that, I don't know," objected Matthew Everett, extending chilled hands to the stove, "but I *do* know the Army has a flotilla on the Ohio right now that pretty soon is going to clear this river down to Vicksburg."

"Them gunboats'll never pass Island Number Ten," Jennings objected while riffling a sheaf of invoices. "My God, man, you ought to see the batteries we got there! And the channel narrows so never a boat can get past 'thout gettin' blowed clean out of the water."

Matt turned, picked up his round felt hat. "Come along, Philo. Seems like these gentlemen prefer to talk strategy, not business. We'll keep on down to Memphis where they understand the situation better."

The chilly office resounded to a thud caused by Jennings' feet being pulled off a counter. He hurried forward, exuding good nature. "Now! Now! Mr. Everett, don't you take on so. Who said yo' prices ain't goin' to be met?"

Haggling continued but it lent Matt no peace of mind to watch a half-company of infantry, wearing blankets and ponchos for raincoats, tramp down to the levee and line up opposite the *Western Arrow's* landing stage.

Pender, when that movement had been pointed out, rose, muttered something in Jennings' hairy ear.

Bullwinkle saw, too, spoke sharply. "Yo' pardner, Major Holmes, seems to be getting horsy. Send down and warn him to get them Butternuts out of the way in a hurry or we'll pull right out and you can whistle for yo' goods—*and profit.*"

"I will," Pender promised. He returned promptly and, without further ado, signed bills of sale totalling something over one hundred and twenty-five thousand dollars, an example swiftly followed by Mr. Jennings and the third contractor, a sallow silent individual who in expression resembled a heartbroken bloodhound.

One and all, the Southern contractors sighed, but licked lips over the prospects in store. Percussion caps, surgeons' instruments, blankets and boots brought plenty of fine gold in this section of the Confederacy, remote as it was from the seacoast and suffering already from the strict Federal blockade of the Passes below New Orleans.

Presently Mr. Pender called his slave Julius and disappeared. At the end of a half hour he returned from the local bank lugging a bulging carpetbag and followed by his retainer bent under two large and heavy canvas sacks.

The Southerner exposed big, horse-like yellow teeth in a friendly grin. "Reckon you fellers air smart enough to reco'nize a good speculation when you see it. Eh, Mr. Everett?"

Matt smiled. "Might and then again, being a damnyankee, as your friend put it, I mightn't. Depends what this speculation is about; be it cotton or sugar, my partner and I will listen. But," he cocked his head towards the two canvas bags, "if it's got to do with Reb-er, Confederate currency, I'll say 'no' so long as you ask."

Color welled into Pender's gaunt visage as he offered a sheaf of crisp new but crudely printed bills. "Now don't be hasty," he urged. "Right here I've got some nice new banknotes fresh issued by the Sovereign State of Louisiana—worth a hundred cents to the dollar."

"And secured by gold or silver?"

The Southerner's lips tightened into colorless lines. "No, suh. This currency will be secured by a tariff on imports and from the sale of cotton in London; they will pay one hundred dollars a bale."

A wide grin spread slowly over Matt's sleet-stung countenance. "Now that's what Philo and I call an A-1 security; duties on goods that can't be imported because of the Union blockade, and unexportable cotton that's piled up and rotting on every levee between Cairo and Baton Rouge."

"Then you won't hazard a part of your price in Louisiana money?"

"No, sir."

Mr. Bullwinkle, the intermediary, took pains to remain cordial. He picked up and surveyed a blue-gray banknote. "Why, it's real pretty, but I'd like to gamble this here bill is so common-printed any counterfeiter owning a job press could run off a couple of thousands in a day's time. He cast Jennings a reproving glance. "Really, Tom, you had ought to know me better. Mr. Everett and Mr. Daingerfield and I don't aim to take our price in nothing but gold or silver or Union banknotes—as usual."

"By God, you *are* a hard lot!" Pender brushed the Louisiana notes onto the floor, heaved the carpetbag he had carried onto the table.

"Christian honesty, forbearance and decency get a man nowhere in this world," snapped Matt. "If you expect justice, you're an almighty fool. Now then, you've on hand the kind of money we want, or not?"

The Southern contractors grimaced and nodded. Then the silent one spoke at last. He snarled, "Reckon you Yankee bloodsuckers hev got us by the tail with a downhill drag, but I'll pray my God some wildcat battery blows you all clean out o' the River on yo' way home."

VIII VISITATION FROM THE EAST

St. Louis on this February afternoon of 1862 appeared to be heartily tired of such a long and unusually cold winter; the city appeared distinctly shabby—and busy. The most obvious change Matt noticed about the brick-paved streets and sidewalks—St. Louis had been very largely constructed of brick—was the absence of any great number of soldiers. He knew where they had gone, for, on the *Western Arrow's* last trip he had sighted one transport after another loaded to their guards with cheering, jeering troops, and towing barges deep-laden with mules, horses, fieldpieces, caissons, forage wagons and a multitude of other supplies.

Upon once more raising the long, low outline of St. Louis the contraband runner cruised slowly towards shore, riding deep under her cargo of cotton bales and hogsheads of brown sugar. To their surprise her officers noticed many gaps along the levee where, in the past, one laid-up steamboat had been crowded against another. The Federal Government must have either bought or chartered these idle craft by the dozen for that forest of rusty smoke pipes, spreader bars and guy wires to become so thinned out.

Still wearing a seaman's pea jacket, checkered woollen pants and a steamboat captain's leather-visored cap Matt Everett swung along towards his office. His tread along a muddy, wooden sidewalk was light because that long-staple cotton taken aboard at New Madrid promised fabulous profits. Even before he had departed on this trip the spinning mills in New England had been clamoring for raw cotton, price no object. Bidding recklessly against the Yankees for that slender trickle of cotton bales finding their way northward were the agents of French and British manufacturers, now truly desperate for raw material. Never in the history of North America had the price of cotton and sugar soared so high.

Matt chuckled while unknotting his muffler. Godreys! He was doing all right these days. In three short months he had banked above a hundred thousand sound United States dollars; probably as much as Josiah Cosby could have amassed in ten years!

He and Philo had been mighty lucky, he told himself, to have commenced operations just when they had. Not many more contraband runners could hope to get through once the Union's Western Flotilla devoted their efforts towards controlling the Mississippi.

To prevent this the Confederate Government now was collecting a fleet of sturdy, ocean-going vessels and river gunboats supposed to be faster and better-built than the Union's sluggish ironclad "turtles."

While in New Madrid Matt had learned the names of some of these gunboats. Owned by the Confederate Army they bore such military designations as *General Price*, *General Van Dorn*, *General Bragg*, *Colonel Lovell*, *General Jeff Thompson* and *General Sumter*, among others.

Commodore J. E. Montgomery, the vigorous and able Officer in Command had commenced carefully to patrol the Mississippi above Island Number Ten and, in accordance with President Jefferson Davis' embargo, he was doing his best to halt a northbound flow of cotton or the export of that invaluable staple. In addition to this hazard, so many independent Confederate batteries were being erected nowadays on both banks that soon it would become impossible for Cassius Bullwinkle, who had remained South for just that purpose, to suborn the commander of each and every one of these mushroom installations. Alas, only a single, well-aimed round shot was required to sink the *Western Arrow* or cripple her beyond repair.

From now on, Matt decided, he would stick to the safer, if somewhat less remunerative, business of inducing through bribery or subtle blackmail, certain Federal purchasing agents to pay through the nose for essential war materials.

Thinking he heard Philo's footsteps on the broad sidewalk he glanced back over his shoulder in time to see that wiry little individual duck into a saloon for a quick drink and the purchase of a bottle of champagne with which to celebrate the completion of this enormously successful cruise.

The hour being six o'clock no clerks were about the offices but night lights were glowing and the stoves were still warm. Matt tramped through the empty outer office and smiled to notice Mouser, the office cat, on guard at a promising rat hole. This feline, it turned out was the only living thing about the Western Arrow Supply Company's premises. On his rolltop desk Matt noted a huge pile of mail, bills of lading, inventories and other documents accumulated during his ten-day absence.

With satisfaction Matt noticed that during his absence two new desks had been added to the original four, graphic testimonial of his expanding business. His chief clerk also had procured some highly colored lithographs of various celebrated steamboats and had hung them about the accounting room walls. Once in his private office the New Englander lit and turned up a pair of lamps adorned by green-and-white ground-glass shades.

He commenced softly to hum "Old Zip Coon" for, come nine o'clock, he'd be driving out to that neat little house on Lucas Street in which he had installed Léonie Dulac. Lord! How wonderful it would be to feel gay and affectionate Léonie's soft and lively mouth upon his, to feel the eager pressure of her arms about his neck and to sniff her French scent so infinitely preferable to the River's damp reek and oily fumes exuded by the *Western Arrow's* engines.

Tonight he planned for the two of them to partake of a quiet and intimate supper but tomorrow he intended to hire a dining room at the Planters Hotel and give a triumphal banquet. To it he would invite key members of the "organization" such as General Mixer, Colonel Buttons and certain other officers who had proved conveniently preoccupied while contraband cargoes were being landed.

Of course Tobias Greenway would be included, along with Simon Quirk, his brother-in-law, if only to prove to the former that he had not misplaced his confidence. Philo would have to be left out on account of Greenway's presence but that worthy undoubtedly would occupy himself pleasantly enough in one of St. Louis' fashionable establishments. Being flush he might very well patronize Mrs. Wilber's Academy for Young Ladies, that most luxurious of all the bordellos.

In her house, so ran the gossip in various gentleman's clubs, Major-General Mixer had encountered an exquisitely lovely girl upon whom he had squandered a small fortune. Not a small part of this had been amassed through a convenient absent-mindedness concerning the *Western*

Arrow's activities—along with those of certain other vessels likewise employed.

Grinning to himself Matt settled into a swivelled armchair. By God, life *could* be good for the fellow who found sufficient courage to ignore conventions and take his chances with the law. He wondered how the redecoration of the handsome brick house purchased for his own occupancy out on Compton Street might be progressing.

Right now he could visualize lovely, dark-haired Léonie flying downstairs to answer his knock. He guessed she'd greet him with her usual scampering leap into his arms and gurgling cry of delight. Most likely she'd be wearing an azure ribbon about her throat, the sapphire-blue negligee with its rose-point lace collar, black garters, and yellow silk stockings with lace insets—and not another blessed thing.

Léonie possessed the invaluable gift of appearing wildly appreciative of anything he did for her; rapturously she would refer again and again to his gifts, even very little ones.

True, she had cause to be grateful. Had he not purchased her release from Madame Henriot's Myrtle Hotel, and the necessity of pleasing a succession of generally coarse and unattractive males? Now Léonie had a place of her own with a coffee-complexioned servant to care for her and only himself to please. Small wonder she was pathetically happy to pamper his sometimes insatiable tastes!

After removing his jacket Matt thumbed through a pile of correspondence, chiefly contracts to be negotiated, receipts and bills of sale.

From the door to the outer office Mouser uttered a chirrup of greeting and strolled in gently waving his ringed tail, gravely to reconnoitre a cane wastebasket which, more than once, had yielded a succulent mouse.

He was occupied in reading a long list of requirements forwarded by the Quartermaster Corps when subconsciously he heard a door open and close downstairs; undoubtedly that would be Philo. His gaze descended the long list of desired supplies. Two hundred bolts of dark blue woollen cloth, twelve gross woollen drawers. Someone cleared his throat. Instantly, Matt realized that it was not Philo who had entered his private office. He whirled about on his swivel chair to behold a complete stranger in stovepipe hat and a brown travelling cloak, standing in the entrance. With his left hand the man raised his hat at Matt's "Come in," and strode in, his small, steel-gray eyes flickering about.

"Good evening. Are you looking for me?" Matt demanded.

"You are Mr. Daingerfield?" queried the gaunt, clean-shaven stranger.

"No, I'm Mr. Everett."

"Mr. Matthew Everett?"

"Yes. And you are?"

"My name is Pennypacker," the stranger informed him in an even tone.

Matt thought he heard the downstairs office door open and close once more.

"Mr. Everett, I have brought you something from the East."

"From the East? I don't understand. I have no undertakings with Eastern firms. We do all our business around here."

"My errand hasn't to do with business," announced Mr. Pennypacker, in a deadly monotone, "This concerns a personal matter." He produced a Colt's forty-four revolver from beneath his cloak and levelled it at Matt's chest. "With Josiah Cosby's compliments, Mr. Everett!"

Matt had only time to realize that he must not have killed his father back there in Bangor before a crashing double report caused his office to resound. Something bit savagely at his right shoulder and spun him half about. Deafened, he lurched and would have collapsed if he hadn't caught the edge of his desk. Then, as the room reeled wildly about him, he was surprised to notice Mr. Pennypacker's stovepipe hat go rolling crazily off over the floor. Turning, he realized that the stranger was swaying, with eyes fixed and grown round as marbles. All at once Mr. Pennypacker's knees buckled and he collapsed onto the office floor like a huge puppet the strings of which had been cut.

Hatless and clutching a still-smoking derringer, Philo Daingerfield came running, an expression of concern on his coppery visage. "You hurt, Matt? You hurt bad?"

"Guess not," Matt gasped, then removed his left hand from the wound to stare incredulous at fingers grown brilliant with blood. "Guess I—I'm all right. Only w-winged me, high up."

Still steadying himself on the desk Matt watched his diminutive partner walk over with his foot to stir that long and sombre figure sprawled so slack upon the office's turkey-red carpet. Philo squatted onto his heels, parted the stranger's travelling cloak, and made a quick inspection. He straightened grinning. "Straight through the heart; pretty a shot as I've ever made."

"But—but—"

"Saw this feller going into our place," Philo explained while uncocking his little pistol's second barrel. "Wondered what his business could be at this hour so I hurried up." He fashioned a compress from a none-too-clean blue bandanna handkerchief. "Hold still, Matt, whilst I peel off your coat. Um. He winged you all right, but you're lucky. Iffen that bullet had struck a half inch lower you'd have had a lame shoulder for life. Here, take a jolt of this forty-rod." With his teeth Philo removed the cork from a flask jerked from his coattail.

"You heard what he said?" Matt demanded presently though his ears yet rang from the revolvers' report.

"Reckon so. Who in hell is this feller?"

Thickly Matt replied, "I've never seen him before."

"Who's Josiah Cosby?"

"My father. Guess he figured he'd better have me killed before I tried again to kill him. Please tighten that compress. I'm bleeding like a stuck hog."

IX THE GARMENT FACTORY

EARLY ON THE morning after her escape from Mrs. Wilber's "Academy" Phoebe hurried downstairs and consumed a meager breakfast before begging the loan of a newspaper. A careful perusal revealed the fact that female cutters and sewing machine operators were in considerable demand so, to Phoebe's infinite relief, she obtained employment in the garment factory of a Mr. A. J. Bulloch. The establishment was on Plum Street right across from the terminal of the St. Louis & Iron Mountain Railroad.

At first the work seemed easy enough, making infantry tunics for the Army, but the light was bad and the loft ill-ventilated and overcrowded.

After two days the dizzy spells recurred, that, and a sharp aching in her head. Worst of all she twice was taken violently nauseated, so much so that on one occasion she had to be sent home and her pay of ten dollars a week docked accordingly.

She managed, however, to keep on, thanks to the kind offices of the forelady who pitied this vague-eyed girl with the numbed expression.

But eventually Phoebe's dizziness increased until she could no longer sew a straight seam, nor could she guide the thread into her needle's eye.

On a Saturday night—they all worked until seven from seven in the morning—the proprietor beckoned her into his office. "Sorry, Miss Whidden, got to let you go. Mrs. Austin has hung on to you as long as she could, but I ain't in business for my health and the Quartermaster's hollering for these uniforms like a pig under a gate."

Like a stone, Phoebe's heart plummeted within her. "But—but Mr. Bulloch, what can I do? Where can I go?"

"God knows," said he carelessly. "I suppose you will land another job when you get to feeling better." He turned his back.

The results of her concussion grew no better, so for a week, Phoebe was forced to lie about watching her pitiful supply of cash dwindle. She had simply had to buy a few underthings, a decent pair of shoes and some toilet essentials.

By the time she had paid Mrs. Mallory her week's rent, a half dollar, a quarter and a twenty-five-cent shinplaster were all that lay on the top of her chest of drawers. Of course there was that little gold and garnet ring Loretta had bestowed; and when she secured, and promptly lost, her next job, she was forced to pawn it for an outrageously small amount, not enough to buy her more than a few skimpy meals. She certainly was missing those hearty repasts she must have enjoyed in the past because she tired so easily nowadays. Her clothes hung with increasing looseness upon her.

Again and again she tried to hold a job but always that dreadful dizziness and occasional nausea sent her out onto the street again to be pushed and jostled by the crowds that seemed forever to be on the move in St. Louis. Never had the city been so populous, it seemed. There was a sharp scarcity of lodgings, particularly of the inexpensive sort, so it came as a particularly damaging blow when Mrs. Mallory, having accorded her a week's grace, curtly informed her that she would have to move elsewhere. Being a poor woman herself, she could not afford to maintain even a single unproductive room.

And so on a chill Saturday evening, Phoebe Whidden stumbled down the worn stone steps and again drifted aimlessly in the general direction of the river.

If only she weren't so hungry! If only she knew of a single friend. Of course there was Loretta Bentalou and Cleodene, but she didn't dare go near the Academy even if she could locate it.

Uncertainly her feet carried her downtown where saloons, restaurants and hotel fronts blazed with light. It was late enough now for streetwalkers, young ones who looked well enough by daylight, to begin plying their trade.

Suddenly overcome by weakness, Phoebe sank onto a bench and listlessly watched the traffic go by. She saw a provost guard frog-marching a pair of yelling soldiers off to some guardhouse.

Had she begun to mend again? Possibly. She hadn't been ill nor suffered a pain for nearly three days now. Perhaps she could keep a job? But this was Saturday evening. No factories would be open until Monday and she was penniless, without a possession in the world save the clothes she wore. Her head sank onto her chest and she huddled into Clairette's mantle. Her feet had become damp clear through due to the heavy moisture on the streets and a wind off the Mississippi was icy. Dully she became aware that someone had halted before her. She looked up into the face of a Union officer, a plump, well-fed looking individual with rather a friendly expression about his eyes.

"May I sit down, miss, or are you awaiting someone?"

She nodded. After all it was something to have someone to talk to. "Now for the life of me I can't understand why a pretty girl like you should be sitting here all alone. Haven't you any friends?"

She shook her head.

"Where are you from?"

"The East."

"Oh." There was a world of meaning in the monosyllable. "Now look," said he, "I have just come in from upriver and I don't know many people here in town, either, so, since we are both lonely, what say we keep each other company?" He spoke eagerly, studying her features by the fading light. "You look like a nice girl and one I wouldn't be ashamed to be seen with." When he took her hand she made no effort to withdraw it. "Now listen, Miss–?"

"Whidden."

"I'm in something of a fix. Friend of mine's giving a big dinner and he invited all the people he does business with to come and bring a partner." He unhooked the front of his overcoat, fumbled and presently fetched out a seegar case.

"When is this dinner?" The very sound of the word made Phoebe faint with longing.

"Tonight, not till about nine o'clock, so you will have time to go home and fix up. I'll call for you whenever you say."

"Thank you, Mr.–"

"Major Tucker, Charley Tucker. I'm from–" but he broke off and said nothing more about his home.

"But you can't come for me, Major Tucker. You see I have no home. I–I was put out of my boardinghouse today. I–was behind in the rent."

"Sa-ay! That's hard lines, Miss Whidden. Haven't you got any clothes, I mean party clothes, put away somewhere?"

A faint shake of her head was all he got for reply.

"Well then, look, suppose–say, you're hungry aren't you? I thought so. Well, tell you what let's do. We will go over there to that restaurant and get you something to line your ribs. Then," he snapped his finger ecstatically, "we'll go shopping; get you a dress and some pretty things. Matt's fussy about how our lady friends are turned out."

There was nothing for it but to agree. "And what about after the dinner?" she murmured as he assisted her to her feet.

He winked. "We'll see about that when the time comes. I guess you'll feel a lot more like being playful after the party."

"I—I—really should tell you that I won't. I—"

"Oh, nonsense! Come along now, and let's have a plate of stew."

X PHOEBE WHIDDEN

THE PLANTERS HOTEL's principal private dining room had seldom appeared so resplendent. In a pair of ornate cut-glass chandeliers, in three candelabra and in several sconces, gleamed dozens of candles to cast a warm, yellow-gold radiance over a long, elaborately decorated table set for fourteen. From one of St. Louis' few hothouses, ferns and great sheaves of pink and white roses had been procured with no regard to expense. Before each place stood a rank of wine glasses ranging from tiny liqueurs to long-stemmed champagne goblets.

Following Mr. Everett's positive instructions the Planters Hotel's management had produced their very best silverware, china and napery. Each dinner chair had arms—lest its occupant become unsteady, as was expected—and a handsome goldbound pigskin case of seegars or a small package done up in pink tissue paper and white ribbon occupied each place plate, while upon a gleaming sideboard sweated a whole battery of champagne buckets. Awaiting guests with plainer tastes stood a formidable array of whiskey bottles for the most part showing famous brand labels yellowed with age. A rich red carpet and yellow-painted walls lent an atmosphere of warmth if not of taste.

"Everything is to yo' satisfaction, suh?" demanded Prescott, the urbane mulatto headwaiter who would officiate.

"Yes. The table looks very well," Matt smiled. Godfreys! What would the folks back in Dexter say to such splendor? Even Josiah Cosby most likely would gape over this lavish display of hospitality. With each passing moment Matt was feeling oddly relieved—not only that he was not in fact a murderer, but that Cosby had sunk so low as to hire an assassin. He, Matt, at least had had the courage personally to confront and to shoot down his enemy. Yessir, he now stood several cuts above his father in the matter of attempted murder.

Prescott said, "Everything has been done, suh, just like when Gen'ral Frémont was here. What with livin' in foreign parts so much that Gen'ral knew how to entertain them Frenchies, Hungarians and Eyetalians he used to keep on his staff."

"Looks elegant to me." A small sigh of relief escaped the New Englander for, of course, he knew mighty little about such fashionable entertaining, and Léonie, giggling and radiant in her new, wide-skirted dinner dress of pale rose looped in green and secured with many little bows of crimson velvet, knew even less. Too bad that when Léonie took a glass too many her speech and table manners became something to blush over; she could sing, however, and, under sufficient inducement, would remove the more cumbersome elements of her raiment in order to execute a sprightly French dance which called for a deal of high kicking. Nor was Léonie averse to revealing the slim perfection of shapely white limbs—she always called them "limbs" during her more refined moments.

Léonie now approached and passed a slender arm about Matt's waist. "Oh, Matt, this sho'ly is the elegantest spread that *evah* was." Ecstatically she rolled liquid eyes upwards, then smiled tenderly. "How's your po' hurt shoulder feel tonight, honey?"

"So–so. The doctor said it's nothing to worry about. Look," he led her over to a mirror. "Do you notice any bulge made by the bandages?"

"No, honey. Dr. Lamson did a real clevah job. I love all them little ruffles on yo' shirt front and that big diamond stud. I do declare, Matt, you are the handsomest man I ever did lay eyes on."

"And you've maybe seen two," he laughed, but continued to inspect his reflection. During the past six months he guessed he had aged considerably and now looked older than his age what with his jaw line hardened and his brow divided by a pair of small V's that had not been there the day he called upon Mr. Stetson. His yellow sideburns now had become real adornments instead of just yellow fuzz and he must have filled out quite a lot, for all he carried no fat at all. Somehow, his high and rather prominent cheekbones had become more pronounced.

He examined the set of his white tie as arranged by Marcus, the dapper colored barber who customarily shaved him and cut his hair. Marcus, or so he claimed, had once been personal valet to Mr. William Harvey, one of the richest men in St. Louis, and it had been he who had told him where to have this elegantly cut dress suit made, and where to purchase his spotless white waistcoat, ruffled dress shirt and gleaming patent-leather shoes.

While standing before a cheery open fire and listening for the arrival of the first of his guests, Matt reached into his coattail and produced a leather-covered small box.

"Prescott," he said to the mulatto headwaiter, "I shan't require your attendance until my guests arrive."

Prescott bowed and withdrew with the impressive decorum of a well-trained colored servant. Matt then kissed Léonie on the mouth and, capturing her right hand, slipped a ring upon its little finger.

"Now look!"

When she saw the size and hue of that emerald glowing between two smaller diamonds the dark girl's breath came in with a sibilant rush, then escaped in an ecstatic squeal as she literally flung herself upon him and caused him to wince from the pain she caused his wounded shoulder. Her eyes filled while she smothered his face with kisses and, cooing, hugged his waist like a small and wildly excited child.

"Oh, Matt, Matt! Why are you so awfully good to me? After all, you know I'm but a cheap little—"

His imperative gesture cut her short. "That will do, my dear. I know only that from the beginning you have been wonderfully sweet and gentle and kind to me during a—a difficult part of my life. I've made a killing this trip, so I'm rich now—it's only right you should have a share in my good fortune." He smiled a warmer and more genuine smile than she had ever remembered. This was because he no longer deemed himself a murderer, but of course she could not know that.

After dabbing at her eyes with a tiny lace handkerchief plucked from between ripe and half-exposed bosoms Léonie peered up in mock horror. "Mercy! Let me wipe off that lip rouge. I hear someone in the corridor."

The private dining room's door of well-polished mahogany swung open to admit big and muscular Colonel Buttons together with that dainty Corybant from Mrs. Wilber's Academy who called herself Clairette Vansant. In a sparkling gold and dark blue dress uniform with black tie Colonel Buttons was looking uncommonly handsome despite receding red hair and a constellation of freckles across his scalp.

"Congratulations on your last voyage," he boomed, taking Matt's hand. "I am delighted on its success." Colonel Buttons should be pleased, Matt mused; he'd just cleared a cool three thousand as his share, and without running the least risk.

The two girls giggled and smiled as, expertly, they appraised one another's gowns and jewellery. Claire immediately noticed Matt's latest gift.

"Merciful Heavens!" she gasped. "What a perfectly *go'geous* ring! My, you're one lucky girl, Léonie!" She cast Colonel Buttons a quick look, managed to pout a little. "Co'se *I* could never hope to have anything so fine." The big colonel only grinned and patted her on the rear.

At this point Tobias Greenway waddled in fairly bulging out of a frock coat and leading by the hand a frightened, big-eyed brunette who could scarcely have passed her eighteenth birthday.

"This here's Pauline. Just come to town," chuckled Greenway.

In a tight and poorly cut gown of flame-colored silk ornamented by much too much jet beadwork the new arrival appeared desperately unhappy as, with lips compressed, she greeted the other female guests. Because this Pauline appeared to possess breeding and her voice sounded rich and well modulated, Matt felt more than a little sorry for her.

"That was great news 'bout our Flotilla capturing Fort Henry, ain't it?" Greenway demanded from the sideboard as he poured himself a half tumbler of bourbon. "Most of them gunboats was built right here."

"Sure is," agreed Buttons shortly. "Unless I miss my guess the River batteries will be firing victory salutes again pretty soon."

"Again?" Matt demanded.

"Saw a telegram this afternoon at Headquarters; claimed Grant's Army is closing in on Fort Donelson from three directions while Andy Foote's flotilla is attacking up the Cumberland. Of course what with this terrible winter weather the Rebels just *might* hold out. We know Donelson's a lot stronger than Fort Henry and held by a powerful garrison."

"We damn' well better take it," grunted Greenway, "else we'll never do business in Nashville this year."

Presently Simon Quirk and another contractor appeared escorting bejewelled, overdressed and excitedly giggling young women.

Promptly all four made for the sideboard.

"Wonder what's keeping the General?" demanded a major in the Quartermaster Corps. "He left before me—"

"Probably he's making his manners to Mrs. Wilber and his Sultana." Buttons laughed, then turned to his host. "I say, Everett, have you ever seen this, er, lady friend of Mixer's? The one known as Loretta Bentalou?"

"No, but I hear tell she's a raving beauty."

"This Loretta's not only extremely handsome," Buttons informed him, "but she's also damned good fun. She's got old Mixer turning handsprings whenever she smiles at him."

Prescott and a discreet assistant appeared; champagne corks popped and gleaming glasses were lifted. None too subtly, Léonie displayed Matt's ring and obviously revelled in the other girls' envy.

The champagne took quick effect on Léonie. She sidled possessively up to the host. "Please, honey, how much longer we got to wait fo' Major Tucker and the General? Everybody else is here and we-all are just starvin' to death."

A quick shake of the head from Prescott warned Matt that the main course of buffalo hump and wild duck could not be held back much longer without disastrous results.

Chattering excitedly over their place favors the guests were about to seat themselves when the dining room's double door was eased open and Prescott's pompous voice announced, "Majo'-General Mixer an' Miss Bentalou."

Every head in the room swung about, epaulettes flashed and the guests hesitated, hands on the backs of their chairs. A flash of golden buttons and a yellow sash encircling a corpulent middle shone at the entrance.

Léonie's hand swung over to nestle within Matt's. "Honey, don't you *dare* to think this—this Bentalou wench is prettier than me!"

"I won't." Matt smiled and started forward to greet his guest of honor.

"Well, well," boomed Mixer, "this *is* quite an affair! Sorry to be late, Matt, but I'd some papers to sign."

"You are not the last, sir. Charley Tucker's not here yet."

"Good. Good," said the General accepting a tall bourbon highball. "Oh, yes, this is my friend Miss Bentalou—Matt Everett, dear."

The girl's carefully made-up eyes widened a trifle. "I've heard a lot about you, sir, but nobody ever said you were so handsome."

Matt bowed laughing. "That's because you evidently don't associate with liars. Some champagne, perhaps?"

In rising impatience Matt glanced at his watch. It showed almost half after eight. What the devil could be delaying Charley Tucker? He was about to signal his guests to seat themselves when the private dining room's door handle rattled. Prescott opened it and announced, "Major Tucker and—and friend!"

Matt had started forward to greet the last of his guests but halted with hand outstretched. His jaw had dropped ludicrously open.

Léonie watched her patron's expression freeze as there swept into the dining room a tall young woman whose red-gold hair had been trained into an overly elaborate coiffure which left a single curl dangling over the pallid perfection of a bare shoulder. In a crinolined gown of garish red satin looped with jet bugles, Major Tucker's companion advanced, with clumsily painted lips forming an uncertain smile.

"How do you do, Mr. Everett?" she cried, dark blue eyes wavering. "Major Tucker has been telling me all kinds of nice things about you."

Suddenly gray-faced, Matt swayed before the dinner table much as he had after Mr. Pennypacker's bullet had struck.

"Phoebe!" The name barely was audible. "What are you doing like this?"

XI MR. EVERETT'S DINNER PARTY

In all Prescott's years of service he had never witnessed a moment quite so dramatic. All in an instant the Planters Hotel's private dining room had become transformed into a well of stillness peopled by wax figures.

The officers, gentlemen and the girls stood rigid, as if confronted by a haunt. Everyone was goggling at this young woman, lovely despite her garish paint and the crude arrangement of her hair, at the obvious bewilderment of her ashen-faced host.

"Phoebe Whidden," rasped Loretta Bentalou. "Oh, my God, you did it after all!"

"I say, Loretta," General Mixer turned a big, blunt and florid head; his flaring black sideburns commencing nervously to quiver. "Why should my friend Everett address this lady as Phoebe?"

"I don't know, but her name *is* Phoebe—Phoebe Whidden."

"How did you know that?" rasped Matt.

"I knew her at Mrs. Wilber's—"

"*Mrs. Wilber's!* Oh my God!" Livid, he whirled upon Major Tucker's companion. "What were you doing in a place like that?"

"As if you didn't know," chuckled Tobias Greenway.

"What were you doing there?"

"I—I was sewing," Phoebe replied in a hushed voice and not for an instant did her great, dark blue eyes desert Matt's frozen countenance.

"Sewing?" chuckled General Mixer. "Wild oats, eh, my dear."

"No!" Loretta started to explain. "She was hurt and lost her memory. She wasn't—"

"Be still!" Matt drew a long, shuddering breath.

So, despite everything, Phoebe Whidden *had* carried out that threat made in her mother's kitchen. Somehow she had followed him out here. Dear God in Heaven! Candelabra, mirrors, faces spun and swayed before Matt's agonized eyes as the appalling truth became inescapable. On his account she stood yonder, still beautiful despite cheap finery and daubed features. She could not be one whit better than Léonie now clinging so tenaciously to his sleeve and hissing, "Don't you dare pay attention to that hussy or I'll scratch her eyes out. *I'm* your gal. Remember!"

Still Matt stood glaring into Phoebe's wide and bewildered eyes.

Léonie in desperate gaiety cried, "Come on, folks, let's sit down and eat. Me, I'm simply starvin'!"

Had her voice been the squeak of a mouse Matt might have paid more attention. He shook himself free, walked the length of the table, turned to plump and definitely bewildered Major Tucker.

"This girl is my fiancée," he announced in a clear, penetrating voice.

To General Mixer he said, "Will you kindly assume my place as host? I must leave."

Major Charley Tucker turned to Phoebe. "What in hell *is* this?" he exploded, but she remained rigid, clutching the back of a chair and staring dazedly at Matt's tall, black-clad figure.

Slowly, wonderingly, Phoebe's gaze then wavered over to her escort. "I don't understand this, really I don't, Major Tucker. I seem somehow to recognize Mr. Everett, and at the same time I can't remember where I've seen him before."

"Of course not!" shrilled Loretta Bentalou. "I tell you her head was hurt, badly, in a train wreck. Beyond her name she can't remember——"

"—Of course I won't take over as host! Really, Matt, this is nonsense, sheer, utter nonsense," the General broke in loudly. "Let's have done with this play-acting, dramatic as it is, and drink a toast to our generous and handsome host and to his luscious Léonie."

"No! Please don't."

"Come off it, Matt, don't act so silly." Again Léonie pulled at Matt's sleeve, causing him to wince because of his wounded shoulder.

Greenway pushed his enormous bulk forward. "Sure you ain't already had a few drinks too many, Matt? Don't blame you what with that mean trip upriver and getting the *Western Arrow* piled up on that sandbar for a while."

"No." The New Englander's voice was hollow, lifeless. "You take over, Colonel. Miss Whidden and I are departing."

"Oh, no. We are *your* guests!" Colonel Buttons protested. Major Tucker stepped before his companions and the double row of buttons descending his solid figure flashed warningly.

"Look here, Matt," he boomed, "I don't know what you have in mind, but Miss Whidden is *my* partner. You're going too far, much too far, with your jest."

"This is no jest. This—this girl is from my home town. We were engaged—"

"Who is she?"

The New Englander's eyes began to glisten. "That's of no importance here. She is leaving this place with me at once."

"Phoebe'll do nothing of the sort!" roared Charley Tucker, going scarlet as an outraged turkey cock. "I escorted her here and she'll stay with me."

Léonie commenced to wail. "Oh, Matt, honey, how can you shame me like this? Ain't I always been good and agreeable to whatever you asked of me?"

The sound of Matt's breathing was momentarily audible in the brilliantly lit dining room. "You have, Léonie," he said without looking at her. He kept his gaze fixed on Tucker's enraged countenance. "Léonie, the house in Lucas Street, the carriage and pair, everything I have given you and five thousand dollars, will be yours."

"Oh, honey boy! Ain't you just too sweet and gen'rous fo' words!" Léonie actually danced a few steps, then gulped a glass of champagne.

"Heah's to you, honey, and yo' new gal." She had the temerity to wink at Greenway. Certainly she should please him better than that skinny, washed-out looking Pauline.

Returning his gaze to Phoebe's immobile features, Matt stepped forward. "Phoebe, you do remember me?"

"No," she replied in a stifled voice. "But you are the first person I have met who knows who I am—who I was, rather. Sometimes I—I almost seem to remember, but I never can quite. I do feel, though, that we knew each other somewhere."

"Dexter."

"Dexter? Where is Dexter?"

Matt drew himself up, offered Phoebe his arm. "I'll tell you later. But now we are leaving."

"Like the devil you are!" roared Major Tucker. "You think I'm going to stand by like a ninny and let you take away a girl I've just squandered sixty dollars on?"

In a calm but menacing voice Matt informed him, "You've made a mistake, Charley. This lady will not be your companion tonight. Her real self, whom you've never met, is sweet and innocent."

"This trollop sweet and innocent?" chuckled Mixer. "God, but that's rich!"

Such a roar of shrill and raucous laughter made the dining room resound that Prescott slipped quietly out into the hall. If he knew the signs he reckoned a couple of police officers would come in handy mighty soon.

"God damn it, Everett, you *are* drunk!" Tucker shouted and doubled his fists. "If you think for one minute I am going to let my little friend go with you—"

"Phoebe," Matt called above the tumult, "will you do as I say? Will you come with me?"

Piteous uncertainty became evident in Phoebe's manner as she glanced first from one then to the other of the principal figures.

"Don't you dare listen to this crazy, drunken fool! Come here to me," cried Tucker.

Certain of the guests, experienced in brawls, caught up bottles while the girls retreated, twittering, across the dining room, not altogether displeased by the drama of this moment.

"Since you seem to know who I really am, Mr. Everett," Phoebe's voice sounded jerky, toneless, "I'll do as *you* tell me."

Moving with a speed surprising in a man of his bulk, Tucker aimed a hard swing. Experienced by now in the matter of rough-and-tumble, Matt easily avoided the blow and countered with an uppercut which, although it caused agony to his hurt shoulder, snapped the major's head back so violently that he reeled into the table, then fell amid a crashing of china, glassware and silver.

"Stop it," roared the General. "Stop it, I say!"

"Jesus God!" Greenway gasped, goggle-eyed. "You gone crazy, Matt? Mixer and Tucker can put every damn' one of us out of business."

"I don't give a thin damn if he does." Matt was standing over the fallen officer.

Aware that blood from the reopened wound was trickling down his shoulder blade, he offered Phoebe an arm and conducted her to the doorway. There he paused long enough to call back, "Sorry my party turned out this way. Good luck to you all. Have yourselves a good time."

"Where are you taking me?" Phoebe Whidden inquired from the depths of Matt's opera cloak.

"To a house I've just bought," came his stony response barely audible above the brisk clatter of the horseshoes over paving. "Although it's only partially furnished I guess we can make out there overnight."

Because a warm rain had washed the brick pavements clear of snow and ice, the rasping of their hack's steel tires sounded very loud. Phoebe peered sidewise at the tall, tight-jawed figure beside her. He had not delayed to borrow an overcoat so his ruffled shirtfront shone crisply in the light of the carriage lamps.

She started. "What's that on the back of your hand?"

"Blood, I expect. During my little debate with Charley Tucker I must have opened a wound I suffered the other day."

At this hour many hacks, omnibuses and private carriages were travelling along Gratiot Street with lights gaily dancing and flaring. By their passing radiance Matt's yellow hair occasionally gleamed bright as polished brass.

"Tell me who I really am. Please, Mr. Everett." Phoebe demanded from the hack's musty-smelling shadows.

"For Heaven's sake don't call me 'Mr. Everett.' Can't you recall me? I'm Matt–Matthew Hovey." He winced, caught her by both hands and peered intently into her great dark eyes. "We grew up together in Dexter, Maine."

"Hovey?" the girl repeated uncertainly. "Hovey? Seems I have heard that name before."

"You have. You've heard that name all your life. My mother, Abigail Hovey, taught you to read, to write and to figure."

"Did we really grow up together?" Phoebe's confusion was pitiful to behold.

"We did," his powerful profile became puckered as he nodded. "Your father is Azel Whidden. He's a farmer." In desperation he queried, "Can't you remember anything at all about Dexter?"

She sighed and, timidly, her hand came to rest upon his. Some of the blood on it stained a black velvet bow gracing her wrist. "Mr. Everett, er, Matt, I wish I could, but I can't seem to recall a thing before I was brought here to St. Louis." Suddenly her eyes flickered up. "No. That's not so. The other day I think I remembered something; a black-and-white collie dog I once owned, but I can't recall his name."

"It was Benjie."

"Benjie! Of course." In the semi-darkness her teeth glistened in a delighted smile. "What can my parents—do I have parents?"

"You had last November," he assured her gently and tucked his uninjured arm about her shoulders.

"Whoa, you Columbus!" The colored hack driver pulled up. "Heah we is, suh. Number Twenty-eight Compton Street. Dat right?"

"That's correct." Once the driver had clambered down to unfold his carriage's step Matt presented him with a silver dollar, rare in these days of little hard money.

"A whole silber dollah! De Good Lawd bless you, suh! Hopes you and de pretty lady has you a right elegant time." The old Negro's teeth shone in the carriage lamps.

"Be quiet!" Matt snapped and led Phoebe across the sidewalk and into the vestibule of his recent purchase. When he tugged the bell handle a melodious tinkling commenced deep within this handsome red brick edifice. It being both cold and raw on the stoop Matt commenced silently to curse Lambert, his valet's slowness. Presently a lamp glimmered through the vestibule door's ground-glass panels.

"Who dat?" quavered a voice.

"It's Mr. Everett. Open up and be quick about it."

Lambert, otherwise clad in a nightgown and cap, was wearing a shawl about stooped shoulders. A fringe of white hair gleamed in silvery contrast to his wrinkled and sable features as, hastily, he slipped off the guard chain, saying, "Why Misto' Everett, Ah figgered you wouldn't come home till mawnin'."

"You thought wrong."

"Mah Gawd, suh! Yo' wound's done opened up again?"

"Yes. But the bleeding has stopped. Go make us a pot of coffee, then get into your clothes."

"Yassuh, directly, suh." Backing away Lambert goggled at this thin young woman with the red-gold hair who stood gazing curiously down the long and completely unfurnished hallway.

"In there," Matt opened a door to his right. Within was a study obviously partially decorated but containing chairs and a sofa. A sea-coal fire blinking redly in a grate gave off a heartening warmth.

Two elaborate brass table lamps soon revealed the girl in red to the last detail, pitilessly betrayed the presence of paint on her cheeks and lips.

"I'm chilled right through." Phoebe for the first time was speaking in her normal voice. "Is there anything?"

In silence Matt disappeared, returned bearing two small glasses and a cut-glass decanter. Frowning, he poured twin drinks, then dropped heavily onto a chair. Phoebe he knew to be barely twenty years of age, yet wearing that absurd coiffure and clad in that outrageously decolleté gown which revealed more than concealed her bosom, she appeared to be years older. The girl settled herself near the fire and held out her hands to its warmth.

Awkwardly, with his left hand he tossed her his handkerchief. "In Heaven's name scrub off that dreadful paint."

Matt jumped up in anguish and for a while stood staring down at her, a tall figure silhouetted against the fireplace's crimson glow. "During the past few months some evil things have happened to both of us. But you are not to be blamed that they happened—only I."

"Evil?" She looked up from the fire at which she was warming her chilled hands. "In what way?"

"You have become a—a fancy woman," he cried in a quivering voice, "and I a shameless traitor. Phoebe, Phoebe, I've cheated and extorted money from patriots risking their very lives in a noble cause. I've gambled, I've whored and guzzled myself into drunkenness more often than I can remember. Oh, Abigail Hovey's bastard son has become a fine specimen of manhood!"

The self-accusations poured from his lips in jerky, bitter sentences. To it all Phoebe listened round-eyed, with lips compressed and sitting bolt upright. "Ah, uh,—what did you say you were, Mr. Everett?"

"Never mind. What tortures me most is, in effect, that I'm responsible for your—transformation."

"You responsible, Matthew? I—I don't understand. How *could* you be responsible for what happened to me?"

He swallowed hard. "I'll tell you. When I learned that my mother had been tricked by an illegal marriage ceremony, and that I, therefore, was illegitimate, I swore I would do three things. First, I'd leave Dexter; second, I'd kill the man who had dishonored and maltreated my mother; and then I'd hunt down the mock minister who had officiated. Don't you remember that time in your mother's kitchen when I told you I was leaving Dexter forever?"

"You told me you were going to leave?" Phoebe repeated wonderingly, and her petticoats rustled softly when she shifted on her chair. "And what did I say to that?"

"You swore that you loved me." His voice deepened in his wretchedness. "You said that if I went away you would follow me, no matter where I went."

"I see. Then *I* was in love with you?" she demanded gravely. "Were *you* in love with me?"

"I've loved you," he told her, "ever since you were a stork-legged little girl with long red pigtails."

"Oh. Then we were really promised, just as you said at the Planters Hotel?"

He flushed. "Well, I felt so and so did you, although we never did come right out and say so." Forgetting his wound, Matt poked the fire, then straightened painfully.

"You followed me," he informed her, "how closely I don't really know, but apparently Mrs. Wilber brought you to St. Louis still unconscious from an injury received in a wreck. You must have been struck on the head hard enough to make you lose your memory. So," he urged in desperate earnestness, "always remember that you can't ever be held responsible for falling into Mrs. Wilber's clutches—and her way of life."

"But—but, Matt. I didn't fall into 'her way of life' as you say."

Infinite pain was in his eyes. "No? Then why are you dressed like this —like a fancy girl?"

"I—I was friendless—desperate. Please, Matt—let me tell you what's happened since I came or was brought to St. Louis."

While the fire crackled and snapped Phoebe talked on and on. Often she paused to refresh her memory. She pressed her temples as, forlornly, she concluded. "I—I hope you'll believe me, Matt. I left Mrs. Wilber's as soon as Loretta told me what was in store. Really I did. As for Major Tucker, when I met him tonight I had no place to stay, no money—and I was hungry. . . ."

A sibilant sigh escaped him. "I do believe you—despite appearances. But will anyone else? Surely everyone there, the General, Colonel Buttons, Greenway and the rest would swear that you're no better than Léonie, Loretta and those other fancy girls."

He stood up. "We're leaving St. Louis as fast as we humanly can. By the first ferry tomorrow. I—I hate this city because of the disgraceful things I've done and stood for. Can't get away fast enough."

Her dark blue eyes lingered on his strong, weather-beaten face.

"So my name really is Phoebe Whidden?" The girl spoke in a confused monotone. "I come from a village in the State of Maine called Dexter. My father's name is Azel and my mother's is Nancy."

He smiled delightedly. "But I *haven't* told you your mother's name. That's come back of its own accord. Oh, Phoebe dear, let us pray God that before long you'll remember everything before your accident."

A knock sounded at the door and Lambert appeared, clutching a battered stovepipe hat. "Yessuh? You got errands fo' me?"

From a billfold Matt counted out fifty dollars in crisp notes on the Exchange Bank of St. Louis. He said quietly but distinctly, "I know it will be difficult to carry out my instructions at this time of night but I want you to buy, I don't care where, this young lady, a complete outfit of decent clothing. Understand, garments which must be plain and warm."

Lambert's white-fringed head bobbed several times. "Yassuh. Ah expects Ah knows right where Ah kin find 'em. Over to Sixteenth Street lives a lady from Arkansaw what been sellin' off her daughter's clo'es. She runned off with a gambling man."

"Good!" Matt once more was the Captain issuing orders. "One more thing. You're to locate Mr. Daingerfield, he's probably at Mrs. Wilber's place." He winced. "Tell him he *must* meet me at our place of business tomorrow morning at seven o'clock sharp. Understand?"

Never had Lambert seen his master wear so grim an expression. He ducked his head several more times. "Yas, suh, yassuh. Ah'll sho'nuff find Misto' Daingerfield."

Once the servant had shuffled out Phoebe rose, came sweeping forward, petticoats whispering under her wide hoop skirt. "What do you plan, Matthew? I want, I need to know. I'm so dreadfully confused."

"Tomorrow morning we will be married at the first possible moment," he informed her gravely. "Then we leave St. Louis forever."

"Oh. I see. But what of you?"

He drew a deep breath. "I intend to leave everything I've come by here to my partner—he's the only loyal and good friend I've found since leaving home. When we board that ferry I'll have with me only the three hundred dollars I brought West with me."

"But you—aren't you abandoning a small fortune?"

He jerked a nod. "I suppose so, but it's a tainted fortune—which I wish to play no part in our future. God willing, we shall live as decent, self-respecting citizens."

She peered up into his drawn features, then kissed him sweetly and whispered, "Where shall we go from here?"

"I don't know for certain. Possibly to Cincinnati or Louisville. I heard recently that a man named Ellet is converting a number of Ohio River boats into steam rams. Perhaps I can find employment with him."

XII NEW ASSIGNMENT

On this uncommonly mild winter's day the water front of Cairo, Illinois, was the scene of more than usual activity. Tied up to a great floating wharf fashioned from flatboats lashed together or anchored close under the town's wholly inadequate levee lay a long rank of those unpainted but still gaudy steamboats which had transported the troops of Generals Grant, Smith and McClernand. Smoke from rust-flecked chimneys often sixty feet tall climbed in sooty spirals.

On this ninth day of February, 1862, a spring-like warmth mellowed the air and encouraged a small army of black roustabouts engaged in loading supplies aboard the transports to start sweating, cursing and singing just as they did in summertime. Sweetly their rich voices rolled out verse after verse of "Buffalo Gals." A crowd of blue-clad troops off duty, loafers and townsfolk were concentrating their attention upon two gunboats lying tied up to the United States Naval Station's wharf.

Although repairmen had been swarming over them for nearly twenty-four hours the Union gunboats *Cincinnati* and *Benton* still revealed numerous scars of battle. For instance, *Cincinnati's* blue-topped port smokestack was missing two-thirds of its length and that section which remained had been so thoroughly riddled by Fort Henry's shellfire as to resemble a collander. It was obvious, also, that one of her stern ventilators would have to be replaced. Many deep shell scorings showed in the heavy two-and-a-half inch armor plate protecting the gunboat's bow and her beam opposite the engines. Bright silver-gray splashes shone everywhere upon the ordinary boiler plate covering the rest of the casemate.

"By Grabs! Will you look at them smashed davits? Them gunboats ain't got a single small boat left between 'em," commented a hatchet-faced flatboatman in hickory jeans.

"Thank God *I'm* not aboard the *Carondelet,* the *St. Louie* nor the *Louieville,* neither," drawled a civilian engineer officer.

The flatboatman spat brownly. "Why not, mister?"

"Overheard one of them Navy officers from the East say old Andy Foote's whole flotilla—what's still fit to fight, that is—are headed up the Cumberland. Reckon they're fixing to tackle that whopping big fort the Rebels have built up near Dover. Dunno what they call it."

"Fort Donelson," supplied a big, black-mustached sergeant of artillery.

"They say it's near three times as strong as that-there fort our gunboats captured last week."

A bandy-legged private in clumsy, spurred boots and showing the yellow stripes of cavalryman on his pale blue breeches, said in awed tones, "I heared it was God-awful aboard the *Essex* when that steamline got cut. One of the fellers in her said steam stripped the hull skin right off them poor bastards nearest the explosion, just like they'd been flayed. Them what breathed the live steam died like they was, lugging cannon balls or pickin' up a rammer. Blew some others right out the gunports and into the river. Their bodies hain't never been found," he added in ghoulish satisfaction.

The muddied and motley crowd's attention was momentarily distracted by the arrival of a train in a huge freight yard sprawling on high ground directly above the Naval Station. A short while later a slight commotion along the top of the bluff preluded the descent, by a long wooden stairway, of a file of seamen wearing the Regular Navy's dark blue. Led by a couple of officers they struggled and slipped downwards, bent under sea bags and attempting to keep their silly-appearing flat caps from being blown away. A senior lieutenant, young but carrying himself with the unmistakable assurance of an Annapolis graduate, drew near. The wind playing all the while with his short yellow-brown sideburns, he addressed an artillery sergeant wearing a two days' beard.

"Sergeant, can you direct me to the landing for the gunboat *St. Louis?*"

The idlers crowded about the naval party which numbered some twenty in all. The sergeant made no effort to salute, only pointed amiably off to his left.

"See that-there gray-painted machine shop? Wal, there's a landin' float lies just beyond. You ain't going aboard the *St. Louie?*"

"Some of us are," announced the second young officer while hooking the catch of a watch cloak over his throat. A wind had begun to beat in from the direction of Camp Defiance guarding the confluence of the Ohio and the Mississippi.

"Wal, mister, jist you traipse on down to that-there gray building; that's where replacements from the East report." The sergeant produced a plug of tobacco already indented by several crescent-shaped bites.

"Have a chaw, mister?"

"Thank you, no." For all his fiercely flaring dark mustache the younger officer smiled in friendly fashion, then ran an eye over the gaping crowd. By God, people certainly went roughly dressed out here; to a man they seemed long-haired, unshaven and mud-caked to the knees. Not a few wore one or more pistols or a Bowie knife jammed into their belts. Were there any drearier spot in North America Augustus Cosby could not imagine where it could be. Why, in this almost treeless ramshackle town there weren't visible more than thirty or forty two-storey buildings. Obviously of mushroom growth, shacks built of slabs and the crudest sort of log huts had been placed upon the high ground without any attempt at plan or order.

"All right, men," called the senior naval officer. "Shoulder your bags and follow me."

"You fellers hev come a long way to fight, ain't you?" called a flat-faced teamster. "Wal, you'll git your bellies full of fighting in a few days—ef you think I'm lyin' just look at the pore old *Cincinnati* yonder."

For the first time the younger lieutenant's dark blue eyes took notice of the shell-scarred gunboat and he caught his breath sharply. So this was how a man-of-war could look when she came out of a punishing action? Think of it! Men actually had been killed and wounded aboard yonder ugly, turtle-like craft. As Augustus picked up a suitcase and stepped off through the ankle-deep mire, his gaze wandered to a series of hills across the river with a line of bare trees crowning the far shore. Yonder lay Kentucky. While not exactly an enemy state, Kentucky had been reported to be strongly Secessionist.

Amid the chill gloom of a temporary naval barracks a harassed-looking commander glanced up from a mound of papers hemming him in at his table desk. "Well," he snapped, "what do you want?"

"Lieutenant Stemble reporting, sir," said the officer, saluting smartly, "with Sub-Lieutenant Cosby and eighteen gunners."

The commander summoned a stiff smile, offered his hand. "By God, you got here just in time, Mr. Stemble. What with the losses we suffered off Fort Henry and so damn' many of these freshwater sailors hightailing for home, we're hard-put to fill out our crews. How do you do, Mr. Cosby." The Commander offered his hand to the slender but well-built young officer whose dark, red-brown hair brushed his collar. "Hope you'll meet with better luck than those poor devils in the *Essex*."

"What happened, sir?" inquired Stemble, in a quiet tone.

"A Rebel round shot cut her steamline and in a few instants scalded to death thirty-four of her company."

The new officers from the East exchanged glances.

"I'm Commander Pennock, Commandant of this station." He raised rough brows. "Either of you gentlemen Regulars?"

"I am, sir. Annapolis 'fifty-three."

A smile creased Pennock's leathery countenance. "Welcome aboard, Mr. Stemble. We need every Regular we can get. He turned to Augustus. "What about you, sir?"

"Sorry, sir. I'm only a volunteer."

The Station commander selected a form. "Your full name, mister?"

"J. Augustus Cosby."

"What's the 'J' for?"

"Josiah. I have never liked the name," he added truthfully.

Meanwhile from the double-breasted front of his long skirted naval tunic Lieutenant Stemble produced a roster and at a nod from Alexander M. Pennock read, "Master's Mate Paulding, J.F.; Gunner Hall, A.B., Gunner's Mate Graham, J. Cooper–" As he tolled off their names man after man stepped up to knuckle his forehead.

Commander Pennock viewed these replacements in evident satisfaction; to a man, they bore the stamp of the Regular Service and were older than the hands he'd recruited locally. Tattoo marks shone blue on the backs of many a fist and even in midwinter their faces were brown and leathery.

Commander Pennock grinned suddenly, pushed a lock of graying hair free from his dark and penetrating eyes. "You men have a lot of surprises in store for you during the next few days. Those marine abortions lying out there on the river are like nothing any deep-sea sailor has ever seen, sober. They're ugly, they're sluggish as molasses in January and they've no decent quarters for their crew, pilots or officers.

"You'll find the guns aboard them familiar, however, and you'd better serve 'em the best you know how! Those Rebel gunners at Fort Henry proved damned handy with their ordnance."

Just before sundown columns of sooty smoke commenced to gush first from the twin chimneys of *St. Louis,* which had been designated flag steamer since *Cincinnati* had been crippled; then from those of *Louisville* and *Pittsburgh.* Presently troop transports, such as *J.T. Wilson, Ike Hammit, Hero, Rob Roy* and a dozen others, commenced to fire up.

Activity also was to be observed aboard a flotilla of tugs assigned to towing a small armada of woodflats and coal barges. A big river steamer, *City of Memphis,* which had been chartered to serve as a hospital ship also commenced to up-anchor.

"Mr. Cosby, until further notice, you have been assigned to command the guns of Number One Division," briskly announced Lieutenant Leonard Paulding, U.S.N., commanding the *St. Louis* for Flag Officer Foote. "You will need to work hard to train your gun crews. Aside from the men you brought from the East you must assign and organize a detail of gunners transferred from the *Essex* and the *Cincinnati.*"

"Aye, aye, sir," Augustus swallowed hard, aware that all at once the gunboat's great stern paddlewheel had commenced to turn. "I will hold drill first thing in the morning."

"Morning? Mr. Cosby, you will select your gun crews the instant you get your gear stowed in your quarters. They lie aft, by the way," Paulding rubbed eyes hollowed by sleeplessness. "You will keep your men at it until they know where everything is, until they're ready to drop. I want every man-jack to be so sure of his duties he can recite them in his sleep."

Paulding turned up the wick of a lantern swinging just above his head. "We have aboard a number of men who were under fire at Fort Henry. Depend on them to learn the worth of your replacements; all your first loaders have been proved to be reliable." He shoved forward a slip of paper. "Here is the name of your only experienced gun captain, together with the names of some first and second tacklemen I fetched out to this godforsaken country. You'd best assign your greenest men to be spongers and shotmen; your best old-timers as first and second trainers."

"Aye, aye, sir." Augustus gradually became accustomed to the rhythmic throb of the engines, the wet threshing noises made by the great stern paddlewheel and the sibilant hiss of steam escaping from the exhausts. He made his way aft along *St. Louis'* very gloomy gun deck. Of course he had intended to become a engineer officer, but back in Boston Navy Yard the Commandant had claimed that no engineer educated in the East could know much about those "revolving scrapheaps" called engines in the West, so, for two months he had been assigned to a training ship upon which to master the fine points of gunnery.

To Augustus' infinite relief *St. Louis'* big forty-two pound rifled guns and Dahlgren eight-inch smoothbores were identical with those on which he had trained. Familiar, too, were the contents of various racks and chests containing battle-axes, shot tongs, shell bearers, priming wires, fuse wrenches and gunlocks. All the training tackles, breeching and preventer gear appeared new and was neatly coiled down; in racks built along the gunboat's side stood spongers, cups and rammers.

The First Division, the new gunner officer discovered, consisted of the three heavy pieces of ordnance: two rifled forty-two pounders and a Dahlgren eight-incher. The gun deck's whole length was weakly lit by numbers of kerosene lanterns under which gun crews already had begun to drill.

Aft of the sternwheel's lightly armored housing, quarters for four officers, mere hutches, were located. The vibration in them when the ironclad was underway proved so violent that when Augustus set his cap down it skidded off a table within a very few moments.

After changing hurriedly into a worn and grease-stained Navy jacket—most of the crew wore civilian clothes—Augustus stepped out onto the gunboat's hurricane deck and descended a wooden ladder affixed to the iron casemate's sloping side. This ugly steamer's interior could not be reached from above save through a gunport or down the pilothouse companionway.

On *St. Louis'* fantail Augustus lingered a moment to gaze in profound curiosity upon the wide, turbulent and slate-hued Ohio. Amid the darkness gathering astern, slender, yellow-red streamers of fire marked the position of various transports or supply ships. Well ahead of this straggling column cruised a pair of fast towboats ready to signal the presence of snags or torpedoes.

A chill wind, rising, brought the insistent staccato coughing of engine exhausts from all directions, it seemed. Augustus found it suffocatingly hot within the casemate because *St. Louis'* four ventilators had been dismounted in anticipation of action. This ironclad's gunports, Augustus noted, seemed uncommonly ample, too much so, perhaps, when jagged splinters from bursting shells commenced to fly and minié balls came hissing from some river's banks.

To each of his gun captains Augustus assigned twelve seamen to serve his piece. Certainly very little sleeping would be done tonight. Not a single canvas hammock had been slung anywhere. Presently the First Division formed up behind their pieces wearing only grimy undershirts and bell-bottomed blue trousers. Then, endlessly, the noisy manual of loading, training and firing was simulated.

The hot, half-lit casemate resounded to barked commands from gun captains, to the grunts of sweating gunners, to the metallic clang of rammers or to the whining protests of training blocks and tackles hard at work. Towards midnight boots rang on the pilothouse's iron steps, and someone called out, "All hands take stations and stand to attention!"

It was then that, for the first time, Augustus Cosby beheld Andrew Hull Foote's neat, spare figure. Holding himself straight for all his sixty-odd years, Foote descended to the gun deck, his belt buckle and buttons flashing in the lamplight.

Augustus received impressions of a thin, boldly jutting nose, ruler-straight brows, penetrating dark eyes and a long, clean-shaven upper lip which overhung a slash of a mouth. Bristling gray chin whiskers had been trimmed into a neatly pointed beard. The Commanding Officer, without comment, inspected Augustus Cosby's First Division, to a man standing rigidly at attention, as became seamen from the Old Navy.

At Foote's left stalked Lieutenant Paulding and, directly behind him, First Master Black and Second Master Kendrick. When, briefly, Paulding presented the First Division's new commander, Augustus blushed, fervently wishing he hadn't been detected wearing a pair of old shooting pants from Sachem Hill.

Flag Officer Foote gazed coolly at the replacement. "You and your men appear to understand your duties, Mr. Cosby; you may dismiss after this inspection, but you will recommence gun drill at daylight."

Andrew Foote had started towards the Second Division with his long tunic skirt fluttering briskly above shoes polished as if for parade when suddenly he halted and, raising his voice, called out, "All hands listen well! During our recent engagement with Fort Henry several lives were lost needlessly because men forgot to bend over when a shot was reported to be ricochetting towards their vessel. When such a projectile is reported every man will bend over from the waist and remain in that position until the danger is past." Deliberately Flag Officer Foote ran his eye along the pattern of men and guns. "Another word of caution. Always make sure when loading that all charges and projectiles are *well and truly* tamped home! I want no guns blowing up in action."

Once the inspection came to an end and the gun crews had commenced to unlash and sling hammocks Augustus turned to Fourth Master Alexander Fraser. "We were told there were seven of these Eads ironclads, but I count only three in this flotilla. Where are the rest?"

Mopping heated features, Fraser replied, "As you no doubt saw, the *Cincinnati's* repairs weren't completed in time to come along, and where the *Mound City* and *Cairo* are right now is anybody's guess. Although she was pretty badly hit, the *Carondelet* never returned to Cairo after Fort Henry, but, after recharging magazines from our powder ship, went off up the Tennessee River. They say she'll meet us at the mouth of the Cumberland."

"I read about the *Carondelet* in the papers. Isn't her skipper something of a fire-eater?"

"Bet your sweet life he is! All he thinks about is engaging the enemy," Fraser grunted. "Commander Walke isn't afraid of man, God, nor Jefferson Davis, and he doesn't mind letting the world know it. They say he raises almighty hell if he doesn't get every ounce of credit due his ship and himself."

XIII A DISPATCH FROM BRIGADIER-GENERAL GRANT

The United States Gunboat *Carondelet* lay at anchor, a low, rusty gray-black outline upon the Cumberland River's lead-hued waters. It would have been difficult, mused Paul Dent after putting away his sketchpad again to study *Piloting Instructions for the Cumberland River*, to visualize a bleaker, more wintry or colorless landscape. Off to starboard towering hardwood forests raised stark black branches against a silver-gray sky. To larboard, as "port" invariably was termed upon western rivers, a long succession of raw, yellow bluffs and snow-bleached hills crawled away to the skyline. Below them huge flocks of mallards and pintails kept rising from great, yellow-brown marshes choked with ice.

On this morning of February 13, 1862, dense, gray-white clouds hung low, threatening still more snow, and wind which came whistling through cracks around *Carondelet's* steel gunport covers bit as sharp as a Bowie knife's edge.

Aside from *Alps*, the transport which had towed Walke's gunboat up from the Ohio, *Carondelet* was entirely alone. She lay at anchor with a rising storm from the northwest wrenching smoke violently away from her red-painted funnel tops. In the ironclad's pilothouse her First Master used a pair of binoculars to scan intently the river's eastern bank, for just now he had sighted, and reported, the presence of various small cavalry units upon it. To which Army they belonged there could be no telling, so rapidly had these horsemen faded back among the woods.

In the chartroom situated immediately below the pilothouse Commander Walke could be heard. "Why, in God's name, hasn't the Flag Officer come up yet with the rest of our flotilla? He's long past due and still there's no trace of his smoke downstream."

"Well," drawled Chief Pilot Hinton in nasal accents, "leastways *we* done what we were told. Reckon Gen'ral Grant's troops heard us lob them shells at Donelson yesterday afternoon?"

"Hope so. That's one whale of a big fort the Rebs have built upstream. 'Twon't prove so easy a nut to crack as Henry."

Dent heard a rustling as of maps and charts being consulted, then Walke's incisive voice continued, "What worries me in particular are those Confederate batteries mounted on the crest of the bluff; they can deliver a plunging fire which will penetrate our unprotected decks like a hot knife does a pat of butter. I presume, Mr. Hinton, that you noticed the enemy has emplaced guns upon three different levels?"

"No, sir, I didn't," came the Chief Pilot's slow reply. "I was a heap too occupied keeping my eyes skun for reefs and snags."

"Which is just what you should have been doing. In any case, the Rebels have thrown up a water battery about ten feet above the river—too low, really, if this river keeps on rising—another lies some sixty feet up the bluff and the last is on the crest. As you say, Mr. Hinton, we're going to have our work cut out. I intend to protect my decks with iron chain, bags of coal and anything else that will check a plunging fire, I—"

A ringing of hammers setting to work within the casemate drowned out further conversation below. It seemed to Paul Dent there was no end to these repairs which had been going on ever since the fall of Fort Henry. Unlike her consorts, *Carondelet* had not returned to Cairo for refitting but had put in to Paducah where only the simplest of repairs could be effected.

Again Dent ran through his mind certain instructions repeated over and over by Chief Pilot Hinton, possessor of considerable experience along the Cumberland River. To the former college student it remained astounding how accurately both pilots could recall even minute characteristics of a given stretch of river. They seemed to know by instinct exactly where and when to look for a landmark, be it eddy, reef, sandbar, wreck or some other hazard.

During the past week Paul Dent had come more than ever to appreciate how much remained to be learned before he could be considered even a halfway competent cub pilot.

Abruptly First Master Wade spun about. "Dent! Go below and tell Commander Walke a small boat's putting out from yonder creek."

Presently a party of pea-jacketed seamen shuffled out onto the fantail to make fast a river pilot's yawl awkwardly managed by half a dozen red-faced infantrymen.

By remaining in the wheelhouse Dent soon deduced what General Halleck and Brigadier-General U.S. Grant intended. An aide, a thick-bodied major of artillery, saluted Walke in weary fashion.

"General Grant's compliments, sir. He will greatly appreciate it, if, at your earliest convenience, you would make a demonstration against the fort. Such a diversion will greatly facilitate the movement of certain of our brigades into position."

Walke tugged thoughtfully at gray chin whiskers. "And what does General Grant mean by way of 'a demonstration'?"

The major, whose craggy features had been burned bright red by the raw wind, forced a stiff grin. "Why, sir, by throwing shells into the fort at intervals throughout the day. It should serve to distract the Rebels."

"'Throughout the day,' eh? Is the General aware that, at present, the *Carondelet* is alone?"

"Yes, sir. He has been conjecturing on what could have happened to delay the other gunboats."

"So am I," said Walke grimly. "Well, this means all the more glory for us." Smiling, he accepted a written dispatch from the aide's stained gauntlet. "Pray inform General Grant that the *Carondelet* will proceed upstream at once and will commence to bombard the fort. I shall maintain my fire until darkness."

"The General will be most appreciative, sir," predicted the aide. "The more you can distract the Rebels, the fewer will be our casualties."

Even before the dispatch yawl had pulled half the distance to the creek's entrance, billows of sooty smoke commenced pouring from *Carondelet's* twin smokestacks. Twenty minutes later Daniel Weaver was steering the ironclad, skillfully utilizing the Cumberland's furious current. Soon the pilot commenced to curse because blinding snow squalls had begun to scurry over the river.

Painfully, *Carondelet,* sluggish under the best of conditions, struggled upstream at approximately four knots an hour. Walke stood in the wheelhouse using binoculars to scrutinize the western bank. In approaching a sharp bend in the river Weaver almost invariably steered along the outer edge where the current was less. He had to use caution, though, because the ironclad was a sternwheeler and therefore not nearly so maneuverable as a sidewheeler.

Standing silent at Weaver's left, Dent strained his eyes to pick up various landmarks called out by the Assistant Pilot. Mr. Hinton, too, devoted full attention to various aspects of the rivers' surface.

Desperately, Dent compressed his lips while awaiting an onset of those soul-shaking fears which had tormented him at Bull Run and again before Fort Henry. But to his surprise there came no sudden drying of mouth, no griping in the bowels even when Weaver remarked in a conversational tone, "Cap'n Walke, sir, we'll open up the fort around that next bend."

By degrees an unfamiliar sense of self-confidence encouraged him when none of those dreaded symptoms manifested themselves. With only a few yards to spare the ironclad's blunt, low bow nosed by the snow-mantled wreck of a steamer into full sight of Fort Donelson. Outlines of the enemy earthworks were clearly to be recognized, sharply etched by newly fallen snow. Away to the westward several dense clouds of blue-gray smoke indicated that Union troops must have fired some buildings.

Commander Walke, thanks to Grant's dispatch, knew that the General himself was advancing from the northwest and that General Lew Wallace would advance directly east from Fort Henry, while General J. A. McClernand was to invest the Confederate stronghold from a southeasterly direction.

When Flag Officer Foote was able to bring up the rest of his gunboats, transports would land yet another Federal force upon the west bank above Hickman's Creek, an estuary which now had become faintly visible.

There was too much snow in the air to permit sight of Confederate colors at Donelson's signal mast, but all hands knew it was flying there.

Walke turned, strong features set. "Mr. Wade, order all hands to their battle station. Mr. Weaver, we will anchor just behind the tip of yonder point. Go in close as you dare without masking the fort."

A few moments later *Carondelet* was swinging to both of her anchors in the lee of the point with bow guns trained upon the fort which lay approximately one and a quarter miles distant. Below sounded the stamp and clang of men's boots hurrying to raise the forward gunport covers, closed until now for fear of sniping. The snowy river bank loomed less than one hundred yards distant.

Presently the First Division's three guns opened fire causing the armored casemate to resound like a beaten gong. Streamers of foul-smelling burnt powder smoke commenced to beat in through the texas' eyeslits and set Commander Walke and the pilots to coughing and wiping their eyes. Every time one of the bow guns was discharged the whole deck of the pilothouse shivered.

To his delighted amazement Dent discovered that he could see *Carondelet's* shot arch up, high up into the gray-white sky. The first ranging shells burst short of their target and so lashed only the Cumberland River with deadly iron splinters, whereupon Commander Walke shook his head and called down through the companionway, "First Division! You'll do better using fifteen-second fuses."

When the First Division's Number One Gun roared again everyone in the wheelhouse watched its shell burst a few scant yards short of Fort Donelson's water battery.

"Elevate five degrees!" they heard Number Two Gun's Captain shout over a roar caused by steam rushing through escape pipes located aft of the smokestacks. This time a cheer arose below, for the gunboat's shell had burst squarely above the water battery. Then Number Three's shot plunged into the parapet and blew a great cloud of snow and dirt high into the air. There followed a dull rumble caused by gun carriage wheels when the rifles were run in for reloading. A moment later Walke observed, "Well, gentlemen, here comes a calling card from General Floyd."

Hairs on the back of Dent's neck lifted when he saw an enemy roundshot climb high into the air and come plunging straight at *Carondelet*. Raising an eerie screech, the shot passed harmlessly above the dingy red bands painted near the top of the ironclad's chimneys; then a tall waterspout arose among floes drifting a good quarter-mile downstream.

Soon shells fired by various batteries crowning that bluff upon which Donelson had been constructed commenced to shatter trees growing upon the point behind which lurked the Union gunboat. Soon a Confederate shell burst almost abreast of *Carondelet* but too far out to cause any real damage. At the ringing *clang! clang!* caused by shell fragments clattering against the ironclad's casemate Dent bit his lip but experienced nothing of his previous insensate terrors.

Carondelet's "diversion" continued; her three bow guns firing in leisurely fashion. Not once but twice Walke called down, "Loaders! Make sure your charges are tamped well home; seat your ball carefully. We can't have those fine guns blowing up."

It came as a heartening miracle that, no matter how close the enemy's shells exploded, Dent's fears faded. Quite calmly he accepted a seegar offered by Hinton during the lull in the ironclad's firing. He even drew a hasty sketch of the distant smoke- and snow-veiled fort.

"The enemy," presently commented Walke, "has commenced to fire one hundred and twenty-eight pound shot and I don't like it. Our armor can stand all the thirty-two and sixty-four pounders they wish to send, but nothing much heavier."

He then ordered crews from other divisions to relieve those which had been serving the bow guns.

Not until late in the morning did *Carondelet* suffer her first hit. It was Dent who first discovered the projectile plunging straight towards the gunboat. Instantly he faced the companionway and yelled, "Ball coming!"

Whereupon various gun captains bellowed, "Bend over, boys!"

A second later there sounded a terrifying, ear-splitting crash caused by a Confederate one hundred and twenty-eight pound solid shot screaming through Number Two gunport to shatter a barricade of logs built to protect the boiler heads. Then, its impetus largely spent, the projectile bounded crazily about the casemate until it burst the gunboat's steam heater which, fortunately, was at low pressure. Hoarse cries and startled shouts beat up the companionway, followed by dense clouds of oily steam.

Presently Second Master John Dorety appeared dabbing at a shallow gash across his cheek. "We have seven men wounded, sir," he reported, "Some of them badly. Shall we resume fire?"

"No, Mr. Dorety. We will fall downriver to repair damage. Mr. Wade, make arrangements to transfer our wounded to the *Alps*. Then," he announced calmly, "we shall return to this spot and resume our bombardment. I do not wish General Grant to find the Navy wanting today."

Armorers, engineers and carpenters were hard at work by the light of rows of kerosene lanterns when the anchor watch sang out, "Wheelhouse, ahoy! Lights! Many lights downriver!"

Carondelet's crew, though still half-deafened and bone-weary from having fired her guns a hundred thirty-eight times, roused up and even raised a cheer as, through the steadily sifting snow, they glimpsed ten, then twenty, then eventually hundreds of lights.

Flag Officer Foote's Western Flotilla at last had arrived, together with the transports it had convoyed up from Cairo.

XIV GRAND ASSAULT

ALL MORNING LONG a sullen thudding of field guns and the lighter rattle of musketry had sounded upstream, attesting the fact that Brigadier-General Grant and his subordinates had completed their investment of Fort Donelson and some twenty thousand excellent Confederate troops under Generals Floyd, Pillow and Buckner.

A little after the dawn of February fourteenth, a series of top-heavy-appearing transports nosed in towards the west bank, lowered landing stages and, straining with both paddlewheels to maintain position, disgorged columns of silent, blue-clad infantry. Unit after unit formed up behind its colors and soon disappeared up a wooded valley; they were headed southwest and, for most of them, a terrible baptism of fire.

While quitting the *Alps* transport, Medical Lieutenant Robert Ashton knuckled eyes grown sunken and hot through lack of sleep. When the Western Flotilla had dropped anchor on the preceding night a small boat had pulled over from *Alps*. Would the timberclad's captain lend the services of her surgeon to care for wounded from *Carondelet?*

By the hot yellow light of many lanterns Ashton and the ironclad's own surgeon, a Dr. Rice, had labored long to remove dozens of lance-like oaken splinters from shuddering flesh, to sew up gashes and, with decoctions of laudanum, to lessen the suffering of their patients.

"Criminently! It's really cold today," thought Ashton while being rowed back to his own vessel. All night long snow kept falling in fitful flurries which repeatedly obscured the flag steamer and the rest of the flotilla. He could make out many small boats pulling from one to another of the snow-powdered ironclads. Their activity had become redoubled since a yawl had put out from the west bank bearing dispatches for Flag Officer Foote. Now rows of brilliantly colored signal flags kept rising to *St. Louis'* signal yard.

This, mused Dr. Rob Ashton, presented a very different phase of the war from that to which he had been accustomed and also a welcome change from attending overcrowded sickbays in the vicinity of Boston. How absurd, he reflected, body yielding to the oarsmen's stroke, that every day five men must perish of disease to every one who succumbed from wounds sustained in battle. Why was it that big, strapping men from farms and the backwoods seemed so pitifully susceptible to all manner of disease? Undernourished, stringy and scrawny youths from cities and towns seemed all but immune to common ailments. There must be some explanation.

At last he was listening to enemy gunfire! What confounded poor luck to be posted aboard a miserable timberclad. A good deal of the contempt for timberclads, however, had evaporated after their effective intervention last year in the bloody little Battle of Belmont. The Confederate General, Leonidas Polk—also Episcopal Bishop of Louisiana—recently had claimed that but for these timberclads General Grant's whole command would have been captured or driven into the Mississippi.

Once he had reboarded *Tyler* Rob Ashton requested her lantern-jawed pilot to point out *Carondelet*. Aboard her, incessant hammering could be heard and she showed new, silver-gray slashes through her rusty armor.

"Now yon's a real man-o'-war," said Mr. John Sebastian squirting a golden-brown stream over the rail. "Heard tell that-there feller Walke who commands her is crazy to win promotion. Dan Weaver, he's her second pilot, claims Walke would walk right up and spit in the Devil's eye if it would win him another stripe. Thank God, *I* am not serving aboard of her!"

Soon Ashton learned to recognize the other Eads gunboats, superficially identical, by the bands of green, blue, red or vari-colored paint applied near the summit of their smokestacks.

"Yes, doc, I'm right well pleased," said Sebastian. "I hear we're goin' in with the second line, account of bein' only a timberclad. Believe you me, them cocky ironclads is going to catch pure hell today."

Gradually this glum and overcast morning wore by and routine duties occupied all hands aboard *Tyler* until, at noontime, orders were received by Lieutenant Given to ready his vessel for departure. After wolfing a plate of corned beef hash in the engine room, Ashton repaired to a tiny hutch aft which would serve as his cockpit, and again mournfully inspected the shaky kitchen table upon which he was expected to operate. This, in addition to a pile of more or less clean towels, several buckets of muddy water, and one of sawdust, constituted the sum of his operating room equipment.

"Thank God, I won't have to work in a seaway—" he thought while laying out instruments, sutures, compresses and bandages.

Curiously enough the young surgeon's mind wandered back to those warships in which he knew his family had served. First of these had been the privateer, *Grand Turk II*, in which, during the Revolution, his great-grandfather had been killed. Then there had been the U.S. Frigate *United States*. Great-uncle John had served her as a lieutenant when she had whipped H.M.S. *Macedonian* to a fare-thee-well. Again, there was Cousin Richard who had sailed in the Steam Frigate *Merrimac* before she fell into Rebel hands at Norfolk. On all those ships, surgeons must, at some time or other, have laid out their instruments and cursed the conditions under which they were expected to operate.

Despite signals from *St. Louis* to remain ready for instant departure, despite the rumbling, grumbling thunder of a furious cannonade taking place upstream, the Western Flotilla's anchors were not weighed until half after two of the afternoon. Then sooty smoke plumes towered above all four ironclads and both timberclads. Presently white water frothed beneath their fantails as their sternwheels commenced to revolve.

At once Rob Ashton went out on deck and, crouched in the lee of *Tyler's* breastworks, watched proceedings. Everyone knew that this promised to be the grand assault upon Fort Donelson. In ragged line abreast, all the Eads gunboats commenced churning upstream, but not until they were about a mile distant did Lieutenant Given, commanding the two timberclads, give orders to get under way. Soon *Tyler's* fabric commenced to throb and pulsate as her powerful sidewheels began to thresh. Originally Ohio River steamers built for speed, both *Tyler* and *Conestoga* were considerably more nimble than their heavily armored consorts.

Loud and long did Lieutenant William Given, U.S.N., curse the circumstance that he and his wooden consort had been condemned to straggle thus ingloriously behind Foote's main battle; a wise decision, nonetheless, for a shot from any one of those great Columbiads mounted in Fort Donelson could have reduced them to drifting wreckage. As it was, Rob Ashton heard the engine room bells jangle when their pilots rang to reduce speed, lest the timberclads advance too rapidly. They surged past the newly arrived hospital ship, *City of Memphis,* and *Alps* sawing restlessly at their anchor cables.

At the end of thirty minutes the chuffing, awkward-appearing timberclads rounded a bend. Then Rob Ashton saw a picture the least detail of which he would never quite forget. Through lightly sifting snow he made out a bluff perhaps a hundred and sixty feet high crowned with a large earthworks over which dense clouds of grayish powder smoke were rising only to be driven eastwards. A good mile upstream all four Union ironclads were drawing into effective range. For some odd reason Rob groped under his overcoat and, inside his tunic, found the key-winding watch his brother, David, had worn in the Japanese Islands when serving in U.S.S. *Mississippi* under Matthew Calbraith Perry. Therefore he was able to time the first burst of gun smoke from *St. Louis'* forward guns at 3:30 P.M. Those ugly, turtle-like ironclads weren't keeping a good line, he decided. First one would outrun the rest, then another would drop several lengths behind.

At the moment *Pittsburgh* and *Louisville* were lagging behind *Carondelet* and *St. Louis*. Now they, too, opened fire and the smoke of their guns trailed like gigantic broken cobwebs towards the Cumberland's east bank until it lost itself among a stark, black forest growing yonder.

A militia artillery officer in command of *Tyler's* fieldpieces raised an imploring, terrier-whiskered face to the wheelhouse, then bellowed through cupped hands, "Fer God's sake, Mr. Givens, let me open fire!"

"No! Wait for my order!" snarled Lieutenant Givens. "That Redleg artillery of yours can't even halfway range the fort."

Now *Tyler's* tight-jawed company could make out the sudden, fiery blooming of bursting shells and brief white spouts raised by Confederate shot plunging into the river all about the Eads ironclads. Soon the thunderous naval cannonade increased until it became incessant, swelling an already-deafening uproar caused by the field artillery of both armies.

For the hundredth time Rob Ashton regretted his noncombatant role. Glory! What he'd give right now to be among those hairy artillerymen; bragging, cursing and fiddling impatiently with rammers, shell carriers and cartridges.

Near the fort a thunderous explosion took place, sent shafts of brownish smoke and a litter of debris shooting high into the air. Pretty soon Rob could discern a flag staff displaying a huge Confederate flag. This flagstaff, the medical lieutenant noted, was equipped with halyards, shrouds and crosstrees, exactly as if it had been mounted upon a naval vessel.

At length the coiling, undulating smoke of battle combined with snow flurries to obscure both fort and the ironclads bombarding it.

Suddenly on *Tyler's* foredeck a fieldpiece roared its flat, staccato report and Lieutenant Givens raged. "By God, I'll see that Army sonofabitch court-martialled. Those pop-guns of his can't begin to range the fort!"

Through his megaphone Givens bellowed, "Damn your eyes, cease fire until I give the word!" But by this time *Tyler's* other forward gun had let fly.

"God above!" groaned Rob when he saw *Tyler's* shell burst directly above the line of Union gunboats. "Those fools down there are murdering our own men!"

In fury Lieutenant Givens jerked out his big Navy Colt's revolver and stormed down the companionway. "Cease fire! God damn it, cease fire, I tell you!"

An artillery corporal grinned amiably. "Shucks, Mister Givens, us was just tryin' fo' range. Didn't hurt nobody, I expect."

The timberclads sped on at half speed cutting cleanly through the ice-dotted water as the Eads gunboats could not. Now the ironclads had advanced to within half a mile of Fort Donelson whose great guns were probing through the gray winter afternoon with fingers of fire.

"Jesus God! Look! There goes the *St. Louis'* starboard smokestack!" gasped a civilian engineer. "And will you look at them yawls on the *Carondelet*. They're sure gettin' smashed to kindlings."

Through a pair of fieldglasses Ashton watched two of *Pittsburgh's* davits snipped off like twigs by a roundshot which allowed her small boats to fall and to drift off downstream, quite unharmed. Perhaps disdainful of such puny adversaries or too fully occupied by the ironclads engaged in hammering their water battery, the Confederate gunners directed never a shot either at *Conestoga* or *Tyler* although both by now had advanced to within three-quarters of a mile range.

Still scarlet-faced with outrage, Lieutenant Givens reappeared in his pilothouse and at last issued orders to open fire, using fifteen-second fuses. Immediately the wheeled fieldpieces below commenced to bark and then recoil savagely against sandbags arranged to check them.

XV FORT DONELSON

IF INFERNO EVER could exist upon earth Lieutenant Augustus Cosby became convinced that it must be within *St. Louis'* casemate. The deafening, fabric-shaking reports of her three great bow guns, the only ones capable of use in so narrow a river, made his head swim. Presently, his ears commenced to bleed. Contributing to the magnitude of this uproar was the incessant roar of the other ironclads and that of the fort looming now not a quarter of a mile away.

Half dazed but fighting for self-control, Josiah Cosby's son ranged back and forth behind the three pieces composing his division. At present they were engaged in hammering Fort Donelson's water battery into a muddied ruin. Concussions slapped at Augustus as with gigantic, invisible hands. Because of acrid gun smoke beating back through *St. Louis'* overheated casemate he commenced to cough and his throat burned. When he attempted to call orders over the rumbling clank made by guns being trained all he could manage was a rasping croak.

"Number Two Gun, depress three degrees!" he gasped through cupped hands, then ran to check the range through the center gunport. God above! The smoke-and-flame-spouting Rebel citadel now loomed terrifyingly close at hand. The water separating it from the four ironclads was churned white by a hail of shell fragments; sudden, plumed geysers spouted whenever a solid shot fell short but, on the whole, the Confederate gunnery was all too effective.

Again and again enemy shells burst above the flag steamer. Successively they sliced off most of her funnels, gashed her armor and carried away the last remnants of her small boats. Shell fragments drummed upon the armor, caused the suffocatingly hot casemate to reverberate like a frying pan beaten with a ladle.

To his own great surprise, Augustus found himself watching, calmly enough, the gunners' movements; every time a piece was being loaded he made sure that a rawhide marker on the rammer handle was driven right up to the lip of the reeking tube thus proving that the load was really home. Then half-naked and powder-blackened tacklemen, three to each side of the gun carriage, would heave and send the long barrel lurching out of the port even while the gun captain cleared and primed its vent and cocked the gun lock. After squinting over its sights the captain might call for a slight correction in elevation or traverse.

Satisfied at last he would dash sweat from his eyes and bellow, "Stand clear!" just before he jerked the lanyard. A shaft of dazzling yellow-red fire would illumine the casemate an instant before fresh billows of blinding smoke came beating back through the gunport. Then the gun would recoil violently against its heavy manila breeching tackles and would be hauled further inboard to afford spongers the opportunity of handling their homely instruments. Meanwhile loaders and shotmen waited their turn to minister to this engine of destruction. Until the sponge, blackened and steaming, reappeared to reassure them that no spark lingered in the bore to blow off hands or arms, they stood clear.

The first loader then would shove a silk-cased powder charge deep into the bore. The second loader immediately drove home with a mighty heave of his copper-capped rammer. Once a wad had been inserted the shotman then heaved up to the cannon's mouth a shell or shot and dropped it into the bore. Finally he drove home a second wad to secure the projectile lest it roll out if the muzzle were depressed.

With each passing moment the raging fire from Fort Donelson became more intense, less tolerable. Successive concussions made the head swim, nerves tauten until they hummed like an overstrained cable. Jagged pieces of shell now commenced to fly screaming through the gunports; they killed two tacklemen on Number Three Gun and sent their mangled bodies hurtling across the casemate. Thereupon Augustus numbly signalled forward replacements from the idle broadside crews; the Cumberland unfortunately remained much too narrow to permit turning the ironclads sidewise and so to employ their maximum fire power.

Promptly the moaning wounded were carried aft to an improvised operating table in a more or less protected corner of the engine room. The unbearable crashing cannon reports and the pandemonium, the outrageous noise caused by shells and roundshot smashing at the armor created a clangor which gradually paralyzed the intellect. Out of a fog of shifting, blinding burnt powder smoke, hoarse voices seemed to scream unintelligibly from all directions.

Something seemed to have gone wrong with Number One Gun so Augustus started groping toward it but slipped on a pool of blood, went down and banged his knee cruelly hard. He was helped up by a wild-eyed black-bearded gunner.

"You hit, sir?" he bellowed.

"No. All right."

"My God!" somebody screamed. "Does that damned ijit in the pilothouse aim to drive us ashore? That fort ain't a—"

The outraged gunner's voice was drowned out by a terrifyingly loud explosion and down from the pilothouse beat brief but blinding flashes of fire. Everyone froze in his tracks when above the hurricane of battle sounds could be heard a thin voice screaming and the unmistakable *thump!* caused by a falling body.

Aloft somebody was coughing spasmodically until he managed to call out, "Wheel's carried away! Back the engines! Quick, for Christ's sake, back!"

Aware of a nauseating, sulphurous bile welling into his mouth Augustus struggled up the companion into a tangled mass of wreckage which was all that remained of the pilothouse. Shells still were bursting all about and the vicious hum of minié balls now filled the air. The shot-churned parapets of Donelson now loomed above rather than ahead of the ironclads!

Flag Officer Foote was clinging to a jagged piece of stanchion more than half stunned and bleeding from a wound which stained his dark blue tunic. At his feet lay the hideously dismembered body of Chief Pilot Riley while the Assistant Pilot, who had called out, lay slumped over a segment of the wheel, vomiting blood.

"Man tiller ropes!" Foote managed to gasp. "Must fall back!"

Perceiving this and the other gunboats' crippled state, the Confederate batteries accelerated their rate of fire.

Augustus, carrying the order to man the tiller ropes, travelled *St. Louis'* length through a maddening turmoil and had to hunt several moments before he came upon the First Master.

"Man the tiller ropes, Foote's orders," yelled Augustus.

"Can't! We'll just have to drift and trust to luck," the other snarled, passing a cuff over a gash in his forehead. "Those Goddamn' timberclads of ours are spraying our decks with their infernal short shots. A man can't live out of this casemate two minutes." He was not exaggerating.

Peering through a loophole Augustus could see the bags of coal, the chains, spare anchors and other gear placed there to minimize damage from plunging fire, stir and jump under lashing shell fragments. Through a ragged wall of gunsmoke he glimpsed a dim outline looming near and his nerves crisped. "Man the tiller ropes!" he shouted, "else we'll foul the *Pittsburgh* and both get battered to pieces."

"Don't go out!" implored the First Master, eyes ringed with white and starting in terror. Augustus, however, beckoned forward a party of five seamen, led three of them to the port steering tackles lying limp on the exposed rear deck and directed the rest to starboard. He had taken up the slack and had just begun to get the helplessly drifting ironclad under some degree of control when a shell from one of *Tyler's* field pieces burst squarely above the fantail.

"To hell with this!" yelled the seaman next to Augustus and started to run back into the casemate but halted. "My God, sir!" Lieutenant Cosby was sitting dazedly upon the mangled ruins of his right leg. A jagged section of red-stained whitish bone was projecting through the dark blue fabric of his trousers.

"Damn it!" he wheezed when they picked him up. "Man tackles—orders. Don't quit—"

Again out of control *St. Louis* continued to swing sidewise across the current and bore relentlessly down upon *Pittsburgh* which also was having trouble with its steering gear. The men were hesitating when still another shell from the timberclads burst over the stern and sent them scrambling back into the casemate bearing with them the wounded lieutenant. The gunboat's surgeon quickly appeared, blood-smeared to the elbows and wearing an apron as red as any butcher's. Quickly Dr. MacDill bent to secure a tourniquet because rhythmic spurts of bright arterial blood were spattering the gunboat's deck. Mercifully Augustus Cosby fainted dead away even as Dr. MacDill commenced to snip away his ripped and sodden trouser leg.

Thanks only to a lucky whim of the current *St. Louis'* threatened collision with *Pittsburgh* was narrowly avoided, but she remained utterly unmanageable and continued to drift downstream and away from the fury of that conflict raging about Fort Donelson on land as well as on water.

Through an open gunport Paul Dent, for the moment substituting for a starboard tackleman recently beheaded by a roundshot, saw the flag steamer commencing to drift away. What would the other gunboat commanders do now? Flag Officer Foote had issued imperative orders that all vessels in the first line must immediately duplicate any and all of the flag steamer's movements. He was straining on a tackle rope when, through eddying mists of powder smoke, he noted *Carondelet's* Number Three Gun being run in for recharging.

Because Dent was acting Number One on the tackle rope he stood abreast of his piece's trunnions, and had bent over to heave when it seemed that a flash of lightning had entered *Carondelet's* casemate. He and such men of his gun's crew as had not fallen, remained in stunned immobility, then, as from a great distance and over a chorus of howls, screams and bubbling moans, a voice shrieked, "Christ Almighty! Number Three's blown up!"

Half blinded and all but deafened, Dent nonetheless guessed what had occurred. In his excitement Number Three's loader had failed to tamp a charge all the way home where the increased thickness of the tube's breech could contain the force of the explosive charge.

Dimly seen figures reeled about screeching, followed by trails of blood; others lay still or squirmed in feeble helplessness. Then the dreadful cries arose. "Oh, God, I'm blind!" "I can't see!"

Fully a minute passed before anyone could recover from the concussion, then Captain Walke appeared, half blinded by burnt powder grains and groping his way. "What ails you idiots?" he raged at the remaining gun crews. "*You're* not hurt. Keep on firing!"

Now the uproar had achieved a crescendo. Fort Donelson lay less than four hundred yards distant. Gunners manning the water battery could be seen running for their lives up the bluff.

"Hammer 'em! By the Eternal Jehovah! Hammer 'em! They're on the run!" Commander Walke himself laid Number Two Gun to such good effect that a whole section of Donelson's middle battery caved in. But *Carondelet* was enduring fearful punishment. Everyone heard the grinding, reverberating crash caused by a smokestack being toppled alongside; jackstaff and signal staff long since had been sheared away. Then, causing a horrible snarling sound, a one hundred and twenty-eight pound shot opened a gash of nineteen feet along the boiler plate inadequately sheathing that part of the gunboat's beam. As if to cap this hellish climax *Carondelet's* pilothouse was struck squarely by a thirty-two pound solid shot which drove a ragged slab of light armor, supposed to protect that vital post, into Billy Hinton's chest and dropped him, writhing in mortal agony, onto the wheelhouse's littered floor. At the same instant a flying piece of timber struck Daniel Weaver in the side, broke three of his ribs and crumpled him, helpless, amid the smoking wreckage.

When, a moment later, *Carondelet* commenced to swerve from her course, Paul Dent without waiting for instructions leaped up the companion where he slipped on rivulets of blood dripping from step to step and finally had to haul himself on hands and knees into the crazy remains of the now uncovered pilothouse.

By some miracle the ironclad's six-foot steering wheel had been but slightly damaged; only a couple of its handholds had been carried away. Pitilessly the enemy's shells crashed and thundered over the river and rendered it difficult in the extreme for Dent to orient himself, but soon a vista opened through a dense wall of battle smoke to disclose *Pittsburgh* bearing down from starboard! Obviously she was completely out of control. Nearer and nearer she loomed. In an agony of apprehension, but otherwise completely master of himself, Dent ground over his wheel at the same time ringing for full speed astern. If only he could see better! To ascertain the position of *Carondelet's* consorts proved nearly impossible.

Nearer threshed *Pittsburgh* with guns smoking idly and the ruins of her wheelhouse draped over her casemate.

"Oh, God, help us!" Dent gasped even as his vessel's sternwheel commenced to revolve in reverse. Almost *Carondelet* avoided her consort's blind charge, but not quite. The two Union gunboats collided, heeled 'way over under the impact of a resounding collision. The wheel wrenched itself from Dent's grip, spun like a millwheel and flung the substitute pilot onto his knees beside the dying Hinton.

"Get up!" Dent ordered his aching, quivering body despite the fact that musket balls were humming through the air like gigantic hornets. "Get up! This time, by God, *you are not afraid!*" Again and again musket balls went *splat!* against remains of the wheelhouse armor.

While Paul Dent was hauling himself erect a slant of icy wind suddenly cleared away the smoke to reveal that *Carondelet* alone was enduring a battering from all the serviceable guns in Fort Donelson.

In rising alarm the bareheaded pilot sensed that during the collision with *Pittsburgh* both of *Carondelet's* starboard rudders must have become carried away. She simply would not answer her helm in that direction.

Commander Walke reappeared at that instant, bareheaded, his blue tunic lacking half its buttons. "Why are you backing?"

Dent told him. "Standing orders from the Flag Officer, sir. *St. Louis* is in retreat."

"You're right, but oh, my God, look!" Walke's long face became contorted with helpless rage. "Why must I fall back now that I'm able to pass above and bring our broadside to bear in enfilade? I'd silence those batteries in twenty minutes."

"Why not keep on, sir?" Dent's hand closed over the engine room signal rope's handle.

"No, Mr. Dent," snarled *Carondelet's* commander. "At Annapolis we are taught to obey orders; Flag Officer Foote's are to follow his flagship."

Enduring the effects of a merciless cannonade which beheaded two men who neglected to stoop when a ricochetting shot was sighted, *Carondelet,* oozing clouds of smoke and steam from her ports, fell downstream. But still she fired her remaining forward guns until the range became too great.

"And to think, Mr. Dent, that we almost had them!" groaned Commander Walke. "I guess we've been repulsed today but, by the living God, we'll come back tomorrow, and the day after that, and the day after that until the fort surrenders!"

XVI HOSPITAL BOAT

The former luxury steamboat, *City of Memphis* lay at anchor a short distance below Fort Donelson bearing "USA Hospital" painted in tall black letters upon her paddlehouses. This designation had been surcharged upon a faded representation of King Saul hurling his javelin at young David while the latter was playing upon a harp. Presumably David must just have struck some extra sour notes, or so suggested the Second Engineer.

The big hospital boat lay ringed all about by yawls, gigs and barges, much like a sow by hungry piglets. It being an unseasonably mild day her colors flapped lazily while two scows from the fort's hastily repaired landing dock put off with bottoms jam-packed by stretchers. The first of these gained the hospital ship's after deck, which rose less than a yard above the river, just ahead of *Carondelet's* pilot yawl.

In deep compassion Dent gazed upon those rows of silent and motionless figures swaddled in woollen blankets of every hue and description.

Proudly wearing the brass-buttoned tunic of a naval officer with unmarked shoulder straps, as became a civilian employee of the Navy Department, Pilot Paul Dent clambered onto the main deck and at once sought the office of the vessel's commander Lieutenant W. R. Wells.

The moment he stepped before the huge, plate-glass mirror in what once had been the palace boat's grand saloon, his nostrils were assailed by the reek of formaldehyde, chloroform, tobacco and a nauseous stench created by suppurating and gangrenous wounds. Cots had been ranged in four ranks running lengthwise along the former saloon. Upon them numbers of hollow-eyed and unshaven patients, soldiers mostly, lay staring vacantly up at lavish designs wrought in gilded and white fretwork or upon a vividly rendered mural depicting the blowing up of the steamer, *Ben Sherrod.*

The pungent reek of pipes smoked by some of the less seriously wounded, or held between the teeth of uncleanly male nurses slouching about on various errands, came as a relief from the other smells.

"Name's Weaver, eh?" A red-nosed clerk, obviously suffering from a streaming cold, opened a ledger. "Let's see, let's see. Um. Warner, Williams, Worthington, ah, here you are—Weaver, Daniel. You should find him in stateroom 'Arkansas' up on the hurricane deck."

While mounting an elaborate "welcoming arms" staircase, Dent was appalled at sudden piercing screams raised by a delirious soldier who lacked his left arm.

"Shut up, you!" "There he goes again!" growled the nearest patients.

"Mina! Mina, darling!" cried the delirious man. "Please wear your white dress."

"Hell! Tell her to peel it off and call me!" mocked a big corporal on an adjoining cot. From sunken eyes he winked at Dent.

That his friend was fortunate indeed Dent discovered on locating him in one of the *City of Memphis'* more spacious staterooms. Upon one of the four cots lay Daniel Weaver attempting to read a week-old newspaper held horizontally. As usual his muscular jaws were steadily at work upon a cud of tobacco bulging in his right cheek. Brown stains marking his pillowcase of coarse, unbleached linen attested that, temporarily at least, the pilot must have lost his remarkable accuracy in spitting.

His pallid features lit. "By God, Paul, yer welcomer'n a shower of bourbon at a rousers' hoe-down!" Weaver also must have lost considerable weight for his always prominent cheekbones jutted out like miniature crags.

"This yere's Lootenant Cosby, a gunnery officer out o' the *St. Louie* and that joker yonder with the bandage 'bout his eyes is my old pal Sam MacBride, Second Pilot o' the *Louieville.* The poor feller yonder's another pilot, Dave Wade, got hit mortal bad in the *Pittsburgh's* texas."

Dent grimaced as he shook hands with his friend. "You pilots surely caught hell the other day. No wonder they've begun to call the pilothouse a slaughter pen."

The man Wade made no move. Either he was asleep or unconscious. The mass of bandages about his head showed a bright crimson patch in the midst of a big, red-brown stain which attested the fact that the stricken pilot had not yet ceased to bleed.

"Howdy," Dent seized MacBride's groping hand. "Hope you'll get your sight back soon. A lot of those men blinded aboard the *Carondelet* when her gun blew up have recovered their vision," he encouraged.

"I sure hope so," MacBride said wearily. "A pilot ain't much good 'thout his eyesight, and me I've six young uns to feed back home in Cincinnati."

"Where are you from?" Dent inquired of Cosby.

Although ghastly pale and showing livid circles beneath both eyes, the young officer sat propped up sufficiently high to permit sight of the passageway along which uniformed orderlies were lugging a long column of stretchers.

Augustus' purple-blue lips parted themselves in a forced smile. "I hail from away up in the State of Maine, a town called Bangor."

"Bangor!" Dent's expression hardened. "Odd. On my way out west I met a fellow who came from right near there. A place called Dexter, I think."

Animation enlivened the wounded officer's drawn features. "What was his name? I might know him; that part of Maine is not overly populated."

"Why, his name was Everett."

"Everett!" Augustus Cosby's dark blue eyes widened. "Do you remember whether his Christian name was Matthew?"

"Yes. How amazing that you should know him."

"I met him only once; only then the fellow's name was 'Johnson' or so he called himself," came the grim comment.

Dent stared. "Johnson?"

"Yes. He came out to our house and tried to murder my father."

Recollections of that midnight confession aboard the westbound train and in the contraband runner, *Western Arrow*, recurred in such amazing detail that Dent could recall almost everything Matt had told him. This then, this handsome young fellow with the wavy, dark red hair, must be the legitimate son of Matthew's father.

Augustus sighed. "Where is he now? Perhaps he'd be interested to learn that he failed in his attempt on Pa's life. My sister wrote Pa's hale and hearty and ornerier than ever."

Dent frowned. "Matt owns a steamboat now and appears to be doing very well for himself. I've seen him just once since we parted last fall. He was in Cairo about a fortnight ago."

"Doing well? In what way?"

"Running contraband, I'm afraid. I gather from what I have heard in Cairo and along the River that our acquaintance isn't what the righteous would term 'an exemplary character.' He's grown hard, bitter and brutally cynical."

Augustus' head sank back against a grimy pillow and his eyes half veiled themselves. "There's some kind of a mystery behind this Matthew Johnson—or Everett, which ever it is—that I haven't yet penetrated. Maybe he is not entirely to blame."

"He's not." Sidewise glances revealed that Weaver was reading and the other two men dozing. He leaned forward and lowered his voice. "He's your half-brother."

Cosby could only stare and gasp. "My half-brother?"

"Yes. He's a little older—and illegitimate."

"Oh, my merciful God! How do you know this?"

"He told me so himself," came the quiet response of the blue-clad pilot. "He had only been aware of this a short while before I met him. I believe he was informed by his mother's lawyer immediately after her death. He intended to kill your father and the false minister who officiated in a mock marriage."

For a brief space innumerable small and hitherto inexplicable incidents clarified themselves in Augustus' mind; Pa's intensive search for his would-be assassin through a hired gunman named Pennypacker, for instance.

"Poor devil. No wonder he's bitter. It—it must be hideous to learn one's a bastard child. I—I wish I could help him—somehow make amends of a sort. Hand me a drink of water, will you? There's a good fellow."

"If I see him, shall I tell him what you've just said?"

"I wish you would. Oh, by the bye," he fumbled under his pillow, "I've just received a telegram from my sister, Flavia. I expect she'll have to break the news about this," grimacing, he indicated his amputated leg, "to my parents. My young scamp of a brother, Decius ran away last January to enlist or so he said—but nothing's been heard of him since. Perhaps Flavia could come on to Louisville and nurse me? I understand that's where my group is headed."

So Lieutenant Cosby had a sister named Flavia? Dent wondered why the Cosby family was so given to Roman names. Unusual. Would she, if she came west, prove to be as pretty as this pallid young fellow was handsome? A shadow fell across the cabin's entrance caused by a benign-appearing, white-haired and bearded man of near sixty. He was garbed in sober black and wore a clerical collar.

The patient called Weaver gasped painfully when he attempted to rise on one elbow. He had to sink back but summoned a smile to his unshaven face as he called, "How you, Rev'rend?"

The minister entered and from mild, gray-blue eyes cast an anxious glance at the pain-racked pilot.

"Afternoon, sir," Augustus Cosby greeted him in obvious enthusiasm. "We've got company for a change. This cabin is growing popular. This gentleman is Paul Dent, temporary pilot aboard the *Carondelet*. Mr.

Dent, this is the Reverend Mr. Adams, David Adams, our great friend and benefactor."

"You fetched my eatin' tobacco?" Weaver demanded weakly.

The minister nodded and produced a plug from a roll of newspapers tucked under his arm. "Here are a few fairly late copies of the St. Louis *Democrat*. They'll tell you a lot about the capture of Donelson that will prove news to you. Their reporter writes that a captured Confederate colonel claimed that 'the Blue Forces hurled such a hurricane of shot' upon them they just had to surrender."

Dent cast the Reverend Mr. Adams a searching glance. "You're from New England, are you not, sir?"

"Yes," he smiled, "I come from Augusta and was pastor to a congregation in Portland before I accepted a call to Peoria nearly twenty years ago. Dear, dear, time really flies doesn't it?"

Augustus chuckled and lifted a water pitcher from the cabin's only chair. "Please sit down, sir. We Maine men get together like swarming bees. Funny, we were just talking about another State-of-Mainer."

The minister dipped a towel into the water pitcher, went to drape it carefully over the unconscious officer's forehead. Dent could see that the Reverend Mr. Adams was trying hard not to gag at the fearful stench exuded by young Cosby's bandages.

"You seem to be coming on a lot better," he encouraged Weaver. "You'll be up and dancing jigs inside of another week."

"Reckon so," the pilot nodded. "But I'd ruther get back to the *Carondelet*. She's a mighty scrappy old gal and I'm fond of her. How's old Andy Foote's wound comin' along?"

"Pretty well. It wasn't as serious as they had feared at first." The minister glanced out of the *City of Memphis'* window, his attention attracted by a long string of supply steamboats churning downriver and towing barges loaded with field artillery pieces. "He prays night and day for recovery, but I fear his age is against his getting back into action. All he thinks of is getting his flotilla repaired and in action again for 'tis rumored the Confederates have been working desperately to increase their defenses on an island at a bend in the Mississippi just above New Madrid."

XVII FLAVIA

Less than a week after Paul Dent had dispatched a telegram to Flavia Cosby, she appeared aboard the hospital boat. Dent and his friend were playing checkers when a rap sounded at the cabin door. It so chanced that, except for the checker players, the cabin was empty so Dent strode over to turn the door handle.

The panels swung inwards and he saw waiting before the entrance one of the handsomest young women he had ever beheld. Her lively bright brown eyes, lustrous black hair and gently arching brows were in delightful contrast to the smooth pallor of features that were quite broad across the cheeks and narrowing to a small, but firm-looking chin.

"You are?" he began.

"I am Flavia Cosby," she declared simply and shifted a net containing various provisions and reading matter. "How is my brother?"

"Hi' there, Flavia!" Weakly, Augustus struggled up on one elbow. "Ready for another frolic?" he demanded with a tremor about his mouth.

She halted staring aghast at the empty space below his right knee. "Oh 'Gustus! You poor darling!" She dropped onto her knees beside the bed and, slipping an arm about the patient's neck, lifted him to her. At the girl's breathless sobs, Dent turned away, started to leave, but Augustus called him back.

"I want you to meet my sister. This is Paul Dent. He's been mighty kind to me ever since I, well, tried to play football with a piece of shell."

Features gone a delicate pink, Flavia stood smoothing full skirts of shimmering gray silk and offered a hand to this tall young chap with the sober-looking blue eyes. Intuitively she guessed he must have suffered from something a great deal during the past few months.

"How do you do?" she inquired in a rich, pleasantly modulated voice.

"Fair enough, Miss Cosby, and I am mighty happy that you are here now. Augustus needs a lot more care than the overworked male nurses and the Sanitary Commission ladies can give him." He smiled slightly. " 'Gustus said you look alike."

"Don't we?" she demanded, unknotting the green velvet ribbons securing a bonnet of black silk.

"Was your journey west very uncomfortable?"

She shook her head. "Mercy no! Papa knows quite a few directors on the railroads I travelled so I simply sailed through in style."

"How is Pa?" Augustus demanded evenly.

"Busy as all get out," the girl returned.

"And making money hand over fist, I'll warrant," supplemented the invalid.

"Yes, he is making so much money people are beginning to talk." She tucked a bright nether lip between her teeth. "I do wish he would do something for the Country. And where are you from, Mr. Dent?" she gazed up at him from sherry-brown eyes that Dent found very lovely.

"From New Haven," he returned carelessly. "I wonder if I could persuade you sometime to sit for a little sketch?"

"Oh, mercy no! I couldn't keep still that long."

"You had better," Augustus advised. "Paul's mighty handy with his pencil. Show her your new sketchbook."

"Oh no, there isn't much in it; only some impressions I made after our battle off Memphis."

"Please," Flavia held out slim hands in black mesh mitts.

Diffidently at first, and then with growing confidence, Paul Dent described his subjects and Flavia's laugh rang out at his caricature of Flag Officer Davis ordering about a slack-jointed naval recruit.

During the three days remaining before *Carondelet* dropped further downstream, Dent found an increasing number of reasons why he should visit the hospital boat, and curiously enough during those hours Flavia would be present. The girl appeared to be immeasurably sobered by the presence of so many sick and wounded and no longer started at the shriek of some wretch on the operating table. She expanded her duties by visiting not only her brother but as many other of the haggard invalids as she could.

On the last night before *Carondelet* sailed, Flavia and her now almost constant escort repaired to the hurricane deck to watch the last of the sunset's glow fade from the sky. From an isloated portion of the deck they stood staring out over the wide river, just now beginning to reflect a few stars.

"I shall miss you, Paul," murmured she, "and so will 'Gustus. He always perks up a lot when you are around."

"I wish I could bring myself to give you that drawing I made of you, bad as it is," he smiled. "But I am going to keep it, if you don't mind."

"I don't mind," she said. "I will be glad for you to have it. Do you suppose you will be able to see us again before I take 'Gustus back East?"

"God alone knows," he said. "The ways of the Navy are deep and mysterious. I could be ordered to any vessel anywhere tomorrow."

"But do please let me know where you are."

His hand crept over to rest on hers. "If I write, you'll answer?"

Her gaze swept upwards. "Of course, Paul. I want to hear from you. In fact, I–I–"

Before he sensed her intent, she lifted her face and brushed her lips across his cheek. "I–I think you are a wonderful man, Paul. I have been hearing of what you did at Henry and Donelson."

He was too dumfounded to do more than beam on her, conscious of the sudden wild hammering of his heart. "I'll write," he promised.

A voice from below called out that the picket boat which fetched visitors to and from the fleet was about to depart.

Not at all gently he caught her to him and, despite the amusement of various invalids strolling the deck, he kissed Augustus' sister as he never before had kissed any woman.

XVIII THE COTTAGE ON CATBIRD WALK

THE EVENING PROMISED to be an especially balmy one, decided Phoebe Everett. Fragrant breezes blowing along the Ohio River valley wafted the scent of new hay grass and the faint perfume of fruit blossoms. Phoebe was gladder than ever that this frame cottage they were renting from a sad, young widow who had lost her husband at the Battle of Columbia, was situated on the eastern side of Louisville, Kentucky. Therefore it mercifully was removed from the almost endless construction noises created at the boatyard where finishing touches were being applied to some very fast Ohio River passenger steamboats which a Mister–now Colonel–Charles Ellet had been converting into rams of his own design. The whole town was talking about the project so even Phoebe knew that the *Monarch* and *Queen of the West* were two of the largest of a new class of supposedly deadly river fighters.

Today it had been unseasonably hot aboard the hospital ships *City of Memphis* and *D. A. January* and so the wards had been smellier than usual. As she followed the River Road on her homeward way Phoebe found it a vast relief to slip a shabby cashmere shawl free from her shoulders, to untie her bonnet's strings and to walk dangling it by her side.

How curious *and fortunate* it was that, throughout her long association with the Sanitary Commission, she had never met anyone from St. Louis. This service had commenced on a bleak February morning the day after she and Matthew had arrived in Louisville. They had brought with them very little more than the clothes on their backs and what was left of that three hundred dollars Matt had fetched West with him. Everything else

Matt determinedly had assigned to Philo Daingerfield and so had rendered that bewildered and most unhappy little man one of the wealthiest contractors in or about St. Louis.

Catbird Walk had proved to be neat and cheerful as the bird for which it had been named. In this immediate neighborhood loomed no pretentious mansions; the houses all were small and often badly kept, but most of the gardens behind unpainted picket fences were shimmering with gracefully drooping and lace-like spirea blossoms. Phoebe recollected that back home these shrubs were called "bridal wreath." Beneath these glowed a few late tulips and bank upon bank of azalea. She smiled in particular upon a hurdle fence enclosing a small pasture. It had mellowed through the years to a soft, silver-gray hue and supported masses of climbing red roses such as flamed before this first home of her own.

To her it remained a source of perplexity that recollections of her life in Dexter should return in unrelated sequences, yet it was encouraging that, almost every day of late, many long-forgotten events or personalities were popping back into her memory.

On arrival before the pretty little gray clapboard cottage Matt had selected, Phoebe glanced hopefully at certain pansy plants she had set out before the front door. Um. They certainly could stand immediate watering!

Once indoors Phoebe hung up bonnet and shawl, then hurried out into a tiny kitchen to poke up the fire and lift the lid of a stewpot. A diffident sniff decided her that supper was not scorched, thank fortune. Next she wandered into her small, green-and-pink papered living room and noted a letter bearing her mother's neat script. Merciful Heaven! It must have been lying in that nut dish for a whole week. Full skirts of brown alpaca a-sway, Phoebe sought Matthew's desk, and, sitting very straight as she had been taught, selected a pen and commenced to write:

Louisville, Kentucky. May 19, 1862.

My dearest Mother:

I am dreadfully remiss in not having written sooner but so much of moment has occurred during the past few days; hospital trains and boats keep on discharging distressing floods of sick and disabled men. Now-a-days, and especially since the Battle of Shiloh, or Pittsburgh Landing as the Enemy insist, we of the Sanitary Commission and Christian Endeavour are kept very occupied often far into the night. So many poor fellows stand in desperate need of cheer and care. I must have penned at least a hundred letters for such during the past few days. If only Matthew and I were not so poor and could afford some of those small dainties for which so many invalids yearn! Such, the Commission very properly cannot supply.

Matthew, too, has been hard at work on some new steam rams which are being finished here. These rams are a curious sort of warship, Matt declares, since they carry no cannon whatever but rely upon sinking an enemy solely by means of striking them with a steel-pointed wooden ram. I am proud to inform you that not much time passed before Mr. Jeffrey, in charge of the reconstruction, noticed my dear Husband's ability and swiftly promoted him. Undoubtedly Matthew would be appointed an assistant engineer if he were not so determined upon obtaining an officer's commission in the First Kentucky Volunteers—*Union,* of course!

Phoebe broke off, to peer through the windows and watch the MacLeans' gray cat make graceful leaps after a big yellow-and-black butterfly. Dear Peggy MacLean! How wonderfully kind and helpful she had been right from the start and in the most tactful manner. Paul, her husband, a native of the city, had taken Matt under his wing and was presenting him to many influential citizens. How nice it would be if she and Matt could settle here in Louisville. But they couldn't. Innocent as it had been in reality, her stay at Mrs. Wilber's would be a blot on her reputation if it became known; they could not be entirely free from anxiety living so near St. Louis. And, of course, there always remained that tragic matter of Matt's birth.

No, as soon as this ghastly war came to an end, they must migrate either to California or to that other Portland reportedly flourishing in Oregon.

She dipped her pen and drove it across the paper in a firm and delicately shaded Spencerian script.

It is truly surprising how many people from our little State have found their way out here. Most of them are seafaring folk come in connection with the serving of our curious gunboats. How well Mr. Eads' creations have proved their worth! Recently they captured some forts on Island Number Ten in the Mississippi. This brave success threw not only New Madrid but also Columbus into our hands, and with hardly any fighting at all.

I trust, Mamma dear, that you have not confided our whereabouts to a soul at home excepting Mr. Stetson. I am most anxious to receive intelligence concerning the present condition of dear Mrs. Hovey's estate.

I feel surprisingly well for all that I am now two months with child.

Among those people in Louisville who had their origins in Maine was that old pastor, the Reverend Mr. Adams, who spoke of once having had a congregation in Portland.

For all his sixty-odd years no one could be more untiring about his labors in behalf of the sick and wounded.

I intend to give Matthew a pleasant surprise because I have invited Mr. Adams to supper tomorrow—provided we all are free to foregather. So often poor Matthew does not return home until late at night and then he is so utterly exhausted from his labors at the boatyards that we find small opportunity to converse.

How very, very much I wish I could see you, dearest Mamma. I suppose, Molly, the heifer, is now fully grown and that Papa is bemoaning those stones turned up by the winter's frost.

As for the shawl you—

The garden gate banged so loudly that Phoebe dropped her pen and so showered her letter with a fine, black spray. Matt appeared, seemingly taller and wider-shouldered than ever and smiling so broadly he must be bearing good news. He rushed over to pull his wife onto her feet, then hugged her tight and executed a dance step or two.

"I trust you are aware, Mistress Everett," he beamed, "that you dance with none other than Lieutenant Matthew Everett?"

Her great, dark blue eyes lit. "Then your commission has come? Oh, Matt, I am very proud, and so happy for you!"

"Yes, the Governor made the mistake of his life when he signed it."

Especially lovely because of the color rushing into her cheeks, Phoebe imprisoned and held him at arms' length. "Oh, you will look wonderful in uniform; a—a modern knight," she predicted, tilting her head a little to one side. "But you will never look finer to me than in those work-worn clothes."

He clasped her close, kissed her so soundly that she fluttered happily in his embrace, then melted, lithesome body pressed tight to his. "Goodness, Matt! I wish we had—oh, just something special in honor of your new commission."

He shot her a quizzical look, then grinned like a great boy. "Well, my dear, I'll confess, that in my lowest bureau drawer I've secreted a bottle of claret—just in case, you know?"

She hesitated, her bright expression ebbing. "Do you think we ought, Matt?"

"—I know, my dear, I know," he replied soberly; then grinned again. "But, Phoebe, I don't believe claret should be classified as a spirituous liquor, do you?"

She brightened. "Nor do I, darling, so for Heaven's sake fetch that bottle!" Laughing, she rushed out into the kitchen and returned bearing a pair of heavy glass tumblers.

"Supper smells wonderful!" he beamed while uncorking the wine. "What are we having?"

Phoebe uttered a plaintive little cry. "Oh, dear, it's only lamb stew! If *only* I had known this was going to be an occasion."

He started to pour more wine when she cried, "Save some, Matt. I've a friend asked to supper tomorrow night."

"Who is it?"

"A minister. I am sure you will like him. He's such a kind old man—one of the few Divines we have who preaches at his patients only a little, and works very hard for their comfort."

"Indeed. Is he a local minister?"

"No. He has a church in Peoria, Illinois, but originally he came from Maine. I'm ever so sorry I've not met him earlier."

"From what part of Maine does he hail, my dear?"

"From Portland originally, I think he said. You will like the Reverend Mr. Adams."

"*Adams?*" Abruptly Matt lowered his wine glass and inquired steadily, "What's his first name?"

"Why, let me see," Phoebe was busy securing a blue calico apron about a middle which had not yet begun to thicken. "I think his name is David."

"D. Adams!" Matthew's mind went whirling back to that unforgettable November morning when Mr. Stetson had produced those damning clippings. So the "Reverend" D. Adams from Portland was near by! A sense of savage exultation seized him.

"Why, what's the matter, Matt? You looked just now as if you'd seen a phantom."

He drew a deep breath then, smiling, raised his wine glass. "It's your always lively imagination at work, my sweet. I am quite all right."

"Have you ever met the Reverend Mr. Adams?" Phoebe presently inquired.

"No," came the toneless reply, "but I've heard of him—quite a lot. You say you have invited him to supper tomorrow night?"

"Yes, darling. I was sure you would enjoy meeting him."

Through a turmoil seething about his brain, Matt heard himself saying, "I most certainly do look forward to meeting the Reverend Mr. Adams, indeed I do."

Because Phoebe had bustled back out into her kitchen to shove a pan of biscuits into the oven she missed the grim expression immobilizing her husband's long and wind-burned countenance.

The "Reverend" D. Adams! Next to Josiah Cosby it was he who had been the one most responsible for the ruin of Abigail Hovey's life, for her shame and for his own illegitimacy.

"You don't have to return to the boatyard tonight, do you?" Phoebe called. "The MacLeans have invited us over for a pitcher of shrub after supper. They would have asked us to dine but Peggy has a cousin visiting her. She's from Washington and has brought all kinds of news about the war."

"Sorry to disappoint you, dear, but Colonel Ellet has requested all of his officers to attend a meeting this evening." Matt spoke, still staring at his half-consumed wine. He had to fight to frame coherent sentences. "It appears the Colonel intends to question a Southern naval officer captured aboard a train during one of our cavalry raids into Tennessee.

"Don't know how much we will learn from him," he added, "but we expect better of a spy of ours who's just returned from Memphis. It's expected he'll give us a pretty exact description of the Confederate fleet's strength and armament. I'm so sorry, dear, that I shan't be able to go over to the MacLeans'."

But really he was glad; he needed to get away from Phoebe long enough to arrive at certain decisions concerning the "Reverend" Adams.

XIX CAPTIVE OFFICER

IT WAS IN Colonel Charles Ellet's own office that appeared, one by one, various military and civilian officers volunteering to serve aboard the new steam rams. Among them were Colonel Ellet's own son, Charles Rivers Ellet, and his brother, Lieutenant-Colonel A. W. Ellet. About half of the assemblage were in uniform, for the most part new and ill-fitting. The rest wore the usual assortment of civilian garb affected by rivermen.

Present were several young lieutenants mostly from Illinois or Iowa volunteer regiments. They had offered their services to defend the big former Ohio River packet *Queen of the West;* she probably would be designated as flagboat for the new squadron, and *Monarch,* another swift sidewheeler. More officers would have been present had not *Switzerland, Lancaster* and *Mingo* and other steam rams already departed to join the Western Flotilla, again in fighting condition and now operating under the command of Flag Officer W. D. Porter. When last reported, the Eads ironclads had been taking on all manner of supplies recently captured at New Madrid.

An air of subdued excitement pervaded the boatyard's office. This would be the first time anyone present ever had beheld a Confederate naval officer, for all that Louisville now swarmed with Southern Army officers on parole.

The realization that the "Reverend" D. Adams was near at hand, and to justice, set Matt's nerves to humming and so fogged his perceptions that he sat staring blankly at the *Monarch's* towering bulk. The steam ram at present lay to her dock with slender spirals of smoke commencing to rise from her chimneys. In his mind's eye he read again that friable brown clipping:

BOGUS PASTOR EXPOSED.

Portland, March 12, 1839. Today a clever and plausible rascal who has been masquerading about this city as the Reverend D. Adams has been exposed as an unordained impostor.

The measured tread of a guard detail advancing along the corridor stilled all conversation in Colonel Ellet's office and various officers turned on their seats to face the entrance. There appeared a single, tall blond figure in a long-skirted, gray-blue tunic. The captured officer's buttons were spaced by twos and descended a tunic cut exactly like that of the Old Navy. On his cuffs, however, were three stripes of which the uppermost was surmounted by a diamond in tarnished gold braid.

A trifle wearily the prisoner tramped in and was peering about when a voice called, "I'll be damned if it isn't Sam Seymour!"

The speaker was Lieutenant J. P. Stanford, U.S.N., of the Cairo Naval Station complement, in town to co-ordinate activities of Colonel Charles Ellet's ram fleet with that of Foote's Western Flotilla.

The Confederate naval officer blinked in the lamplight until he identified the speaker. "Hello, Jim. Still play the guitar?"

Before the assembled officers in blue the two men warmly shook hands. "We graduated from Annapolis in the same year," Stanford presently explained, "and served together in the old *Mississippi*. Seen her lately?"

Sam Seymour's yellow head inclined and he grimaced. "Yes. She was in the battle below our forts at New Orleans. When I last saw her she was shooting the lights and livers out of our fleet."

"You were in that battle?"

The Confederate's shoulders in weather-beaten gray-blue rose in a resigned sigh. "No. I was assigned to the other *Mississippi*, the Confederate ram. After New Orleans fell we had to burn her because she lacked her engines and would have fallen into your hands." His jaw tightened. "She'd have smashed Farragut's wooden frigates to kindling if she'd been ready."

At the word "ram" Colonel Ellet rapped on his desk. "We would be most interested, Commander Seymour, to hear anything you care to relate concerning the ram *Mississippi's* construction. Pray seat yourself near the window. It grows warm in here."

"Since she now lies at the bottom of the River," commenced Seymour, "there's no harm in telling that the *Mississippi* was built largely by house carpenters; we in the South are terribly short of shipwrights, you know." The prisoner, with enthusiasm manifest in his voice, then went on to describe the lost ironclad's battery plan, armor and her terribly weak engines.

"Are all your vessels so badly powered?" demanded Matt quietly.

The Southerner's gray-blue eyes swung over to meet his. "Thank God, no! You'll learn that if ever you meet the *Bragg*, the *Van Dorn* and the rest–"

"How many are there?" Lieutenant-Colonel A. W. Ellet of the *Monarch* demanded so smoothly that the Confederate replied without hesitation.

"Our River Defense Fleet numbers eleven all told. Most are protected with railroad iron bolted to–" Suddenly Seymour broke off, flushing furiously. "I shouldn't have said that. I was surprised into it."

"Care to describe any of the vessels, Sam?" Lieutenant Stanford demanded, standing with one arm resting on the mantelpiece over a cold fireplace.

"No, nothing beyond the fact that most of our vessels are very fast and mount the most modern of guns." A wan smile curved the prisoner's broad brown features. "In fact, gentlemen, I predict that you're in for a hell of a hot time around Fort Pillow and Memphis."

"Ain't two of your ships big, ocean-going steamers out of the Gulf?" demanded a civilian.

"I can't answer that," Seymour flecked a speck of dust from his belt's brass plate. "Reckon I've been talking too freely, already. But, as I said just now, you will find Pillow and the defenses there a far tougher nut to crack than Donelson. This time you'll have to fight our fleet–I know you're aware it's commanded by Commodore J. E. Montgomery–in addition to the land batteries–"

"Commander Seymour appears fatigued," observed Colonel Ellet turning his fine, big-nosed head over one shoulder. "Is there any refreshment about, Mr. Chippendale?"

One of the civilian officers nodded, then crossed to a desk and produced a bottle and several glasses. He splashed a little whiskey into them. "I say, Jim," the captive officer called, "seen anything of my cousin Rob Ashton Seymour lately? Heard he was aboard the *Congress* at Hampton Roads."

"No. But he must be all right—if he'd been killed or hurt I'd have heard about it."

For some time now Matt had been studying this big solid figure in gray. Whom did he resemble? Painfully aware of his brand-new uniform's poor tailoring he moved over to the prisoner.

"Your pardon, sir, but didn't you just mention the name Robert Ashton?"

"Yes. Robert Ashton Seymour is my first cousin—fighting on your side. Why?"

All-too-painful recollections of that stormy winter's evening in Dexter were flooding Matt's mind. "Well, Commander, there's a Robert Ashton who was born and brought up right next to where I come from in the State of Maine. I've been noticing a sort of family resemblance."

"Did this Rob Ashton have an ancestor who fought as a privateer during the Revolution?"

"That's the one. He owned the famous *Grand Turk II*," Matt smiled. "My friend Rob's family always was almighty proud about him."

"Then we must be cousins," Seymour said, accepting a glass of whiskey and water. "The main branch of my family are settled in Portsmouth but some of them moved up into Maine, so my mother used to tell me. Her maiden name was Ashton, too. Where is this Rob Ashton you speak of?"

"He's a medical officer in the Union Army. Don't know where he'd be serving right now."

Although various officers attempted more or less subtly to elicit further information, Commander Seymour, C.S.N., dexterously evaded reply, sipped quietly at his bourbon and water.

During the course of a brief conversation Matt ascertained that Commander Seymour had been captured aboard a train by Federal cavalrymen near Grand Junction on the Memphis & Charleston Railroad while on his way east to report for an assignment.

"It was bad enough being taken prisoner," he observed ruefully while setting down his empty glass, "but to be captured on one's honeymoon is really hard lines. I wonder where poor Louise has gone." His expression hardened.

"Back to her people, perhaps?" suggested Lieutenant Stanford. "She's a Southern lady I presume?"

"Yes, her home was in New Orleans which, of course, is now in your hands, so she can't go home. I am afraid there is no one else but my sister-in-law, a widow who lives in Richmond."

Bitterness invaded the Southerner's voice. "If only we hadn't had that damned, fatal division of command at New Orleans. Can you imagine it, Mr.—?"

"—Everett," Matt supplied, warming to the fact that this prisoner evidently also was a new bridegroom. Poor devil, imagine being torn apart like this!

"We had three independent squadrons of gunboats all fighting *on the same side*—our Regular Navy, the Louisiana Navy and an Army abortion called the River Defense Flotilla."

"We are pretty near as badly off," Jim Stanford put in gloomily. "Our Army owns and commands the ships that we of the Navy serve and fight in. And now, here's this ram fleet of Colonel Ellet's—which is *all* Army!"

Colonel Ellet frowned but the Southern naval officer's gray eyes lit. "Thank God! That makes it all the better for Commodore Montgomery. You gentlemen will soon appreciate the folly of such arrangements."

"We have already," grunted Lieutenant Stanford, "But Mr. Lincoln remains obdurate."

"I think," Colonel Ellet observed stiffly, "that we have taken up more of Commander Seymour's time than we should have. I thank you for coming here, sir." He offered his hand and said gravely, "May your personal fortunes soon mend."

Commander Samuel Seymour picked up a képi-type cap across the front of which a fouled anchor of gold braid slanted. Above it were two small gilded stars which matched those adorning his tarnished gold-edged shoulder straps.

"Good-bye, Jim," said he somberly. "See what can be done about arranging an exchange, will you? I'm worried about my wife."

"I will," promised the Regular. "I'll set things in motion as soon as I return to Cairo. Commander Pennock's one of the best and will always help out fellow Annapolis graduates."

In departing Seymour called to Matt, "My regards to my unknown cousin, if and when you see him. Good evening, gentlemen." He bowed with that grace peculiar to Southern officers, then fell in between four blue-clad privates waiting in the hall with shouldered muskets and fixed bayonets. Evilly, those slender blades gleamed yellow-gray by the lamplight.

XX HOSPITAL TRAIN

BREATHLESSLY PAUL DENT ascended a long flight of wooden steps leading from the Louisville ferry slip to the railroad yards on the heights above New Albany, Indiana.

"Hospital train hasn't left yet?" he panted through a wicket.

"No, mister," a bushy-whiskered clerk informed him from beneath a green eyeshade, "but she air due to pull out, come twenty minutes, on Track Number Three. You'll find her easy what with all them ambulances backed up along the platform."

Only twenty minutes? Dent, red-faced and sweating profusely, groaned. Imagine having travelled all this distance from Cairo to have so short a time with Flavia Cosby and that, of course, not in private. Why had the delivery of her telegram announcing departure for the East been delayed some forty-eight hours? Of course such was not an uncommon occurrence because of precedence granted to official and military messages.

That New Albany, its railway terminal and its boatyards had achieved a sudden and probably transient importance, seemed obvious. Here, as in Cairo, Mound City and Paducah, it was the same old story of hastily built warehouses, freight platforms, barracks and shacks thrown together and not on any appreciable plan.

The hospital train proved to be long—twenty-three coaches not counting some freight cars and cabooses. Blue-uniformed hospital orderlies wearing more or less white aprons were still pulling stretchers out of crude four-wheeled and mule-drawn ambulances that kept backing up to Track Number Three. Everywhere along the wide wooden platform limped casualties in every type of uniform from Zouaves wearing blue-and-yellow boleros and baggy scarlet trousers, to Militia cavalrymen in black-frogged shell jackets. Most wore plainly visible bandages or swung awkwardly along between crutches. Ladies from the Christian Commission and the Sanitary Commission or pious, serious-faced young men from the newly established but very active Y.M.C.A. circulated about, assisting various patients up the steps and into the cars.

The day being overcast and barometer readings low, coal smoke from the bell-shaped funnels of half-a-dozen locomotives panting gently about the freight yards hung low, but failed to dampen the enthusiasm of certain lightly wounded men who obviously were in raptures to be starting homewards. Some of them were singing a newly popular song entitled "Oh,

Lord, Gals on Friday!" to the accompaniment of a wheezy accordion.

Complete exasperation commenced to harass Dent. To find Augustus and his sister amid this dense and shifting crowd was proving difficult. Suddenly it occurred to him that Lieutenant Cosby, being a rich man's son, probably would have engaged one of the train's few private staterooms. Therefore he hurried along through the train and only vaguely noted how stretchers had been slung within solidly built tiers of frames from canvas slings cushioned with rubber and designed to lessen the inevitable jolting of a car in motion.

Suddenly through an open door he glimpsed voluminous, dark gray skirts and a mulberry poke bonnet trimmed in black lace framing Flavia Cosby's dark hair and pale, classically handsome features.

"Flavia!" he called and as he rushed forward she sped out into the aisle and swayed into his arms amid the curious grins and pointed comments of various patients in the bunks.

"Oh, Paul! Paul, my dearest! What agonies I have suffered for fear my telegram failed to reach you."

"It came two days late, darling," he explained between kisses, "but then I travelled as fast as I could. Luckily I'm on a fortnight's leave, but oh, Flavia dear, isn't it wicked we've been granted so little time and you lovelier than I've ever seen you!"

"It is, Paul. It's downright inhuman." Her brilliant and expressive dark eyes intently examined his well-tanned features. "By this uniform I deduce you've joined the Navy? How wonderful! You wanted to so much."

He hugged her firmly slender young body again. "For some reason Commander Walke took a favorable view of my trifling services at Fort Donelson so I expect I have become about the only commissioned pilot with the Western Flotilla." He smiled. "Since there are plenty of experienced civilian pilots available, men who've forgotten more than I will ever know about the rivers, I will shift to the Naval Ordnance Branch come the first of next month." Suddenly he remembered. "Augustus? How is he?"

Flavia turned aside, darkly shining red lips compressed. "Oh, 'Gustus has picked up considerably over the prospect of going home."

"Is he reconciled to–?" He clung to her hand.

"Not entirely, and I can't blame him. After all, the prospect of being crippled for the rest of his life must be hard to face."

Dent, summoning a cheerful mien, entered the stateroom to find Augustus sitting in a chair placed beside his bunk. His still pale and wasted features relaxed when Dent strode in.

"So the bad penny turns up." He grinned. "Thank goodness you have.

Never thought you'd make it. Flavia's been languishing like a heroine of Sir Walter Scott's. Can't you ride with us part way?"

"Lord, no!" Dent shook a head as dark as Flavia's. "I must catch a ferry back to Louisville. I'll be cutting my leave very fine if I'm to report aboard the *Carondelet* on time and God alone knows whether I'll find a boat heading downstream tomorrow."

"Where is the *Carondelet* now?"

"On the Mississippi somewhere above Fort Pillow, I expect. Oh, Flavia, I–I've brought you something." Flushing he groped into the front of his double-breasted blue tunic and produced a ring box. "Picked this up in Louisville," he explained apologetically. "I'm afraid a fire opal isn't much to offer Josiah Cosby's daughter."

When she pressed the box's release button, Flavia emitted a small squeal of delight. "Oh, Paul, Paul! Why, this is the loveliest engagement ring a girl could hope for!" She hugged him delightedly but when, watched by Augustus, Paul slipped the ring onto her third finger, she sobered.

"Expect I'm privileged to be the first to offer congratulations and conventional good wishes?" Augustus pecked his sister's cheek and wrung Dent's hand. "Hope Pa won't prove difficult. Money's the yardstick with him."

"Oh, Paul! How long will it be before you can get leave enough to come East? I'm impatient for you to meet Papa and Mamma and to visit us all at Sachem Hill."

"Only the good Lord knows, darling," came the sober reply. "Unless I miss my guess–along with Commander Walke and a lot of others–the Western Flotilla is in for a lot of hard fighting. I don't expect we'll rest until Vicksburg is taken and the River opened all the way to the Gulf."

A voice was penetrating a babble of conversation in the hospital car, the chuffing of passing locomotives and the cries of vendors busy upon the platform.

"Which is Lieutenant Cosby's stateroom?"

"See who it is, dear, will you?" Flavia demanded while tucking a quilt about her brother's leg.

Dent thrust his head into the passage. "Here! What– Why, it's the Reverend Mr. Adams!" He drew breath to call a cheery greeting, but something in the white-haired minister's expression restrained him. Very grave in his rusty black frock coat, the Reverend David Adams entered the stateroom, closed its door behind him and removed a tall stovepipe hat.

His gaze shifted quickly from Augustus to Flavia. "Alas, my poor young friends, how little did I suspect that when I bade you farewell yesterday I would see you again so soon and bearing such ill tidings."

Flavia Cosby's sherry-brown eyes opened wide. "Ill tidings?"

"Yes." The Reverend Mr. Adams with a quivering hand passed a blue telegraph form over to Dent. "Perhaps you, my friend, had better read this while I say a little prayer that you," his gaze included Augustus and Flavia, "will bear this tragic news with truly Christian fortitude and resignation."

While a freight train clanked by beyond the stateroom's smoke-grimed windows Dent unfolded the telegram and read:

MAY 10, 1862 BANGOR, MAINE
MISS FLAVIA COSBY, CARE CHRISTIAN COMMISSION, LOUISVILLE, KY. YOUR FATHER INSTANTLY KILLED THIS MORNING BY POORLY FELLED TREE. GOD'S WILL BE DONE. COME AS SOON AS YOU CAN. YOUR SORROWING MOTHER.

XXI SUPPER AT THE EVERETTS'

PHOEBE EVERETT, BUSY about her kitchen, could hear Matt tramping around upstairs collecting such of his meager possessions as he intended to take aboard the *Monarch* now scheduled for unexpectedly early departure. In fact various minor bits of carpentering remained to be done on the trip downstream. Only by an effort was she able to hum while basting the fowl; she would have preferred to sob. Gradually it was becoming borne in upon her what it would mean to see Matt depart tomorrow at daybreak on his way into the path of humming musket balls, screaming round shot and bursting shells.

She bit her lip while mashing potatoes with unnecessary vigor. Of course she had seen other wives clinging to and weeping over their departing menfolk and had pitied them from the bottom of her heart. She imagined she could guess the poignance of their grief but she had not, not until this evening. Well, she for one wasn't going to blubber on the dockyard wharf—she would bid him a smiling farewell if it killed her.

Only twenty minutes earlier Matt had come swinging through their white picket gate affecting a lightheartedness and enthusiasm over this sudden and premature departure. It was due, he'd explained gravely, to the fact that the Western Flotilla had suffered a serious defeat off a place called Craigshead Point. Two Eads ironclads had been reported sunk; apparently the Federal Fleet on the Upper Mississippi had been making heavy going following its triumph at Island Number Ten.

In a way Phoebe rejoiced that the Reverend Mr. Adams was expected for supper; it should be easier to maintain an unworried air, with him present, and to manufacture cheerful small talk.

Matt called down the backstairs. "Where have you put my brown flannel shirt, darling? Don't I own more than two pairs of whole socks?"

She reassured him and completed the setting of her table by decorating it with a spray of yellow roses brought over by Peggy MacLean earlier in the afternoon. A horrible possibility occurred. This was the first time she and Matt had ever entertained in their home—might it also be the last?

Matt meanwhile was finding it difficult to concentrate upon packing even so simple as this. Any moment now the "Reverend" D. Adams—he could recollect just how that name had appeared in those faded clippings back at Newport Junction—would arrive.

At the moment he entertained no notion what he was going to say, or what he might do, to that pious fraud. In vain he attempted to remain calm, not to dwell on those long years of humiliation and shame suffered by his mother. From a drawer of his bureau he produced that same pistol he had purchased in Bangor, the one he had employed to shoot down Josiah Cosby. A wave of wild and bitter hatred engulfed him. Not only had Cosby callously and cruelly betrayed Abigail Everett but, too cowardly to make the attempt himself, he had paid an assassin to attempt his end!

During a long moment Matt stood gazing down at his ugly little pistol with unseeing eyes fixed upon a copper percussion cap shining dully on its nipple. The weapon he knew to be loaded; he had kept it ready in the event of thieves. Following an instant's hesitation he grimly slipped the weapon into a side pocket of his single-breasted blue uniform tunic as it hung to a peg behind the bedroom door.

Almost before he realized it the gate giving on to Catbird Walk had banged gently and, glancing out of the window, he beheld a lean, black-clad figure advancing slowly up the nasturtium-bordered walk. He received instant impressions of gold-rimmed spectacles, long white hair, and of a white patriarchal beard trimmed square across the new arrival's throat. There he came, the "Reverend" D. Adams. In how many other wickednesses and betrayals had yonder charlatan participated?

He heard his wife's rich voice calling, "Oh, Mr. Adams! How *glad* I am to see you! I was beginning to fear that you might have been detained at some one of the hospitals." From the foot of the stairs Phoebe cried, "Come down, Matthew! The Reverend Mr. Adams is here."

"Just a minute," he called and, despite himself, his heart commenced to hammer. Deliberately, in order to master his nerves, he took time to place a couple of clean nightshirts in his carpetbag. Next, and with fingers steady again, he buttoned the single row of brightly new gilt buttons. In a mirror he noted with satisfaction the presence of single silver bars set at either end of his shoulder straps against a background of light blue velvet—his commission being in the infantry. The weight of that little pistol tugged reminiscently at his pocket—just as it had at Sachem Hill. Halfway down the short flight of stairs he drew a deep, shuddering breath which somehow steadied him.

"It is so pleasant to see your home, Mrs. Everett," Reverend Mr. Adams observed a little later, "and to meet your husband." He smiled brightly at Phoebe. "May I observe that you seem very fortunate in both? I wish I could tell you, Lieutenant, how fortunate I deem you, too. If ever there was an unselfish and tireless worker in the service of the Lord and an example to her sex, it is your wife."

After removing her apron Phoebe led the way into her tiny sitting room where all three seated themselves and sipped glasses of raspberry shrub.

Matt sat stiffly erect, surveying the self-styled "minister" with a subtle intensity. This Adams fellow he decided certainly was a convincing actor. What with his kindly air, gentle voice and straightforward manner small wonder poor young Abigail Everett should have been taken in so long ago!

"What kind of a day did you have, Mr. Adams?" Phoebe presently inquired through the kitchen door. She was bustling about dishing up the fowl, biscuits and half-a-dozen kinds of vegetables.

"Busier than usual, but also it proved to be an uncommonly sad one."

"Why?"

"It became my melancholy duty to inform a gravely wounded young officer and his lovely young sister, who had been nursing him, that their father had been accidentally killed; just when they were looking forward to a happy family reunion." The minister removed his glasses and shook his silvery head. "Dear, dear! It seems sometimes as if the Lord indeed must be wroth with His children. Poor young Cosby had appeared so excited and cheerful over the prospects of returning home at long last."

"Cosby?" An icy rivulet commenced to course down Matt's spine.

"Yes. By a curious coincidence I happened to know the deceased man as well as his children; in fact I performed his marriage service." The Reverend Mr. Adams' voice sounded clearly to Matt's ears but as from a great distance. By God! Here he calmly was admitting his crime.

"And what was the father's name?" Phoebe queried in a hushed voice.

The Reverend Mr. Adams slipped his spectacles back into place before lifting his glass of shrub.

"It was Josiah. I well remember marrying that sturdy young fellow to a lovely young lady who was the daughter of a fellow clergyman."

Fighting to keep his voice level despite a furious pounding of blood in his ears Matt inquired. "Where did you marry them?"

The minister laughed softly. "In Portland, Maine, back in the year 1839."

"What a perfectly marvelous memory you must have!" observed Phoebe, flushed and pink. "Do you remember all the people you have married?"

"Mercy, no! During the course of my life I must have married hundreds of couples that I couldn't for the life of me remember, but I always have remembered that Cosby couple. They were so handsome and so very much in love."

The skin commenced to grow cold and to tingle on the back of Matt's big hands.

"Why," he demanded in a taut monotone, "should you have remembered these two out of all the rest?"

"Probably because they were in such a hurry to be off and alone together that they rushed away leaving behind their wedding lines."

"Left their wedding lines behind?" An emotional whirlwind assaulted Matt's mind.

"Yes, I recall that wedding as clearly as if I had performed it yesterday. The bride's name was Abigail Everett—spelt the same as yours, Lieutenant. Josiah and Abigail. Good biblical names if ever there were any. And to think that after having comforted Cosby's son I should be forced also to become the harbinger of his death."

Matt heard his own voice inquiring, "You signed a marriage certificate?"

"Indeed I did; in the vestry of my church. As a matter of fact their certificate is still in my possession."

By a supreme effort Matt, controlled himself, did not cock the pistol. "When did you leave Portland?"

"Very shortly after the Cosby nuptials," came the quiet reply. "You see, Lieutenant, I was offered to a congregation in Peoria. I had often thought of posting the certificate—"

"One moment," Matt said. "Where were you ordained?"

"At the Divinity School of Harvard University," came the prompt reply. "But why do you ask in so strained a tone?"

"Is there record there of your ordination?"

"Dear me, young man," frowned the minister, "you do seem to be frightfully perturbed. What, pray, is the reason?"

"You should know!" burst out the New Englander.

The Reverend Mr. Adams suddenly got to his feet blinking nervously behind his spectacles. "Are you by any chance confusing me with a certain impostor bearing a very similar name?"

The whole cottage seemed to shift and sway under Matt's chair.

"Then there *was* an impostor?"

"Yes. A scoundrel by the name of Donald Adams who arrived in Portland shortly after I had departed for the West. Calmly, he passed himself off as my brother. Heaven alone knows how much he stole from church funds or how much mischief and sorrow he caused to innocent persons."

In a furious torrent, soul-shaking realizations flooded Matt's brain. "You are positive that Josiah Cosby's bride was named Abigail Everett?"

The minister stared at this young officer's vehemence. "Yes, I am as sure as my name is David, and *not* Donald Adams."

"And you still have possession of that certificate? You are positive of that?" The words fairly crackled from Matt's lips.

"Have I not just told you so? Young man, I fail to see why you should become so fearfully overwrought."

Matt stalked over to stare for a little while out of the window. "Would you not be concerned, Mr. Adams, if you suddenly learned that you were not a bastard child after all, but conceived in honorable wedlock?"

The intensity of Phoebe's joyous cry caused robins hopping about the lawn to flutter away. "Matt! Matt! Then it's *not* true!"

Such an expression of indescribable joy lit the young lieutenant's features that the Reverend Mr. Adams never forgot it. "Then *I am not* illegitimate. It is Augustus, Flavia and Decius who are the nameless ones!"

"Dear Lord forgive us!" gasped the minister. "So you deemed your parents married by that charlatan?"

Regardless of hissing noises caused by a pot's boiling over, Phoebe, face radiant, rushed over and, weeping for joy, clung to her husband. "Oh, Matt, how wonderful! How very wonderful! If only your dear mother could have learned the truth."

"Perhaps she does know," suggested the Reverend Mr. Adams. "Who can be sure that she does not?"

Matt suddenly slipped onto his knees and with Phoebe kneeling beside him offered a brief prayer of thankfulness. Then, in unison with the minister, they recited the Lord's Prayer.

Wonderingly Phoebe remarked as they arose, "Isn't it strange to realize that our name is really Cosby?"

Matt looked startled. "Why, that's true, of course," he hesitated, "but I don't intend to alter our name immediately. It would cause a multitude of complications, my commission and such; there's no time since we're to sail early tomorrow. Besides Mother's wedding certificate must be registered and Mr. Stetson must take certain steps to prove who legally is entitled to the name of Cosby." Smiling widely he kissed his wife. "Phoebe, after dinner I'm going to write to Mr. Stetson. And may I ask you, sir, to pen my lawyer a brief explanatory note?" He drew himself up, squared his shoulders. "Do you know, Phoebe, I shall be acutely interested to learn the provisions made in Josiah Cosby's will?"

"Then you intend to return home to claim your birthright?" inquired the Reverend Mr. Adams.

Startled, Matt peered at the venerable minister. "Certainly."

Silence ruled the cheerful little sitting room until Phoebe said, "Isn't Matthew perfectly justified?"

A long slow sigh escaped the Reverend Mr. Adams and thoughtfully he stroked his short silvery beard. "Legally he has every right, but—but—"

"But what?" Matt's dark eyes bored into those parchment-hued features across the room.

"I was only thinking, Lieutenant, of the tragedy that will engulf four innocent people when the truth is published."

"Whom do you mean?"

"First, there is the second Mrs. Cosby. She undoubtedly was wholly innocent in her bigamous marriage to Josiah Cosby." He broke off. "I am becoming inclined to think that your father really believed that the 'Reverend D. Adams' was indeed an impostor who had married him to Abigail Everett and so deemed himself unwed."

"Perhaps he did," Phoebe murmured. "In any event let us not speak ill of the dead."

"Next to suffer," the minister elevated a second finger, "is young Augustus Cosby, as fine a young officer and Christian as I have ever encountered. Recently he has lost a leg in action and faces the existence of a cripple."

Matt's jaw hardened. It had always remained a source of amazement to him how clearly he had retained that brief impression of Augustus Cosby received last autumn.

"—And then there is his sister Flavia."

A mental image of that darkly vital young woman, too, had lingered inexplicably sharp in Matt's mind.

"During the past two months she has been here in Louisville nursing her brother and others. It may not interest you, Lieutenant, but I have watched her transformation from a spoiled, willful and ill-tempered chit to a thoughtful, useful and unselfish young woman."

The Reverend Mr. Adams' gaze stole outdoors, lingered upon a glory created by the sunset beating through fresh green leaves of a big maple onto a flower bed next door. "Is it not curious that her fiancé should have given her a ring this very afternoon, only a very few moments before I was forced to bring the sad tidings of her father's sudden demise."

"So Flavia Cosby is engaged?"

"Yes. To a brave young officer who has been, and still is, serving aboard the *Carondelet*. Poor children, they had but a very few moments together before the hospital train departed."

Gently the minister raised a fourth finger. "And then there is another brother, Decius, of whom I know nothing save that Augustus holds him to be a bit of a scamp. We've just learned he is serving in Maryland in a Union cavalry regiment. So, you see, four, if not five, people will suffer when the truth concerning Mr. Cosby's marriages becomes known."

"I can't help that," Matt said stiffly. "I can only remember that my mother was condemned to suffer twenty-one long years of lonely shame and that I was deprived of family relationships. No, I don't owe the Cosbys the least consideration and I shall claim what is mine by right." Smiling, the tall figure in blue suddenly turned to Phoebe. "And now, my dear, isn't our supper almost ready? I trust that Mr. Adams isn't anywhere near as hungry as I."

"But I am," the older man admitted as he and Matt seated themselves, "There was so much to be done today I fear that I quite forgot to partake of a midday meal. Shall I invoke a blessing?"

XXII RIVER SOUTHWARDS

THERE WAS BARELY enough dawn light to reveal a scattering of handkerchiefs being waved on the dock which had just been quitted by the big steam ram, *Monarch*. This particular spring morning promised to be glorious and a multitude of stars paled and yielded swiftly to the advent of day.

From behind heavy timber breastworks recently erected upon *Monarch's* hurricane deck, Lieutenant Matthew Everett strained his eyes until he picked out among the tumbled freight Phoebe's more than average tall figure. She was further distinguishable by the long white apron she had promised to wear. He caught his breath and peered intently downwards. Was this the last he would ever see of his wife, or she of him? Those ever-mounting casualty lists rendered such a possibility more than likely.

The slow, squattering beat of the steam ram's enormous sidewheels—she had been one of the fastest "palace" boats on the Ohio—swiftly widened the expanse of water boiling between steamboat and dock. Soon it grew too great for him to read Phoebe's expression yet he knew that she still would wear a mechanical smile frozen on her lovely lips; just such a smile as he had noted on the faces of too many women during the past few weeks.

Curious, how profound was that turmoil which had pervaded his being since the night before. Right now his mind suggested a cardtable upon which pasteboards have been carelessly scattered. The cards were awaiting collection and arrangement into order of some sort.

Even now he simply couldn't get it through his head that he was no nameless bastard but, beyond doubt, the legitimate eldest son of Josiah Cosby.

His shoulders seemed to rise and square themselves suddenly as if relieved of that heavy load of shame. Up until this morning he had thought to leave for combat recklessly, carelessly, seeking perhaps subconsciously, a redeeming solution to his dishonor. Now he was departing determined fully to discharge his responsibilities, yet inwardly dreading the possibility that he might never come back or that he might return among the wretched hobbling ranks of the sick and wounded.

He felt infinitely reassured over one realization: as the widow of Josiah Cosby's only legitimate heir, Phoebe and her child need never want, and all this in addition to that surprisingly large estate amassed by Abigail Hovey.

With Colonel Charles Ellet aboard, and towing two big barges loaded to the guards with sacks of coal which must keep her in operation for weeks to come, *Queen of the West*, flagboat of the new squadron, already was standing downstream under a dense pall of smoke. *Monarch* likewise was towing a trio of coal barges.

Matt experienced a queer little thrill of excitement once the steam ram's thirty-foot paddlewheels ceased to back and commenced to propel the vessel forward at an ever-increasing clip. He had always deemed *Western Arrow* to be mighty fast but the way this former River greyhound travelled made his previous command appear positively sluggish as they travelled down the Ohio towards that rendezvous somewhere downstream where the smaller steam rams *Lancaster* and *Lioness* were supposed to be waiting together with various tenders, dispatch boats and supply vessels. Once the squadron had become united it would steam down the Mississippi until it found and joined the Western Flotilla.

Determinedly averting his gaze from the familiar outlines of Louisville, Matt strode to the opposite side of the deck where a detail from the Fifty-ninth Illinois Volunteer Infantry stood about amid their knapsacks and other equipment. These, he already had ascertained, were commanded by First Sergeant and Acting-Lieutenant E. W. Bartlett of Company L. He wondered whether Sergeant Bartlett could be as miserably ignorant concerning infantry drill, tactics and administration as himself. Fervently he hoped not.

Simply because he had proved himself a most excellent rifle shot, a natural leader and personally had recruited a dozen-odd lantern-jawed Kentucky mountaineers who could shoot the eyeballs out of a gnat, Matt had been ordered, out-of-hand, to command *Monarch's* military guard and so would rank senior to Sergeant Bartlett.

Certainly there was nothing in the least smart or soldierly about his two squads of Kentuckians. They were lounging about the hurricane deck with blouses unbuttoned, exposing hairy chests or grimy hickory shirts. To a man their jaws were working on cuds of chewing tobacco.

Long since Matt had decided that so long as they remained loyal, stuck to their posts and drove off Rebel sharpshooters, he wouldn't care a hoot how they dressed, or what they said, so long as they didn't become downright insubordinate. Most of these rangy, loose-jointed and soft-spoken individuals had fetched long-barrelled rifles down from the mountains. Just like their ancestors who had fought in the Revolution and that second war against England they had brought along little pigs of lead and bullet moulds cut to suit their particular piece for, in the course of years, a long rifle generally got rebored so often that each developed a calibre peculiarly its own. Too bad their graceful, old-fashioned flintlocks had been replaced by ugly but infinitely more practical percussion-cap locks.

The acting sergeant for Matt's two squads, a gangling mountaineer by the name of Abel Sneed, came ambling across the dew-sprinkled deck.

"Mawnin', boss," he drawled while making a vague motion towards the brim of a round black wool hat. "When do we-uns get to tangle with some vittles? Us boys air gittin' mighty peckish."

"I don't know," Matt admitted, "but breakfast should be pretty soon. I expect the steamboat's crew will ring a bell or blow a horn or something. You men have got plenty of powder and shot?"

"Yes, sirree, sir." A freckled youth of perhaps eighteen years ceased rumpling shoulder-long yellow hair and spoke from the lee of *Monarch's* starboard chimney. "Reckon we all kin pick off 'bout all the Rebs you wants. Me, Ah promised my Maw to knock off a baker's dozen just fer her."

The Illinois Volunteers evidently had been exposed to discipline for now at Sergeant Bartlett's command they fell into line and answered roll call. Matt looked on and tried to memorize various commands. He was taken aback when smartly turned-out First Sergeant E. W. Bartlett advanced and threw him a precise salute.

"Sergeant Bartlett reporting, sir," he informed, "with a detail from Company L, Fifty-ninth Illinois Volunteer Infantry."

Clumsily Matt returned the salute and tried to copy the crisp manner of various officers observed about the boatyard. "Very good, Sergeant. Dismiss your men to draw rations and to prepare for mess. After breakfast, er—say seven o'clock—the guard units will parade for inspection and instruction."

While hoping that he spoke in a convincing military style he consoled himself with the reflection that at this period in the war there must be thousands of officers serving in both armies who knew no more than he concerning military etiquette, tactics and drill. He wished he were able to execute a creditable "about face" but he couldn't, so held his ground until First Sergeant Bartlett had marched his men below.

"All right, you fellows," he hailed his ungainly command, "go below and draw some blankets and a mattress. You can stow them in cabins along the main deck."

There was room and to spare aboard this great converted steamboat and the faded elegance of her empty public rooms echoed hollowly to the boot heels of the seventy souls serving aboard.

The shivering note of a brass gong sounded below—no doubt it was the same which once had summoned elegant ladies and gentlemen. Loudly it reverberated through the hull stripped of ornament, furniture and glassware. Before going below Matt glanced down the wide, tea-colored Ohio flowing smoothly past a neat little village backed by a softly green forest. *Queen of the West* and *Switzerland* were surging along now, trailing dense clouds of black, woolly-looking smoke from tremendously tall twin stacks.

At the foot of the main staircase—so-called aboard river steamboats—he all but collided with a solid figure in dark blue.

"Sorry. I wasn't looking," he apologized and turned to make for a private dining saloon in which he messed together with Captain David M. Dryden, First Master Thomas Chippendale and Colonel Charles R. Ellet.

A hand gripped Matt's elbow and a familiar voice mocked, "You certainly are damned short with an old friend." It was Paul Dent and wearing a naval uniform! After shaking hands warmly the two surveyed each other in undisguised curiosity.

"What in God's name are you doing aboard this weird craft?" Dent demanded.

Matt laughed briefly. "I'm supposed to command the detail of sharpshooters aboard," he explained humorously. "That's a naval officer's uniform you're wearing isn't it?"

"Yes. I'm that amorphous creature known as a contract pilot—at least until I rejoin the *Carondelet*, then I'm supposed to be regularly commissioned at last." Warmed by Matt's friendly interest he lingered at the entrance to the main saloon.

"Then you've conquered your 'Bull Run trouble'?"

The other nodded. "Aboard the *Carondelet* I had to."

"What are you doing aboard the *Monarch?*"

"I'm only a passenger. I am supposed to be on my way to rejoin the *Carondelet* after a leave." He started to continue but broke off.

"What are you doing in that infantry officer's uniform? What made you quit your *Western Arrow?* You were doing so almighty well."

The two paused, reflected by huge mirrors at either end of the great empty main saloon; why these had been left to become shattered in the first collision was inexplicable.

"I was doing too well, you might say," Matt replied quietly. "Then something happened and, well, I discovered a sense of duty."

"I'm so very glad, Matt. Do you mind shaking hands again?"

After they had introduced themselves to Lieutenant-Colonel Ellet and *Monarch's* civilian captain the two seated themselves at a long table covered with red oilcloth and attacked a really formidable breakfast. They lingered over cups of coffee "strong enough to float hoss-shoes," as an ugly but enormously cheerful Negro orderly put it.

While draining the last of his coffee Dent said, "I travelled up to Louisville a while back to inquire after a friend of mine, a pilot by the name of Weaver who got wounded at Donelson, and who do you suppose was aboard the same hospital ship? Augustus Cosby, your half-brother."

"Oh?" Matt said as if it were all news to him that Augustus also had been in Louisville. "And what was he up to?"

"Poor devil's lost a leg," Dent explained while following a design in the oilcloth with a forefinger. "Seems he's something of a hero because he exposed himself to a storm of shot while trying to use the *Louisville* gunboat's auxiliary steering gear after her pilothouse had been shot away at Donelson."

"So he lost a leg? Sorry."

The Yale man treated him to a searching glance. "Isn't it extraordinary how things sometimes work out? Young Cosby's sister came West to care for him and I—I—, Matt, I've fallen head over heels in love with Flavia." He smiled almost shyly. "I know it's a lot to ask, but please wish us luck. We became engaged only yesterday."

XXIII CRAIGSHEAD POINT

In *Carondelet's* ETERNALLY hot, dim and humid wardroom as she lay at anchor with the rest of Flag Officer Charles H. Davis' flotilla above Craigshead Point, Medical Lieutenant Robert Ashton pushed to one side a tin plate containing the remains of a slab of very soggy apple pie. He pulled out a pencil and a sheet of paper stained with perspiration and prepared to write after cleaning crumbs and a splattering of gravy from the cracked and red-checkered oilcloth before him.

Two fellow officers were similarly engaged, hunched over the table in their shirt sleeves with their grease-marked work tunics dangling from the backs of the chairs they occupied.

Ashton wrote:

Aboard U.S. Gunboat *Carondelet*.
May 10, 1862, Above Fort Pillow,
Tennessee.

My dear and Respected Parents:

Today has proved one to be remembered and to tell you about.

As I wrote to Sister Ellen in my last, I am now posted to temporary duty aboard this famous gunboat which has fired more shots at the enemy and has suffered more hits than any two other ships in this flotilla. The *Carondelet's* regular surgeon has come down with a low fever which is so common in these parts it has decimated the crews of several vessels.

I arrived aboard but forty-eight hours ago—the same day on which gallant Rear Admiral Foote, he having recently been promoted, regretfully relinquished command of this fleet to Flag Officer Charles H. Davis. The wound Admiral Foote sustained at the siege of Fort Donelson, combined with arduous duties and advanced age, rendered this gallant old gentleman incapable of continuing in command.

Duty aboard the *Carondelet* is proving most interesting, infinitely more so than it was in the *Tyler*. This vessel is run in Regular Navy fashion, although she actually is owned by the War Department and operated directly under the orders of General Halleck, our Commander in the West.

Rob Ashton broke off to relight a seegar black as a licorice stick and about as thick.

In any case we all lay at anchor, our flag steamer *Benton*, the *St. Louis*, *Cairo* and *Mound City*, when, very early this morning, the *Cincinnati* dropped downstream to protect a mortar boat which had been dispatched to continue our bombardment of Fort Pillow—a massive fortification dominating the River a few miles below us.

Although this flotilla had already suffered an unexpected skirmish with the Confederate River Defense Fleet, for some reason steam was kept up only aboard the *Carondelet* and *Mound City*.

About six this morning a lookout stationed on our pilothouse hailed the chartroom crying that he had sighted several dense clouds of smoke arising on the far side of Plum Point, which is the extremity of a peninsula called Craigshead Point. To me it was a revelation how swiftly this crew of veterans ran to battle stations and prepared for action. Training tackles were manned, gunports raised, spongers, rammers, and all the other paraphernalia useful in fighting the guns were readied in a matter of three minutes. Captain Walke—the commanding officer of all naval vessels is called "Captain" no matter what his actual grade—several times hailed the *Benton*, a huge, ugly former snag boat serving as flag steamer, but on receiving no reply Walke ordered our anchor lines let go and immediately got the *Carondelet* under way, for around a bend downstream a furious cannonading had commenced.

Presently we sighted the enemy fleet rounding Craigshead Point, one after another, to the number of six. Then indeed did drums and bugles sound throughout our flotilla. Signal flags appeared directing our vessel and any other having steam up to proceed at once to the *Cincinnati's* rescue.

The presence of a light fog rendered our progress downstream hazardous but we raced for the enemy at the top of our pitifully slow speed and had proceeded about a mile before any of our other gunboats could quit their moorings.

After setting out my instruments and otherwise preparing the cockpit for the reception of wounded men I stepped out onto our fantail and presently perceived the enemy's leading vessel, I am told she was the *General Bragg*, big, brig-rigged, side-wheel steam ram, rushing down upon the *Cincinnati* with the obvious intention of striking her. At a range of about three-quarters of a mile we opened fire upon the *General Bragg* with our bow guns but soon were forced to desist because the enemy was too near the *Cincinnati*. A groan arose from our brave gunners when the Confederate man-of-war at full speed plowed into our gunboat like a bull into a thicket and struck her in the vicinity of her chartroom. Her ram opened a great gash in the *Cincinnati's* side into which the river water gushed in a resistless tide. Feebly our consort was attempting to retreat upriver when another enemy said to be the *General Price*, also rammed our luckless ironclad, for all that we had been pouring solid shot into the *Price* from our three bow guns. We then headed straight for the balance of the enemy's squadron and passed close by the *Cincinnati.* She was oozing steam at every port and obviously was in a sinking condition as she headed for shallow water. Just then a third Confederate vessel struck her—

The point of Rob Ashton's pencil had broken and while he used a Barlow knife to create a new one he noticed sounds of hammering—carpenters still were at work effecting repairs. The young surgeon absently blotted his forehead with the sleeve of a none-too-clean checked cotton shirt and wrote on:

Rounding-to, Captain Walke ordered our starboard broadside fired into the *General Bragg* and vessels later identified as the *General Jeff Thompson, General Beauregard* and *Colonel Lovell.* So thick and so low did mist and gunsmoke lie over the River at this early hour that we were quite unaware that two of the enemy, the *Little Rebel* and the *Van Dorn,* had passed and were now upstream of us. Therefore we now found ourselves alone and surrounded by the enemy. At once the *Jeff Thompson, Beauregard* and *Lovell* opened such an intense fire upon us that the *Carondelet's* casemate rang like a beaten gong under the impact of their shot and shell—none of which, I am glad to say, penetrated our armor.

At this moment Captain Walke ordered our new rifled fifty-pounder Dalghren gun to be trained upon the *Sumter* and struck this enemy just forward of her wheelhouse. Immediately furious clouds of white steam gushed from the *Sumter's* ports and we plainly saw her crew running out to jump overboard or to throw themselves flat upon her deck.

Throughout this engagement, my dear Parents, I never ceased to marvel over the perfection of the discipline obtaining aboard this vessel. There being no wounded to care for thus far, I remained where I was and so became witness to the first true fleet action of this war, although there may have been another fought below New Orleans, upon which we hear Rear Admiral Farragut is advancing.

Someone hailed from behind a wooden breastworks which recently have been built upon our hurricane deck that the *Mound City* had just been heavily rammed by the *Van Dorn.* I tried to see her among the drifting mists but at this point charges of grapeshot commenced to lash the water about us so I deemed it prudent to retire within the casemate. The action, however, to all intents and purposes, now came to an end but we had been taught a sharp lesson with respect to the courage, ability and gunnery of our enemy. Two of our best gunboats had been sunk in shallow water and several of our vessels had been badly punished by Confederate fire.

As for the enemy's loss, only the *Sumter* appeared to have been badly hurt and she was preserved from capture through being carried away by the current. Right now the Mississippi is in very high stage and runs swiftly.

It was typical that although the rest of our fleet retired behind Plum Point, Commander Walke alone elected to drop anchor on the scene of conflict and voluntarily assumed the duty of guardboat over the mass of supply vessels, tugs, coal barges, hospital boats and such, which accompany our expedition.

Hourly we anticipate the arrival of some steam rams, strange new vessels reported to have been designed by a civilian called Ellet. These craft are the subject of much hilarious speculation among our Regular Naval officers who insist that these so-called steam rams will be punctured like market baskets and sunk by the first broadside from Commodore Montgomery's fleet.

A Negro mess boy entered the wardroom and commenced in lackadaisical fashion to load his tray with dirty dishes. Although he looked mournful he sang softly all the while about "Ol' Dawg Tray."

A sound of voices aboard picket boats posted downstream carried clearly over the water while through an open gunport Rob glimpsed a scattering of yellow-red lights along the heights above some plantation's deserted landing.

"More coffee, Rastus." The surgeon held up a tin cup, whereupon the two other letter writers followed suit.

"Hope to God the damn' Rebs will leave us be for a while," grunted the officer opposite Rob, "and I wish to hell they would send us more ironclads in place of those silly steam rams."

Rob swallowed a gulp of coffee powerful enough to float an ax head, then returned pencil to paper.

As I wrote Sister Ellen, my friend Dent, the one who met Matt Hovey earlier this year is on leave, but is expected to return aboard within a few days. It appears that he has lost his heart to the sister of another neighbor of ours, a Miss Flavia Cosby from Bangor. If she is indeed half of what Paul Dent claims, this Miss Cosby must be a paragon of beauty, virtue and wit.

Dear me, how much I miss our lovely green mountains, the rushing of clear brooks and the smell of the pines. Here are only ugly hills, raw yellow or red, and naked bluffs, while the water! Well, in the glass before me lies a quarter inch of sediment, which is rather less than usual. This sediment, incidentally, affords our engineers no small concern they being forced because of it to draw fires and clean boiler tubes every few days.

As a medical man, Pa, you would appreciate the wonderful opportunities offered me. In the course of a few weeks I have set more bones, dressed more wounds and doctored more sick than would most physicians in a lifetime of practice at home. Alas, that the use of anaesthetics out here is almost unknown. We have on this expedition only a very limited supply of ether which is reserved for high ranking officers or other important patients. For the rest brandy or laudanum must serve the needs of such luckless wretches as get wounded.

I often wonder what has chanced with our neighbor Matt Hovey. Paul Dent informed me that when last heard of he was living in high style in St. Louis where apparently he has made a fortune through illicit traffic with the enemy. I can't imagine what has come over him. He used to be such a Godly, sober youth.

A drum has commenced to beat the retreat so will reluctantly have to close.

Please give my love to Sister Ellen, Aunt Mable and Uncle Will.

Your ever dutiful and respectful son,

ROB

XXIV EVACUATION

THE SPRING OF 1862 never proved lovelier or more balmy than during that week which was required to bring the new steam rams, *Queen of the West*, *Switzerland* and *Monarch* down the Ohio and the Mississippi to their destination above Memphis. Now they lay side by side securely moored to trees on the Arkansas shore, with landing stages lowered and taking on fuel from the barges they had towed south.

During this week Colonel Charles Ellet's civilian crews and the military guards had been required again and again to rehearse their various duties. Small boat drills had been frequent and accompanied by instruction in the use of life preservers; hardly one man in twenty was able to swim.

At all hours of the day and night Lieutenant Matthew Everett had sent his men scurrying to their posts where, sometimes, they conducted target practice upon passing snags or turtles which had come out to sun themselves upon a sandbank. Crouched behind narrow loopholes let through the solid oaken breastworks constructed atop the hurricane deck, mountaineers and infantrymen alike attained a more than satisfactory proficiency.

Happily, Sergeant Bartlett of the Fifty-ninth Illinois Volunteers, proved to be a willing subordinate, intelligent and keen over his duties. At first the Illinoismen's marksmanship with short-barrelled Spencer carbines proved anything but admirable; therefore Matt ordered case after case of cartridges to be brought on deck, ordered his command to blaze away at any likely mark—preferably one also in motion—he being anxious that they should learn to adjust fire from a moving platform on a moving target.

It proved some consolation to the blue-clad country boys that their mountaineer companions, magnificent sharpshooters though they were, never in their lives had been called upon to handle those long-barrelled rifles, for which their State was famous, from an unsteady base. Consequently they missed incredibly for quite a spell—to a flood of livid and picturesque Elizabethan profanity.

Night after night, Matt had strained his eyes by a smoky kerosene lantern studying infantry drill regulations so thoroughly that soon he gained Sergeant Bartlett's respect and friendship.

Wisely, Matt made no effort to convert his loose-jointed, lanky Kentuckians into smartly marching, well-turned-out infantrymen. He still merely insisted that they salute at proper times and desist from squirting tobacco juice while in ranks. It had been hard work to get them to participate in small boat drill because not one of them could swim so much as a stroke. They only yielded to persuasion when their commander explained that the theory of fighting these steam rams was peculiar—to sink an enemy even if it meant going down themselves. This was directly at odds with the Regular Navy's dictum that the preservation of his vessel must be a captain's first consideration. He even described for these long-haired volunteers a conference held aboard *Queen of the West* and presided over by quiet and high-minded Colonel Ellet.

"Gentlemen," he had declared in his soft yet commanding voice, "my steam rams have been designed for but a single purpose; to sink the enemy by ramming, *at any and all costs!* We shall rely only upon our superior speed, on our rams and on God's help. I shall expect none of you to swerve one foot aside once you steer for your enemy! Therefore, I charge you all," his gaze had included all the young-old bearded faces of his captains, "to be especially industrious in instructing the routine for abandoning ship." He had smiled faintly. "As a motto for this ram fleet may I suggest 'Come what will, press home the charge'?"

It had been a mighty serious group of officers who then had dispersed.

Lieutenant-Colonel Alfred W. Ellet, the Commander's brother, had grinned wryly at Matt while they were being rowed back to big, high-sided *Monarch*.

"A nice prospect, eh, Mr. Everett? Well, every man aboard our boats is a volunteer, so there shouldn't be too many shirkers or deserters."

Because there was space and to spare aboard these former palace boats and the mess was both plentiful and good, civilians and soldiers were getting along well enough together.

Soon after *Monarch* had quit Louisville Matt made successful efforts to secure the confidence and friendship of Captain Dryden, First Master Chippendale and Tim Collins, a rotund, red-nosed rascal who, with sallow and morose Charlie Jackson, were the steam ram's pilots.

Paul Dent, naturally, spent the bulk of his time in *Monarch's* pilot-house. Obviously, he was dreading that pending transfer to Ordnance. When the civilian pilots learned that he had been in *Carondelet's* wheelhouse at Forts Henry and Donelson they accorded the shy New Englander a respect granted to few others of the steam ram's little company.

During the long voyage southwards *Monarch's* crew and guards were afforded ample opportunity to familiarize themselves with the least details of their steamboat's construction and reconstruction. They scrambled over massive oaken beams lying parallel upon her bottom which, anchored into *Monarch's* original fabric at numerous points, supported a blunt, iron-sheathed wooden ram projecting beyond the former palace boat's stem. This ram bow was blunt, as the celebrated civil engineer, Charles Ellet, explained to his officers, and not knife-sharp because he intended to break in an enemy's side and leave a hole too great to be plugged.

On and on the ram fleet had cruised past innumerable bends, tow-heads, shoals, bars, wrecks and snags. Recently *Monarch* and *Queen* had become reinforced by a pair of sternwheeler rams—*Mingo* and *Lioness*. Former towboats, these craft were more powerful but not nearly so large or swift as their sidewheel consorts. To the ram fleet also were added a brace of dispatch boats, the former river tugs, *Fulton* and *Horner*. These fleet little craft were supposed to make themselves useful by bearing communications between units of the ram fleet and also by conveying suggestions from the flagboat of the ironclads. There were no timberclads accompanying this expedition; *Conestoga* and *Tyler* being fully occupied in keeping the Tennessee open towards Nashville.

After supper, meals aboard the ram fleet were seldom if ever termed 'messes," there was opportunity for Matt and Paul Dent to sit on the hurricane deck beneath the stars and watch a succession of shadowy, moon-silhouetted landscapes slide silently by; absently they watched streams of jewel-bright sparks from their consorts' stacks go trailing off over the presently peaceful Mississippi. Every so often they would recognize the empty, crumbling and pathetically inadequate parapet of some abandoned

Confederate battery. After considerable persuasion, Dent related for Matt's benefit his impressions and showed sketches made during the attack on Fort Henry and that fiery hell which had been endured before Fort Donelson.

On several occasions Matt was tempted to touch on the subject of Dent's recent engagement, yet he did not; the former Yale student obviously was aware now that he and Augustus Cosby had met. Characteristically, neither New Englander mentioned the metamorphosis which had overtaken them.

Matt wondered how Dent would react once the fact of Flavia's illegitimacy became established. How? It was curious, he reflected, that they should both become regular worshippers at Divine Services held at sunup every day by big-nosed and black-bearded Lieutenant-Colonel Ellet. He had elected to follow an example set by his brother aboard *Queen of the West.*

On May seventeenth the Ellet ram fleet rounded a sandy, willow-shrouded bend a few miles above Fort Pillow. Promptly *Queen's* engine room bells jangled and the rams slowed down for, dotting the broad expanse of the Mississippi downstream, could be seen the low and ugly outlines of four Eads ironclads which, with ungainly *Benton,* formed the core of Flag Officer Davis' Western Flotilla.

For Dent it was easy to identify the various "Pook turtles," as well as the former snag boat now displaying a Flag Officer's pendant.

Matt, too, recognized *Benton* at once. Lord! How long it seemed since that raw day he first had beheld her on the ways at Carondelet! Anchored apart lay certain advance elements of the Ellet ram fleet together with the tender, *Dick Fulton.*

This afternoon seemed especially glorious because radiant sunlight was bathing the angular, red-gray ironclads, the yellow River and its freshly green shores in a golden effulgence.

Soon signals were flown aboard the flag steamer instructing the new arrivals either to tie up to the Arkansas shore or to drop anchor. *Queen of the West's* hook hardly had gone splashing overboard when her yawl was manned. Everyone in the Western Flotilla saw Colonel Charles Ellet's spare figure swaying in its stern. His yawl's coxswain steered straight for *Benton,* and a conference with Flag Officer Charles H. Davis. Everyone also noted that Colonel Ellet did not remain aboard the flag steamer very long but with disconcerting speed returned to *Queen of the West.* From her signal staff at once was flown the "Council of War" signal.

Presently it became evident to the ram fleet's officers, hurriedly rowed over to the ex-palace boat, that their Colonel's conference with Flag Officer Davis must have proved something less than satisfactory. Charles

Ellet's cavernous and expressive dark eyes were flashing and the nostrils of his thin, curved beak of a nose closed and opened quickly. He forebore comment, however, beyond stating that the naval commander had refused to issue the ram fleet instructions of any sort; in short, he, Colonel of the ram fleet, was free to do just as he saw fit, without reference to the ironclads and on his own responsibility.

A distant dull, rumbling, grumbling sound suggestive of distant thunder cut short Ellet's speech. All of his officers ran out onto the main deck in time to hear a second, and louder, series of reports come reverberating up the Mississippi Valley.

"Sounds like artillery fire," someone commented, staring off into the lantern-studded darkness. "You don't suppose General Lew Wallace could already have come up to attack Fort Pillow?"

During the next few moments several more increasingly violent detonations sounded, then silence again settled upon the Mississippi.

Once the council had reconvened Colonel Ellet cleared his throat and quietly addressed the browned faces above those dark blue tunics and winking brass buttons. "I have decided that, with the coming of dawn, our ram fleet will undertake a reconnaissance. You, Alfred," he turned to his brother, "will take the *Monarch* downstream and come as near to Fort Pillow as you dare—without risking being hit."

Lieutenant-Colonel Ellet queried, "And what, Charles, if enemy gunboats appear? Am I to attack them?"

Momentarily Ellet debated, stroked his long, clean-shaven chin. "I fear it would afford our friend, Flag Officer Davis, some small satisfaction were we to lose a boat so close upon arrival. No, you are not to fight. With your speed you can easily run away from the Confederate vessels. They are fast, but also they are weighted down by guns and armor."

That night Matt wrote another long letter to Phoebe trying, but not succeeding, to make light of the impending action. Tenderly he inquired into her health and that of the MacLeans and other friends. He concluded by sending warm regards to the Reverend Mr. Adams. Despite himself, his fingers still quivered whenever he wrote that name. He then pondered briefly on the probable fate of the false minister; also on whether Josiah Cosby had *at the time* really believed himself to be married by a charlatan.

Dog-tired, yet stirred by anticipation of tomorrow's reconnaissance, Matt retired to his once-palatial stateroom, palatial now only with regard to spaciousness, since all furniture, saving a plain wooden table, a folding chair and an Army cot, had been removed. A handsomely engraved plate-glass mirror, however, remained so situated as to afford a satisfactory view of that spot upon which a big, brass bed must certainly once have stood.

Sometime during the night Matt roused to a sound of more heavy firing and by rushing over to the stateroom window beheld a series of orange flashes briefly brightening the sky downstream.

Just before dawn a gig came threshing over from *Queen of the West* with orders for *Monarch* not to make the projected reconnaissance downriver but to send her yawl to undertake the mission.

It proved to be suprisingly cold on the River when, at four of the morning, Lieutenant Everett and Lieutenant-Colonel Alfred Ellet stepped into the pilot's yawl together with a detail of six sharpshooters, and as many more rivermen at its oars.

How very still it was save for a faint gurgling of the current. Right now the world appeared vast, dim, empty of life save for a scattering of lights indicating various units of the Union flotilla. Gradually Matt's pulses quickened. Yonder lay the enemy, ready to kill him. But he realized he wasn't anxious or afraid. Probably certain tense hours aboard the *Western Arrow* might explain it.

Those friendly yellow-red lights soon became eclipsed by one of the Mississippi's innumerable bends and all alone *Monarch's* yawl pulled along, silent save for the rhythmic *clunk!-clunk, clunk-clunk!* of oars against rowlocks.

Sergeant Bartlett from the bow called back quietly, "Lieutenant, sir, I'm sure I smell burnt gunpowder and wood smoke."

A moment later the entire reconnaissance party glimpsed the throbbing glow of some minor conflagration on a bluff above the eastern shore.

"Have your men cease rowing," Alfred Ellet drawled to his civilian coxswain, so for the next twenty minutes *Monarch's* yawl and her company of shivering, tense humanity was borne downstream in utter silence.

The east paled, darkened again but commenced to glow in earnest as dawn broke with disconcerting rapidity and startled oaths rang out from the boat's crew because their craft was drifting close under the shadowy parapets of Fort Pillow. But, as Matt and his companions quickly perceived, there came no challenge, there seemed to be no one beyond those embrasures which soon were discovered to be devoid of cannon, while, from further back on the heights, numerous woolly, whitish spirals of smoke lazily were ascending.

"Say, Misto' Ellet, hadn't we-all better turn back?" demanded one of the civilian oarsmen. "Missis Beasely's boy ain't hankering to git curried by no charge o' grapeshot."

"Quiet!" hissed Ellet as through night glasses he surveyed an imposing line of earthen parapets.

Robins and thrushes commenced to chirp and pipe on shore while the sound of someone chopping wood somewhere upstream came ridiculously loud and distinct.

A few stove-in flatboats and a sunken tug lying half submerged off the fort's landing caused glimmering streamers in the River's suddenly silvery surface.

"Rebs seem to have pulled foot," Ellet commented with a sibilant sigh. "See anything to the contrary, Matt?"

"No, sir."

"Of course the Rebels have evacuated," Ellet spoke as to himself. "With Corinth fallen into our hands they've become outflanked along the River all the way down to Memphis. Steer for the wharf, George."

On the wharf was found no sign of life beyond a shaggy mongrel puppy which came trotting eagerly out over the worn planking. By now the fires raging above were gaining in intensity. At Matt Everett's curt order his six sharpshooters shuffled away and fanned out in a line of skirmishers and, holding carbines ready, advanced along a rutted road zig-zagging up the face of the bluff. Matt, his heart thumping strangely, loosened in its holster his long-barrelled Navy Colt's revolver.

Every few rods the reconnaissance party halted to listen but still caught no sound of voices or of any activity above. When they gained the summit of the bluff, it was to behold by the dawn's light a desolate vista of empty gun emplacements, shattered casemates, burning barracks and what must have been magazines sullenly smouldering.

The only living things discovered in or about Fort Pillow were a handful of Negroes skulking timorously about, obviously salvaging cast-off shoes, blankets and bits of broken equipment. At first challenge they fled like rabbits and vanished into the underbrush back of Fort Pillow.

"I think," Alfred Ellet smiled suddenly through his curly black beard. "I think, fellows, we can use our yawl's flag to advantage up here."

"Yessuh!" A sharpshooter went pelting down to the landing and soon returned carrying the National Colors draped carefully over one arm. Through someone's oversight the halyards of Fort Pillow's flagstaff had remained intact and were neatly secured to a cleat.

Lieutenant-Colonel Ellet drew himself up, set a round, black felt hat straight on his head and called the sharpshooter detail to attention. "Will you be good enough to bend on and hoist our Colors, Mr. Everett?"

The civilian oarsmen removed their hats and the soldiers presented arms while Matt, his heart hammering, ran up the Stars and Stripes. Then all joined in a cheer which echoed and re-echoed thinly, eerily, about the great, abandoned fort.

XXV OFF "PADDY'S HEN AND CHICKENS"

THE WESTERN FLOTILLA'S acitvities proved to be varied and extensive once the sun had come up to reveal in dramatic hues an absurdly small Federal flag at the top of Fort Pillow's towering flagstaff. Lazily Old Glory curled above smoke rising from burning magazines, barracks and from a large number of cotton bales. Details of troops were sent ashore to take possession of the abandoned fort and restore the place to some kind of defensible condition.

Shortly after sunup the ironclads got up steam and with *Carondelet* leading, as usual, disappeared downstream. Not a word of explanation had been vouchsafed to the commander of the ram fleet.

Because Colonel Ellet, like so many other Union officers, was profoundly religious he did not swear out loud at this, but certainly outraged profanity was to be read in his looks while he watched *Carondelet, Benton, St. Louis* and *Cairo,* go churning off downstream with noon sunlight picking out the distinctive bands of paint about their smokestacks. With them went the auxiliary dispatch boats, tugs, supply boats and even a small floating hospital. Presently *Queen* hailed *Monarch* and Colonel Ellet, through a speaking trumpet, shouted over to his brother, "Guess we's might as well get along and learn what might be happening at Fort Randolph."

Accordingly, all four steam rams, *Queen of the West, Monarch, Switzerland* and *Lancaster,* headed downstream, soon overtook the lumbering ironclads and so arrived off Fort Randolph a good hour before Flag Officer Davis' plodding gray-black "turtles" hove into sight around a wooded point.

Fort Randolph, also having become hopelessly outflanked by General Wallace's Blue Army, had been evacuated. Yonder lay the smashed casemates, the empty gun emplacements and familiar pillars of smoke and flame.

While, one by one, the gunboats cast anchor and sent shore parties to take possession of the deserted fort, Colonel Ellet meditatively stroked his long chin, then sent orders by the dispatch boat, *Horner,* directing his smaller sternwheel steam rams, together with their tows of coal barges, to remain at a safe distance in the rear of the ironclads. After the affair at Craigshead Point and the way the gunboats had been caught napping there he intended to take no chances.

Still no instructions or communications of any sort came from *Benton* which, with her consorts, up-anchored in midafternoon and dropped down to the foot of Island Forty-five situated some two miles above the populous city of Memphis. Again the sidewheeler rams followed suit and participated in this general advance. As night came on *Queen* made signal for all four of the bigger steam rams to tie up along the Arkansas shore some eight to ten miles above Flag Officer Davis' anchorage.

The steam rams' crews sat up late eating a huge supper, slapping mosquitoes, and drinking many toasts in raw bourbon to the easy conquest of two forts which had been expected to fall only at the cost of many lives and some vessels. Speculation, some of it downright uneasy, was rife as to what the morrow would bring. Even the stupidest coal-passer was well aware that a victorious and powerful Confederate squadron lay anchored off Memphis. Undoubtedly it would come out to defend, at all hazards, the otherwise unprotected town.

Tomorrow *Monarch* might reel under the impact of solid shot and shell or her thin sides might be smashed by murderous charges of grapeshot. Tomorrow? At breakfast her officers, sunburned and generally bearded, considered one another in sudden curiosity. Whose face might be missing tomorrow from this long, oilcloth-covered table? *Whose?*

"Better have a full head of steam ready by half-past three tomorrow morning," Lieutenant-Colonel Alfred Ellet instructed First Engineer Hiram Lanahan.

The engineer wiped a large and plentifully mustached mouth on the sleeve of his sweat-stained checkered shirt. "Say, Al, ain't that a mite late in the day?" came his sarcastic query.

"No," grinned the younger Ellet. "Charlie's figuring to get the jump on those brass-bound Navy heroes who've not even been looking down their noses at us."

In his stateroom Matt, by the light of a bull's-eye lantern, penned a long letter to Phoebe, became abruptly and shockingly aware that this might well be his last to her. In detail he described his landing at Fort Pillow in the dawn and his sense of exhilaration on hoisting the National Colors over a Rebel stronghold.

"And to think," he wrote, "not six months ago, I cared not a hoot about our Flag or what happened to it!"

After sealing his missive, Matt knelt beside his cot to pray as long and as earnestly as ever he had in his little room back in Dexter. He prayed God that he might on the morrow bear himself without fear, that he and his comrades might be spared wounds or death and that God would look with favor upon the Union cause.

As he arose and unbuttoned his now wrinkled and spotted blue tunic he wondered how Paul Dent was making out now that he was back aboard his beloved *Carondelet*. Until now he had failed to realize how greatly he missed that quiet, well-bred individual's company. Would Paul perhaps be writing to Flavia Cosby much as he just now had been pouring out his soul to Phoebe?

Because of the return from sick leave of *Carondelet's* own excellent surgeon, James S. McNeely and a sudden sickness of *Benton's* surgeon, John Ludlow, Medical Lieutenant Robert Ashton once more found himself on temporary duty. He welcomed the change. Here aboard the flag steamer he should be in a position to witness Flag Officer Davis' command decisions and to grasp more readily various phases of the impending battle. Besides, it was something to be thus honorably relieved from dangers attendant to service under impetuous and ambitious Henry Walke.

Everyone in the Western Flotilla claimed a man's chances of survival were reduced fifty percent if he served in *Carondelet*. Over a game of piquet after supper with the Executive Officer, Lieutenant Joshua Bishop, U.S.N., he heard restated the Regular Navy philosophy in fighting an enemy—to damage them to the maximum *without losing the ship*; unless, of course, orders were to the contrary.

"The engagement we'll fight tomorrow," predicted Bishop, riffling worn and food-marked cards, "is going to be vastly different from our attacks on Henry, Donelson, Island Number Ten and all the rest."

"In what way?" queried Rob while cutting and dealing.

"Why, in this case, we're going to fight a classic naval battle. Ships—" the Regular couldn't bring himself to call them "boats—" "—against ships, and for once with no shore batteries to reckon on." Bishop nodded his big yellow head to himself. "Thank God, opposite Memphis the River's wide enough to allow plenty of room for maneuvering.

"Yes, Doctor, I venture to predict this will be the first fleet action, pure and simple, to be fought thus far."

Rob started to make some mention of Craigshead Point but the other anticipated. "Tomorrow or the day after there will be fought a full-dress battle, and a desperate one. The Rebels have simply got to sink us or lose Memphis, together with all its rail communications and the vast hills of cotton bales stored in warehouses there." Wrinkles appeared on his high pink brow and solemnly he shook his head several times. "I fear, Doctor, you will find yourself a very busy man come tomorrow night."

XXVI THE FLEETS ENGAGE (I)

THE SOUNDING OF a gong which aboard *Monarch* effectively, if vulgarly, supplanted the more martial summons of a bugle or drum, aroused Lieutenant Matthew Everett from a curiously uneasy slumber, set him to yawning and knuckling eyes. Feet commenced to clump along the deck aloft while he tugged on white-striped blue trousers and a uniform jacket beginning to grow baggy at the elbows.

A glance out of his cabin's window—it was indeed a window and not a port—confirmed the fact that an opaque mist as usual was shrouding the Mississippi. Although dense this fog proved to be so low-lying that only the pilot houses and chimneys of *Queen, Lancaster* and *Switzerland,* moored to a grove of cottonwoods, loomed dimly above it. All these stacks were commencing to spout Stygian smoke and to vomit torrents of vivid, wildly spiralling sparks.

Breakfast as usual consisted of coffee, "flannel" cakes and molasses, fried salt pork and doughnuts wolfed at an undigestible speed. Then, to a shivering clangor of engine room bells, the vessels cast off their mooring lines. Huge paddles commenced to splash and thresh as, successively, the steam rams backed out into midstream by the light of a waning moon.

Matt found it surprisingly cold on the hurricane deck where his unshaven guards waited shivering and hawking in a poorly dressed double rank. From this elevation one could discern occasional puffs of fire from some steamboat's smokestacks briefly flooding the mist with crimson radiance. The chanting of various leadsmen feeling their way downstream echoed eerily through the ghostly, gray-black mist: "Mark twain! A quarter twain! Mark three! Mark a quarter fo'."

In *Monarch's* big, oak-encased wheelhouse Matt knew both pilots must be straining their sight once her sidewheels ceased to back, hesitated, then commenced to churn, speeding her downwards towards the ironclads, towards Memphis, towards the enemy and whatever Fate held in store for her. On how many lives would Atropos use her shears today?

Off a bar called "Paddy's Hen and Chickens" the mist raised briefly, just long enough to reveal the dark outlines of Flag Officer Davis' command still at anchor but obviously preparing for action because dense columns of smoke were rising straight above all four gunboats.

From over the water sounded a ringing of boot heels hurrying along iron decks, the whine of tackles raising a gunport cover, and the rasp of coal scoops over fire plates as stokers gorged their fire boxes.

While tramping about the hurricane deck and swinging his arms Matt suddenly saw *Queen*, which had stopped her engines, get under way again and, at a half-speed, commence to shape a course towards the Arkansas shore. Presently Colonel Ellet's craft made signal for the ram fleet again to tie up.

"What in Tunket does this mean?" Matt muttered to himself after ordering his men back to the warmth below. If only some, even a rudimentary, liaison existed between these two elements composing the Union Fleet!

Nobody aboard the steam rams entertained the least notion of what might be Flag Officer Davis' strategy or objective; nor more could that taciturn worthy guess what plan of action Colonel Charles Ellet had decided to follow.

By five of the morning dank river mists smelling like water left too long in a flower vase had closed in, thicker than ever. Nothing was to be heard for a brief space but the threshing of paddlewheels out on the River and the sibilant hiss of steam roaring through some escape valves. Then, with terrifying suddenness and no warning at all, a shell burst opposite *Switzerland's* stern, luckily at a safe distance. Out on the smoke and mist-blanketed River, commenced a heavy cannonade. With a convulsive gasp Matt realized this gunfire *had not come from the direction of the Union ironclads' last known position!*

Through a baffling, blinding stratum of fog Colonel Ellet's deep voice hailed from *Queen's* wheelhouse. "Steam rams! Back immediately out into the channel and follow me in order."

At once followed the squattering beat of the quite invisible *Queen's* paddlewheels, commencing to revolve in reverse. Cursing in their excitement *Monarch's* pilots nonetheless waited until the flagboat's engines stopped in order to proceed forward. Immediately *Monarch*, appearing positively huge in this half light, followed suit.

To identify *Queen's* approximate position proved easy because above the single stratum of low-lying mist a column of fiery sparks could be seen gushing from her chimneys. Once *Monarch's* backing had ceased, everyone listened for *Switzerland's* departure from her berth; instead ensued a grinding crash and a mad jangle of bells followed by ringing volleys of curses.

"You blind sonofabitch! You've fouled me!" roared an outraged voice. "Why'd you shove off 'fore yer turn?"

"You were too damn' slow, blast your ugly eyes! For Christ's sake back your labbord wheel, you sister-seducing bastards!"

Further obscenities became lost amid the increased splashing of *Monarch's* paddles. Matt ran the length of the hurricane deck posting his sharpshooters at their appointed loopholes; also he made certain that they had a plentiful supply of cartridges.

Long since he had decided to command the starboard rail while Sergeant Bartlett would be responsible for the port. Gradually Matt's nerves crisped and his throat grew tight for now the cannonading sounded much closer beyond that wavering barrier of mingled mist and coal smoke. The air became filled with the whining scream caused by passing cannon balls. The rhythmic, whistling gasps made by steam escaping through the ram's exhaust pipes quickened.

Glancing backwards he found that he could still make out the smokestacks of *Lancaster* and *Switzerland*. Apparently the two boats had remained entangled and were drifting slowly downstream. Perhaps a third of a mile below, *Queen's* iron-crowned chimneys led towards that line of Union ironclads which, spouting torrents of smoke, were entering the main current above a comfortably wide stretch of river known to exist opposite the city of Memphis.

A vagrant slant of wind came bearing down and, as if some magician had waved his wand, the smoke and mist whirled away, all in a moment revealing a line of housetops upon which spectators had gathered to watch. Dense crowds, too, had collected upon the bluffs to view this action which would, beyond any doubt, determine their immediate fates and fortunes.

Nervously Matt again and again checked the mechanism of a carbine selected for his own use, then twirled the cylinder of a heavy Navy Colt's dragging at his brass-buckled belt. Occasionally his sharpshooters, their lean and bearded faces encrimsoned by the newly risen sun, stood up to get a better view. Some of them bent cautiously half forward, but others lounged with hands carelessly crossed over the muzzles of their long rifles.

It came suddenly to Matt that aboard the enemy gunboats, now in plain sight and steaming in two long and irregular columns, there must be hundreds of men whose sole intent this day was to kill him and as many of his fellow Yankees as possible.

He counted eight Confederate vessels, of widely varying size and design, which soon would pit themselves against four ironclads and two weird-appearing steam rams. An acrid taste entered his mouth when he reflected that aboard the enemy vessels might well be found not a few of those small arms and percussion caps he and Philo Daingerfield had sold at New Madrid.

Fortunately no one noticed a guilty flush rising above his uniform's dark blue roll collar. It came as only a small consolation that what he was about to risk today might, in a measure, atone for his treachery.

The enemy vessels, without exception single-stacked, steamed steadily upstream led by big, brig-rigged *General Bragg*. Her gracefully tall spars and trim crossyards stood out among these ungainly rivercraft like a peacock among cowbirds.

Curiously Matt noted the presence of a recently smashed small boat drifting soddenly southwards and crewed by only a pair of rusty black cormorants which stupidly craned snake-like necks in order to watch *Monarch* go rushing past, raising graceful white plumes to either side of her ram.

For want of something better with which to occupy himself Matt strained his eyes, tried to pick out *Carondelet*. Um. There she was, recognizable because of her famous red-banded chimneys. Godfreys! Aboard her Flavia Cosby's lover must be serving.

Now *Queen*, supremely independent, plunged through a gap between slow-moving *Cairo* and *St. Louis* and raced straight towards Commodore Montgomery's array. As she did so a sound of cheering, undoubtedly derisive, arose from the ironclads.

Her superstructure towering briefly above the "turtles," Colonel Ellet's flagboat rushed on, sketching a creaming, lacy carpet across the water in heading straight for *Colonel Lovell*, the foremost Confederate vessel.

Before Matt was well aware of it *Monarch*, too, had passed between *Carondelet* and *Benton*. It was possible to discern that the muzzles of their heavy ordnance were painted scarlet in Regular Navy style.

At amazing speed the stretch of water between the steam rams and the enemy narrowed and the Confederate vessels became disconcertingly larger to look upon.

"Down behind the breastwork! Down, everybody!" Matt shouted over a sudden thunder of cannon fire and the consequent eerie shrieking of enemy shells. The enemy's leading vessels, *Colonel Lovell* and *General Jeff Thompson* had commenced to fire on the steam rams with their heavy bow guns—a fire to which neither *Monarch* nor *Queen* could reply. The sun, rising higher above those bluffs, to the eastward tinted gold a succession of brief waterspouts raised by enemy shot in narrowly missing their targets.

"Keerist!" gasped one of the mountaineers who answered to the name of Absalom Magruder. "Take a look at the Old Whore, will ye?" By this appellation was *Queen* known through the ram fleet.

Matt swallowed hard on nothing and took comfort in glimpsing Colonel Charles Ellet's slim, erect figure stand exposed outside the flagboat's pilothouse. He was waving a brown slouch hat, evidently trying to indicate that *Monarch* should attack a chunky, low-to-the water gunboat later discovered to be *General Price.*

How curious, Matt reflected during these last instants of inaction, that the Eads ironclads were forced because of their weak engines to go into action stern first, barely maintaining steerageway and allowing themselves to be carried along by the five-mile current. Otherwise they would have small chance of escaping in case of trouble. All the same their stern guns now were blasting away regularly. He saw *Queen* head for *Lovell,* a craft of approximately her own size. Both vessels steered straight at each other over the glassy, yellowish water until, at the very last instant, the Confederate gunboat's commander seemed to lose his nerve and veered away.

Lovell's evasive maneuver was poorly timed for, in thus turning aside, she offered to the onrushing steam ram not the small, strong target of her bow, but her whole vulnerable broadside. A grinding, crackling, crash as of a hundred tall trees being felled simultaneously sounded over the River.

Spasmodically gripping the rough oak of the breastwork before him Matt watched the Confederate vessel roll far over onto her starboard beam, saw her funnel torn from its supports, and fall, still smoking, across *Queen's* bow. Paddles still churning furiously the Union vessel all but rode over her steam-spouting and nearly-cut-through enemy.

Under the impact *Queen's* tall and slender chimneys swayed like reeds in the wind but they remained erect although one of them canted slightly off the perpendicular.

As in a dream Matt watched *Queen's* paddles come to a halt, then reverse themselves, backing her out of a welter of steam and smoke created by the mortally wounded Confederate. He saw, too, brief white and flower-like blossoms of smoke burst from the steam ram's breastworks. Her sharpshooters were picking off men still clinging to their posts beside *Lovell's* forward gun. Then all near-by enemy gunboats opened upon the victorious ram which seemed to have suffered no serious damage, but their aim was poor and presently Colonel Ellet's flagboat started swinging forward in an attempt to meet a furious charge made by *General Beauregard.* The thunderous tumult of incessant cannonading became ear-splitting.

"Keerist, Matt! Poor Old Whore cain't nohow get out o' the way!" panted Absalom Magruder. This was true. The former Ohio River packet could not regain sufficient steerageway to evade *Beauregard's* rush and so suffered a ramming which half tore away and completely disabled her larboard wheel. When a bank of drifting, acrid-smelling gun smoke mercifully concealed her, *Queen* was squattering like a wounded wild duck and lurching towards shallow water on the Arkansas shore. Obviously her participation in this action was at an end.

Directly opposite Memphis and witnessed by dense crowds of townspeople, the battle now achieved maximum fury as this whole broad reach of River became dotted with gunboats all blasting away and raising dense clouds of coal smoke which, mingled with gun smoke and remnants of the morning mist, created blind areas over the Mississippi.

An imperative jangling of bells in *Monarch's* engine room and a further acceleration of her paddlewheels' beat apprised Matt that she was about to play her part in the battle. Out of a wall of smoke and not a hundred yards distant burst the Confederate gunboat *General Price* steering straight for Alfred Ellet's command. Her captain evidently had determined not to duplicate *Lovell's* disastrous error and wavered not an inch from his course.

"Fire at will!" Matt heard his voice shouting, but in that tumult the command sounded faint as a gull's mewing amid a gale. Matt raised his carbine and sought a target. He became absurdly conscious of *Monarch's* laboring engines, creaking fabric and the excited curses of his sharpshooters.

"Fire at will!" Matt repeated and sighted his carbine at an officer directing gunners on the foredeck of the smaller but well-armored *Price*. Just as he was about to squeeze his carbine's trigger the hurricane deck seemed to slide out from under him. He heard the smokestack guys hum like gigantic harp strings, a deafening crash, then a tortured groaning of *Monarch's* timbers.

Knocked onto his knees Matt clutched the breastwork, stared dazedly down onto the roof of *Price's* pilothouse. In it two men in checkered shirts were struggling to control her madly spinning wheel. While he ran to pick up his carbine he saw Magruder's ramrod flash as the Kentuckian reloaded, but by the time he managed to cram a fresh cartridge into his piece *Price* lay astern, still reeling from the glancing blows she and *Monarch* had exchanged.

To Matt *Monarch* appeared undamaged, but her late assailant was showing a jagged, yellow-brown gash in her bow. Her starboard paddlewheel now was motionless and steam, escaping in great, screaming clouds soared high above her. Visibly she commenced to lower by the head.

At once Flag Officer Davis' ironclads concentrated their fire upon the crippled Confederate. *Monarch,* meanwhile, regained speed and headed for *General Bragg,* biggest of the enemy. She was a large Gulf steamer effectively armored with railroad rails bolted together and mounted, among other pieces of ordnance, a thirty-two pound Parrott gun on her bow. *Bragg* did not approach as swiftly as *Price* so Matt had opportunity to call out to his mountaineers, "Pick off that bow gun's crew! Bartlett! Have your men concentrate on their pilothouse!"

At once a crackle of musketry rippled along the steam ram's hurricane deck, became intensified as the enemy fired in return. Matt could hear musket balls going *ta-chunk!* into the oak before him mingled with the tinkle of expended cartridge shells and the steady, inspired cursing of his mountaineers. With incredible rapidity they were reloading their antique but deadly muzzle-loading rifles, sighting and, with bearded jaws working steadily, firing at the enemy gunners.

As calmly as he would have drawn a bead upon a buck back in Penobscot County, Matt sighted at a fair-haired officer commanding the gunners. He was hardly aware of his carbine's recoil but he saw the yellow-haired officer suddenly clutch at his chest, reel sidewise and fall sprawling over a rammer.

When two more of their number were picked off survivors of the bow gun's crew dashed back within the rusty casemate. The pilots at *Bragg's* wheel, too, must have been driven from their posts for suddenly the big steamer veered and, from following a course capable of dealing *Monarch* a crippling if not a deadly blow, dashed harmlessly by, her crossyards wavering over the steam ram's deck.

Matt was aware she was flying a Confederate naval flag, not the famous red Battle Flag carried by the land forces, but the Stars and Bars, a flag dangerously similar to that of the Union. It showed two wide red stripes separated by a single wide white stripe and a circle of eleven white stars within a blue canton.

While cramming yet another cartridge into his carbine's chamber the New Englander abruptly became aware of the near proximity of another enemy, *Beauregard*. As it was, *Monarch's* pilot, capitalizing on her tremendous speed, managed to slip her between *Bragg* and *Beauregard*.

"Keerist!" shouted Magruder. "They going to ram each other!" It was so. *Beauregard* in missing *Monarch's* stern by scant feet had struck her consort a grinding, glancing blow shrewd enough to cause the paddlewheels of both gunboats to stop and tall plumes of steam to gush through their escape tubes. They lay momentarily motionless, affording tempting targets for the deadly gunnery of Federal ironclads now closing ponderously in.

The water had become littered with broken planking and other debris but through it *Monarch* regained her amazing speed and commenced to circle about, eager for another ramming. *Bragg's* people now had swarmed out onto her deck and were waving anything white. A couple of her crew wrenched off their shirts and commenced to brandish them frantically because shells from *Carondelet* and *Cairo* were bursting all about the disabled vessels and sketching great gray cloudlets or lazy rings of smoke above the current.

Again *Monarch* sped straight for her former enemy, the already-damaged *General Price*. She had not struck her flag but did so when the steam ram slammed into her, left her stove in. With smokestack wrenched off at deck level and filling rapidly amid a litter of broken rails and bulwarks, she started to sink.

The next quarry selected by calm but pale-faced Lieutenant-Colonel A. W. Ellet was *Little Rebel*, the enemy's flag steamer. She already was fleeing towards newly green cottonwoods fringing the Arkansas shore, all the while peppered by shells flung after her by the ironclads.

Matt found opportunity, while leaning over a fresh case of cartridges, to glance back along the hurricane deck. To his overwhelming joy he saw that although bullets had sketched jagged yellow grooves in the breastwork and bits of flying shell had punctured the big steam ram's smokestacks not one of his men appeared to have suffered hurt.

Faster and faster rushed *Monarch* until, at the top of her amazing speed, she was able to overhaul the fleeing flag steamer. Just as she was about to pounce upon her prey Matt's attention became momentarily diverted by Sergeant Bartlett's hail. More ammunition needed to be brought up from below. Matt had arisen to pass over a surplus of his own when *Monarch* drove her ram so deep into the smaller vessel's starboard quarter that her own progress all but ceased and her whole hull shook and groaned as if she had been run onto a reef.

Matt, caught in the act of rising, was thrown off balance and hurled reeling crazily across the deck until he struck the opposite breastwork with such violence that fiery comets whirled before his eyes. All breath was driven from his lungs and a series of excruciating pains stabbed at his right side.

All he could do was to cling gasping in agony to the breastwork while men to either side fired at the half-drowned *Little Rebel*, and watch the enemy flag steamer pile up on the shore. She began to ooze smoke in a dozen places.

By fives and tens the enemy were leaping overboard into water not even waist-deep and floundering through a wide reed-bed towards clumps of alders and willows screening the river bank.

Alfred Ellet began bellowing fruitless commands for these fugitives to halt and a few of them did when the sharpshooters cut down a couple threshing in the muddied waters. Sergeant Bartlett suddenly noticed Matt's ashen complexion.

He came running over, eyes wide. "You hit, sir?"

"No," wheezed the ghastly pallid New Englander. "I–guess I just got my wind–knocked out. Get back to your post. I–I'll soon be all right."

But he wasn't.

XXVII THE FLEETS ENGAGE (II)

To VETERANS SERVING in *Carondelet* this was by far the tamest, if noisiest, action in which they had thus far participated. To them it was an almighty relief not to be exposed to a disastrous plunging fire directed from land batteries situated high on some bluff.

Off to larboard the city of Memphis sprawled, bathed in morning sunlight and displaying a brave array of Confederate flags at various staffs and signal yards. Ever denser throngs of onlookers crowded the levee and wharves to survey the battle through a weird array of spyglasses and binoculars.

Paul Dent, busy cutting fuses in *Carondelet's* shell room, silently cursed his inability to witness and make sketches of what might be chancing aloft. On several occasions he heard roundshot clang viciously against the gunboat's armor. More commonplace was the rumble caused by the ironclad's gun carriages being hauled in or out, the barked commands of the gun captains, and the thunderous report of the Fourth Division's twin cannon.

Among the shadows of the wheelhouse Commander Henry Walke frowned, viewed the River with mingled satisfaction and chagrin. His satisfaction was derived from the facts that, within the brief space of an hour, the enemy had lost three ships sunk and that now the Rebels very probably could not assemble another effective naval force.

Critically, Henry Walke tugged at his side whiskers and watched the precise, effort-saving movements of his Number One gun's crew which at that moment were firing at *Jeff Thompson*, then he snapped fingers in delight when their roundshot struck *Thompson* viciously in her stern and raised a dense cloud of splinters. The Confederate gunboat lurched violently under the impact and, smoking furiously, veered off to starboard. Barely had the stricken vessel joined a string of sunken or burning wrecks along the Mississippi's Arkansas shore than *Jeff Thompson* blew up with a stunning, thunderous report which broke windows in Memphis.

Because he had decided to quit fighting rear-end-on Walke had ordered cut away logs chained about his command's waterline to protect her from such a ramming as had sunk *Mound City* and *Cincinnati*. *Carondelet*, free of these encumbrances, now was steaming well in advance of her consorts.

In the wheelhouse's gloom Walke shot a glance at his chief pilot, observed crisply, "That's better, but I presume there's no hope of overtaking the *Van Dorn?* Don't like to see even one of them get away."

"No, sir, we ain't got no chance at all," the pilot drawled. "*Van Dorn's* their fastest boat by a long chalk."

Conversation ended when the gunboat's Number Two bow gun roared and, by a matter of yards, missed the fleeing *Sumter*, but Number Three succeeded in detonating a shell directly above the fugitive and sheered off her tall funnel as neatly as an ax severs a sapling; dropped it riddled and smoking into the current. Promptly the enemy's ensign was struck and a white flag raised in its stead as members of her crew ran out to line the rail with hands uplifted.

"Damned if that isn't a mighty small prize we've captured," Walke chuckled and, as a well-trained naval officer should, pulled out his watch to note the time as seven-fifteen. The action between the two fleets had required little over an hour to be fought to this decisive termination. Then his grim smile faded. "I expect, Mr. Judson, we will have to eat plenty of humble pie before the men aboard those crazy steam rams. They certainly did a magnificent job." He pulled his sketchbook out and prepared to jot down various positions and maneuvers still fresh in his memory.

From time to time he caught up binoculars slung about his neck to scan the river bank opposite Memphis and the remains of the defeated squadron stranded upon it. Furthest north and barely visible was the funnel and wheelhouse of the luckless *Colonel Lovell* which had gone down so swiftly as to drown most of her crew. Next downstream lay the disabled but still floating *Queen of the West*. Her position was directly opposite the northernmost buildings of the city. Next in order were the wrecks of *General Price* and *Little Rebel*. Both had been successfully run ashore so the majority of their crews had jumped onto the bank to make good an escape. Next came the shattered *Thompson*, furiously afire now and raising a tall pillar of bluish gray smoke.

Far downstream twin torrents of sooty smoke attested the fact that *Van Dorn*, sole surviving element of the Confederate fleet, was fleeing with *Monarch* in hot pursuit.

"Ring for half speed and stand in towards the Tennessee shore," Walke instructed his pilot. When *Carondelet* threshed closer to Memphis Walke went out on deck and heard above the laboring of his engines screams, yells and shouts of fury arising from the water front. People, singly and in groups, could be seen running along an embankment and upon the levee. On the outskirts of town appeared at first a few, then many vehicles of all sorts heading a panic-stricken exodus born of terror and uncertainty as to what might chance when the city should, as it must very soon, fall into Union hands.

"We'll soon have that rag down," growled *Carondelet's* Chief Engineer emerging on deck, scarlet-faced and smeared with grease and coal dust for, from a staff above the Custom House still flapped a large Confederate flag.

Gradually the rest of Flag Officer Davis' ironclads came chuffing up to drop anchor even as *Monarch*, returning from her fruitless pursuit, steamed boldly up to an empty pier near the Custom House and tied up.

"By God, that fellow Ellet has gall and to spare!" grated Walke. "Looks like he's landing a detail to take possession without reference to the Navy."

First Master Wade grinned to himself on imagining just how well choleric Flag Officer Davis would relish this move by an independent Army colonel.

Seldom had Medical Lieutenant Robert Ashton heard such inspired profanity as resounded in *Benton's* chartroom while Navy Regulars cursed Ellet's presumption and boldness, which, added to the painful slowness of their ironclads, had permitted the Army's boats to snatch up so great a share of the laurels.

Rob was feeling at once relieved and considerably let-down because aboard *Benton* few casualties had been suffered. When, later in the day, he was summoned to *Monarch* by Matt Everett he went gladly. He found Matt racked by excruciating pains every time he drew a deep breath. Nonetheless he was able to summon a wry smile.

"Aren't I clumsy as a cow on ice?" he wheezed. "Here I'm all stove in and I've not even a little battle wound to brag about."

"You've got something better than that," Rob pointed out after a tentative examination. "With half a dozen ribs cracked or broken like yours you're going to linger on the casualty list a good long time; three months at least. Means you can convalesce at home."

Because Matt was the only occupant of *Monarch's* vast sick bay the place was quiet and the two were alone now that Dr. Robarts had departed for *Queen* there to consult upon Colonel Ellet's wounded leg.

Through a window opened to a warm spring breeze came sounds from the sullen and still rebellious city. The barking of dogs, a clattering caused by hooves and steel-shod wheels travelling a cobbled street. From nearer by sounded the rich and plaintive singing of Negro roustabouts exulting that their slavery promised soon to end.

At sundown Paul Dent, sketchbook in hand appeared and, smiling encouragingly, dropped onto a campstool beside Matt's cot. He spoke of drawings made of gunboats, of the battle, and of those wild scenes which had ensued at the Custom House when *Monarch's* men had hauled down the Rebel flag.

Under the injured man's probing regard Dent flushed. Wasn't it the purest irony of Fate that his great good friend and his fiancée should prove to be half-brother and sister—one of them necessarily illegitimate?

"I presume, Dr. Ashton," said he, replacing a rubber band about his sketchbook, "that when Matt gets well enough to travel he will be permitted to return East on sick leave?"

"I've just told him so," replied the dark-haired physician.

"Will you go home—to Maine, that is?"

Matt's eyes never wavered and seen by lantern light his face seemed perceptibly to age as it rested upon a pillow. "Yes. I intend going East. I have an important account to settle."

"Important account?" What in the world was Matt's intent? Surely he knew that Josiah Cosby had been dead these many weeks?

Rob Ashton stood up. "I expect you will be transferred to the hospital boat in the morning. I'll see you there. I've put the laudanum bottle on the shelf above you in case the pain increases. Try to get a good night's rest."

Presently Dent also got to his feet and said, "You don't mind if I stop aboard the *Red Jacket* and get you a little packet of jewellery to give my fiancée—if you would be so good as to take it East for her—the mails are so damned chancy and irregular these days."

He hoped for a quick assent. That would mean that Matt intended to go to Bangor, but the injured man only dropped his eyes, muttered, "There isn't any certainty of when I'll be going."

"Nevertheless, I'll leave it with you, anyhow," Dent said, then added, "If necessary you can post it anywhere in the East. I don't care to risk Miss Cosby's gift in the mails out here unless it's unavoidable." Uncomfortably, he offered his hand. "I'm afraid I won't be seeing much of you for long."

"Why, Paul?"

"It's understood that the combined flotilla will move to attack at Vicksburg and then destroy certain rams the Rebels are reported to be building downstream." His wide warm smile flashed. "Get well enough to travel quickly, Matt, and I'm sure you will, what with that wife you love so dearly waiting for you."

As he tramped out of the *Monarch's* sick bay he remained conscious of Matt's eyes stabbing at his back like bayonet points.

XXVIII STETSON & STETSON, COUNSELLORS-AT-LAW (II)

LIEUTENANT MATTHEW EVERETT HOVEY was deciding, as he rode down towards Newport Junction, that it had proved a wise move to resume the name under which he had grown up. In fact, he had all but decided legally to change his actual name once the true nature of Josiah Cosby's offense against his first wife had become public knowledge. He wanted no use of the Cosby name.

Mr. and Mrs. Whidden, in whom Phoebe, under oath of secrecy, long since had confided the supposedly shameful secret of Matt's origin, of course had been delighted with his notion. Steadily the engine "General Todd" puffed along towards Newport Junction spouting showers of sparks from its bell-shaped funnel and drawing after it a long train of timber cars ending with a battered passenger car instead of a caboose.

Seldom, Matt decided, had his native State appeared more glorious than on this early September day. Through an open window came whiffs of air redolent of fragrant spruce and balsam. Various low patches of ground along the right-of-way shone with huge clusters of blueberries, while on higher levels goldenrod glowed amid clumps of sumach already commencing to flame with autumnal hues.

In Matt's ears yet were sounding the awkward and often curt but always wholehearted welcomes of various old friends and neighbors. Mrs. Whidden, of course, had spread far and wide the news of Matt's service aboard *Monarch*, that now-famous steam ram which, singlehanded, had sunk three Confederate gunboats!

The selectmen of Dexter and representatives from half-a-dozen adjacent villages had been at the log railway station to greet Phoebe and himself upon arrival. Mr. Parker, the postmaster-grocer, and almost everybody who was anybody within a radius of ten miles stood up in their carts and buggies to raise a ragged cheer when Matt appeared on the platform first, in order to mask Phoebe's swollen abdomen. Indeed those gruff, hard-handed citizens, in their undemonstrative fashion had managed to make him feel quite the hero despite his earnest protestations that he had not even been wounded, had only been clumsy enough to break several ribs through carelessness. Only in the eyes of Mr. and Mrs. Whidden had there been an anxious, searching expression which nobody noted.

Bent old Dr. Ashton had driven over from Garland, eager to glean news of his son and had appeared vastly pleased to learn that Rob was proving so steady and useful to the Western Flotilla.

"Rob always was a sober and industrious one. Tell me, Matt, when do you suspect he might get a mite of leave?"

"Not for some time, I fear, sir," Matt had predicted. "Right now our whole flotilla is mighty busy above Vicksburg."

"Hi, Matt, how many Rebels you shoot?" had shrilled Caleb Barton's freckle-faced younger son. "Hope it was lots and lots, cuss their bones!"

At the Whiddens' farm had appeared an irregular stream of shy, patently anxious visitors most of whom were girls and women with menfolk away at the war. It had proved a heart-warming experience to perceive how honestly glad they had been to welcome home Phoebe and himself.

Unhurriedly the train chuffed on and on through a countryside every detail of which was intimately familiar. Subconsciously, he noted that Walter Willis had put up a new and quite pretentious backhouse that boasted clusters of grapes cut into its twin doors. Peleg Watson must at long last be doing well with his timbering, if that big new barn rising in the clearing behind his newly painted house was any indication.

A shrill screaming of the locomotive's whistle warned that Number Nine was entering the outskirts of Newport Junction, so, with a very taut expression hardening his mouth, Matt rehooked his military cloak, caught up his black felt campaign hat and braced himself for the grim session ahead.

While picking his way over a weed-grown spur towards the law offices of Messrs. Stetson & Stetson, he attempted to recall his appearance when last he had strode in this direction. How gawky he must have looked back last November, a powerfully built but still somewhat awkward young man wearing a hickory shirt, duroy pants tucked into cowhide boots and a heavy winter jacket. Now he had become transformed into a tall, solidly built officer in the Union Army showing a lot of fine new lines about his mouth and forehead and with a thoughtful look in his wide-set brown eyes. Of course last fall he hadn't been wearing these short yellow-brown side whiskers with which Phoebe loved to toy.

Again and again voices called out, "Hi, Matt! Got them Rebels on the run yet?" "How long you going to tarry?" "Come on over and stop a while." "Seen anything of my brother Billy?" and so on.

He stalked past a group of red-cheeked lads playing at "duck on a rock" in the middle of Newport Junction's dusty main street and smiled. Here was home indeed. Certainly the war had brought to this little town a considerable prosperity. No less than five new stores, gleaming with fresh paint, had been put up on the Widow Hanson's vacant lot and a structure that appeared big enough to become a hotel was being built across from the depot. Through the dusty golden sunlight carpenters' hammers rang loudly, incessantly, over the rasping whine of saws at work.

On this occasion Matt was not required to wait but was shown directly in to Mr. Edwin Stetson's presence. He came hurrying forward, both hands outstretched.

"This is indeed a happy and a proud moment, Matt! Although I expect a lot of people have said the same before, none could mean it more than I. You can hang that fancy black hat of yours," he pointed to the deer's antler hatrack, "over there. By cracky, you certainly have filled out considerable. Last year you looked all legs and feet—like a Newfoundland puppy."

"It's fine to be home," Matt admitted quietly as he seated himself beside the desk; but, thought Mr. Stetson, he didn't say it quite as if he meant it.

"I have your portfolio right here," the lawyer informed while polishing square-lensed glasses. Briskly he then undid a bit of tape securing a big folder of brown cardboard. "Oh, yes. Forgot to tell you how glad I am over you and Phoebe. Her ma was dreadfully worried when Phoebe lit out from Portland like that, whilst I, knowing what I did, was Almighty concerned over you and what you intended to do. It was the mercy of God, boy, that you didn't manage to kill Josiah Cosby—richly as he deserved it. And now everything has come out all right." He chuckled dryly. "Mrs. Whidden sent an account of your exploits aboard the *Monarch* both to the Bangor and Portland papers and they printed every word of what you wrote. Like to see them?" Edwin Stetson glanced inquiringly over the tops of his spectacles.

The big man in blue and gold buttons shook his head. "Later, Mr. Stetson, if you don't mind. By now I presume Mr. Cosby's—my father's—" even now his voice quivered when he said that "—will has been probated?"

"It has. So moreover, the certificate of his marriage to Abigail is now on file at Penobscot County Court House. Filed it myself. What with the Reverend Mr. Adams' sworn and notarized testimony there isn't a doubt in the world but that you stand on the firmest of legal ground."

Matt listened intently, while gazing without seeing, upon the familiar mildewed print of "The Surrender at Yorktown." How much had happened since last he had viewed that patriotic scene! St. Louis, the *Western Arrow*, St. Louis again and then Louisville, Memphis and finally, Boston.

Edwin Stetson's usual dry accents were stating, "I have here a copy of Josiah Cosby's will. In it, he leaves two-thirds of his estate to his eldest legitimate son." He broke off, little steel-gray eyes boring steadily into

Matt's. "Mark well that phrase, 'eldest legitimate son'; because that, my dear Matthew, means you beyond any peradventure, doubt or question."

The lawyer's usually expressionless features formed a brief smile. "Congratulations, Matthew. You should inherit something—at a rough estimate—close on a quarter of a million dollars. It will likely amount to more. Your mother's estate which, I am glad to inform you, has prospered under my care, adds another ninety thousand. So, all of a sudden, you are about to become a wealthy young man."

"Ninety thousand dollars?" Matt stared, incredulous, fingers spread wide on light blue knees. "I had no notion Mother's estate amounted to even half as much."

"It didn't. Not until I sold off a tract of prime hardwoods when the railroad ran a spur to within a mile of it. That brought a pretty piece of change."

Matt got up, the skirt of his long blue tunic rippling gently about wide white stripes descending his light blue trouser legs. "That's a lot of money, all right," he observed and stood at the window to watch a string of freight cars go clanking through the Junction.

"Indeed it is."

Matt faced about, thumbs hooked in his gold-buckled uniform belt. "What about the rest of the Cosby family—or whatever their name is legally?"

Mr. Stetson hesitated. "Well, I expect that while they won't exactly starve they'll have to scratch hard to live in even modest circumstances."

"Let 'em. That's no skin off my nose," Matt grunted. "So the bulk of old Cosby's money will be mine and there are no two ways about it?"

"Correct. But it'll bear mighty hard on the Cosbys when the truth about that bigamous marriage comes out. Mrs. Cosby's said to be a fine, proud woman."

Said Matt grimly, "It's only justice that she and her brats taste a sample of what my mother suffered twenty years and more."

A small double V appeared between the lawyer's brows. He jerked a nod. "True. But it won't lessen the fact of your mother's unhappy life an iota." Briskly Mr. Stetson pushed forward a sheet of foolscap covered with neat Spencerian script. "Here is a list of your holdings through your mother's estate."

Lower lip outthrust, Matt bent his yellow head and scanned them. Thanks to his operations in St. Louis, he could sense with half an eye that the lands his mother had purchased and the securities Edwin Stetson had bought were of excellent quality, promised considerable further profit. "You have done very well, Mr. Stetson; my earnest thanks. I trust you have taken a sufficient commission?"

Mr. Stetson again summoned that faint smile of his. "Remember my profession, Matt?"

Matt stood up, took a turn before Stetson's desk. "Tell me, truthfully, Mr. Stetson, is anybody around here aware of my activities out West? I mean that er—contracting business I conducted?"

"I can solemnly assure you no one except me—and your wife, of course—knows anything about it. May I add that I deem you wise in resuming your original name upon your returning home? As near as I know, nobody except the Cosbys, their lawyers and myself are aware that Matthew Everett and Matthew Hovey are one and the same person."

Settling back in his chair, Mr. Stetson steepled pallid, ink-stained fingers. "Is it your intention eventually to assume your legal name of Cosby?"

Matt tugged at his short side whiskers a thoughtful moment. "I think not. I believe I shall have my name legally changed to Hovey. That wouldn't effect the matter of the will, will it?"

"Not one jot or tittle," the lawyer told him. "Nothing can alter the fact that you are Josiah Cosby's eldest legitimate son."

Matt ceased his restless parade up and down the sunny little office, raised his bent head. "Have you yet communicated with the Cosby family lawyer?"

Edwin Stetson's silvery head shook slowly. "No, Matt. I deemed it best to postpone any action whatever until you, personally, arrived. I hope you approve?"

"I do." Matt laughed harshly then strode over to take down his hat. "Tomorrow I intend making a visit on those cuckoos occupying Sachem Hill that they'll never forget."

Once his door had banged shut behind that erect figure in blue, Mr. Stetson fondled his chin a long five minutes then heaved a sigh and prepared a telegram directed to Mrs. Josiah Cosby in Bangor:

LIEUTENANT MATTHEW HOVEY INTENDS CALLING TOMORROW. SUGGEST IT YOUR BEST INTERESTS RECEIVE HIM POLITELY.

XXIX SACHEM HILL (II)

AT THE ENTRANCE of the drive of Sachem Hill, Matt Hovey pulled in his hired nag and sat for quite some time staring blankly out over the oily-looking and rapid flowing Penobscot now rendered dark brown by the refuse of sawmills and tanneries upstream. Absently he noted how water boiled about cribs built in midstream to assist in log driving. Along both shores scratched, scored and muddied logs left over from last spring's drive lay among the shiny boulders like basking saurians. To Matt's surprise he felt himself icily calm now that the moment of retribution was at hand. He turned on the buggy's seat again to view with curiosity and interest Sachem Hill—his property! How beautifully it was situated with fields and woods sloping gently away and to either side.

In some surprise he noted that since his last visit there were subtle differences about the property's appearance. For instance, pickets here and there were missing from the fences paralleling Sachem Hill's long driveway and a farm cart with a broken axle had been abandoned near the center of a field glowing yellow-brown under the September sun. Weeds, too, were sprouting along the course of the driveway; mute testimony that Josiah Cosby was no longer there to order them cleared away.

How odd, mused the big figure in blue as briskly he slapped reins against his horse's broad rump, that he, Phoebe, Augustus and Flavia should all have dwelt in Louisville for so long a period without ever encountering each other. Perhaps it was just as well: if what Paul Dent had said were true he would now find it hard steeling himself to the task of informing the widow and her children that they must soon quit Sachem Hill.

Slowly the buggy's steel-shod wheels ground up the unevenly gravelled drive. The mansion itself, however, and the lace curtains at its windows appeared to be as fresh and trim as ever. Um. What was that hanging to the door? It looked like a black bow. When he pulled up his horse before that well-remembered front door he saw that a crêpe bow had been tied to its handsome brass knocker.

He had expected his heart to commence pounding when he passed the windows of that room in which he had shot down Josiah Cosby; but it didn't. He jumped down from his buggy and snapped the hitching rein to a ring let into a cast-iron post topped by a horse's head. A vagrant puff of air stirred the crêpe bow tied to the knocker. Who might have died here? The most logical explanation was that that wound Augustus had taken before Donelson at long last had proved fatal.

The door was opened, not by the butler but by an aged maid servant wearing a rusty black uniform and a white apron.

"What do you want?" Stolidly, almost hostilely, she regarded the tall figure who came clumping up, dusty black campaign hat with well-polished brass wreath-ornament still held in one hand.

"I am Lieutenant Hovey," Matt informed her shortly. "Pray tell Mrs. Cosby and any other members of the family who are at home that I must see them at once."

To his astonishment, the gray-haired servant said, "They are expecting you. Come, sir, into the parlor, please."

"Expecting? Did you say?"

"Yes, sir. Them was Mrs. Cosby's very words."

Behind the parlor's sliding doors, Flavia Cosby drew a deep breath and straightened her slim figure into rigid erectness. What, oh, dear Lord, was about to happen?

She glanced sidewise at Augustus, still desperately haggard and pale, sitting in an invalid's chair with a brown velvet throw over his lap; a throw which rested there unevenly because of the missing leg. Her mother, grown very gray of late, looked smaller and yet somehow more stately than ever in her mourning as she waited behind the invalid chair beside Flavia. A sombre trio they presented, all in deep black. Gently Flavia's hand crept out to press her mother's.

"Don't worry, dear. I don't think there is much Lieutenant Hovey can do to hurt us now." She forced a smile as the front door closed out in the hall. "Who knows? After all, he was a very close friend of Paul's so perhaps this is a friendly visit."

When the parlor's silver door handle clicked, Augustus straightened in his chair. Then the doors slid apart and the opening became almost filled by Matt's stalwart, blue-clad figure. Augustus attempted a smile.

"Welcome to Sachem Hill," said he with a ghost of a smile. "I presume you recall meeting my sister, Flavia? May I present you to my mother?"

Matt remained standing in the doorway gazing steadily upon that pallid figure in the wheelchair and the black-clad figures behind him. This sombre little group appeared isolated in the center of a huge, lavishly furnished parlor brave with a handsome mantelpiece, sparkling crystal chandeliers and a pair of round Federalist mirrors topped by American eagles.

It was upon Augustus that Matt centered his attention. Dear God! How vastly he had changed from that lively, humorous young fellow of nearly a year before. He was as handsome as ever, but his features had become refined, more sensitive. The subtle sadness of his expression was scarcely to be wondered at. Here he was condemned, without hope of reprieve, to the life of a cripple who never again could dance, ride a horse or take the field with his gun, or do any one of many things an energetic young man might enjoy.

Matt bowed stiffly. "It is a pleasure, to make your acquaintance, Mrs. Cosby," he managed to say, though his voice sounded not in the least familiar. He bowed again in Flavia's direction. "It is a pleasure also, Miss Cosby, to meet you once more; even under such sad circumstances."

When the ladies silently inclined their heads he advanced two steps into the parlor, then halted and returned his attention to Augustus. Flavia, Matt had noted, now wore her dark and glossy hair parted in the middle and swept back into a gleaming black bun at the nape of her neck.

"I had feared, when I noticed that crêpe bow on the door, that it might have been you," Matt told the cripple. "I am glad it was not."

Mrs. Cosby straightened her slight figure which involuntarily had sagged. "No, Mr. Hovey, that crêpe is for my son, Decius. Yesterday the War Department telegraphed us that he had been killed in a cavalry skirmish at a place called Leesburg. It's somewhere in Virginia, I believe."

A nerve in Matt's cheek began to tighten.

"We were all very proud of Decius," Flavia said softly. "He had just been breveted a lieutenant."

"Please accept my heartfelt sympathy, Mrs. Cosby."

All at once Matt seemed to hear Abigail Hovey's serene voice reading, " 'Vengeance is mine; I will repay, saith the Lord.' "

Surely, the Lord had smitten down Josiah Cosby and had afflicted his family for all that they were entirely guiltless of Josiah Cosby's crime.

Matt drew a long, slow breath, his dark brown eyes shifting from one pale face to another. How well could these people bear up when the shameful truth came to be known? What lay in store for this family now? For Mrs. Cosby the shame of a bigamous marriage, the brand of bastardy for her children, and poverty for them all.

Phoebe. He wondered how Phoebe would feel at this moment of triumph?

All at once Matt found himself advancing to take Mrs. Cosby's thin hands in his. "I deeply deplore, madam, to hear of this new loss—especially of so gallant a young officer as your son seems to have been," said he quickly. "I came here—I came here," he repeated, forcing a smile, "to deliver something from your fiancé, Miss Cosby."

He fumbled in his tunic's tail pocket and produced that long, flat box which, so many weeks ago, Paul Dent had pressed upon him off Memphis.

Finis